Jill Paton Walsh

The Wyndham Case
and
A Piece of Justice

D1513370

HODDER

The Wyndham Case Copyright © Jill Paton Walsh 1993
A Piece of Justice Copyright © Jill Paton Walsh 1995

The Wyndham Case first published in Great Britain in 1993
by Hodder & Stoughton
A Piece of Justice first published in Great Britain in 1995
by Hodder & Stoughton
An Hachette UK company

This Hodder paperback edition 2009

1

The right of Jill Paton Walsh to be identified as the author
of the work has been asserted by her in accordance with the
Copyright, Designs and Patents Act 1988.

All rights reserved. No part of this publication may be reproduced,
stored in a retrieval system, or transmitted, in any form or by any
means without the prior written permission of the publisher, nor
be otherwise circulated in any form of binding or cover other than
that in which it is published and without a similar condition
being imposed on the subsequent purchaser.

All characters in this publication are fictitious and any resemblance
to real persons, living or dead, is purely coincidental.

A CIP catalogue record for this title
is available from the British Library

ISBN 978 0 340 99312 5

Typeset by Hewer Text UK Ltd, Edinburgh
Printed and bound in the UK by
CPI Mackays, Chatham ME5 8TD

Hodder & Stoughton policy is to use papers that are natural, renewable
and recyclable products and made from wood grown in sustainable
forests. The logging and manufacturing processes are expected to
conform to the environmental regulations of the country of origin.

Hodder and Stoughton
338 Euston Road
London NW1 3BH

www.hodder.co.uk

Jill Paton Walsh

The Wyndham Case

HODDER

1

Imogen Quy looked out of her office window into the Fountain Court of St Agatha's College. It was just after nine in the morning. The famous turf maze of the court, with the 'Arab' fountain in the middle, was shining with dew in the soft sunlight of a February morning. The exquisite Jacobean brick of the court, with its Barnack stone windows and doors – reputedly the finest door cases in Cambridge – showed, she thought, better in the cool fenland light of winter days than in the warmth of summer. Imogen liked her view. So many of her colleagues, college nurses in other colleges, had offices in dark basements and remote, ugly corners. It was not so much the rooms themselves, she often thought, but the clear indication they gave as to what degree of importance the senior members of college attached to the health and welfare of themselves and their students. She had had her share of bad luck in her thirty-two years, but she was lucky in St Agatha's.

Sir William Buckmote was coming towards her down the southern side of the court. She frowned. She was very fond of the Master, and she could see at once that he was very agitated. He seemed in haste, but he was walking a wavering course, as though his right foot were taking a different direction from his left. His hands were flapping about. Imogen sighed, and used the little key on her châtelaine to open the medicine cupboard. Before the Master had got halfway across the court, his tranquillisers were on her table, and she had counted out a day's dose for him. She frowned more deeply. She would have liked a word or two with the doctor who had started the Master on these.

The Master was trying to get himself off the things. They damped him down, and took the cutting edge off his wits when he was working. They were, in fact, a disaster for him. But he had so many worries. The crisis over the Wyndham audit was barely over, and now he was intolerably harassed by a possible benefactor to the college, whose generous intentions were hedged round with detailed conditions, and who seemed to think the Master should be at his beck and call for days on end. So Imogen had charge of the bottle of pills, and kept them under lock and key. He had made a rule for himself that he was to take them only one day at a time, and only when he could give his college nurse a reason for being under special pressure. She confidently expected him to arrive in her office, sit down, push his glasses up on to his forehead, and tell her some tale of woe, before taking two with water, and departing with the rest of the day's pills in his pill-box.

But she was wrong. The Master stumbled in without knocking, and said, 'Miss Quy, you must come at once, please! There has been a calamity in the library – oh, do please hurry!'

Imogen was hurrying. But she was not going anywhere leaving pills on the desk and the cupboard unlocked. 'I'll be right with you,' she said, putting the pills away and turning the key.

'What has happened, Master?' she asked him as they descended the staircase on which her room was located, and emerged into the court.

'I hardly know – I hardly know – I shudder to think!' he said. 'We must be quick!'

Imogen turned through the arch towards the Chapel court, but the Master seized her sleeve and drew her the other way.

'You said the library?'

'Not the real library; the Wyndham Case!' He broke into a lumbering run.

They reached the door to the Wyndham Library, with its elaborate decoration, and the words FINIS EST SAPIENTIA carved above it.

Imogen's duties did not take her into the Wyndham Library very often. It was a large vaulted room, lined down one wall with the famous 'Wyndham Case' – a huge two-storey bookcase of ancient oak, with a set of steps at one end, and a little gallery running along it from end to end to give access to the upper shelves. It was glazed and polished, and the magnificent books it contained in sombre bindings scented the whole room with a fragrance of old leather, saddle soap and dust. There was no time to admire it now; the Master almost pushed her through the door, stepped after her, and locked it behind them. The room was not deserted. Crispin Mountnessing, Wyndham's Librarian, was standing by one of the tables provided for readers, with a shocked and tense expression on his face. At his feet, spread-eagled on the floor, a young man was lying. He was wearing a lilac silk shirt with a narrow white tie, and a black leather jacket with a wilted white carnation in the buttonhole. He had long, tousled, mousy hair. His bland, unlined face wore an expression of mild surprise. His right arm was extended, palm upwards, at shoulder level. Under his head there was a large pool of bright red blood, which had flowed widely, towards and around the leg of the table. It was now edged with a darkening rim, like an island on an old map. All three of the people in the room knew very well who he was. He was Philip Skellow, a first-year undergraduate, the first student St Agatha's had ever taken from his provincial school: a very bright young man, who had been expected to get a first.

'I found him like this when I unlocked the library this morning,' said Mr Mountnessing.

'We can't rouse him,' said the Master.

Imogen knelt beside Philip, and took his wrist between her fingers. He was quite cold. She tried gently lifting his head. His neck was stiffening. Blood flowed over and between her fingers, cool and shocking. Looking up, she saw there was blood and hair on the corner of the table above him and a little to the left.

'Too late, I'm afraid,' she said. 'No one can rouse him now.'

The Master put a hand to his eyes. 'Dead?' he said.

'I'm afraid so. Master, I'm afraid you must call the police,' said Imogen. She noted with clinical detachment that she herself was trembling very slightly. She was surprised. The eminent and unworldly men in the room had probably never seen a dead body before; but Imogen had. She had seen injuries much more gruesome than the violent blow of head against table that had apparently killed Philip Skellow, and though death is an extreme kind of injury, and always, she knew, an outrage, she had seen many deaths. Only, of course, though on very slight acquaintance, she had liked young Philip, and... She looked at her blood-smeared right hand, baffled.

'A doctor?' the Master was saying. 'The next of kin?'

'The police, Master. This looks like murder.' She had never seen murder before. This was different from other deaths.

'Murder?' wailed Mr. Mountnessing. 'Oh, no! Surely he just fell, and...'

'I do not see how a fall could have been hard enough. I think he must have been pushed. But we do not decide; we just call the police. Master, you absolutely must call them at once. Think of the scandal.'

'Yes,' said the Master. 'I see that. Where is there a phone?'

'I have one in my study,' said Mr Mountnessing.

'We should not touch anything,' said Imogen. 'Where can I wash my hands?'

The three of them went through a doorway at the end of the room into a side-room where Wyndham's Librarian had a cosy study. A little lobby with a tiny window had been made into a kitchenette for him. While Imogen washed her hands, the Master picked up the phone. He seemed not to have dialled 999 but the number of the local police station. Imogen had spotted an electric kettle on the side-table, and was hastily making therapeutic tea. She thought the next hour would be rough on everyone.

The Master was saying, 'We have found a body in a locked library at St Agatha's... Yes, there was a college feast last night... What do you mean, tell you another? No, I do *not* read detective stories...'

Imogen took the handset from him. On impulse she asked for Sergeant Michael Parsons, the only police officer in Cambridge whom she knew.

'Who shall I say is calling?' demanded the voice on the other end.

'Imogen Quy. No; it rhymes with "why" but it's spelt Q-U-Y. This is a very urgent matter...' To her relief, the operator put her through to her friend. 'Mike, this is Imogen Quy. I'm sure you remember me from that St John's Ambulance training course. 'Good. Mike, there's been a... an accident. It might be foul play. Please get

9

someone over here as quickly as you can.'

An hour later, Imogen was sitting in Mr Mountnessing's study, overhearing conversations in the library next door, and sunk in misery.

'But who could have done such a thing?' the Master kept asking. 'A perfectly inoffensive young man like that!' His interlocutor was a policeman – Detective Inspector Balderton.

'First find out why, and then it's usually easy to find who,' said the Inspector. 'What do we know about the body? Debts? Girlfriends? Enemies? Supporter of silly causes?'

'You must talk to his tutor,' said the Master. 'Mr Benedict will tell you anything the college knows about him.'

'Later,' said the Inspector. 'When the pathologist and the fingerprinting boys have done their stuff. Hallo; what's this?'

Someone had found a book. It was lying on the floor, under the lethal table, and wedged against the skirting, as though it had been projected from the outflung right hand of the dead young man.

'Where does it belong?' asked the detective. 'Was he stealing it, perhaps?'

'No,' said the Master.

'Why do you say that, sir?'

'Well, it would be such a wicked thing...'

'Does it come from one of these shelves?'

'I'll tell you if you let me look at it,' said Mr Mountnessing.

'Look without touching, please, sir. There may be prints.'

'*Nova et Antiqua Cosmologia*. Yes: it belongs in the Wyndham Case.'

'Valuable, is it?'

'Fairly. Not by any means the best book here.'

'This room kept locked?'

'Always. It is a condition of the Wyndham Bequest.'

'Can I see the keys? Strewth! That might be the bloody murder weapon! Where the hell did you get one like that?'

'It's Christopher Wyndham's own design. Made in 1691.'

'If you could possibly do without me...' said the Master. Imogen walked back to her office with him and shook out three more of his pills. He sat in front of her little fire, sunk in despondency, while she tried to comfort him.

'Would you like me to contact his parents for you?' she asked.

'No, no. That's my responsibility. Can't shirk that. But thank you. A kind thought,' he said.

The day was getting worse and worse. And the Master had hardly left her for five minutes when a girl undergraduate appeared, looking upset. 'Miss Quy, could you come, please? There's someone locked in the girls' toilet on E staircase, crying her eyes out, and we can't make her come out.'

Imogen accompanied the girl to the toilets. The sound of racking weeping filled the chill, tiled little room.

'Who is it?' she asked.

'We think it's Emily – Emily Stody – but we haven't seen, only heard her,' the girl said.

It took Imogen ten minutes of exasperating pleading to talk Emily into unlocking the door and emerging, tousled and red-eyed, a picture of misery.

'What's it about, then?' Imogen asked, kindly enough.

'Philip's dead,' said one of the bystanders.

How had it got round the college so fast? The body had not yet been covered and taken away. 'Oh, well,

11

colleges are like that,' thought Imogen.

Emily at once began to weep again, gasping for breath between sobs.

'Emily, you'd better come to the sick room,' said Imogen, leading her away. Emily was a healthy, a positively glowing young woman who had never visited Imogen's 'surgery', not even for the kind of advice young women in a mixed college usually requested, so Imogen knew nothing about her except by repute. Her friends were an assortment of classy youngsters – Jack Taverham's crowd – given to wild parties about which wild rumours went around. A confident and dominant sort of girl. But she was certainly in something of a state now. Imogen – with a motherly arm round the girl's shoulder as they walked – could feel her trembling. And yet, once she was sitting comfortably in Imogen's room, with a cup of hot sweet tea in her hands, and confronted with Imogen's professional kindness – 'Now, what is all this about? Can I help you in some way? '– Emily suddenly sobered up, and clammed up.

'Miss Quy, I'm awfully sorry. I'm a bit of a pig to take up your time like this. I'm all right now, really.'

'Don't worry, Emily; that's what I'm here for. Of course you don't have to tell me what has upset you, but you can if you want to. I keep people's confidences, and often I can help.'

The girl said nothing. Imogen risked, 'Is it about Philip?' At that Emily looked up at her, as if startled. Her pale blue eyes met Imogen's.

'Everyone is upset,' she said.

'But not everyone is bawling in the loo,' thought Imogen, though she said only, 'Were you fond of him?'

'No,' said Emily. 'Why should I be? I hardly knew him. Only at parties.'

'But you did know him; and now...'

'Oh, Miss Quy, people are saying he's been murdered! That's not true, is it? It *can't* be true!'

'I honestly don't know what happened, Emily. The police are here to find out.'

Emily's face looked about to crumple into tears again.

'Anyone would be upset the first time someone they know dies very suddenly,' Imogen said, gently. 'It's perfectly natural.'

Then, when the pause she left open in case Emily changed her mind about confiding in her was left in silence, she returned to her brisk manner and insisted on taking Emily back to her room, and helping her to bed with a hot-water bottle.

'You honestly don't have to bother,' said Emily. 'I'm all right.'

But she obviously wasn't all right. Imogen escorted her back to her room, which was in the Garden Court, high up; a pretty attic with sloping ceilings and a view of the castle mound rising from the immaculate lawns and trim flowerbeds which were the pride and joy of the college gardeners. The room was chaotic, full of discarded clothes and scattered books, but the bedder had cleaned around the mess, and the bed was made. Emily dropped her culottes to the floor, pulled off her Benetton sweatshirt, and climbed into bed in her peach satin undies. 'I expect I've got flu,' she said.

Imogen opened the cupboard in which the architect concealed the washbasins, looking for a tap to fill a kettle for a hot-water bottle. The basin was heavily stained, and there was a large number of test tubes and glass bottles around. A strange and pungent smell was released into the room by the open door. On the mirror above the basin a sticky note bore the message:

'Please conduct experiments in the laboratory, not in your room. M. Hillaston (your bedder).'

Imogen was hardly surprised at this. She filled the hot-water bottle, and brought it to Emily with two aspirins and a glass of cold water.

'I can't go to sleep,' said Emily. 'I've got a supervision this afternoon.'

'I thought you had flu,' said Imogen. 'I'll cancel it for you. You just sleep it off.'

'Whatever it is,' she added, under her breath.

2

When Imogen got back to her room she found Roger Rumbold waiting for her. Roger was the college librarian – 'the *real* librarian' he always called himself, in ironic contrast to the Wyndham Librarian.

'I thought I'd drop in and see how my favourite nurse is surviving,' he said. 'I expect you're having a bloody awful day. Come for a drink?'

'I mustn't, Roger, thank you. I've hardly been in my room all morning, and I don't suppose the usual crop of student ills is suspended just because of poor young Skellow. Another time. How's your mother?'

'She's all right in herself,' said Roger. 'But her roof still leaks. I can't get our blasted Bursar to do anything about it. Couldn't you mention to him that damp brings on bronchitis, which brings on death in the aged, and the college might be liable?'

'I could vouch for the damp to bronchitis part of that,' said Imogen. 'You're right, Roger, I could certainly do with a drink. If you'd care to have a whisky with me right here…'

'Yes, please, Imogen.'

She set out two plain medicine glasses, and produced her bottle of The Macallan from the back of the cupboard.

'Mmm,' said Roger. 'Just the ticket. I didn't know you were a secret drinker, Imogen.'

'I'm very careful, Roger, as it happens. It takes a dire emergency to drive me to drink as a pick-me-up. And I never drink alone. A person who lives alone can't afford to.'

'That's a touch puritanical for me, Imogen. Your health. Besides, you don't live alone. Your house is packed to the attics.'

'Well, I do and I don't,' said Imogen, collapsing into the other armchair in her room, 'like you.'

Roger lived in college. Rather few of the college fellows did that nowadays, most of them having families to go home to. A live-in fellow was so valuable that when, a few years back, Roger had announced that he would have to live with his mother in future, as she was becoming too frail to manage, the college had hastily found Mrs Rumbold a place in Audley's Almshouses, just a step from the college in Honey Hill, and belonging to some trust entangled with the college by the Wyndham Bequest. Ever since then, Roger had been grumbling in a mild way about the administration of the almshouses, which he said needed money spending on them. Personable and hard-working as he was, he was one of life's grumblers.

Roger was always nice to Imogen. He chose to regard himself, though he was a senior member of college, as, like herself, an employee, and brought a conspiratorial tone to their relationship. Imogen thought of this as a game, and mildly enjoyed it. She also enjoyed Roger's company when, as he did from time to time, he took her in to High Table, or out to dinner or a theatre. Life had rather side-tracked Imogen, although she enjoyed male company as much as anyone did, and Roger's friendship was welcome to her. If, sometimes, she wondered what motivated him, she remembered a line of Hazlitt her father used to quote: 'The art of pleasing consists in being pleased.' Only right now she wasn't feeling pleased by Roger.

'The whole place is humming with rumours like a wasp's nest,' he said. 'My favourite theory is that Crispin did it. The handsome boy rebuffs Crispin's lewd advances, and there, in Wyndham's sacred chambers, the Wyndham Librarian does him in. What do you think?'

'That you are disgraceful, Roger. I know you and Mr Mountnessing have been feuding for years, but accusing him of murder is OTT.'

'Perhaps he has flipped his lid. Being in charge of all those books of ancient rubbish might push anyone over the edge, I would think. *I* would go dotty in his position. But of course, you have the advantage of us all; you may *know* what happened.'

'Well, I know that Philip Skellow fell, or was pushed, hard enough to crack his head open on the library table. Mr Mountnessing found him. He was very upset.'

'I can't understand why that should count as an alibi. Of course the murderer would be upset. *I* would be upset if I had done someone in.'

'*And,*' thought Imogen, sipping her whisky, observing her companion, 'you are a little – not quite upset, but uneasy, Roger.'

'A murder is very disturbing,' she said, 'to everyone's peace of mind.'

'Why, Imogen,' he said, suddenly concerned. 'I believe you are upset yourself. I'm so sorry. How crass of me to joke about it! Forgive me.'

'There was blood all over my hands,' said Imogen, suddenly near to tears. 'Poor young man! It's such an *outrage*, Roger!'

'There, there,' he said, leaning forward from his chair and taking her hand. 'Couldn't it have been an accident?'

'I'm not sure. Perhaps, just possibly. I think it's almost

17

as much an outrage anyway, even if only God or chance are to blame.'

'That's too deep for me, I'm afraid,' he said, getting up. 'And one can't help wondering, you know, what the victim was *doing* in the Wyndham Library. Perhaps he was nicking books.'

'Perhaps we should not make slanderous accusations until more is known,' said Imogen, crossly. Just for once she was glad to see the back of Roger.

It was a great relief when her 'surgery hours' were over. Imogen locked up and went on her little round. She looked in on Emily Stody, and found her safely curled up fast asleep. She visited a third-year flu victim and released him from bed, starting tomorrow, and then – it was hardly a duty, but she was concerned – she called on the Master.

The Master lived at the far end of Castle Court, rebuilt by Christopher Wren after the depredations of the Civil War, when the castle had briefly returned to military use, and the college had been exiled to Barnwell. An austerely beautiful colonnade led at the far end to a wide black-painted door with an immense brass plate, which Imogen always thought ought to read 'Mr Badger's House' but which actually said 'Master's Lodge'. The Master was sitting at his desk in evening dress. He looked ten years older, and his face was a crumpled ashen grey. When Imogen entered, he looked up at her and said, 'I've just been talking to the dead man's parents. He was an only child.'

'How terrible,' she said. 'I'm so sorry. Master, forgive me, but do you think you should dine out this evening?'

Behind her the voice of Lady B. said, 'At last! The voice of common sense. Do listen to her, William.'

'I can't,' he said. 'I'm dining with Lord Goldhooper.'

'Couldn't you make some excuse? Say you are ill?'

'But that wouldn't be strictly true, my love, would it?' he said. 'I am perfectly well, only a little distraught.'

'Nobody else I know would worry about a technical untruth like that, in the circumstances,' said Lady B.

'Wouldn't the strict truth do?' asked Imogen. 'Someone has been murdered.'

'We don't know that,' said the Master. 'And I am in no hurry to tell Lord Goldhooper about it, even if it is true. He would be only too likely to take his three million pounds somewhere else!'

'That dreadful man!' said Lady B. 'I really wish he would do just that! He is leading you such a dance, William.' She turned to Imogen. 'Miss Quy, you have no idea! One ridiculous condition after another! Endless meetings with lawyers! The college has perfectly good lawyers, but he will only negotiate with William in person. And whatever he asks, William feels obliged to do, for the good of the college. Lord Goldhooper has the finest astrophysicist in England dancing attendance on him like his valet! It really is too bad!'

'Don't, my dear,' said the Master, looking pained. 'You mean it kindly, I know, but you are merely rubbing salt. How many more of these oblivion pills can I take, Miss Quy?'

'No more till bed-time, I should say, Master,' said Imogen.

'Going to the Pink Geranium at Melbourn,' lamented Lady B., '...and driving, in such a state...'

'Not driving,' said Imogen. When her professional view of things surfaced she was capable of bossing even the Master. 'Let me order a minicab for you, and another to bring you back.'

'Could one rely on a minicab?' asked the Master.

'We can rely on Zebedee's,' said Imogen. 'I was at school with him; he's a good sort.'

19

She waited to give moral support until the Master was collected by the cab. A malign coincidence resulted in their having to wait in the gatehouse archway while the ambulance and several police cars at last took their leave. Imogen's friend Mike Parsons was driving the last car. He waved, and wound down the window to greet her.

'What can you tell us, Mike?' she asked him.

'Not a lot,' he said.

'Will it be a murder enquiry?'

' 'Fraid so. You must have realised. We'll be back in the morning, talking to everybody.' With that the car ahead of his eased out into Chesterton Lane, and he was gone, leaving room for the cab from Zebedee's.

'Good luck, Master,' said Imogen, closing the cab door on him.

And she felt like a wrung-out dishcloth. She just didn't feel like the bike ride home to Newnham straight away, and on impulse she went into the college gardens. She climbed the castle mound, on the zigzagging path. She loved to see it as it was now, lined with crocus and aconite naturalised in the grass. She felt both delight and envy – her own little garden gave no scope for effects like that. She observed with pleasure that the steepness of the path caused her no breathlessness, barely affected her pulse. 'You'll live, Imogen,' she told herself.

Below her, in the rapid dusk of early spring, Cambridge lay outspread. St Agatha's was nowhere near the famous Backs and had not even a glimpse of river or river bank to its name; but it had, indeed it encompassed, the highest point in the city, and topped the only hill. From the summit of the mound Imogen could command a view across the rooftops, starting with the backs of a row of seventeenth- and eighteenth-century houses along Chesterton Lane that were now all part of St Agatha's, and the tiny, ancient church of St Giles, with its simple bellcote – luckily a plan to knock the houses down and replace St Giles by a huge new church in 1875 or so had been rejected by the then fellows. Beyond, the Cambridge roofscape was punctuated by towers and spires and cupolas and the avenue of delicate Gothic turrets along the sides of King's College Chapel. From here the fundamental shape of the town was clear, its two main streets jostling as they shouldered their way towards Magdalene Bridge, to become Castle Street and mount the gentle incline past St Agatha's. Imogen liked to reflect that one of these ancient alignments had carried the Roman road from Colchester to Chester. From the west the open countryside still seemed to come right up to the edges of the town, the massive tower of the University Library was backed by green distance, and the just perceptible rise of the last hills in England before the fen; ahead the gentle wooded rise of the Gogmagogs impinged modestly on the wide sweep of evening sky.

Imogen drank it in, and sighed. She loved this townscape, this town. She was Cambridge born and Cambridge bred. Even her name was that of a local village – Quy, once a Saxon 'Cow Island,' in a fen long since drained and dry. All her disasters in life had happened somewhere else; she had usually been happy here. She would never like to live anywhere else. But she was harassed tonight, and a half-remembered quotation was nagging at the back of her mind. Only as she descended again, in quest of her bike, did the quotation surface clearly:

'...On a huge hill,
Cragged and steep, Truth stands, and he that will
Reach her, about must, and about must go...'

A good motto for a detective, Imogen thought, ruefully.

[illegible faded text from previous page showing through]

3

Imogen's house was in a terrace. The three slotted slabs for parking bicycles which occupied her front garden were all assigned to the lodgers, so Imogen wheeled her bike down the tiny alley between garden fences that led between her road and the next, to the back garden gate, and put it in the shed that leaned against an ancient apple tree. She noticed that the dark buds on the tree were beginning to swell, and smiled at her little colony of snowdrops beside the fence as she walked up the path. Opening the back door into her trim little kitchen, she was reminded at once that one day last week she had found it left ajar.

The comfortable battered chairs beside the Rayburn in the breakfast room were both occupied – it was cheaper to sit beside Imogen's wonderful cosy stove than to put coins in the gas meters in their bedrooms – by two of her lodgers, Simon and Liz, who were amiably arguing about something.

'Kettle's hot, Imogen!' Liz called. Imogen hung up her coat, wondering uncharitably whose tea and milk were in the mugs her two scapegrace students were holding, and then, seeing the packet of tea-bags and the bottle of milk they had brought down from their rooms, she was repentant, and opened a packet of chocolate digestives for them. In theory, Imogen's lodgers helped pay the expenses of staying on in the large and comfortable house she had inherited from her parents; in practice they cost more in biscuits and such like than she would have thought possible, and kept her washing machine running non-stop day and night, though the obsession with clean clothes that possessed them all did not extend to clean rooms. Sometimes she thought it would be easier to stop taking student lodgers. But they had inveigled themselves into her way of life.

'But the climate *must* have changed!' Simon said.

'Well, but climates just don't change that easily,' Liz replied. She had done Part One geography before changing to law. 'It's an ignorant speculation, Simon. Every time the weather changes people say the whole climatic system has shifted for good; but really it has changed very slowly, oscillated between narrow limits, and very slowly, until very modern times. Of course the greenhouse effect is another matter, I grant you, but...'

'Don't you go throwing words like ignorant at me!' said Simon, still amiable. 'The fact is, your assertions are based on nothing but theory, whereas when I say the climate has changed I am basing the assertion on historical documents. Not theory, but fact.' Simon was a historian.

'I have a bone to pick with one of you,' said Imogen. 'I know I explained to you about the back door. And last week I came home and found it open.'

'Sorry, Imogen, but it can't have been me,' said Simon. 'I was away last week, reading in the Newcastle County Archive for the Prof. Don't you remember?'

'Liz, then,' said Imogen sternly. 'It really is important.'

'Well, I know,' said Liz, frowning. 'But...'

'No buts,' said Imogen. 'I won't have that door left open.'

Liz, who was blonde and rather pretty, usually had that vacancy of very young faces, and looked suddenly interesting when she frowned. 'But I'm sure, Imogen, really sure, that it wasn't me.'

Imogen, who had expected denial, realised that Liz genuinely was sure. Of course people can be sure, and mistaken. How many times had someone in Imogen's care been sure they had remembered to take their pills?

But Liz was a steady, trustworthy sort of girl.

'Well, never mind about last week, just make sure it doesn't happen again,' she said, and set about making herself her supper. There was a problem there, though. Not that Cambridge was much troubled with burglary; when Imogen was a child every front door in the street was left unlocked. She well remembered her mother saying, when advised to lock up on going out, 'But one of the neighbours might want to borrow something, and then they couldn't get in!' However, that was then, this is now. The little alley at the back was not overlooked, and the kitchen door had a defective catch. If it was closed but not locked, it was likely to blow open in gusty winds, and could stand wide all day. She really ought to put a Yale lock on it; no – she could imagine only too well getting locked in the back garden every time she put rubbish out.

'But there was snow before Christmas nearly every year, for centuries!'

'Well, whatever the reason was, it wasn't climactic change!'

'You mean *climatic*, I think. And don't be ridiculous.'

Imogen put her chop in the oven – she couldn't imagine living without the Rayburn, always warm and ready to cook, and she felt a guilty pleasure every time she used it, since having the coal-fired one which had dominated her mother's life replaced by a gas-fired one. All the benefit and none of the work – whatever would her mother have said? Pretty much the sort of thing

Roger Rumbold said about the Wyndham Librarian!

And while the chop cooked Imogen left the youthful disputatious voices in the breakfast-room, and did what she had done the day she found the back door open: she went up to the top of the house and inspected Professor Wylie's flat. Professor Wylie was in Italy; he usually was. He was a fellow of St Agatha's, but had retired from active involvement and now spent all his time in pursuit of the ancient books he collected. He needed a *pied-à-terre* in Cambridge, and Imogen's flat suited him as well as he suited her. For him she had broken her usual rule that her lodgers were never from St Agatha's: a good rule usually, she reflected. She would otherwise have come home today not to innocent and irrelevant chat about snow before Christmas, but to more frantic talk of death by violent means.

The flat did not have its own front door; it was simply the top floor of the house with a kitchenette installed under a skylight on the upper landing. Professor Wylie's books filled it; they were piled high on the floor in stacks, carefully made with the spines alternating with the page edges, so that no undue pressure would damage the squeeze on the spines. The rooms were lined with crammed and crowded bookcases, the table was piled high, the piles of books even advanced down the stairs, occupying every tread left and right. To Imogen's eyes nothing looked disturbed: the Piranesi prints which decorated the chimney breast in the room the Professor used as a sitting-room were still there; his bronze of Laocoon with serpents was still on the mantelpiece; his heavily tarnished Georgian silver teapot – full of cold tea, Imogen discovered, picking it up to put it away – was still on the draining board of the tiny sink. If the flat looked chaotic, the chaos was home-grown. Imogen knew the books were hugely valuable; but if several dozen had been removed she wouldn't have known any different. Reassured by the unfingered dust on every pile – she was absolutely forbidden to dust the books – she rinsed out the teapot, and returned to her chop.

Later, when the young had disappeared on their evening amusements and Imogen had cleared the kitchen, she lit the gas fire in her sitting-room, spread herself in her cosy chair and, at peace for the first time that day, began to think. At first her thoughts were troubled; poor Philip! And what a calamity for his parents! Of course, Imogen knew only too well that not everyone in the triumphant flock of the gilded and gifted young people who won places at Cambridge every year would enjoy it; a considerable minority would spend some or all of their too-brief three years being very miserable, and some would shipwreck drastically – taking their own lives, or getting into dire trouble. Many more would merely disappoint their ecstatic parents and school teachers by getting indifferent degrees, or taking diplomas in sociology, or getting pregnant. Not that that was the problem it used to be now that everyone was so ruthless about abortion. Idly Imogen wondered if Emily Stody's flu was anything to do with being a little overdue. She must keep an eye on that girl.

By and by Imogen got up and fetched a battered notebook from her bookcase. It had a pretty flower-printed cover, and a pencil tied to the ribbon place-marker. Imogen had learned long ago how to take patient histories, sitting at hospital bedsides asking questions, ordering the answers carefully, and never, never (her professor was very insistent) failing to explore and eliminate the significance of anything that looked merely coincidental. If the flu patient has, completely coincidentally, just returned from West Africa, then the flu may be Lassa fever; if this is the third member of a family, completely coincidentally, to get sepsis in a surface wound, then hygiene in the home in question may be poor; if an unduly large number of people who happen to smoke get emphysema... Imogen had learned this lesson well. As she had learned the benefits for clear thinking of writing things down. And there was, of course, an oddity about Philip's death in the Wyndham Library. The Wyndham Case, which was normally of very little interest to anybody except Roger Rumbold – to him it was like a raging toothache – had now figured, coincidentally, in two successive college crises. Imogen set herself to recall and set down everything she knew about Christopher Wyndham.

Scholar, poet and eccentric, friend of Andrew Marvell and Samuel Pepys, passionate opponent of Sir Isaac Newton... she got up and looked up Wyndham in Chambers' Cyclopaedia. 1629-92. The entry called him an 'occultist'. He had been extremely wealthy. St Agatha's, of which he had been a scholar, was impoverished by the Civil War, during which it even lost possession of its buildings for a short time. Wyndham had made large bequests during his lifetime, on which the prosperity of the college still depended. On his death he had bequeathed his books to the college, in a settlement hedged about with conditions. Imogen wrote down what she knew about those conditions.

Fundamentally the Wyndham Bequest had been a scheme like that of Samuel Pepys' bequest to Magdalene College. Like his friend, who had died a few years after him, Wyndham had left to his old college a library of books, complete with cases, on condition that in perpetuity no book should ever be removed, and no book should ever be added to the cases. But while Pepys had merely contributed to a handsome building which eventually housed his bookcases, Wyndham had commissioned

Wren to design from scratch. In almost every respect he had tried to go one better. His bookcase, the great two-storey affair with gallery and steps, that dominated the Wyndham Room, had been made and decorated by Grinling Gibbons. A permanent library keeper was to be appointed, who should enjoy 'the usufruct' of four farms. Wyndham had probably intended simply to make his library-keeper as comfortable as any other college fellow; but the four farms were now under Bayswater.

Two aspects of Wyndham's bequest caused trouble in the present day, and the first troublesome matter was just this. Wyndham's 'keeper', known now as the Wyndham Librarian, the post currently held by Crispin Mountnessing, was hugely overpaid. Essentially his job – merely making sure that no book was ever removed and none added to the collection – was a sinecure, although now that the books were very old some conservation work was entailed. He also had to supervise any scholars who wished to consult the volumes, which they were allowed to do at the reading tables provided in the room. There were not very many of these visiting readers, a matter which provoked the particularly vitriolic comments of Roger Rumbold, because the books in the Wyndham Case reflected Wyndham's opinions as clearly as those in the Pepys Library, just down the road in Magdalene, reflected the culture and urbane interests of Samuel Pepys. But Wyndham had been a Ptolemaic astronomer. He was equally opposed to astrology, still relatively respectable in his time, and to Isaac Newton. And there was not a soul left in the world, leave alone in the University, who did not nowadays espouse one or other of those two radically opposed opinions about the celestial world. The books with which Wyndham had thought to make an intellectual ark for his beleaguered opinions were now of interest only as objects – valued as incunabula, or for the light they cast on the history of typography, or for their splendid bindings – reverently inspected, but never read.

Of course the college had a real library, and, in Roger Rumbold, a real librarian. He was paid the going rate for academic librarians, no doubt, but it did not amount to more than a fraction of what Bayswater ground rents bestowed on Crispin Mountnessing. Crispin did not need to be, and was not, according to Roger, much of a brain. Of course he was *supposed* to be a brain – or at least, a scholar. He could not have been appointed otherwise. He had written the definitive critical work on Alfred Austin.

'Who?' Imogen had asked Roger, on being told this.

'Well may you ask!' Roger said, grimly. 'The next Poet Laureate after Tennyson, that's who.'

'Did he write anything good?' Imogen had asked.

'In a word, no,' Roger told her.

Mountnessing was working now on an edition of the works of Colley Cibber. No wonder hard-working, devoted Roger, whose real library was always short of money, whose own research languished for lack of time, grumbled and sniped at Mountnessing across the common room!

The other troublesome aspect of the Wyndham Bequest, as Imogen understood it, was the codicil. As Wyndham got older it seemed he got nuttier. His books were installed in the college, the will was written, the gift accepted, the conditions understood. But Newton's hated *Principia* was setting the world aglow – the Ptolemaic system was everywhere in disrepute. Wyndham spent his twilight years trying to disprove the law of gravity, and becoming ever more paranoid. He became convinced that everyone was waiting for him to die, in order to violate his sacred collection wholesale. The result was his codicil. Imogen methodically wrote down what she knew about the codicil. It provided for a system of audits to be carried out to check that the contents of the Wyndham Case were intact. The Wyndham Room was to be kept locked at all times, except when the keeper-librarian was present. The college was to have only one key. Wyndham himself designed the lock, and the key. The lock was never to be changed, nor any second lock added to the door. But there was a second key, to be used by the auditor. The audit, for which Wyndham had made undisclosed arrangements, was to be carried out once, on a date chosen at random, in every successive century from the date of the bequest. It was to be carried out without warning. If all was found to be in order, the auditor would announce the fact, and the college was to have a feast, paid for from the Wyndham estate. But if ever any book was found to be missing, or any spurious book was found to be present, then the college was to lose all benefit under the will. The books were to be sold, the keeper 'sent forth into the world', and all the money raised by the sale of every part of the Wyndham Bequest was to be applied to Audley's Almshouses, a modest charity for housing twelve elderly poor men and women of the parish of St Giles, which a friend of Wyndham's had set up in 1689.

Imogen put down her notebook, and sat deep in thought. She very well remembered the panic the Wyndham audit had generated last term. It was on one of the rare occasions when she dined at High Table. Roger had invited a suitably eminent guest – a lady from the Library of Congress – who had then gone down with flu, and was confined to her hotel room in London. Of all the senior fellows, only the Chaplain was likely to raise an eyebrow at Imogen's appearance as Roger's guest. He had once complained bitterly that some provision or other under discussion in the college committee 'reduced the Chaplain to the level of the college nurse', whereupon such a fury in defence of Imogen had browbeaten him that he kept clear of her ever after, though, as Imogen said to Roger, how could this be her fault? Anyway, that night – it must be about a year ago, Imogen supposed – there were quite a few fellows dining in, and one or two other guests, including an economics don from Oxford and a Queen's Counsel.

The Wyndham Bequest was mentioned, and the Master outlined the provisions of the will to his guests.

'Was this extraordinary audit ever carried out?' asked the lawyer.

'Crispin?' said the Master. Mr Mountnessing was something of an expert on college history, having, as Roger so often said, few more urgent demands on his time.

'Yes, indeed; the first time some thirty-five years after Wyndham's death, in 1728. There was a most splendid feast, involving five dozen roast swans. Everybody seemed to have forgotten about it after that, so that the second audit caused considerable surprise. But it was carried out in, I believe, 1855, and another feast was given.'

'But it was out of time, surely,' said the Oxford economist, 'if more than a hundred years had elapsed since the previous audit.'

'No,' said the Master. 'Crispin will correct me if I am wrong, but as I understand it the crucial date each time is not the date of the previous audit, but remains the date of Wyndham's death. An audit must occur at some time within each successive one hundred years after that. It could be nearly two hundred years since the last audit, and still be within the relevant century.'

'However,' remarked the lawyer, 'if no audit has been carried out since 1855, you must be expecting one daily.'

'Must we?' said the Master. A sort of hush had fallen over adjacent conversations.

'Well, the third century since Wyndham's death is nearly up. What month did he die in?'

'January,' said Crispin. 'January the eighth, 1692.'

'Then there has to be an audit within a month, I should think,' said the lawyer.

'I imagine that whatever arrangements Wyndham made have lapsed by now,' said the Bursar.

'Why do you say that?' enquired Roger.

Imogen offered her only general observation of the evening. 'If the purpose was to surprise the college, then it has been left too late. It won't be a surprise if we can be certain it will happen within a month.'

'I wouldn't call any such antique farrago a certainty,' said the lawyer. 'I imagine there is a trust of some kind, set up for the purpose. But you know, over great lengths of time trusts become moribund, people die, solicitors get taken over... a secret trust in particular could very easily get lost in the mists of time. Does the will provide what is to happen in the event that the audit does not get carried out?'

'We would presumably acquire control of the bequest,' said the Bursar. 'Who could say us nay?'

'Would you say we had nothing to worry about?' asked the Master. And, Imogen thought, nobody did seem very worried. They were talking about the whole matter in the tone of voice normally used for discussion on varying the procedure with the rose-bowl, that college tradition asserted should be brought out after dinner.

'I think I would be worried enough to make sure that there is nothing out of order with those books,' said the lawyer.

'What happens if there is?' asked the Oxford economist. He was told. For a while the conversation dallied with the vast sums of money that would be lavished on the twelve pensioners in Audley's Almshouses.

'We could billet them all in the Garden House Hotel for life on a fraction of it,' said the Bursar.

'Then I think I shall give you some excellent financial advice,' said the man from Oxford. 'Tamper with the books; make sure the audit will fail. When it does, apply to the Charity Commission to vary the terms of the Wyndham Bequest, on the grounds that it is unreasonable in present conditions, that the intention of the benefactor is impossible to fulfil. You get a splendid windfall. You would of course do something for the Audley's pensioners.'

'What a shocking idea!' said the Master.

'It rather appeals to me to divert some of Wyndham's loot to some useful books,' said Roger.

'Or to a new hall of residence,' said the Bursar. There was a sort of glint in people's eyes, a certain hopeful, wistful tone in their voices.

'There is, and will be, nothing wrong with Wyndham's books,' said Crispin stiffly.

'Oh, well, you would have to bribe the curator lavishly, of course,' said the Oxford man, laughing.

'What price Crispin's honour?' asked one of the younger fellows.

'Oh, it needn't affect his honour,' said Roger, with a glint in his eye. 'All that is needed is for some of the books to be at the binder at the crucial moment. Didn't you tell me, Crispin, that *A Treatise on the Astrolabe* was being rebound right now?'

Wicked Roger! He took malign pleasure – Imogen, sitting opposite him, could see the glee on his face – in the bombshell he had dropped. Mountnessing had turned a distinctly paler shade.

'Come, come,' said the Master briskly. 'We mustn't

bore our guests with this sort of thing. Ghosts of the past. We must turn our eyes to the future. We must have a care; even joking about a dishonourable manoeuvre such as we have been adumbrating tonight, leave alone putting one into practice, might deter future benefactors. Would you fetch the rose-bowl, Mr Sharkin?'

The most junior senior member present rose and brought from an ancient sideboard behind the high table a large shallow silver bowl, exquisitely chased, full of water topped with floating rose petals. Gravely the company passed the bowl round the table, and each person in turn dipped a corner of his extensive damask napkin, and wiped himself on the forehead and behind the ears. Some pleasantly nutty earlier benefactor had bequeathed the bowl for the purpose, having apparently believed that cold water behind the ears was a sovereign remedy for gout.

'Shall we go up?' said the Master, rising as soon as the ritual was complete. He led the way across the Fountain Court to the common room, where dessert was laid out in a splendour of old silver, overlooked by portraits of past Masters, and the company talked pleasantly of other things.

There had followed two weeks of the most appalling anxiety. Imogen recalled, wincing, how the Master and Mountnessing had both needed moral and pharmaceutical support while frantic efforts were made to retrieve the books from the binder. Mountnessing had refused to leave the Wyndham Case, but spent all day there, and all night on a camp bed in his office, so that should the auditor appear, he could be reasoned with. Of course the whole senior common room knew what was afoot, and the college buzzed with excited gossip. The discomfiture of one of their own members, and the associated windfall of money for college affairs, had just the elements to make eyes sparkle and tongues wag, and living-out fellows come in to dine in flocks.

Crispin's discomfiture was acute. The three books being rebound had gone to an eccentric lady who for many years had worked for the British Museum Department of Printed Books, and was incomparably skilled at her job, but who on retirement had moved to Skye, where she worked on a few special commissions. She was, luckily, on the telephone, but not co-operative. She very nearly refused to get the books finished at once, saying they should not be removed from the presses so soon. Then she agreed to complete the work in haste; but she absolutely refused to drive the books to Cambridge at short notice. She would deliver them, as arranged, in three months' time, in person, or she would send them by courier, at the college's own risk. Crispin wouldn't hear of that, and so somebody had to drive to Skye to fetch them. And Crispin wouldn't leave the Wyndham Case.

The Master was tied down with multiple onerous duties – Imogen thought he was already dealing with Lord Goldhooper, and he was on numerous weighty committees of the great and the good. It was held to be unfair to ask a college servant to take responsibility for priceless, uninsurable, irreplaceable objects. Crispin was beside himself.

'How did he get them there?' Imogen had asked Lady B., with whom she was discussing the wear and tear on everyone's nerves.

'The lady comes down from Skye once every six months. She fetched them.'

'They've been gone six months?'

'Four, I understand. Anyway, Imogen, everybody senior enough to be trusted is either too doddery to drive or too busy to be spared. Do you fancy an excursion? I

35

think we shall have to go ourselves, don't you? To share the driving.'

It had taken them five days for the round trip. Imogen had called on the 'Babysitting Circle' – an informal freemasonry of college nurses that arranged for them to cover each other's duty hours when required. Lady B. had booked them into an excellent hotel in the Forest of Bowland to break the journeys, and she was very good company. Though Imogen would have said the two of them had nothing in common except affection for the Master, it turned out that they had read a lot of the same novels, that they both liked gardening, that they both secretly thought St Agatha's in many ways laughable. The books were retrieved from a very cross lady book-binder and driven away, wrapped in blankets, in the boot of Lady B.'s car.

Sitting comfortably after dinner in the hotel, on the return trip, Lady B. had suddenly quizzed Imogen. 'Come on now, my dear, tell me about yourself.'

'What do you want to know?'

'Primarily, what you are doing apparently unattached.'

'Well, there was somebody once. It didn't work out.'

Under gentle probing, Imogen had told Lady B. the whole sad, commonplace story. She had been studying medicine at Oxford. The young man was older than her and universally thought to be brilliant. She had been deeply in love. When his professor offered to take him to Harvard with the research project they were working on, they couldn't bear to be parted; she had thrown up her studies and gone too. It had never occurred to her that the ruthless dedication to science which she admired so much in him included ruthlessness about her. Not, that is, until he left her, abruptly, in favour of an American girl who was nearer his own level of brilliance, and had good connections – her father was a college president.

Coming home penniless, and without a right to a grant, she had not felt up to resuming a medical degree, and had trained as a nurse. She had intended to work in India, but then her mother had broken a hip, and her father needed her. She came back home to Cambridge, found part-time work as a nurse at St Agatha's, looked after her parents...

Lady B. offered no sympathy. She simply said, 'Luckier is not necessarily happier, you know. And there will be somebody for you, sometime.'

'Perhaps,' said Imogen. 'If I want. One gets to like independence. It puts people off.'

'Does it, still?' mused Lady B. 'I would have thought nowadays there were those who found strong-minded women a turn-on.' Imogen redirected her thoughts sternly to the matter in hand.

By the end of the following day, the precious books were safely returned to their places on the sacred shelves. The auditor had not turned up in the meantime, and a grateful college had given Imogen a generous bonus.

The auditor had not turned up while Imogen and Lady B. bowled along the high roads; he had not turned up at all. January 8, the tricentenary anniversary of Wyndham's death, came and went. There had been no audit in Wyndham's third century; the arrangements for enforcing his will had collapsed. And, as Imogen would have predicted if she had been asked, nothing happened. The college fellows voted to continue Mountnessing's emolument as before, to continue to respect the terms of the Wyndham Bequest. Any deviation from these immemorial arrangements would be bound to attract notice; and the practice of making generous donations to ancient colleges with conditions attached had not ceased in the seventeenth century; Lord Goldhooper was busy arranging just such another right now.

But the crisis was over, the audit now out of time. A body in the Wyndham Library was, in relation to the events Imogen had been carefully mulling over and noting down, just a coincidence. It had to be.

'A person perfectly well *could* have come back from West Africa without Lassa fever, and then caught ordinary flu. Coincidences do happen sometimes,' Imogen said aloud, addressing the remembered medical guru under whom she had trained. She closed her notebook, put out the lights and went to bed.

4

The college was uncannily quiet the next day. The weather was cold, and a grey drizzle descended from a sulky sky. From her window Imogen saw the unfamiliar sight of policemen coming and going to the Wyndham Library, and to the college office on the opposite side of the court, where they had set up an operations room. They were interviewing people all day. All day a uniformed officer stood guard at the foot of the staircase where Philip Skellow's room was; the other occupants of the staircase had to give their names coming and going. Everyone, it seemed, had other things to worry about than the usual aches and pains they brought to the college nurse. Imogen had a quiet day.

She checked up on Emily Stody; the girl was better, and out of bed. She opened the door to Imogen's knock and stood her ground, stony-faced. No, there wasn't anything she needed; only to be left alone. As Imogen left she added ungraciously, 'Thank you.'

As Imogen had fully expected, the Master dropped in for his quota of 'oblivion pills'.

'I am ashamed to confess that I need them again today,' he said.

'Be easy on yourself, Master,' said Imogen. 'The time to cut back on them is when things are normal. Not when a major disturbance is going on.'

'Disturbance?' he said. 'You will think badly of me. But

39

it isn't the police, Miss Quy, nor yet that poor young man's death, however distressing that may be. But if Lord Goldhooper can be persuaded to act sensibly as well as generously it will benefit the college for many, many years to come. It is that question that is agitating me.'

'The only aspect of it that I should ask you about is how long you think it will continue to worry you, since that has some bearing on the rate at which we can reduce these pills.'

'I don't know. It has been getting more and more tricky. I don't mind telling you about it, in confidence of course; perhaps an outside opinion would clarify my mind. The problem is this. We start from Lord Goldhooper's wishing to unload his fortune on the college. He wants to endow three fellowships, and nine student scholarships, for work using computers to advance science. He wants to give the college funds for these positions, and for highly advanced personal computers for these new fellows and their students to work with. It would make the college independent of what the rest of the university has available, and there would be money to update the hardware and software indefinitely. It would put the college in the world class for computer projects in science.'

'But?'

'But there are conditions. Lord Goldhooper is an admirer of what he calls hard science: physics, astronomy, inorganic chemistry. He dislikes – he positively *despises* – what he calls soft science: sociology, statistical analysis, economics, that sort of thing. He wants to tie us up so that we can never use his computers or one second of any of his scholars' time on any such thing.'

'Is there any problem doing what he wants?' asked Imogen. 'There would never be any end of projects that he would approve of.'

'No. But there would certainly be very tempting projects that people would badly want to embark on, that he would definitely *dis*approve of.'

'Do you have to decide this all by yourself?' Imogen asked. 'What do the other senior members think?'

'Oh, that we should take the money and run, to use a cliché. The decision is mine, but I shall be very unpopular indeed if I refuse to take the gift.'

A thought struck Imogen. 'Is medicine a hard, or a soft science, according to Lord Goldhooper?' she asked.

'Soft, I'm afraid. Out of the question.'

'And the difficulty is that you yourself disagree with the great man's value judgment?'

'Well, no; not entirely. I agree that the great thing is to work in areas of science which are capable of yielding precise answers to precise questions. We would have no difficulty keeping the terms of the donation for the next few years. The trouble is, Miss Quy, that I don't think it will long be possible to distinguish hard from soft science. Organic and inorganic chemistry, and molecular physics, and genetics, and probability theory applied to genetics, are all going to collide and coalesce. Nearly always good new science takes place on the boundaries of subjects. I can foresee the college entangled hopelessly in futile and intellectually disreputable attempts to maintain distinctions which everyone else has abandoned, forced to do so on pain of losing the Goldhooper trust. Allowing one project, disallowing another on the advice not of scientists, but of lawyers. Distorting projects to make them fit; becoming notorious for such things. A result compared to which overpaying Mountnessing is a mere pinprick. It is this I am fretting over when I can't sleep!'

Imogen offered sympathy. She doled out a day's pills with a gentle admonition to try to have two left at bedtime, to help with that sleep problem.

As the Master left she asked him, 'Is the dreaded Lord Goldhooper a scholar himself? What did he study?'

'Sociology,' the Master said. 'That's the trouble.'

The Master was Imogen's only visitor until just before five o'clock, when Mike Parsons, her policeman friend, suddenly appeared.

'Sit down, Mike,' Imogen said. 'Are you off duty? I can offer tea or whisky.'

'I won't have a drink, thanks,' he said. 'I'll be off to the Pickerel in a mo. Am I off duty? Well, that rather depends. The chief doesn't know why I'm calling on you, but it wouldn't be a sacking matter if he did.'

'Hum,' said Imogen. 'I ought to tell you before you start that college medical records are private property. College permission to see them, or a warrant, Mike, even if we are old friends.'

'Well now,' he said, rocking his chair back on its legs, and swinging himself gently, 'perhaps I would like a cup of tea, after all. And while you're getting it, maybe I'll just do a little thinking aloud. I take it I don't need a warrant to have a little talk with you?'

'Of course not. Milk and sugar?'

'Milk and three, please.'

'*Three?*' Imogen looked at Mike's lanky form sprawled in her chair, and decided he must be burning sugar as fast as she could supply it. He was wearing a suit which looked as though he had borrowed it for the day: his natural foliage would have been a track suit.

'You saw the body, Imogen,' he was saying, 'so you will realise there's a time-of-death problem.'

'Rigor setting in, and blood still wet. Yes, I realise,' she said. 'But he wasn't haemophiliac, Mike. I would have known about that.'

He nodded. 'We haven't had the path. report yet. Maybe that will cast light on it. It wasn't that I wanted to think aloud about, really. I thought to myself, "I bet that nice Miss Quy gets fond of these little perishers. In the course of her work."'

'Some of them,' said Imogen, cautiously.

'We're having a little trouble interviewing victim's known associates, otherwise known as students in this blessed college. I thought it just possible you could help.'

'I'll help you in any way I can that doesn't conflict with my duty.'

'Well, thanks. But really I was wondering if you could help *them*.'

'Tell me about it. As far as allowed, of course.'

'Some of them are bloody rude. It gets you down, having people be rude to you all day.'

'Sorry, Mike. The Cambridge citizenry doesn't hate its police force, I know, but these youngsters come from all over the place, and they bring their attitudes with them. I can't do anything about that!'

'I didn't think you could teach them manners, love. Too late for that. Look, here's what it comes down to. We've been buzzing about trying to find young Skellow's friends, and ask them simple questions about him. You know the kind of thing. When did you see him last? Did he have a quarrel with anyone that you know about? What were his interests? – the usual things. And we have a problem I could put to you like this. We have a list of young sprigs to see. Some of them are very rude; all of them are uncooperative.'

'Which makes things difficult?'

'Which makes things slower. They always tell one more than they mean to. We can piece things together.'

'But a few little jigsaw pieces from me might help?'

'Look, why don't I put you in the picture – off the record? And you fill in where you can – likewise off the record?'

'All right, Mike. The sooner you get to the bottom of this the better.'

'Natch. Well, the one thing nobody minds telling us about is the victim. A pansy boy, one would gather. Didn't row, didn't play rugger, did play chess; a swot. Dubious honesty, I am led to believe.'

'You amaze me, Mike. A perfectly nice young man. I'm sure he had girlfriends.' Imogen remembered seeing him in a pub, drinking and holding hands with a young woman. 'And why does anyone think he wasn't honest?'

'He seems to have had more money to spend this term than his friends reckoned he ought to have had.'

'Now if you had said he had *less* to spend than they expected I wouldn't have been surprised. He was sharing a set – a set of rooms – with Jack Taverham, and Taverham is very wealthy. Has money to burn. Has well-off friends.'

'I gather Skellow's presence in the set of rooms was an embarrassment to Taverham,' Mike said.

'Yes, perhaps. I think they had both asked to be moved.' Imogen got up and opened her filing cabinet, and looked at her notes. 'Taverham asked to have Skellow moved and replaced by someone else at the end of the first week of their first term. About six weeks later Skellow also asked to be moved. The Domestic Bursar sees to such things, but I make a note in case it casts light on some upset they bring to me.'

'Psychological?'

'We are talking about very clever young people. Or perhaps I mean very young clever people; sometimes they get upset badly by what seem like small difficulties.'

'So why didn't the Bursar move these young prima-donnas?'

'Rooms are always short; moves hard to arrange. And besides, the college had almost certainly put them

44

together deliberately. Taverham came from Brummer's School; he had six schoolfellows arriving in the college at the same time, and at least as many ahead of him in the second and third years. We like to split them up – they are very cliquey, as it is. Skellow was a grammar-school boy. As a general thing the college puts unlike people together, and they rub each other's corners off, and widen each other's view, and become reasonably cordial. Looking at this note now, I can see exactly why Taverham's request was ignored. They had a very nice set of rooms, overlooking Garden Court. He didn't ask to be moved; he asked to have Skellow moved, leaving himself in possession. The Bursar offered to move Taverham, to a room in a college house in Honey Hill; Taverham preferred to keep the rooms in college and put up with his companion. I should think the Bursar didn't even consider allowing Taverham to get his room-mate removed from a pleasant set.'

'And when Skellow himself asked to be moved?'

'That would have been different; but by then there really were no rooms available.'

'So they were stuck with each other?'

'Till next year.'

'And it seems Skellow was a pain in the neck at Taverham's parties. Cast a gloom over the fun. Made a fuss.'

'Maybe.' Imogen had no knowledge of that.

'But people don't get themselves murdered because they whinge at parties, Imogen, even though there was a helluva party the night before last. Or so we understand. There's got to be more to it.'

'Mike, I know it doesn't look like an accident, but...'

'We are to believe that nobody, but nobody, who was at that party can remember whether Skellow was there or not. If he was, he wasn't having much of a time, because everybody is absolutely certain that they didn't talk to him.'

'Why not ask Taverham?'

'We'd love to; but we can't find him. You wouldn't know where he might be, I suppose?'

'Haven't a clue, Mike, I'm afraid. In the old days people needed permission to be away from college during term, but not any more. As long as he doesn't miss a supervision nobody will notice for days. He could have gone fishing, gone home, gone to London...'

'His supervision isn't due till five o'clock tomorrow. He didn't go home. If he went to London, it wasn't on the train.'

'Nobody keeps tabs on a student's movements any more. Certainly not me. I can't help.'

'Let me go back to the beginning,' said Mike. 'We are interviewing people who were at a party on the night of the murder, that the victim was probably at. It was in his rooms, anyway. And some of them are rude, most are uncooperative, and all are frightened. Imogen, they are all very scared. You get a feel for it in my job; they are holding something back. And I thought you might like to try to help them; to limit the damage a bit. Murder is a very serious matter. Withholding information from the police in a murder enquiry is a very serious matter. They could get themselves into unpleasantly deep water. Someone ought to tell them to be sensible; someone ought to tell them to be careful. They can't *all* have murdered Skellow. The ones who didn't are digging an elephant trap for themselves. They could do very urgently with some friendly advice, and they won't take it from the police. So do you think...? Does your pastoral care extend to that?'

Imogen sat thinking. 'I could try,' she said at last. 'I could try talking to people and see if I got anywhere. To be honest, Mike, I think it would be easier to get them to tell me if Skellow was at the party, and when he left, than to get them to tell you, although I can try to persuade them to help you.'

'Then I'll make a little friendly deal with you,' he said. He looked at his watch. 'I'm definitely off duty now. I'll keep you abreast of the investigation, as far as duty allows me; you'll ferret around for me a bit and let me know anything you find out, as far as duty allows you. Here's a list of people who admit to being at the party.' He put a piece of paper on her desk. 'The ones I rather think aren't coming clean with us have a tick against them. Done?'

'Done,' she said.

5

Imogen took the list of names to her filing cabinet. It had been a big party, evidently – there were at least thirty names on Mike's list. Five of them were ticked. She began methodically to look them up in her case notes, reminding herself whether she had seen any of the young people, apart from the initial medical, and if so why, and what they were studying, and where they came from. Nick Sanderson. Reading economics. From Felixstowe. In the college first eight. Imogen had seen him twice: to bind up a pulled ligament in the left knee and then to give him simple exercises to speed recovery. She remembered him perfectly – he had the sort of sharp, intelligent features that often went with a weedy physique, set atop a massive athletic frame. He had been very agitated about his slight injury, in case it took the edge off his top performance. If he went to wild parties, she reflected, that would take the edge off him for a day or two, without any other cause required.

Frances Bullion. Reading English. From Taunton. She had never consulted Imogen on her own account; nevertheless, Imogen had seen her several times, when Mary Jakes, her room-mate, became depressed. Fran Bullion had turned up and consulted Imogen on how to befriend a person in psychological deep water. A cheerful, uncomplicated, well-meaning girl, very good-looking. And kindly: she had visited Mary in hospital, for Imogen had

48

bumped into her there. Hers was really not a name Imogen would have expected to find on a list of those withholding information from the police. One of the most likeable undergraduates in the college, Imogen thought. But then, she told herself wryly, the fact that I like someone isn't evidence!

Terence Masters. Languages – Persian and Bengali. From Finchley. Imogen knew him well: he had picked up a very nasty tummy bug in Bangladesh last vacation, and been chronically ill for months. He had missed a lot of term, but he was bright. He was repeating the second year. A lanky, rueful lad with a sarcastic tongue.

Felicity Marshall. Medicine. From Birmingham. Must be healthy; Imogen knew nothing about her.

Catherine Brack. Zoology. From Bournemouth. Ah yes; that one had needed Imogen's services a lot. She had had detailed contraceptive advice, and several tests, both for pregnancy and Aids. The fact that Imogen had not seen her recently might mean her turbulent life had settled down somewhat, and it might mean that she had acquired the expertise her lifestyle required. A dark-haired, delicate-looking girl with large blue eyes and an elfin appearance; Imogen could well imagine her as the centre of attention.

While she was at the filing cabinets, Imogen looked up the missing Jack Taverham. Agriculture. From Wood-bridge. Had never consulted her. Imogen frowned. Why did she think he had? Then she remembered – he had dropped in on her last term to borrow her typewriter over the weekend. She had been reluctant to lend it, she recalled, and he had beamed charm at her, and she had given in. He needed it to fix up a newsletter for some undergraduate society or other. He promised the machine would be back on Monday morning. She remembered a great handsome oaf of a fellow, standing in the doorway with her trusty Olympia in his arms, saying, 'Just to reassure you that your kit is safe with me, Miss Quy, I should tell you that I was at school at Brummer's.' The typewriter had been promptly returned, undamaged.

And last – why hadn't she thought of it before? – she looked up poor Philip Skellow. History. From Helmsley. And there was a recent note on his file. He was going trekking in Kashmir at Easter, and he needed jabs – the usual holiday inoculations. He was supposed to pick them up at the chemist and bring them to Imogen to inject for him. He should have come the day before yesterday, and he hadn't turned up. Had he forgotten? Had he cancelled his trip? But within hours of the missed appointment he had been dead.

Imogen considered the list of names again. Then she checked a room number, locked up for the night, and set out across the college court to see if she could find Fran Bullion and entice her home to a quiet supper in Newnham. Fran accepted very willingly, saying, 'I'd love to get out of college for a few hours!'

Imogen biked home ahead of her to prepare the meal. Her quickest way home involved wheeling her bike through the Castle Court of the college, past the Castle Mound, and through the little churchyard surrounding St Giles, all now within the college perimeter; then through the Chesterton Lane gate of the college. Imogen liked graveyards, usually; she liked idly reading inscriptions, and indulging the pleasing and poignant melancholy they brought on. Somehow, since the murder enquiry had begun, she was avoiding thoughts of death, those having become altogether more immediate and sharper. She had been coming and going via the main gate. But now she was in a hurry. The gravestones stood about among the leaf-blades of daffodils about to break into golden trumpet voluntaries, and the shorter darker blades of the promised lake of bluebells that would follow. The gardeners left the graveyard unmown until midsummer, when they would scythe the herbage down, and already the footstones and the little headstones that marked the places for the poor and the very young were obscured by the marching armies of advancing daffodils. Imogen had no time to linger today, anyhow.

Once in Imogen's house, Fran got on famously with Liz and Simon, who were again sitting in the breakfast-room, warming their toes by the Rayburn, and still arguing about snow before Christmas. They were only too willing to exchange their half-drunk mugs of powdered coffee for some of Imogen's sherry in honour of her guest.

'It wouldn't take *much* of a change in the climate,' Fran offered, when the problem was put to her.

'Come again?' said Simon.

'Well, as you say, we pretty well never have snow before Christmas; but we quite often have it in January – just after Christmas, in fact. The change required would only be about a fortnight on one of those season maps.'

'What's a season map?' asked Simon.

'Imogen, do you have a good gardening book?' asked Fran, wandering sherry in hand into the kitchen, where Imogen was dealing with supper.

'Second shelf on the left in the sitting room,' said Imogen.

Soon they were all three poring over the 'Advance of Spring Isothermic Map' in Imogen's *Climate and Gardening in the British Isles*. The wiggly lines on the map showed spring a fortnight later at Wisley in Surrey than in Penzance; ten days later in Cambridge than at Wisley. With renewed zest Simon and Liz began to explore the possibility that the interpretation of Simon's historical records needed the assignment of a place on the isothermic map for every one before it could be held to prove anything. The conversation flourished until Imogen began to set the table for two. 'Supper is chops,' she said firmly, 'and there are only two of them.'

'Time we were off, Liz,' said Simon, amiably. 'Never let it be said we were slow on the uptake.'

'Hints uptaken instantly, that's us!' said Liz, getting up.

'How d'you get lodgings here?' asked Fran. 'If only I'd known!'

'You go to Clare rather than St Agatha's,' said Imogen. 'I don't like mixing work and home.'

'I think you *are* mixing work and home, though,' said Fran while Imogen was making coffee, when chops with three vegetables and apple pie with cream had been dealt with. 'I can't think why you should suddenly invite me otherwise. But whatever you did it for, it is nice to be here. In a real place for an evening.'

'Isn't St Agatha's real?'

'Well, not really. Not like someone's house. It's a stage set, sort of, isn't it? For playing dramas in. Comedies most of the time, but... You want to ask me about Philip?'

'I need to talk to somebody sensible.'

'About Philip?'

'About that party on the fifteenth. And about why people won't help the police.'

'You can't blame them,' said Fran.

'Let's go and sit by the fire and be comfy,' said Imogen. 'Would you bring that box of chocolates, and I'll bring the coffee tray. Why can't I blame people for not helping the police?'

Fran curled up in Imogen's fireside chair and stared at her with wide, candid grey eyes. 'They give young people a hard time. They rough them up outside pubs, looking for drugs, they pick on their black friends, they are pretty well always rude to anyone in denim or under forty, and then suddenly they turn up saying 'Help us'. What do they expect would happen? People are actually afraid of them. People may have been beaten up...'

'Is that what it is?' said Imogen, pouring the coffee. 'Let me think aloud at you, Fran. We are talking about my friend Mike Parsons, and his chief. And we are talking about attempts to find out who murdered one of a group of friends. I find it a little hard to believe that anyone thinks Mike might be going to beat them up; and I would expect, I think, that Philip's friends would be more afraid of the murderer than of the police. Now, where am I wrong?'

'Well, for one thing, everyone seems to think that the people at the party were Philip's friends. Just because it was in his rooms. But they were Jack's rooms, too. Jack's party. Jack's friends. They didn't all like Philip. Some of them loathed and despised him.'

'Enough to want him dead?'

The girl shook her head. 'No, I don't think so. I wouldn't have thought so.'

'So where does that get us? I think the police want to know if Philip was at the party...'

'He was. I saw him there.'

'...and when he left.'

'I don't know. If it was me who knew that, I wouldn't mind saying. But I didn't see him go. The rooms were packed, and I wasn't paying much attention to Philip.'

'It's a nice big set of rooms, isn't it? Doesn't it have two little bedrooms off a big main room? Couldn't Philip have just gone to bed and closed the door on the party?'

'His room would have been – well, borrowed. Occupied.'

'Continuously?'

'Repeatedly. He used to get browned off. He used to push off somewhere else; all night sometimes. So perhaps he didn't go straight from the party to the Wyndham Library. And no, I don't know where he used to go. And I don't know what he was doing in the library. And I have answered every question about Philip the policeman asked me. Honest, Miss Quy.'

'Fran, I'm not accusing you of anything. But if I tell you that some of your friends may be getting themselves into deep trouble by not "helping with enquiries", what would you say?'

'I wouldn't say anything,' Fran said, glumly.

'Suppose the police were right in thinking that people were holding something back? Suppose that I am right in thinking that if they are it must be for some better reason than just dislike of policemen in general? What then?'

'What sort of trouble would they be in?'

'Obstructing a police enquiry – and a murder enquiry, too! Accessories to murder. Even simply making themselves suspects for a crime they didn't commit; surely only one person did the deed. There are some half a dozen people clamming up when asked questions, I understand. Any friend of the innocent would advise them strongly in their own best interests to cooperate with the police.'

'Have you heard of E. M. Forster?' asked Fran, suddenly.

'The novelist. Yes,' said Imogen. 'My father took me to tea with him once,' she added.

'Do you know what he said about treason?' said Fran. 'That if he had a choice between betraying his friend and betraying his country, he hoped he would have the guts to betray his country.' But she was looking more unhappy than defiant.

'It sounds wonderful, doesn't it?' said Imogen. 'Are you

telling me you think it would justify concealing evidence in a murder enquiry?'

'You see, I, personally, myself, wouldn't conceal anything about murder,' said Fran. 'But there might be lots of things apart from murder that people wouldn't particularly want to tell the police about. I mean, just because people are concealing something, it doesn't have to be murder.' She stopped, and coloured. 'I can see it's dangerous to talk to you. I like you; and if I'm not careful...'

'You will betray your friends?'

Fran looked up at Imogen. Her eyes gleamed with a trace of tears. 'I'm in a blue funk,' she said. 'I'm just scared.'

'Not for yourself,' said Imogen gently, 'but for your friends?'

Fran nodded, dumbly.

'Well,' said Imogen, pouring more coffee, 'I'm going to think aloud at you again. All you have to do is listen. You can't betray anybody by listening, can you? Here are a group of people behaving stupidly. They have drawn attention to themselves by their attitude. If they think the police will just go away and stop asking questions, they are very mistaken indeed. The police will ferret around till they find out what they want to find out, and anything else that may be carefully concealed is more likely to be discovered than hidden in the process. If these were my friends I would advise them to tell the police everything they know about Philip and the party. That's good advice. Perhaps, like you, I would draw the line at telling the police myself. But I would try very hard to talk people into coming forward on their own two feet. Of course, if there really is a murderer among them, then that person is in really terrible trouble. I would say there was no saving that person. But whatever the others may be concealing, it can hardly be as serious as the risks they are running. I wouldn't expect it to be any good my trying to talk them round. I'd say I needed a kind of Trojan Horse for good advice, some way of smuggling through to them what I have been saying to you, without them refusing to listen to it.'

'I see,' said Fran. 'I suppose I could try.'

'E. M. Forster would be proud of you,' said Imogen.

'Did you really have tea with him?' asked Fran, brightening. 'What was he like?'

'I was only a small child at the time. I don't remember much. He was doddery, and kind. He served very sticky buns,' said Imogen, launching into reminiscence. From reminiscence the talk got round to the novels. Was he a misogynist, they wondered? If so, not the usual kind, Fran asserted. Far from thinking women were inferior minds, and only of interest sexually, he seemed to think intelligent women had superior minds, and only when they acted sexually did he deplore them.

'Come to that,' Imogen observed, 'he wasn't so good at describing *men* acting sexually.'

'Well, he wasn't allowed to write as himself about that,' said Fran. 'He was a persecuted minority, wasn't he? He couldn't publish *Maurice* in his lifetime.'

'Well, I sympathise with him, biographically speaking,' said Imogen. 'But when I'm reading a novel, either it has got the sexuality of the characters convincingly described or it hasn't. No excuses possible.'

They talked happily till Fran had to go.

'Come again, any time,' Imogen said.

'I will,' said Fran. 'Trust me.'

Thinking it over, before going to bed, and making notes in her book of what she had learned about Mike's delinquent five, Fran herself included, Imogen rather thought she did.

6

Imogen's day began with the usual small medical emergencies, and a visit conveniently near coffee time from Roger Rumbold.

'I haven't got any biscuits,' she said, looking at him severely.

'Now, would I come for the biscuits?' he said, reproachfully. '*Would* I? How could you, Imogen? As a matter of fact I came to see if I was still in bad odour. Naturally enough hoping to find myself restored to your good books.'

'What do you mean, Roger?' she asked.

'Well, I thought you were rather tart with me last time I was here. Perhaps I just imagined it. But I say, Imogen, murder does rather seem to put everyone in bad humour. The senior common room is glum and jumpy, like the junior one just before exams.'

'Well, it's reason enough,' said Imogen.

'Of course. Not that being glum about it helps. It neither resurrects the dead nor apprehends the killer. I said as much to Mountnessing, and he near snapped my head off. Particularly hard to live with at the moment, is our distinguished Librarian.'

'Well, what do you expect, Roger? How would you feel if it had happened in *your* library?'

'Oh well, if it had happened in *my* library it could have been anyone,' he said, looking slyly at Imogen. 'My library isn't supposed to be kept locked, you know. Rather the opposite; it's supposed to be available to all. That's part of the idea. The police have got a full-powered watch-the-docks search going for Jack Taverham; did you know?'

'He didn't turn up for his supervision yesterday, then?'

'No. And his supervisor says it wasn't like him. Bit of a lad, it seems, but not given to skipping supervisions. His parents are distraught; say he hasn't been home, or been in touch. So it seems he's done a bunk.'

'Well, why would he have done that, unless...'

'Unless indeed!'

Imogen was frowning at him across the table. 'Somehow I'm surprised,' she said.

'Oh, good. I thought that frown was displeasure, rather than simply thought. And I'm hoping to entice you to dine at High Table on Sunday. The Master is bringing the dreaded Lord Goldhooper, and I thought you would be pleased to get a glimpse of the persecutor... oops, benefactor, I mean.'

'Won't you be neglecting your mother?'

'Not at all. Crazy Uncle Arthur is visiting from Gloucester, and she's as good as let me know my company would be uncalled for.'

'Then I'd love to come,' said Imogen.

Fran must have got busy right away, for shortly after Roger left a little procession of visitors began to call on Imogen. Terry Masters came first. A lanky, energetic-looking young man with a faded sun-tan, left over from those far eastern travels, no doubt. He sat down on the very edge of the chair, looking uneasy.

'I, er, gather that you would like to know when Philip left that blasted party,' he said.

'The police would like to know.'

'But we could tell you instead, and you'd pass it on?'

'Yes, if you preferred. Of course they might just come straight back to you, asking supplementaries.'

'He left early, as a matter of fact.'

'When would early be?'

'Before ten.'

'Did you see him go, Terry?'

'No; but I wanted to, well, borrow his bedroom for a bit, and someone told me he had gone, so never fear, so I had a quick look round the crush of people to make sure, and he wasn't there. You see, Miss Quy, I can hardly tell that to a policeman, can I? He'll want to know which girl it was, and that's none of his damn business, and it doesn't make any difference which girl it was, it just means I happen to know that Philip had gone by ten.'

'Terry, were you surprised he had gone?'

'Nope. I thought he might have been feeling a bit off. Gone to bed early.'

'Somewhere other than his own bed?'

'Well, there wouldn't have been much peace in his own pad.'

'Why did you think he might have been feeling dicey?'

'He was having jabs. The whole lot for India: typhoid, typhus A, polio and tetanus, meningococcal... you know. They made me feel very ropy every time I've had them, and I had warned him the party might be a bit much. He was there earlier, though.'

'You saw him?'

'He was there when I arrived. Look, Miss Quy, it would be really good if you could tell the fuzz what they want, so I don't have to go naming girlfriends. If there's a chance.'

'Terry, why don't you go and tell them yourself? You've got a little piece of hard information there; Philip had left by ten. Why not go and tell the police that you looked for him at ten, and couldn't find him. Just say you wanted to ask him something. There's a good chance they won't be interested in what you wanted to ask. And if you did have to say what it was about you could ask them to be discreet.'

'I'll think about it,' he said. 'But just in case I decide against, you tell them. OK?'

Imogen's next visitor was Catherine Brack. Such a pretty girl, Imogen thought. She was looking tense and pale; it appeared to suit her. 'Miss Quy, I gather one could tell you things instead of telling the police.'

'Not really instead of, Catherine. The police might want to ask you questions, whether you tell me things or not. But you could try telling me, if there is something you think they ought to know.'

'Philip left early. Definitely before ten.'

'You saw him go?'

'No, but...'

'But you're sure?'

'Everyone was looking for him. He wasn't there.'

'When was everyone looking for him?' Imogen spoke patiently. Long training in teasing out of people what they dreaded to tell you, long training in eliciting lists of symptoms was bearing fruit.

'Ten. So he had gone by then.'

'Catherine, *why* was everyone looking for him at ten?'

Catherine looked down at her hands. She hesitated. 'They wanted to play a joke on him.'

'What kind of joke?' asked Imogen.

'Does that matter?' asked Catherine, looking up in alarm. 'Nobody did it. He wasn't there.'

'I don't know if it matters, love,' said Imogen. 'But I think the police might want to know what it was.'

'I thought it wasn't very nice,' said Catherine. 'He was always being picked on; well, he asked for it, really, in some ways. He was a bit of a wimp, you know, Miss Quy. But this was a bit much. Well, it would have been a bit much, only Philip wasn't there. He left early. Someone warned him.'

'And you don't want to tell me what the joke was?'

Catherine shook her head.

'Even though it was you who warned him?'

Now the girl was really startled. 'How did you know?' she wailed.

'Not hard to guess,' said Imogen.

'You mustn't tell anyone it was me!' Catherine said. 'Please, Miss Quy. Promise. Please.'

'Catherine, since the joke wasn't played, since Philip is now dead, does it really matter who warned him?'

'It does to me. Please don't tell anyone.'

'I'm not going to tell anyone if you don't want me to. But Catherine, you're going to have to tell the police yourself. You really are. If only to fix the time at which Philip left the party.'

'If I start telling them things they're going to ask me more and more.'

'You must help them find who murdered Philip.'

'I don't know who. Somebody killed him in the Wyndham Case; it wasn't anybody at the party. We were all in Jack's rooms until late, whooping it up.'

'Including Jack?'

'Jack was there all the time, and right till the end.'

'When was that?'

'About half past one. He said he had to go to bed, and we all went.'

'OK, Catherine. Now, what I suggest is this. Go and see Detective Sergeant Mike Parsons, and tell him what you have told me. Ask him to keep it all confidential if he possibly can. Don't be afraid; you haven't really any option, and it's much easier to offer information than

61

have it pressured out of you, believe me.'

'I'll think about it,' said Catherine.

Imogen also thought about it. She turned over what she had been told. So when, just before her office hours were up, Nick Sanderson came in to see her, without waiting for him to tell her when Philip left the party, she said, 'Now, Nick, what is all this about a practical joke?'

He didn't show signs of surprise or guilt. 'Oh, that,' he said. 'Very stupid really. Someone was going to bop Philip one; give him a nosebleed. That's all.'

'That would have been funny?'

'Well, he was goofy about blood. Even a drop of it. The first week he was sharing rooms with Jack, Jack came in with a cut cheek from being booted at rugger, and Philip fainted clean away.'

'It does happen,' said Imogen. 'I trained with someone who had a terrible time with it. Used to get a needle into someone's arm, practising injections, and the needle would smoothly slide out again as the pupil nurse fainted holding it.'

'That's it,' said Nick. 'He was like that. Bit soppy in a man, don't you think?'

'I don't think soppiness has anything to do with it,' said Imogen crisply.

'Well, I didn't think it was that funny myself,' said Nick pleasantly. 'As a matter of fact I was going to come to his aid; fend off his assailant, you know; get bopped myself if need be. Doesn't worry me. So I was keeping an eye out for Philip and any sign of an ambush anywhere near him. And it didn't happen. He stood around having a few drinks. Talked to Emily a bit. Talked to Terry. Then he left. At about ten.'

'Nick, what exactly is the objection to telling the police about this?'

'Can't think, really. Perhaps it seems a bit off, telling a

policeman you were going to give some poor bloke a bloody nose and have a good laugh when he fainted, when the bloke in question has just been found seriously dead.'

'Well, I do see that. Nick, you are quite sure nobody hit Philip at that party?'

'Absolutely sure. I was all ready to interpose my person, in the famous phrase. And nobody followed him out, either; I was on the look-out for that. Jack was pouring drinks at the other side of the room.'

'Was it Jack you were expecting to do the bopping, as you call it?'

'No, it wasn't. I'm not saying who.'

'But lots of people knew about it?'

'Quite a few, yes. I suppose it sounds a bit naff to you, Miss Quy?'

'It does rather, Nick. I'm glad to think there was one person ready to try to stop it.'

The young man blushed slightly. 'Yes, well...' he said, getting up to go.

Imogen had quite a lot to tell Mike Parsons, she reflected on the way home. And she didn't like the feel of things at all. There was something both poignant and nasty about the thought of a young man with a horror of blood lying dead in a pool of his own.

7

Imogen had Tuesday mornings free. Barring emergencies, she arrived in college at around midday, and dealt with the day's enquiries then. One of the benefits of her way of life was a good deal of freedom. For a while she had done a second job, as a college nurse at another college, for the hours required at each made it perfectly possible, and only in the frenzy before finals was the work too taxing. But the small legacy from her parents and the mortgage-free house they had left her eased her need to earn money, and after a while she had decided that the most splendid luxury money could buy was a modicum of free time.

The job at St Agatha's, which was officially a half-time job, expanded in practice to more like two-thirds. Imogen was not cut out to be a clock-watcher, and interpreted her duties to the college very generously. Nevertheless she did have time to herself.

Tuesday was her day for pottering around the town, inspecting the garden plants and produce on sale in the market, window-shopping, and if she felt self-indulgent, buying herself a tiny box of exquisite chocolates from Thornton's or the Belgian Chocolate Company in All Saints Passage. Somehow these delights were less enticing than usual with murder on her mind, and she was nearly an hour early at the foot of Castle Hill when she passed the hairdresser's shop. Glancing in she saw it was nearly empty, and on impulse went in and asked if they could manage a cut and blow-dry without an appointment.

The manageress seemed uncertain. She disappeared into the staff quarters behind a curtain at the back of the shop, and re-emerged a few moments later to ask Imogen to take a seat. Then the stylist appeared: a young woman with a very tall hair-do, a very short skirt and very red eyes, who had obviously been copiously weeping, and for some time.

'It honestly doesn't matter if you're not well,' said Imogen. 'I can come back another time; I work quite near.'

'I can manage,' said the girl tearfully. 'Gives me something else to think about...'

'As before, but shorter,' said Imogen. It didn't seem like the moment to embark on a discussion of changes of hair-style. Then, looking at the woebegone face of the girl in the mirror, she said, 'Cheer up; it's probably not as bad as you think,' and was appalled at the expression of anguish in the girl's face before she again burst into tears. The manageress rushed over to her. 'You'll have to go off sick, Tracy love,' she said. 'You can't cope.'

And to Imogen she said, 'Please bear with us, Madam. Tracy's boyfriend has...'

'...been murdered,' the girl said. Her voice was suddenly cold and calm. 'They've bloody murdered him.'

Imogen took several seconds of shock to recover. A hairdresser's shop is such a refuge normally; such a palace of triviality, a shrine to harmless vanity. One sits being preened before a mirror, and vacuous conversation is administered to one's mind like the conditioner to one's split ends; the last thing she expected was this sudden face-to-face with real disfiguring grief, and the word 'murder'. She reeled inwardly, shuddered, and said softly, 'He wasn't called Philip, by any chance, was he?'

'How do you know?' said Tracy, through her tears.

'It's in the *Cambridge Evening News*, love,' said the manageress. 'Everybody knows.'

'I work at St Agatha's,' said Imogen.

'She's bloody one of them!' cried Tracy, 'I'm not doing *her.*'

'I'm sorry, Trace,' said the manageress, 'but whatever has happened, I can't have you insulting the customers. Do you understand? You're off sick, this minute. Upstairs with you, before you get the sack!'

'I just don't know what to do,' she continued, to Imogen, as Tracy fled, weeping. 'She needs a bit of looking after, and I'm short-handed without her as it is. She's such a nice girl, normally, too. Very pleasant with the clients, and reliable. I hope you'll excuse her, madam... exceptional circumstances...'

'Look, don't worry about that,' said Imogen. 'I'm not offended. But I don't think she should go home alone. I'm a nurse; do you think she would let me walk her home?'

'Well, it isn't a walk,' the manageress said. 'She lives in the flat above the shop here. Top floor. But it would be most kind of you if you would go up and see if she's all right. She could do with her Mum, *I* reckon, but her people are in Manchester somewhere, I think.'

Imogen climbed the stairs. She wondered what she would do if Tracy wouldn't let her in, but when she had climbed past the store-rooms full of cardboard cartons of shampoos and dyes, and reached the door of the flat in the attics, she found it open, and the bedroom door open, and Tracy lying face down on her pillows, sobbing in a muffled frenzy.

Imogen found the little kitchenette and made tea. Making tea, she reflected, stirring sugar into the brew, seemed an immediate and recurring consequence of murder. She took the cup in to Tracy, sat on the foot of the bed, and began to try to open a line of communication.

'I'm the college nurse, Tracy. I knew Philip a little because of that. I didn't murder him.'

The sobbing gradually quietened while Tracy took that in. At last, 'He liked you,' she offered. 'He said you were kind.'

Imogen winced inwardly. Of course she was kind; it was her professional duty. It came naturally to her; otherwise she would have hated her job. But there was an important difference between duty-kindness and real liking. If only more people understood that! Roger Rumbold, for example. To Tracy she said, 'We need to know who murdered him, Tracy. Can you help in any way?'

'I don't know,' the girl said. A deathly calm had replaced the sobs. 'I don't know if I ought to tell the police, or what. It was funny, what he said.'

'Would you like me to help you sort out what to tell the police?'

The girl nodded. She had hair of so beautiful a colour, rich honey-blonde, that Imogen had at first assumed it came out of one of the bottles on the floor below. But a longer look showed it to be natural. The eyes red with weeping were a pale golden hazel colour; the figure disguised rather than displayed by cheap ultra-fashionable clothes was shapely and full – a very beautiful young woman, Imogen realised. 'Tell me about Philip,' she prompted.

'Well, we're unisex here,' said Tracy, improbably. 'He come in for a haircut. Then he asked if I wanted to go to the cinema. Then we went out together. He came back here sometimes,' she added. 'He said I was a million times better than those stuck-up frumps up there!' She waved in the vague direction of Castle Hill.

'Tracy, did you see him last Wednesday?'

'Yes, I did. We were supposed to go for a walk in the afternoon, my half-day, but he didn't make it. Then he came here late, and we went to bed. I thought he'd maybe stay till breakfast, but he said he had to go. And I've been thinking ever since, what if I'd talked him into staying? It wouldn't have happened. He'd still be alive.' She began to cry again, silently this time, just brimming and overflowing tears.

Little by little, gently prompting and leading, Imogen got her talking. She learned a lot about Philip in the next hour. And also, of course, about Tracy. Tracy had been brought up in a children's home. She had an aunt in Manchester, who was kind to her but had six children of her own and couldn't cope with doing much for Tracy. The thought that Cambridge was romantic, and the flat above the job, had tempted her south; her only friends, apart from Philip, were the other stylists, all very young and wrapped up in their hectic love-lives. There didn't appear to be an available adult on whom Tracy could lean.

'What am I going to do, Miss?' asked Tracy, by and by.

'Well, you've got the afternoon off, haven't you? I think the best thing would be some sleep.'

'I can't seem to sleep a wink.'

'Are you registered with a doctor here?'

'No. I'm never ill.'

'Well, I have to be on duty in college in a few minutes. Why don't you come with me? We have a doctor in the college for a couple of hours on Tuesdays, and he will give you something to help you over the next few days. And you can talk to the police there too, instead of having to go to the station. And then you can come home here and get some sleep, and I'll pop in on my way home and make sure you're all right. How's that?'

'Thanks,' said Tracy. 'Are you sure I won't be bothering you?'

'Quite sure,' said Imogen.

A few minutes later this plan gave her an interesting sidelight on Tracy, who came through the archway of the college gate into the Fountain Court, and stopped short. 'Cor!' she said.

'It is beautiful,' Imogen offered.

Tracy was looking round it, wide-eyed. 'It's wacky,' she said. 'It's really something else! Philip didn't say.'

'Haven't you seen it before?' said Imogen, surprised.

'No; I didn't like to come bothering Philip here. Are they all like this?'

'Are all what like this?'

'Colleges.'

'They're all different. Many people would say that Trinity or King's is finer by far than St Agatha's. Haven't you seen any of them?'

'No.'

'I'd love to take you round and show you some of them, when you feel up to it,' said Imogen. She felt rather rueful about Tracy. Someone who could, from a baseline of complete ignorance, appreciate at one glance the qualities of the Fountain Court lacked neither brains nor eyes. What was she doing languishing in a hairdressing salon, uncultivated, unnoticed? Well, of course, Philip had noticed, and done some cultivating of a kind.

Imogen took Tracy to see Dr Feltham, explained the circumstances, got her a few doses of Valium, properly prescribed, and took her to the enquiry room, where Mike, glancing up, seemed instantly to realise a gentle manner was called for, and became avuncular and kindly.

A woman police officer was summoned to chaperone him, and he escorted Tracy into the interview room, saying 'See you later' to Imogen.

Imogen had a quiet afternoon. She pulled her notebook out of her handbag and began to record meticulously what she had learned from Tracy. Philip felt ill at ease with the toffs in Jack Taverham's circle. They were rotten to him; he despised them. They didn't do any work, just messed around, but he had come to Cambridge to learn things. 'He really loved his books, Miss Quy.' It was desperately uncomfortable in the set of rooms, never quiet for him, so he had to study in the library all the time. People kept playing jokes on him. He spent a lot of his spare time with Tracy, and was sleeping with her fairly often, but they were very quiet about it. He would have hated any of his college friends to find out and mock; she was worried about losing her job and her little flat if she wasn't respectable.

Last Wednesday Philip hadn't met her as arranged for a walk. He was supposed to be having his travel inoculations done by Imogen. Tracy had picked up the stuff at the chemist for him and given it to him the day before, but when he went to get it to bring along to Imogen he couldn't find it anywhere. He ransacked the rooms and got very cross. He went through all Jack's things as well, and he still couldn't find it. It got too late to keep his appointment with Imogen. When Jack came in, Philip challenged him. He thought the stuff had been hidden as yet another tiresome joke. Jack said he didn't know anything about it, and somehow, although Jack could well have done such a thing, Philip thought it was true. The two young men together went round knocking on people's doors, asking if anyone who had been in their rooms yesterday or earlier that day had seen, moved, hidden, or whatever, the chemist's sealed paper bag. One of the girls produced it at once, saying she was very sorry, she had thought it was hers. It had been on the floor near where she was sitting last night, and she had a prescription herself, likewise unopened. She had just picked it up, sorry, here it was... Tracy thought Philip had said which girl, but she couldn't remember. Anyway, Philip had complained that he had missed his appointment, and the jabs had to be given by a certain day, to give enough time between first dose and booster dose. Jack had said not to worry, one of the medical students could give it, it didn't need a nurse, and so they had gone off and found somebody to inject the stuff; sorry, Tracy didn't know who. She had just listened to Philip telling her all this without realising that any of it mattered specially; it was just why he hadn't gone for a walk with her. The explanation had been given to Tracy when Philip turned up a little after ten o'clock, maybe ten past, or quarter past. (That would be about right; the hairdresser's was about ten minutes walk from the college.) Imogen deduced that they had been in bed, talking, but not only talking, and Tracy's blurred recall of details like people's names was perfectly understandable.

What she did remember perfectly was that Philip hadn't stayed long. She knew there was a party in full swing, and he couldn't hope for any sleep till it was over, so she was hoping he would stay all night. But he said he had something to do. 'A little night work,' he had said. She had said surely he couldn't have work to do so late, and he had said it was important. He had kissed her, and left by midnight.

Imogen finished writing and sat thinking. She could well understand Philip's fury about missing the appointment for his inoculations. She, Imogen, was not allowed to give them except when there was a doctor on the premises. Dr. Feltham would not be there till the following week, and she must have warned Philip – she warned everyone – that they could not just drop in any time they liked to have inoculations. A whole week's delay would have entailed throwing out the recommended time-lags and intervals for the important ones.

Two contrary emotions contended in Imogen's mind below the surface of conscious thought. On reflection she identified them. One was sharply escalating unease at the possible pattern of events, at things which might just be coincidence, but perhaps were horribly significant. The other was relief. Real relief and gladness about Tracy. Someone had loved the young man who now lay dead in the morgue; someone had cared about him. Someone could talk about him without using the word wimp, and someone, now he was dead, shed bitter tears. Imogen couldn't at first think why she thought this was a good thing: a less upsetting thing by far than the picture of the victim as universally despised and unwanted. Wasn't his parents' grief enough for her? Nevertheless, Imogen did feel glad that Philip had inspired love as well as scorn.

8

When Mike Parsons turned up to talk to Imogen it was six o'clock, and he suggested driving out to a pub somewhere. 'Not in Cambridge. Do you know the Ship at Sutton Gault?'

Imogen agreed to be shown. They drove northwards, through Cottenham and across the bleak acres of the fen at dusk, flat as a map, and ruled with lines of brilliant golden dykes by the setting sun. A thin moon waited faintly for the sun's last exit. The Ship crouched behind a grassy river bank, beside a lonely bridge. It was quiet, beamed, panelled, quarry-floored, with open fires, local history books on the bar, real ale, and Palestrina on a very muted sound system. Before they settled in a corner pew they wandered outside and climbed the bank to look at the river, almost in darkness now, and with a flock of swans moon-faint against the water, quietly gliding. As Imogen and Mike watched, something startled the swans into flight, and they took off, lumbering into the air with wings that cracked like sheets in a high wind, and then creaked overhead.

'Wow!' said Imogen. But it was cold on the Ouse bank; they went indoors and settled comfortably at a table in the corner, within sight of the blazing fire.

'How are things, Mike?' Imogen asked. It was two years – must be at least two – since Mike, with three other policemen, had taken the St John's Ambulance training course, to help them cope with medical emergencies on the streets, in the cells, at football matches and the like. Imogen had taken it herself, to keep up to date on emergency resuscitation and the treatment of burns, which had moved on since she trained in casualty. At that time Mike had been living apart from his wife, and was having a hard time. He had confided in Imogen once or twice. This was the first chance she had had to talk to him personally during the current ruckus.

'Could be worse, I suppose,' he said, pulling a rueful face. 'That course wasn't much good to me, except for meeting you, naturally.'

'Why not? Did the citizenry stop fainting in Petty Cury as soon as you had learnt what to do?'

'I got promoted,' he said. 'I'm not on the beat any more.'

'What about your little girl? Do you get to see her a bit more?'

'Barbara relented, and took me back. We're rubbing along together somehow. And at least I'm there, bringing up the babe. She can talk now – rattles away like ninepence!'

'I'm glad,' said Imogen.

'Things could be better,' he said, 'but they could be worse. I haven't forgotten how lousy they were back then, and how good your advice was. What will you drink?'

'Glenfiddich, please, Mike. No water, no ice.'

While he fetched it she dealt with the rueful feeling which beset her. You reach an age at which all your contemporaries are entangled, and any fresh start involves hacking through tendrils of connections, leaving the sound of weeping behind closed doors. It seemed an insoluble conundrum. Those who hastened to marry or become long-distance 'significant others' proved so often, as soon as hindsight became available, to have been rashly mistaken. But those who lingered found equally predictably that they had left it too late; that barring amazing luck or amazing unscrupulousness in wreaking havoc, everyone normal and personable was spoken for. And of course, as you get older you become much more demanding and difficult yourself. Imogen liked something very rare – what she thought of as a ballasted boat – a personality that could sail, could take life gracefully, leaning to the wind, but which still had some weight, some load of seriousness to give it purpose. Roger's wit, and Mike's earnestness, combined. Whoever he was, she hadn't met him.

Mike returned with drinks and peanuts, and then the waiter brought menus and they chose their food. The administration thus dealt with, Imogen asked, 'Did it work? Did anyone come and see you, and come clean? Apart from Tracy, I mean. I know about her, of course.'

'Three of them did. One Terry Masters, one Nick Sanderson and one Catherine Brack. So we know three times over that Skellow left the party at ten. And thanks to a bit of lucky deduction we know from Tracy Jones where he went.'

'I've never heard of lucky deduction,' said Imogen. 'What's that?'

'It's what amatcher detectives do,' said Mike, grinning. 'Like you.'

Mike settled down beside Imogen on the pew, and pulled out his notebook. 'Right,' he said. 'So what have we got?'

'Mike, it's just a little difficult for me,' she said. 'People tell me things… I might need to respect their confidences, even if I have urgently advised them to tell you.'

'Fair enough. I'm not promising to tell you the entire state of the police enquiry, come to that. We each have our guidelines. All we're doing is synchronising our watches, to coin a phrase. But I did think best we should come out of town a little way, all the same.'

'All right. Sorry to be jumpy.'

'So. Philip first. Left the wild party at ten; visited his bird in nearby flat. Left her around midnight, saying he had something to do. Whatever it was took around eight hours, or something like that...'

'Time of death around eight in the morning?'

'Or thereabouts.'

'What are you going on?'

'Blood still wet and tacky when you saw the body.'

'Yes, it certainly was. But – I lifted his head from the floor. The neck was a little stiff. Not rigid; but stiff. I thought rigor might have started. What does the path. report say?'

'We haven't got it yet. You've been watching too much television. Anyway, doesn't it rather look as though the little job he had to do in the middle of the night was a spot of breaking and entering in pursuit of theft?'

'Theft?'

'Well, the room is stuffed with valuable books, and kept locked, Imogen!'

'Books aren't that easy to steal,' said Imogen thoughtfully, sipping her whisky. 'Well, I suppose they are as easy to steal as anything else, but much harder to dispose of. Famous books like the Wyndham Collection would be known to every dealer, every scholar, every librarian in the world; you couldn't just take them down the road and flog them to a local villain.'

'That doesn't stop people stealing Impressionist paintings.'

'No, I suppose not. But look, this is just a boy from Yorkshire...'

'Someone has got to him. Someone is using him.

Someone wants the books; particular books, perhaps.'

'Perhaps is the right word, isn't it?' said Imogen. 'Where's the evidence?'

'You really have been watching too much television,' said Mike. 'Police work isn't like something on the box, Imogen, with everyone mystified till they build a case with one scrap of evidence after another. The world is full of evidence: evidence for everything, down to the prowl-paths of the local cats. You make a guess what happened, and then look and see if any of all this evidence supports it.'

'You could be wildly out. What about proof?'

'Seldom necessary. People usually confess when confronted with a true story, even if it is based on guess-work. The trick is to guess right. Evidence does help one guess right... are you shocked?'

'Horrified,' said Imogen.

'The boss says,' Mike continued, 'find why, and you find who, find who and you find how.'

'Well, go on, then. Philip is stealing books in the Wyndham Case, and somebody comes in and kills him. Who?'

'The prior question was why?'

'Someone tries to stop the theft... there is a scuffle...'

'Victim is knocked over, bangs his head hard, drops book he is stealing...'

'It doesn't work, does it?' said Imogen.

'Sounds all right to me,' said Mike.

'Your boss's theory, not yours. Why doesn't lead to who, if this is why. And, Mike, what about that massive lock?'

'Well, I reckon your ineffable Mr Mountnessing forgot to lock it. He swears blue that he locked it that night, as always; but then he would, wouldn't he?'

'So perhaps the door was open; anyone could get in;

anyone could have discovered a theft, if there was a theft.'

'Well, the one person who isn't where they ought to be is Taverham; and we gather there's no love lost between him and the victim. So at first we thought, well, Taverham followed Skellow into the library, pushed him over, panicked, and ran. On one level this enquiry isn't getting anywhere until we find Taverham.'

'And hear what he has to say?'

'If he says anything.'

'You mean he might clam up and refuse to help you?'

'I mean he might be dead.'

'Why?' asked Imogen. 'I mean, why do you think so?'

'He was in for breakfast the next morning.'

'So?'

'About a hundred people saw him calmly eating breakfast in hall, looking perfectly cheerful, at nine the next day, just about the time when Mountnessing arrived and opened the library. So it makes an odd sort of story, doesn't it? He panics because he's killed his room-mate, so he runs away; but not till after his bacon and eggs and three toasts. We're still looking for him, but it's alive or dead.'

'You mean, someone killed both of them? Why?'

'It's got to be about what those books would fetch on some black market or other. South America or somewhere.'

'Like Impressionists. Somehow, Mike, I think books are different.'

'Humm,' said Mike. 'Meanwhile, back to the body. Someone has pushed Skellow and killed him.'

'But perhaps not deliberately,' said Imogen.

'Yes, indeed. Or do I mean no, indeed? A fatal blow to the skull caused by falling backwards against a table might easily be the result of an accident.'

'It just *might* have been an accident,' said Imogen. 'Mike, if it wasn't done on purpose to kill, is it murder?'

'Maybe not,' said Mike, 'but it's certainly something. I've been trying to imagine it. Suppose I – you – somebody pushes someone over hard. We don't mean to kill, but there to our horror is a dead body at our feet. What would you do?'

'Fetch help; hope against hope…'

'Or fetch the police, explaining vociferously how you hadn't meant it, how he just happened to bang his head I've known assailants do both those things. But if you were just an honest thug going in for a little bit of GBH, and you just happened accidentally to kill someone, would you leave them lying there and run away?'

'Mike, some of the students here are somewhat half-baked; they don't necessarily behave in ways that we middle-aged folk think of as mature and rational. You have to be able to remember being very young to understand the things they do.'

'Like what, for example?'

'Locking themselves in the loo and bawling when upset. Coming to see the nurse or doctor in such a state of terror in case they have some disease that they lie about their symptoms to make sure you don't tell them what they think they've got; throwing each other in the fountain; copying each other's essays; spending their grants on fruit machines; I could go on and on.'

'And these are the flower of the nation's youth, hand-picked for privilege?'

'There is an imperfect correlation between brains and sense. And of course, I'm slandering the majority of them; most are perfectly sane, most of the time.'

'So a jolly joke like sloshing someone to make their nose bleed and see if they fall fainting would not be typical undergraduate humour?'

'Oh, good,' said Imogen. 'Someone told you about that. I rather think natural shame about that explains why they all clammed up when you first interviewed them.'

'Ah,' said Mike. 'I don't think so, Imogen. I mean the resistance we were meeting, and the fright, seem to me out of proportion to the natural but not paralysing embarrassment the jokers might feel describing their proposed jolly jape to a reasonably decent fellow human. Now if that joke had actually been played, and gone badly wrong...'

'But it wasn't played.'

'So it doesn't explain much, does it?'

'I'll tell you another thing that needs explaining,' said Imogen. 'Emily Stody. Weeping her eyes out in the ladies that very morning. Wouldn't say why. Might be coincidence, of course, but a mention of Philip caused further convulsions of grief.'

'Tracy's rival for victim's heart?' said Mike. 'More your line of enquiry than mine, I think.'

'Not as easy as you think, Mike,' said Imogen. 'One can't go around asking the young about the state of their hearts. Emily has rebuffed several offers of a sympathetic ear from me. I don't think I'd get anywhere with that young woman.'

'Asking her pals?'

'They probably wouldn't tell. And in any case they may not know. Perhaps she keeps her secrets kept.'

'Well, I could always escort folk into the interview room, and caution them, and demand the information. Would that work any better?'

'The trouble is, shedding tears isn't a crime. You can't investigate that with criminal enquiry methods.'

'I keep warning you off television,' said Mike amiably. 'All we do is try to cotton on to what happened. Then, with luck, people admit it all; without luck we go ferreting around for forensic evidence. Why the girl was weeping might just be the clue that helps us cotton on. I have to admit that most of the time it's pretty bleeding obvious what happened, and the only problem is to find the villain. This is a bit different. Interesting case. Makes you think.'

'Well, I'm willing to find out what I can about the child's love life,' said Imogen, sighing.

'If you would, friend,' said Mike. Then he added, suddenly sombre, 'and while we're treating it like a holiday crossword, let's not forget it's a murder, shall we?'

'What did I say to deserve that?' asked Imogen, surprised.

'Sorry. Nothing. Sorry. It's just that we all run about tidying it up, explaining, understanding, forgiving, punishing, and all the while the poor damn body is bloody well dead; and from its point of view nobody is going to put *that* right!'

Imogen looked at Mike with interest. She remembered very clearly her own sense of outrage.

'His parents' only child, with a good hope of a happy and useful life in front of him... I know,' she said gently.

'It's just as bad if it's a sodden old meths drinker, butchered for fifty pence,' said Mike. 'We still run around tidying up, and collar somebody for it, and say to ourselves, "That's all right, then." Don't we?'

'Obviously you don't,' Imogen pointed out. 'Are you in the right job, Mike?'

'Somebody has to do it,' he said lugubriously. 'Or there'll be more murders, not less. And the somebody needs all the help they can get.'

'Yes; I did say I would try,' said Imogen.

They talked of other things on the drive back across the fen in darkness, through Cottenham, into Cambridge, round the Backs to Newnham. Mike had an allotment, Imogen discovered, and they chatted about sweetcorn, and the worthwhileness of growing one's own, compared with buying it in Cambridge market.

She was entirely unprepared for what met her when she opened her front door.

Professor Wylie was sitting on the bottom step of her stairs, unkempt as usual, his passport sticking out of his jacket pocket, his tie askew. 'I have a bone to pick with you, Miss Quy,' he said portentously.

'Oh, hullo, Professor Wylie,' she said. 'What's the matter?'

'What is the matter?' he said, obviously struggling with exasperation. 'You know all about it, I hope. It is, after all, your responsibility. I have relied on your assurances.'

'What about, Professor?'

'The safety of my property. I returned just an hour ago to find one of my books is missing. I cannot imagine why you should have abstracted it; it is of interest only to scholars. But, Miss Quy, I want it returned, *now!*'

She would have been angry if it had not been so apparent that he was genuinely upset. There were actually tears in his childlike old eyes.

Imogen was in for a hard time. The first problem was to comfort Professor Wylie and persuade him to look for the book. His flat was in such chaos, it seemed to Imogen at first that the book was simply mislaid, and it was impossible for him to have walked into his room an hour ago – for he had arrived on the ten o'clock from King's Cross and could not have been in very long when she got home herself – and immediately and correctly spotted the absence of one volume among so many. She would have liked to calm him down with cups of cocoa and motherly talk, and then help him look for it.

But he was by turns inconsolable and enraged – sitting

on the stairs hugging himself and rocking to and fro, like a two-year-old, with tears in his eyes, and saying, 'My book, my Bartholomew, oh, my Bartholomew, oh, my rarest book!' so that he sounded like nothing so much as an undergraduate actor playing Shylock, crying, 'My ducats and my daughter! – a thought which made Imogen struggle with the urge to laugh – or ranting at her about her responsibility, and her promise that the house was kept locked, that the lodgers would be honest, that his treasure would be safe... most of which she did remember having said.

By the time she contrived to get him upstairs in his flat and looking for the book, his shouting had roused the household and Liz and Simon had appeared in pyjamas, round-eyed, to hear their innocuous landlady accused of wicked neglect, or even of actual theft, since the Professor was imploring her to tell him where the book might be and get it back for him.

'Just tell us what it looks like,' said Liz cheerfully, 'and we'll help you find it. I expect it's just got moved.'

The three rational beings in the room looked round expectantly at the crammed shelves and tottering towers of piles of books, through which the Professor's narrow trade routes wove paths between chair and door, door and bed. In accordance with her promise not to touch books, even to dust them, Imogen had let dust accumulate on the volumes till the piles looked well on the way to resemble Miss Haversham's wedding cake.

'Where exactly was it, sir?' asked Simon helplessly.

'There, of course!' said the Professor, as though any idiot would have known. 'In that pile there!'

Simon picked a book off the top of the pile. 'Near Newton's *Principia*?' he asked, opening the book.

'Don't drop that!' said the Professor sharply. 'It's a first edition!'

Simon put it back, very gently. 'What does the one we are looking for look like?' he asked.

'No good; no point! It isn't here! Do you think I couldn't find it if it were?'

'Just the same, humour us; tell us what it was like,' said Imogen.

'A calf-bound quarto; a nineteenth-century library binding, with "Bartholomew" gold-tooled on the spine, nothing special from the outside,' he said, grudgingly.

They looked for it. They looked all down the pile the Professor said it should have been in, and then in every nearby pile. Liz and Simon crawled around on the floor, reading the titles, since handling the books seemed to increase the fury and grief of the Professor.

Imogen helped. By midnight they were certain the book was not in any of the piles; by one-thirty they were certain it wasn't anywhere in the flat.

They were all very tired, rather grimy from all the dust, and very fed up with Professor Wylie. 'Theft!' he was saying, his head in his hands, as they finally finished searching. 'I have been a victim! I hold you all responsible!'

'What was this thing worth?' asked Liz.

'I have no idea. Beyond price.'

'Well, I suppose you had it insured,' said Simon helpfully. 'What was it insured for?'

'Insured?' said the Professor, staring at him. 'You really have no idea, have you? One insures a *car*, or a *refrigerator*! Bartholomew is irreplaceable. There are no more copies known. The last one was bought by Pierpont Morgan in 1923 for ten thousand dollars. Now it would fetch three million; but there are no other copies. I shall call the police.'

Rather to Imogen's surprise the police sent someone round at once; she had thought they would wait till morning. A young woman arrived, who took down details, said she hoped nobody had touched anything, especially window or door handles, said it was a rather unusual burglary and someone from serious crime would be round in the morning, drank a cup of cocoa with the exhausted company, and left, saying kindly, 'Don't take on so, sir. I expect it will turn up!'

Imogen was so tired when she finally persuaded the Professor to go to bed that she only took off her outer clothes before scrambling between the sheets. Above her she could hear the Professor ranting away and weeping to himself. She lay awake. Of course she was remembering, as no doubt Simon and Liz were, the little matter of the back door left open one day, not so long ago... when exactly? She couldn't remember. But even if the lapse with the back door had given some evil person a chance for thieving, it really was a weird kind of theft, wasn't it? Imogen tried to imagine it. A sneak thief enters her house. He ignores the hi-fi and the television in her front room, takes no notice of money or documents in the bureau, takes no notice of anything belonging to Simon or Liz – well, admittedly, most of their kit looks more like the trawl from a jumble sale than desirable loot – and goes upstairs. He ignores the Professor's silver teapot, does not ransack the place for money, but takes a book. In a treasure trove of old and rare books he takes just one, and that one something in a nineteenth-century binding: 'Doesn't look like anything from outside...' the Professor had said. You would need to be imagining a hugely knowledgeable thief, frankly someone who knew what was there. How do thieves dispose of rare books? If on the market, then the Professor could put out a red alert for his Bartholomew round all the antiquarian dealers in England – in the world. It could only make sense if someone wanted the book and had briefed the thief; no getting away from it, somebody had to have known that the blasted book was there; and the Professor, even when he was in England, had few visitors. Glumly Imogen foresaw the suspicion that would fall on herself and her lodgers.

Even more dismal were her thoughts about the unhappy man still groaning and pacing around upstairs. How awful for him to lose something he seemed to love more dearly than an only child; how dreadful to have such an attachment for any material thing; how arid, how terrible a life, which leads to a grown man weeping inconsolably for such a thing as an old book, however magnificent! Imogen wondered what she herself valued as much as that.

Pacing restlessly, going to the bathroom for a glass of water, she stared at herself in the cabinet's mirrored doors. A full and rounded face stared back at her – how Imogen admired hollows below cheekbones! Tousled, curly hair haloed her face with bright red. Most of the clothes in any shop were ruled out by that colour. And, already, thirty-something. Well, admittedly, not thirty-very-much. She peered anxiously at the reflection, looking for the onset of wrinkles. Being a college nurse was such a motherly role, she felt she ought to look at least fifty; she often *felt* at least fifty. The mirror didn't tell her what she looked like, of course – mirrors are bad at that. It didn't show the attentiveness of her expression when others talked to her, or the tilt of her head, which tended to shade her eyes. She didn't sparkle at people; instead, her dark eyes looked mysterious – kind enough, but keeping an inward kingdom in reserve, like Saskia painted by Rembrandt. No bathroom mirror, no bathroom striplight in the middle of the night was going to show Imogen to herself, and in daylight she was too busy even to look.

9

Imogen woke to the sound of Professor Wylie's footsteps on the floor above. It was only five-thirty, she saw, blinking wearily at her alarm clock. Even so, she got up and plodded downstairs to make coffee. Her only reward for taking coffee and toast to the sufferer however was another half-hour of his desperate ranting for his book. In the end she simply walked away from him, withdrew to her room and got dressed. She was sorry for him – truly she was – but she had a day's work to do. No sooner was she seated in the little breakfast-room eating her own breakfast than he appeared in the door.

'I have come to apologise,' he said, sweetly. 'Do forgive me. I am aware that I love my volumes with an uncommon love – I do not expect anyone else to sympathise with such a passion, but if only you knew, Miss Quy, if you could only imagine what it means... to lose... treasured... irreplaceable... glory...' He began to catch his breath as he spoke, and then burst into tears and sat down abruptly on the step into the room, dropping his head in his hands.

She sighed, taking what she supposed would be her only bite of breakfast.

He looked up at her. His expression was wild, but his voice was suddenly calm. 'I am beside myself,' he said. 'I never knew what the expression meant! But what am I to do, Miss Quy? How does one, so to speak, *recover*

87

oneself? Do I require a tranquilliser? Do I require a psychiatrist?'

'No,' she said. 'You are not irrational in being distressed at losing something you love. What you require most, I think, is sleep. And then a plan of action. Whatever can be done to alert booksellers to the theft, you should set yourself to do it, carefully and methodically. And now you must excuse me.'

She escaped the house and rode down the street, eating her cold toast with her right hand, and steering with her left on the handlebars. Luckily there were no horrors awaiting her at work. She came home early to change for dinner at High Table as Roger's guest, thinking that she would have to struggle through more of the Professor's demands while getting into her posh clothes, but she found the house dark and empty. It was half-past five. Liz and Simon might have been in, or might not have; one could never tell. Her relief at the Professor's absence, her liberty to soak in a hot bath and to change at leisure and undisturbed was great. She was only mildly surprised at his absence. And in spite of the pressure of events piling up round her, she had preserved some curiosity about Lord Goldhooper, which the evening promised to satisfy.

Lord Goldhooper was not what Imogen had expected. She had somehow thought of a man of power as having bulk – as being tall, or at least stout. Actually he was a bird-boned little man, with a slight stoop and nervous, somewhat fluttery gestures. He had a hooked nose, and gold-rimmed glasses, and a shock of untidy white hair, in contrast to his Savile Row dinner jacket, his boiled shirt and black tie. Everything about him which was in the care of his manservant was immaculate, whereas he himself was unimpressive and rather unkempt, giving a curious impression of letting his own show down. The senior common room had turned out in force to entertain the great man; all the 'hard' scientists were there, and all the most glorious of the college fellows. Debenham, a junior research fellow in laser-optics, had invited a very famous woman fellow of the Astronomical Institute, who had recently discovered a new star and been very prominent in the papers. The most splendid college silver was in use, and everyone was on their best behaviour.

Crispin Mountnessing, still looking strained and pale, and displaying as his guest the eminent curator of antiquarian books for the University of Salamanca, was actually wearing a baroque decoration, mounted on a primrose yellow sash, which he had received from a Jesuit Institute in South America. Wryly amused and mildly shocked at it, Imogen perceived at once what kind of competition was going on between him and Roger, who had brought her. Some time she would have to explain to Roger that she didn't like being played as a low-scoring card in a private poker game, but for now she accepted the opportunity to observe her college in full force, and form an opinion of its prospective benefactor.

Roger might have intended only mischief in having her as his guest, but the Master, as she came into the combination room, said, 'Ah, Imogen!' and introduced her to Lord Goldhooper. Instead of the cool greeting and indifferent reaction she expected, Lord Goldhooper looked brightly at her, and asked her for a professional opinion of acupuncture. While she and Mike had been supping at the Ship, it seemed, everyone else had been watching a surgical operation shown on television, carried out in China without anaesthetics but with acupuncture. The patient had chatted cheerfully to the surgeons with his abdomen slit open. Imogen expressed a willingness to consider acupuncture, if it was explained to her, and the conversation became animated. The Master said it was a typical western attitude to suppose that something would work only given an explanation, only if we could understand how and why it worked; perhaps if the patient had been a western intellectual instead of a Chinese peasant the acupuncture would *not* have worked.

As the company filed in to the great hall and took their places for dinner, the conversation had turned to Chinese science, and the strange tangents to western science which it had taken. Chinese emperors had adored western clocks, but used them as toys; the Chinese had invented gunpowder, but used it for fireworks; had not invented computing, but made a simple abacus perform amazing calculations... In the discreet scramble for seating at the long narrow tables, Imogen and Roger fell back and sat modestly at the far end from the Master and the great man. The clear and confident voices from above the salt were speculating as to what it could be which had made the Chinese fail to exploit their discoveries, western style.

'Wisdom, perhaps,' said Imogen quietly, and the group around her laughed.

'Hush,' said Roger. 'We must all worship the great God Western Science, or we won't get the money!'

'Well, as I understand it,' offered Debenham, 'the case is worse than that. We must worship a particular kind of science only.'

'I have no difficulty over it,' said Pearce, a fellow in English. 'It's all the same to me.'

'Just look at that gewgaw Mountnessing is wearing,' said Roger. 'What does he think this is – a carnival ball?' The conversation became amiable and sociable. The college chef had excelled himself, and the food was engaging their attention. Later, however, a certain urgency of tone, or perhaps a rise in the volume of the conversation, at the upper end of the table communicated itself to them, and they began to quieten and listen.

'What is your subject?' Lord Goldhooper was heard asking.

'I am the tutor in English,' said Fred Barnes.

'I admire you,' said Lord Goldhooper. 'You have found a way of earning a living by enunciating your private opinions. But at least you make clear that your wares are simply opinions. I take it you would not claim any special authority for them?'

'Only what authority a lifetime of thought and reading may confer on them,' said Fred stiffly.

'Whereas this fellow here,' said Lord Goldhooper, indicating Soppery, 'is a sociologist, he tells me. I take that to mean that he falsely claims for his private opinions the status and the authority of science. He is a charlatan, I think.' This view was delivered with a smile of great sweetness, which nearly, but not entirely, drew the sting of his words.

Soppery began to defend himself. The degree of certainty available in certain sciences – those Lord Goldhooper described as 'hard' sciences – was simply not available in other fields of knowledge; one managed with whatever degree of certainty could realistically be aspired to, otherwise one would have to abandon large areas of human understanding entirely.

'Guesswork, pure guesswork,' said Lord Goldhooper. 'A natural resort of primitive thinking. Of course, in a subject like yours, Soppery, it is inevitable; you have my sympathy. But you don't get a penny of my money. I have no intention of *investing* in guesswork!'

Dr Forshaw spoke up. 'Might you perhaps be over-estimating the degree of certainty available in even such a subject as physics?' he asked. But the conversation around Imogen resumed; she caught only phrases from the other end of the table – '...uncertainty principle... probability theory...' Nearer at hand, among the more junior members, the conversation had turned to the prospects of the college rowing club in the Lents. Mr Pearce, it seemed, was wrestling with his conscience. He really ought to send down the young man who was stroke in the first college boat; he had done no work at all this year. Was it an abuse to postpone his banishment until after the Lents? The less sporting the fellows, the more they were inclined to think it was, Imogen noticed.

'Being head of the river won't cut any ice with that lethal little gnome up there,' Roger observed, and then hushed at once, for the Master had risen, and the lethal little gnome was moving into earshot, as the diners proceeded to effect a ritual change of places at the tables, so that everyone sat next to someone different while pudding was served.

Over an elaborate confection of whole pears in port wine the conversation continued animatedly. 'You may have the wrong picture, to some extent,' Dr Forshaw was saying as they took their places round the table. 'Scientific knowledge does not usually advance inch by inch, pure empirical deduction every step of the way. Someone gets a brilliant hunch – someone guesses what the truth may be – and then of course one sets up experiments to test whether it be so. It is hard to set up experiments in the absence of a theory to test.'

Imogen sat carefully eating a pear with a knife and fork. The redistribution of the company had left her sitting between a paralytically shy and silent research fellow in ophthalmology, and Dr Forshaw, intensely occupied with talking to Lord Goldhooper and the Master. Roger was seated out of conversational distance. She could simply listen. Dr Forshaw on science reminded her of Mike Parsons on detection. She was fascinated by an image of the universe as a recalcitrant suspect. But if you correctly guessed a truth, the universe usually confessed...

At the same time the worldly-wise element in Imogen was touched and amused by the unworldliness of the college fellows. Although they could not all like each other, and visibly did not, a profound brotherly respect for each other, often suffused with affection, gave them solidarity. What was happening, in effect, was that the 'hard' scientists were riding to the defence of Soppery, even if that imperilled the prospect of enjoying Lord Goldhooper's money. They were trying to argue him round, as though he were a slightly obtuse undergraduate. He would not win support for his project by calling one of them a charlatan; though any of them might have called Soppery that among themselves. The college was putting on a good show – the glories of its architecture, its fine silver, the discreetly hovering college servants, the haughty faces in the portraits, all giving the sense that the discussion now in progress was part of a conversation that had been continuing for five hundred years.

Once more following long-established custom, when the pudding was eaten, and after the circuit of the rose-bowl and a two-word benediction pronounced by the Dean, the diners rose and left the hall for the combination room, where port awaited them, and dessert in sumptuous silver dishes, and yet another redistribution of the company could be effected. The combination room was eerily beautiful, being in the Jacobean court, in a Gothic room with vaulted ceiling which had been the college chapel before Christopher Wren built the dauntingly austere and symmetrical present chapel. The lovely little late Gothic room made a perfect setting for dessert by candlelight; the only snag was that reaching it from the dining hall entailed crossing the Fountain Court in the open air. It was a night of bright stars, and sharply cold, and the members of college were disposed to hasten. But Lord Goldhooper, less familiar with the staggeringly beautiful effects of moon and starlight on the glories of the court, lingered beside the great basin of the fountain. The water jets had been turned off at midnight, and the surface of the basin was glass-smooth and reflected the stars between the remaining water-lily pads and the creeping web of paper-thin ice which was beginning to draw lines defining matt areas in the mirror made by the water.

Reluctantly but politely, the company halted beside the pool. They hugged themselves and drew the fronts of their gowns together across their dress shirts. Crispin Mountnessing stamped his feet on the worn flags of the path; the Master more discreetly blew warm breath at his curled fingers. Lord Goldhooper extended an arm in a wide gesture to embrace the scene; he opened his mouth as though to make some comment, but not a syllable emerged. Instead he remained frozen, he and everyone else watching while the tissue of ice was disturbed by something surfacing in the pool and floating. The moon sailed up from behind the tower over the porters' lodge and showed them what it was – the body of a young woman, her hair drawn in strands across her face, her mouth open, submerged and full of water, her skirt ballooning gently among the lily leaves, releasing bubbles at the hem.

Like a green and pallid Lady of Shalott, she floated among the reflected stars, slowly surfacing to the sound of a woman screaming.

10

The moment Imogen realised that it was she herself who was screaming, she stopped, abruptly. But her legs were shaky under her; she sat down on the freezing pavement, shivering, while a revealing theatrical scene was played around her. Fred Barnes sped away to the porters' lodge, roaring for help and the police. Mountnessing turned his back, walked to the frozen moonlit flowerbed in the corner of the court, bent double and was sick. The Master began to dance – to perform his wavering uncertain walk on the spot, while the Dean put an arm on his shoulders as though to hold him down. Lord Goldhooper, however – the object of so much desire to impress that had now, everyone must have been certain, terminally miscarried – assumed the wicked, gleeful expression of a little boy, and, turning to the Master a face full of moonlit *schadenfreude*, said, 'This young person seems to have met with a mishap. Isn't this your second dead body in as many weeks? What an *interesting* college St Agatha's must be!'

Roger helped Imogen to her feet. She stood, still dazed, and watched the porters running across the lawns towards them. Then, as though she had pressed her own inner emergency button, she stepped forward, edging the Master out of the way, and took command of the porters. They waded into the basin and lifted the body between them. The moment it was laid on dry ground Imogen saw it was not who she had thought it was. She told them to lift the girl by the legs. Kneeling, she lifted the head backwards by the hair, and held it while water drained from the girl's lungs. Then they laid her down and Imogen began the kiss of life. John Fairfield, the tutor in medicine, joined her, and began pounding the girl's chest in the drumbeat rhythm of cardiac massage.

'Who is it?' voices behind Imogen were asking.

'It's Flick Marshall, I think,' someone said, in a low voice.

'Who?'

'Marshall. Third-year medicine.'

'We shouldn't be watching this!' said a distressed voice.

'And I was looking forward to the port!' said Lord Goldhooper. He was led away to the dessert by a group of the junior fellows. When the ambulance men arrived they found only the Master and Roger watching Imogen and John Fairfield doggedly at work. A brief muttered agreement between the medically knowledgeable, and they stopped trying. The body was lifted on to a stretcher, and covered with a blanket. Then the police arrived. They were unknown to Imogen; the inspector in charge seemed young and world-weary. He spoke as though it was accident or suicide; he would take statements in the morning. No, there would be no need to detain Lord Goldhooper; his chauffeur could drive him home as long as his name and address were available...

Eventually Imogen found herself wrapped in a blanket beside the fire in Roger's room, sipping brandy and being comforted. The terrible possibility of encountering Professor Wylie on a midnight wailing walk on her stairs in Newnham – she could hardly bear the thought in her present shattered state – had led her to accept the offer of the spare bed in Roger's set.

'That wasn't like you, Imogen,' he observed, pouring

himself a brandy, and sitting in the opposite chair.

'What wasn't?' she asked. The shivers produced by shock and cold had worn off, leaving a deadly weariness in their place. She felt as though she could hardly summon strength to lift her glass.

'Screaming like a girl at the sight of a body. We were all very shocked, of course. Did you see Mountnessing cross himself?'

'No, I...'

'And our poor Master! What a calamity for him; oh dear, oh dear!'

Imogen didn't want to talk to Roger. It had been a mistake to accept his brotherly attentions. But she was hardly in a state to walk home.

'But you, to whom bodies are an everyday affair? You certainly were very upset. Who did you think it was?'

'*Dead* bodies are not an everyday affair for me, thank God!' she said.

'Aren't you going to tell me who you thought it was?'

'No, Roger, I'm not.'

'But your cries *were* from distress at mistaken identity? How fascinating!'

'*Fascinating?* Roger, are you really a reptilian, cold-blooded monster, or are you just pretending?'

'Sorry, sorry,' he said. 'I'm just pretending, of course. One way of dealing with it.'

'Yes, I know. Didn't mean to bite your head off.'

'We both need some sleep,' he said. 'Have you any idea how late it is?'

But Imogen was too weary and over-stressed to fall asleep quickly in an unfamiliar bed. She lay looking at the sloping eaves ceiling above her head, and the moonlight slanting through the uncurtained little dormer window. And thinking, painfully. Of course Roger had been right: she had thought the body in the pool was

Fran's. Felicity Marshall was faintly similar in build; her drenched hair had looked dark enough, her height and build similar enough… Half submerged, she had looked like Fran. And if it had been Fran in the lethal water, Imogen would have known several things clearly. Several terrible things. It would have been murder. And it would have been Imogen's fault. Her remorse was sharp and biting. How could she have so lightly involved Fran in a trawl for information, when a murderer was at large? How could she not have thought of the danger she might be getting the girl into? All very well to rebuke Roger for taking it lightly; he was only bandying flippant remarks; what she, Imogen, had taken lightly was the safety of an unoffending student.

Tossing around in the darkness left by the setting moon, Imogen identified the source of her own wickedness. The reason why she had so cheerfully tried to recruit an informer, the reason why she had actually been as concerned about Professor Wylie's blasted book as about helping Mike Parsons. The reason why she hadn't, till now, actually been afraid. The trouble was she hadn't really believed Philip Skellow had been murdered. Obviously she had known, and therefore believed, that there had been some puzzling skulduggery or other. But murder? It had looked to her like a nasty accident. Or rather, like something which was possibly a nasty accident. So that, however much she had been thinking about it, she hadn't actually imagined malice – a will to kill, stalking among the quiet courts, among the young and unworldly people she worked with.

She was very sufficiently frightened now.

Only where did that leave her? Should she refuse to have anything more to do with helping Mike Parsons? The police are paid to take risks, she tried telling herself. Fran is not; I am not. Or was it more reasonable to think that another death made it twice as urgent to help the police all she could?

She slept at last, fitfully. Only in the grey light of a late winter dawn did it suddenly occur to her that death by drowning is often accidental; haven't strong swimmers been known to drown in shallow water? Neither a suicide nor an accident would give rise to grounds for cold terror. It might have nothing to do with anything; it might be just another, separate, coincident disaster. A person straight back from West Africa with a burning fever might – they really might, mightn't they? – just have plain simple flu.

11

In the morning Imogen woke, uncomfortable and promptly at her usual time. She considered what to do. Roger must be still asleep – there was no sound of movement in the flat. She had slept in her underwear, and found the thought of spending the day in it, unchanged, distasteful. Should she go home to Newnham for clean smalls? But her bicycle was left behind in Newnham – she had walked to college last night rather than cycling in a heavy silk skirt – and walking home now would take some time. She borrowed a dressing-gown from the hook on the bedroom door, slipped her shoes on bare feet, and, bundling up her underwear, she let herself out of Roger's rooms, leaving the door on the snib so as not to lock herself out, and descended to the student laundry room in the basement three staircases along the court.

She had thought it would be empty at six in the morning, but it wasn't. Another dressing-gowned figure was there, slumped in a chair in front of a lumbering dim kaleidoscope of clothes — Emily Stody. Imogen dropped her clothes into the machine and set it going. Emily glanced up and scowled deeply.

'You're up early, Emily; can't you sleep?' said Imogen.

She got no reply. And Emily really had been up early, for her washload was just clicking and humming into its final spin. It made too much noise for conversation, and

Imogen waited until Emily had pulled the clothes into a plastic basket and moved them to one of the driers.

'Are you still upset about Philip?' she asked. She wasn't expecting a reply to this either.

'Philip?' said Emily, exploding. 'That...that...why does anyone think I would give a damn about *him*?'

'Sorry, Emily, but lots of people were upset that day, including you. I just thought...'

'Well, you thought wrong. He was beneath caring about, he really was. I wouldn't have sunk so far.'

'As to mind about someone being murdered?' exclaimed Imogen.

'As to give a damn about *him*! He was a rat, Miss Quy. An absolute rat!'

'That's harsh. Do you really mean it?' Imogen persisted, doggedly.

'A pest. Scuttling around where they aren't wanted, that's what rats do.' Her drier came to a halt, and she bundled the contents into a pillowcase. 'Like you, really, nibbling around getting crumbs of information for the police. And you know what happens to rats, Miss Quy, don't you?'

'Philip was a nuisance to Jack Taverham, you mean?' said Imogen mildly. 'Emily, you must have realised that the fact that Jack has disappeared looks very bad...'

Emily turned on her a furious gaze which rapidly became crumpled with distress. 'If I knew where he was, do you think I'd be moping around here?' she wailed. 'And you stop sucking up to me with your sicky pretend sympathy and your leading questions! You just fuck off!'

'When my washing is done,' said Imogen calmly.

'Well, mine is done now, I'm glad to say. I'm off!' said Emily, scooping up her hot smalls, crackling with static, and removing herself.

Later, back in Roger's spare room, dressing herself,

Imogen reflected. Emily had a point really. She might have been deeply stung by those remarks, and spent time thinking and rethinking; only she was rapidly becoming numb. Too much was happening, too many shocks and panics and re-evaluations. She simply hadn't time and strength to meditate on a childish outburst from a girl like that. A girl like what? Well, Emily couldn't get to Imogen with any accusation, however violent, as Fran could have with the mildest rebuke. Imogen disliked Emily with skin-hardening intensity.

However, she had a day to manage. She got herself dressed, carefully pocketing the sparkling tourmaline Victorian ear-rings she had been wearing for dinner, left a thank-you note propped on the kettle for the still sleeping Roger, and crossed the courts to her office. There she would cover her grand shirt with an old cardigan, kept in reserve against the whims of the college central heating system, swap her evening skirt for the old washable twill one that she kept in her office cupboard in case she needed a change of clothes in emergencies, and be ready for whatever ills the students might be suffering from.

As she unlocked the door she saw a white rectangle lying on the mat. A note pushed under her door, some time after she left yesterday. It rang no alarm bells, and she dropped it on the desk, put the kettle on for some coffee, rattled the biscuit tin and found two digestives for breakfast, found and put on her cardigan. It was some few minutes before she sat down at the desk and opened the note.

> Miss Quy, I need help. I'll come and talk to you tomorrow, only I need to tell someone this RIGHT NOW – it may be my fault. I forgot to check the seals. I'm so frightened. F. Marshall.

Fear, Imogen found, was like being punched very hard

in the stomach. The implications of the note unfolded and reverberated in her mind, appalling all the way. Neither suicide nor accident seemed possible in the case of a girl who had written that note only hours before she surfaced, so horrifying, so moonlit and beautiful, in the fountain pool.

Her hand shaking, Imogen picked up the phone to the incident room the other side of the court. 'I was coming across to see you as soon as I got a mo,' said Mike Parsons, cheerfully.

'Please come now; please come yourself,' said Imogen.

He came in and sat down. 'Is this another enquiry, or another body in the same enquiry, we wonder,' he said pleasantly. 'You'll need to make a statement about last night's little drama, either way. Golly, you look peaky.'

She pushed the note across the desk to him. He read it in silence. Then, 'Another body in the same enquiry, I conclude,' he said. 'Do you understand this, Imogen?'

Imogen shook her head. 'No. I didn't know her at all. But ... I had thought perhaps it was accidental; or suicidal, maybe...'

He shook his head. 'No, m'dear. Not unless someone accidentally held her under. There are marks of struggle on the body, and what look very much to us like bruises left by the grip of someone thrusting her down. I would have thought the whole thing would have been in view from the porters' lodge, but they tell me not. They say the water jets would screen the view, and cover the sound of splashes. Anyway, this note makes it rather clear, don't you think?'

She nodded. 'It doesn't read like someone intending to quench themselves,' she said miserably.

'She was going to tell you something; someone stopped her. The someone didn't know she had already spilled the beans in a note,' said Mike. 'That's what it looks like. But what are these beans? What might be her fault? What seals?'

'I need time to think,' said Imogen. 'I'm very shaken, Mike.'

'Over a girl you didn't know?'

'Someone *murdered*. A second someone; someone, somewhere, capable of that, and prowling around among us...'

'Are you afraid for yourself?'

'It had crossed my mind to wonder if I was doing the right thing, trying to help. I thought for a moment it was Fran Bullion.'

'You should be. Afraid for yourself, I mean. We'll be keeping an eye on you, here and at home, for a few days.'

'Watching my house?'

'Discreetly. Do you mind?'

'I rather think I'm relieved,' she said.

'I must take this to the chief,' he said, getting up.

Imogen had a number of students to advise. One or two perhaps really sick – one silly great fellow ignoring a probable fracture under the impression that it was a sprained ankle – the usual things. She left her door ajar, her 'Back soon, please wait' notice displayed, and crossed to the Garden Court twice, looking for Fran, but she wasn't there. Just after twelve Lady Buckmote came in.

'How's the Master?' asked Imogen.

'He's very distressed,' said Lady B. 'Another set of parents to be told terrible news. But no more distressed than you are, by the look of you. You look distinctly green this morning. It's all rather nasty isn't it?'

'Nasty and...'

'Frightening?'

'Yes.'

'I know,' said Lady B. 'But it isn't about that I've come

across. I've had a frantic phone call from the man who organises the Banks Lectures, wanting to know what's happened to Professor Wylie. It seems he hasn't turned up. I thought I saw him in the market only yesterday – he has come back from Italy, I take it?'

'Yes, he's been back three days. The Banks Lectures?'

'Tremendous honour. He's supposed to be sipping sherry at a reception packed with bigwigs right now, before delivering the opening lecture in the Mill Lane Lecture Rooms in fifteen minutes. The house is filling to the doors and he hasn't turned up, so they got hold of the Master, since Professor Wylie's a fellow here. He doesn't seem to be in college; the porters haven't seen him this morning and they can't find him. I thought you might know.'

Imogen picked up the phone and began dialling her own number.

'No good,' said Lady B. 'They can't get an answer. They've even sped round to your house and hammered on the door without result. Have you any ideas?'

'He's in a funny state,' said Imogen. 'He's lost or been robbed of an important book. The night before last he was prowling all night, lamenting. He's very upset...'

'Upset enough to stand up the Banks Lecture that he's manoeuvred for years to be invited to give? Or so William tells me.'

'No, I shouldn't think so. I'd better go home and see if he's there.'

'Imogen, when did you last see him? Was he OK this morning?'

'I don't know; I didn't get home last night, what with finding poor Felicity Marshall.'

A tiny spark of interest showed in Lady B.'s expression, but it died instantly in the immediate concern.

'I'll go at once,' said Imogen.

'I'll drive you,' said Lady B. 'It will be faster.'

Imogen let them in to her narrow front hall, and called. No reply, except Liz, leaning over the banisters.

'Oh, hullo, Imogen.'

'Is Professor Wylie up there?'

'Don't know. Don't think so. Haven't heard a sound. But I've only just come in.'

'Was he around this morning, do you know?'

'Didn't see him. Sorry.'

Imogen led the way up to Professor Wylie's floor. The usual chaos. But alarm bells began ringing for Imogen at once when she saw the bed neatly made.

'I don't think he slept here last night. I made the bed for him yesterday, before going out to dinner. He never makes it himself.'

'I can see that the hand that arranged these books and the hand that neatened the bed were not the same,' said Lady B. drily. 'So you haven't seen him since yesterday, and he certainly isn't here. It looks as if they can whistle for their lecture.'

'He was very distracted. Perhaps he'll remember, and turn up. Didn't you say he had come back from Italy to give it?'

'Mill Lane Lecture Rooms, next stop,' said Lady B.

But at the lecture rooms the panic was unabated. The Professor had not turned up. A few disgruntled members of the audience were beginning to leave.

'You don't know what he was doing yesterday, by any chance?' Lady B. asked as they returned to her car, parked on double yellow lines in Mill Lane.

'I think he was touring book dealers, to report the loss of his book.'

'Could have been in London; could have been here; could have been anywhere in the nation.'

'Well, there wouldn't have been much point in

confining the news to Cambridge. But he didn't actually say where he was going. To tell the truth I was in a hurry, and I just walked out on him. I·hope he's all right.'

'Well, the thought that he might not be all right has occurred to me, I won't deny. The Banks Lecture is quite something, Imogen. People only give it once. It crowns careers. Now, I'd love to take you back to the Lodge with me, and make you some coffee, and mother you a bit. You look in need of it. But when I left him, William was overcome with irritation and rage at the irresponsibility and criminal negligence of the missing guru; it hadn't yet occurred to him to wonder if the man was all right. And I don't want to cross that bridge before I have to, so...'

'I'd love a quiet coffee, but I'm going to report this to our very own college police force, first.'

'It's that bad, is it?'

'It might be,' said Imogen, unhappily.

'I'll come with you,' said Lady B.

Inspector Balderton rocked back on his chair as they laid the situation before him. At a trestle table to his right, Mike Parsons looked up from his reading and listened to every word.

'Well, I won't conceal from you, ladies,' said the Inspector, 'that in the normal course of events I wouldn't put a missing person enquiry in hand for an absent-minded academic gentleman until he had been gone for some days. All sorts of things might have happened. He might have forgotten the date. He might have missed a train. He might have gone back to Italy...'

'Without telling his landlady?' said Lady B.

'...He might have rushed to the bedside of his ancient mother or his dearest friend.'

'But...'

'But I admit to being uncommonly nervous just now

about anyone having any connection with St Agatha's. So if you would like to make statements to my sergeant here, we'll see if we can find him for you. Dead or alive,' he added, and then, seeing both his visitors visibly blanch, he said hastily, 'I'm sorry. That last remark was in poor taste. It was meant facetiously. You must forgive us, Lady Buckmote, Miss Quy. We have to get through the nasty details of nasty doings every working day, so we do tend to be a bit flippant between ourselves. If we took it as seriously as it merits, we couldn't do our job.'

'You are forgiven, Inspector,' said Lady B. They sat down in the battered armchairs from the common room that had been provided for the police, and made their statements to Mike.

'Do we have a file on this theft, then?' the Inspector put in, when Imogen's explanations reached the scene over the missing book. 'Get it over here, Mike. Send Mason to fetch it pronto.'

The statements made – Lady Buckmote's being of nothing but the raising of the alarm about the lecture, Imogen's being of all she could remember about Professor Wylie's proposed course of action yesterday morning – they were leaving when the Inspector said, 'Miss Quy!'

She stopped.

'We thought you were in college. Sitting peacefully, and safely, in your office, fixing ingrowing toenails or whatever it is you do. When in fact you were haring round the town, popping home, inspecting the state of the audience for a public lecture... We'd like to be kept appraised of your movements for the next few days. If you wouldn't mind.'

'Well, for the next hour she will be having coffee in the Master's Lodge,' said Lady B.

'Then I'll be in my office till five.'

'And then my sergeant will escort you home. That will do for today.'

Imogen sank gratefully into the deep cushions of one of the huge armchairs in Lady B.'s little sitting-room, and stretched out her feet to the glowing coals of the fire. The coffee tables were laden with gardening catalogues, rose-growers' lists, plant dictionaries and garden plans.

'Are we having something nice?' Imogen asked.

'They won't let me touch a daffodil here!' said Lady B. 'I'm thinking of replanting a rather tired border in the garden of our cottage in Norfolk. Now, tell me, do you know a rose called "The Old Glory Rose"? Someone recommended it, and I can't find it.'

'It's a nickname for "Gloire de Dijon", I think,' said Imogen.

'Of course! Why didn't I think of that? Do you want a choc, Imogen?' She produced from under her knitting a huge box of Belgian chocolates. 'I find these a comfort in troubled times. Have as many as you like,' she said. With talk of roses and of needlework they soothed each other's nerves, and kept the devils at bay.

'Do you ever remember snow before Christmas?' Imogen enquired by and by, an idle curiosity stimulated by the peaceful crackle of the fire, the furry cling of chocolate on her tongue.

'Snow at Christmas? Once in the last ten years or so. Well, everything is longer ago than I think these days – once in the last twenty years. Just a dusting. But Cambridge looked so pretty as we went to the midnight service.'

'Not at Christmas; before. I thought, as a keen gardener, you might remember.'

Lady B. considered. 'Frost often; very severe frost. But snow? Now you come to mention it, no. Can't remember any. Frost is much harder on plants of course.'

Neither of them mentioned the troubles of the times. Only when Imogen reluctantly rose to leave did Lady B. allude to it.

'It's an ill wind,' she said. '*Nothing* harasses William as much as Lord Goldhooper did; and we shall surely have lost all hope of Lord Goldhooper's largesse over all this! William can have some peace again on that front.'

12

Mike duly saw Imogen home. 'I'll be all right,' she told him chirpily. 'One thing about having lodgers is there's nearly always somebody around.'

She was hoping – she was more than half expecting – that Professor Wylie would be around, lamenting a forgotten lecture as well as a lost book. But the house was empty. Usually, on those few occasions when she had her house to herself, Imogen felt a wonderful, cosy relief. But today it felt bleak and chill. She made herself a mug of instant coffee, and began to prepare her modest supper and reason with her inner qualms. Was there any risk to her? To suppose there was, one would need to imagine that her modest role in helping Mike by gently persuading people to come clean with the police had made her a threat, or an object of hatred, to a murderer. Honestly, that seemed preposterous, not to say paranoid. But something *had* made Felicity Marshall a threat; and heaven only knew what – something about seals? Imogen's tired mind threw up an image of a seal with a large ball on its nose, and she shook her head and tried to think of something else.

She was sitting with the *Cambridge Evening News* propped on the mango chutney jar, reading about the design of a new building on the Science Park, when a little sound in the kitchen caught her attention. She froze. Someone trying the back door. She could hear the little knock of the lever – the door, thank God!, was locked. But the person neither knocked nor went away. Imogen heard soft footfalls moving past the breakfast-room window, and the sound of someone trying the handle of the french windows. Her heart pounding, Imogen stood up and went quietly through to the sitting-room. She stood in the doorway, without turning on the lights. Her curtains were undrawn, and she could just see a shadowy figure outside the window. She stepped back into the hall, heart pounding. Should she call the police? But it was probably only one of Simon's friends, or Liz's, coming to see them. How stupid she would look if it was a false alarm! And wasn't there supposed to be a policeman somewhere nearby?

Then she had an idea. She turned up the volume on her phone and pressed the Answerphone button. That would produce the sound of voices in the hall. The hall duly filled with voices – urgent and increasingly frantic messages about Professor Wylie, and two softly spoken calls from Fran, asking to see Imogen at home some time, as soon as possible. Suddenly fearless, Imogen marched through the house to the kitchen, opened the window a crack, and called 'Who is that?' into the darkened garden.

'Me!' said Fran's voice. Imogen let her in. 'What are you doing creeping about like that, Fran?' she asked crossly. 'You gave me quite a fright. I almost called the police!'

'I'm sorry,' said Fran, automatically. She looked at Imogen, wide-eyed. 'You're frightened, too,' she said.

'Sit down by the fire, Fran. You look freezing. How long were you lurking in the garden?'

'It seemed ages. I had to talk to you. But I didn't want anyone to see me. Not even that policeman out at the front.'

'Is there really a policeman out at the front?'

'There's someone reading a newspaper sitting at the wheel of a car parked opposite,' said Fran.

'God, he must be cold; shall we invite him in for coffee?' said Imogen, grinning.

'Please don't. I want to talk to you *alone*.'

'Well, surely it can't do any damage for the police to know something, Fran?'

'Oh, yes it could! There are lots of us in trouble because of what they know. They're like leaky sieves; they keep telling people things! They give away as much as they find out, if you ask me!'

'What do you mean, lots of you in trouble, Fran?' Imogen was making black coffee and lacing it with whisky. Fran burst into tears.

Imogen comforted her as best she could. Remembering the calming effect of Lady B.'s chocolates she raided the biscuit tin, and offered it. When Fran seemed recovered she said gently to her, 'Time to betray your friends, my dear, before anyone else is hurt?'

Fran nodded. 'I can't tell you how I hate this. But poor Felicity… You remember how you asked me to try to get people to come clean and help the police?'

Imogen remembered only too well.

'Well, it wasn't easy, because they had all promised not to.'

'Good God! To *whom* had they promised not to?'

'Someone. Each other. About eleven o'clock the morning after Philip… after Philip was killed. I was in a lecture, so they couldn't find me, but they found as many as they could of Jack's friends, and they had a little confab together. The someone told them that there had been a bust-up of some kind between Jack and Philip after the party the night before, and when Jack heard – someone ran into the dining hall and told everyone there that Philip had been murdered in the library,

113

and the police were there – when Jack heard that, he had decided to do a bunk.'

'He had gone when this conference was held?' asked Imogen.

'Yes.'

'He did a bunk – but only when someone told him Philip had been murdered? He didn't already know that, having done it himself?' Imogen was thinking aloud. 'But if he hadn't done it, why run away?'

'I think the idea was to lie low for a bit, and let his Dad get lawyers ready, and make sure the police couldn't frame him up and pin a duff confession on him.'

'So he hadn't murdered Philip, but he had done *something*?'

'He thought Philip's death would get pinned on him. I honestly don't know why, but several of his friends thought so too. They called another confab, and they made everyone promise to keep mum. When I appeared, asking them to let you, or the police, know things, they all told me about it. About having promised not to, I mean.'

'But why would people promise such a thing?'

'To help Jack. Everyone liked Jack. Nobody thought he would kill anyone; they thought he might get framed. I know that's going to sound potty to you, Miss Quy, but people did think it.'

'So they all swore not to tell the police what time Philip left the party?'

'That's the trouble. They swore not to tell about the joke someone was going to play. They swore not to tell anything that could possibly matter in any way, or implicate Jack in any way. And they swore not to tell that they had sworn. But of course, we all got pressed very hard to tell things. Lots of people decided that what time Philip left the party wasn't something that mattered, so they could tell that. And Nick decided that since the joke never happened that didn't matter, and he could tell *that*. He's in dead trouble over that; there are people who will bloody kill him if that turns out to be something you can blame Jack for…' She stopped, realising what she had just said. 'I'm frightened,' she said; and then went on, 'and *someone*, nobody knows who, seems to have thought that Philip losing his prescription wasn't something that mattered, and they told the police that. Right now there's a witch hunt going on to find out who told them that!'

'How does the protect-Jack committee know that anyone knows about lost prescriptions?' asked Imogen.

'The police began asking about it. So somebody told them.'

'I know who told them,' said Imogen, 'and it wasn't anyone in Jack Taverham's circle; it wasn't any of you.'

'But it must have been,' said Fran. Imogen didn't volunteer any more information.

'Fran, do you think that the somebody you keep mentioning might have killed Felicity Marshall?'

'*Killed* her?' said Fran. 'But I thought… I assumed…'

'That it was an accident?'

'No; too silly, too much a coincidence. But I did think she had killed herself. She was very upset. Very worried.'

'Do you know why?'

'Not really. Not except that we were all worried. But Miss Quy, if she didn't do it herself…'

'Then someone on the protect-Jack committee did it to shut her up?'

Fran dropped her head in her hands. 'I don't think so. I can't believe it. I mean, it's one thing to keep quiet and not get a friend into worse hot water… to keep quiet and give them a bit of time to get sorted out… it's quite another thing to kill someone. Isn't it? Wouldn't you have thought?'

'Yes, I would. But Fran, dear, this is looking very ugly, isn't it?'

'I know. You can't believe how nasty. Everyone accusing everyone, and getting upset. I don't want anyone to know I've seen you, I can tell you; they're all going to think that everything the police know has come from me to you!'

'But you have taken the risk, and here you are talking to me. I'll do my very best to cover your back for you. But Fran, having gone so far, you might as well tell me one more thing. There must be a ringleader of some kind in this pro-Jack brigade. If people are being threatened there must be a threatener. Shouldn't you tell me who it is?'

There was a long silence while Fran considered. 'There are several people,' she said at last. 'But it's mostly Emily. She's desperately in love with Jack. Frantically. The rest of us don't like it much; it's a bit sleazy. She was playing up to Philip to get invited back to his and Jack's rooms at first. Then the moment she had got to know Jack she dropped Philip and joined the what-a-wimp campaign about him. And the funny thing is, you know, she hasn't a hope. Jack doesn't give a damn about her except to annoy Philip. And everyone could see that except her.'

Imogen thought for a while. Emily's all too visible emotions, then, were about Jack. Well, that made sense. What had she said? If she knew where Jack was, she wouldn't be hanging around here? Something like that. However, she had more urgent matters to think about than Emily. 'Fran, love, mightn't you be in danger? Believe me, when I asked for your help it hadn't occurred to me there was any risk in it; but if Felicity could be attacked, mightn't you be? Shall we ask for protection for you?'

Fran considered. 'There's two things. One is I'll be

116

safest if I don't get any special protection. Above all if nobody sees me anywhere near you. They all know I didn't promise anything, but I said very loud and clear that I didn't know anything to promise about, and I think they believed me. Why wouldn't they? It's true. I've stopped suggesting that anyone else comes and talks to you. I think the safest thing is for me to creep out of here unseen and lie low. And that way I might get to hear something; I might be more use to you.'

'Fran, the last thing I was suggesting was that you should continue to take risks in order to help the police ...'

'Fuck the police!' said Fran. 'There's two people I knew and liked lying in the morgue, Imogen. If I got my hands on whoever hurt Felicity you wouldn't need to bring back capital punishment! There wasn't a gentler, kinder person... she'd do anything for anyone, and she never hurt a fly! I'd love to help get the bastard that went for her!'

'I'm afraid for you, Fran,' said Imogen. 'I feel responsible. I'd like to ask the police to keep an eye on you, too.'

'And keep me safe from prowlers, like they are you?' said Fran, grinning. 'Well, they didn't stop me from practically breaking in, did they? And if I had been a murderer, you'd be dead and cold by now, and your minder would be doing the crossword outside at the front!'

'So he would,' said Imogen, and the two of them began to giggle helplessly.

'It isn't funny,' said Fran, and that set them off again.

'You'll have missed hall dinner,' said Imogen at last, looking at the clock. 'Have some supper, won't you?'

'Is there enough for two? I thought you always had a chop with your vegetables.'

'It's natural self-defence, when dealing with hungry

lodgers,' said Imogen. 'We could phone for a take-away.'

'Oh, yes, please,' said Fran. 'And if I've got to avoid you, I'd like to make the most of this time.'

'It won't be for ever,' said Imogen. 'We'll have a public feast at the Chato Singapore to celebrate when this is over!'

But just for then they ordered a modest Chinese dinner, with prawn crackers for Fran, and ate it quietly by the fire, interrupted only by a phone call for Professor Wylie. The caller wanted to know why he had not turned up for lunch as arranged, and hoped he was all right. Imogen, of course, couldn't say on either count.

Just after Fran left, a soft tapping on the front door alerted Imogen. A policeman was standing on the doorstep. 'I have a message for you, Miss Quy,' he said.

'At this time of night? How did you know I wouldn't be in bed?'

'Your guest has only just left,' he said.

'You knew she was here?'

'We're keeping an eye on her. You didn't think we hadn't noticed her prowling in the back garden?' He smiled slightly.

'I'm glad you've got an eye on her,' said Imogen. 'What's the message?'

'The Inspector is getting a whole lot of people together in the morning and giving them a lecture. Mostly on the subject of the whereabouts of Taverham. He thinks it might help if he read them the Riot Act. He would like you to be there, if you would be so kind.'

Imogen agreed, and said goodnight. She was very tired, but she was even more uneasy. She could see various possible trails of significance in what had been happening, and she didn't like the look of them at all.

13

Inspector Balderton's 'Riot Act' was a quiet one. It was deliberate and emphatic. He was addressing all the undergraduates who had attended the notorious party, several of their tutors, Imogen, the Wyndham Librarian and the Dean, all assembled in the small lecture-room.

'I want everyone present to consider this,' he said, starting in without preliminaries. 'In this college, in the course of the current term, there have been two violent deaths and two unexplained disappearances.' A little murmur answered him.

'Two disappearances?' said someone behind Imogen. 'Who...?'

'One of the disappearances may be coincidental; that of Mr Jack Taverham certainly seems to be connected to the first death. We are increasingly interested in interviewing Mr Taverham. He may be able to help us in connection with the death of Mr Skellow. And in the light of the death of Miss Marshall...'

He was interrupted by Emily Stody, shouting at him. 'Well, at least that lets Jack out! Jack wasn't here when that happened! *Was* he?'

'I don't know where he was,' replied the Inspector. 'And if you do know, I think you should tell us immediately. Well?'

Emily scowled at him. 'I don't happen to know,' she said. 'But if I did I wouldn't tell you to save my life!'

The chief regarded her steadily for a few moments. Then he said, 'You illustrate our problem rather well, I think. Of course, if Mr Taverham was nowhere near the college the night before last, then, as you put it, that lets him out of the death of Miss Marshall. But because we don't know where he was, or is, we don't *know* that he was nowhere near the college at the material time. He has disappeared; he might be hiding in the nearest cellar, or lying low in a friend's lodging in the next street, or he might have fled to Timbuctoo. Has anyone here seen him since the morning of the sixteenth?'

Silence.

'Until he appears and explains himself he cannot be ruled out of the enquiry into either death. However, I will not conceal from you a nastier possibility. It is that he is another victim of the same murderer. Very possibly he is himself in danger; perhaps in serious danger. Whoever killed Miss Marshall is very ruthless and dangerous; if it is the same person who killed Mr Skellow, then we have to face the fact that a person who has killed twice is well capable of killing a third time. Miss Stody has told us all that she would not divulge the whereabouts of Mr Taverham – if she knew them – to save her life. I am asking her in front of all of you if she would divulge them to save his life. Or perhaps the life of some other person present in this room now, or going unsuspecting about innocent business elsewhere.'

He paused, but Emily did not respond.

'Now I imagine I and my team are the only people present in this room who know anything at all about murder. Murder in general, I mean; I have every reason to think that somebody present here knows something about these particular ones. Murder is very nearly always a private matter; it is as domestic as a pet cat, generally speaking. Once they have rid themselves of a wife, or son, or husband, or lover, or blackmailer, the average murderer is no more dangerous to the general public than the average cyclist, and much less dangerous than the average motorist. The average murderer has no stomach for further killing. But just occasionally a very unusually wicked person kills, and then kills again, perhaps to cover their tracks; and such a person is spectacularly dangerous. They don't think like you and me; it is easily possible to think of them when all is discovered as more crazy than wicked, precisely because we realise that no ordinary person would ever do what they have done, and because their motives seem very insufficient for the havoc they have caused. It is very urgent to find and stop such murderers, because they are unlikely to stop until prevented by main force; that is, by discovery. It is very difficult, however, to find and stop somebody whose thought processes and reasoning are unlike those of ordinary people; ordinary logic doesn't help us. Now I think you will all understand that it looks as if this latter kind of murderer is at work in St Agatha's College. We need to stitch together every scrap of information we can get. In particular we need to find and interview Mr Taverham.

'Now, make no mistake. We will find him. The killer will be stopped. But if another death takes place before we have succeeded in our task, then a very heavy responsibility will rest on the people in this room who have information which they are withholding from the police. Now you know where you can find us. Or perhaps you would prefer to phone us, and arrange to talk where nobody can see you coming and going. We will respect confidentiality, as far as the law allows us. Think over what I have been saying to you.'

With that the Inspector left. A glum silence hung over the company as they dispersed. Emily Stody stood up in her place and glared at her friends as they passed her towards the door. Imogen watched. She felt deeply oppressed. Somehow she didn't think the Inspector's approach, dignified and reasonable as it was, would bring results. There was, after all, that promise these young people had made to each other not to tell anything that could be used against Jack. Perhaps the police should be talking to whoever had organised that? But she herself had become chary of innocently helping; she had still not forgotten the terrible moments when she had thought it was Fran lying dead beside the fountain pool, killed for helping her, Imogen, to help Mike.

She left almost last, and walked across the court with Dr Bent, the Dean, beside her.

'How distressing,' he said to her. 'Surely our young people cannot be assisting in the concealment of murder? Haven't the police got it wrong, Miss Quy?'

'I think there has been some reluctance to speak to the police,' she said. 'They are very suspicious of the police. Not like our generation.'

'I fear that none of those present would be among those I might hope to influence myself,' he said. 'Except Miss Bullion. She sings in the choir. She has a lovely voice.'

'Has she?' said Imogen. She herself did not often attend college services, preferring St Benet's. 'I don't think she is being recalcitrant, though.'

'No; I wouldn't have expected that. I'll do what I can, of course... but you know, Miss Quy, the ascendancy of religion in directing people's conduct is a thing of the past. Medicine is the new fount of authority. Now if people would regard a risk, however slight, that sin put you in danger of hell, as they do a risk, however slight, that eating butter puts you in danger of heart attack...'

'When it comes to students, pretty well all authority is

counter-productive,' she said. 'I'm afraid the Inspector's pep talk has been in vain.'

'What can one do?' he asked, taking leave of her at the foot of his staircase.

But Imogen didn't have very long to reflect on the question. She had only been in her office a short while when Mike appeared.

'News,' he said. 'We think we have found your Professor Wylie. Can you come and identify him?'

Imogen sat down abruptly. 'Oh, no!' she said.

'Sorry,' said Mike. 'Shouldn't have put it like that. He's not dead; or not if he's him, if you see what I mean. He's in Addenbrooke's, rambling away. Seems to have lost his memory. But neither dead nor dying. Answers the description we put out, but obviously you could confirm or deny at a glance. Can you come?'

'Coming,' she said, putting on her coat, and hanging her 'Unavoidably called away: please leave note in my box' sign on her door. She felt weak with relief.

As Mike drove her out through the leafy prosperous southern suburbs, he modified the relief somewhat. 'I ought to fill you in,' he said. 'The loss of memory and rambling and such seem to have been caused by a bump on the head. They expect him to recover, but...'

'A fall?'

'Quite a fall; concussion from behind and above. Looks much more like assault. Possible failed attempt at murder.'

'When and where?'

'Search me. He doesn't make sense, unless he does to you.'

'Where did they find him?'

'Drummer Street. The bus station.'

'Where was he going?'

'He didn't know.'

'But, Mike, he's been missing for three whole days. He can't have been sitting in Drummer Street all that time...'

'Indeed not. A taxi driver saw him alighting from a bus, but can't remember which one. Then he just sat around for a while. Eventually somebody asked him where he wanted to go, and he didn't seem to know. They called the ambulance.'

'And the hospital called you?'

'Not at first. But one of our men calls regularly to chat to the admissions desk. There are always missing people, and anonymous people in the hospital, whose kin can't be found. The constable this morning noticed that the age and hair/eye colour description of one of the anons matched Professor Wylie. They had him down as a Mr Bartholomew.'

'Oh, it's him all right,' said Imogen. 'That's the name of his missing book, though, not his name.'

They had a distance to go within the building. Lifts, corridors. The Professor was in a side-room, with a woman police constable sitting, hands folded, in the corner of the room. His head was bandaged, and a drip was being administered. The Professor looked grey and drawn. Oddly, he looked younger – the slackness and stillness of his sleeping face smoothing away the familiar deep crinkles. Imogen and Mike moved quietly, but the slight stir their arrival made caused him to open his eyes.

'Have you brought my book?' he asked Imogen.

'I'm sorry, Professor. No. It hasn't been found. How are you feeling?'

'Terrible. What a terrible place this is. Not only is one robbed, one is incarcerated for mentioning the fact.'

'I expect they're doing their best for you,' said Imogen, 'and you can leave as soon as you're well enough.' But most people hate hospitals, even while their lives are being saved, she thought.

'I'm all right *here,*' he said. 'It's that bloody dungeon I'm complaining about. Like the hellish Middle Ages. And if I've been robbed, why *shouldn't* I say so? I used to think Cambridge was a civilised place: rather fine, in fact. But it's terrible now. Back to Tuscany for me. I think I'll take my books away with me. Any I have left after the thieves have finished with me, that is!'

Imogen and Mike stared at each other. A male nurse arrived, and took the patient's pulse. 'Not too much talking, Mr Bartholomew,' he said, looking sternly at Mike and Imogen. 'You mustn't get excited.'

'Why do they keep talking about my book, if they haven't found it?' the Professor said plaintively to Imogen.

'We will find it for you, sir,' said Mike. 'That's a promise.'

Everyone retreated at once into the corridor, and thence into the ward office.

'That was a rash promise, surely,' said Imogen to Mike, *sotto voce*, as they followed the nurse out of earshot.

'It's what the poor beggar needs to believe till he gets over the shock of a bashed skull,' said Mike. 'If we can't do it, he can be cross with me when he's better.'

Turning to the policewoman once they were all behind a closed door, he asked, 'Has he remembered his assailant?'

'No, Sarge. I have asked him every two hours, as instructed. I have listened to every word he has spoken. Nothing yet.'

'Has he made any sense at all yet?'

'No, Sarge,' she said. 'That is...' She stopped.

'That's what?' he prompted. The young woman blushed. She had a plain, sharp face, Imogen noticed, with an expression of puzzlement.

'Sarge, he has been talking about being locked up

somewhere. It sounds like a nightmare of some kind. Like a horror movie; you know the sort of thing, underground, dripping sounds, mildewed walls, iron bars, dreadful stuff to eat... but... '

'But?'

'Well, last time I had to sit and listen when someone was rambling it wasn't like him. This one says all these preposterous things, but he doesn't wander, exactly.'

'I don't think I understand you.'

'Whatever has disturbed his imagination hasn't disturbed his sentences. What he is saying doesn't make sense, but the way he says it does.'

'Who did you sit with last time?'

'Road accident victim, Sarge. A Mr Moduli.'

'Not an educated person?'

'I don't think so, Sarge.'

'Well, that's the explanation of the difference, don't you think?'

'Perhaps, Sarge.'

'Go back to your post, constable, and keep up the good work,' said Mike.

Imogen said to the nurse, 'How badly is he hurt?'

'Skull fracture. No impaction of the bones. A good deal of loss of blood from superficial scalp wound. He will recover fully, we believe. In fact the most disturbing symptom is the unexplained memory loss. The psychologist suggests perhaps he wasn't fully *compos mentis* when attacked. Can you cast any light?'

'He was very eccentric. Rather an obsessive. And when he went missing he was deeply upset over the loss of his book. It's the book that is called Bartholomew, not the owner. It might help a lot if you made sure people stopped calling him Bartholomew. It will be reminding him of his troubles every time.'

'We can do that,' said the nurse. 'But I'm not surprised

we got it wrong. He really was very incoherent when first admitted.'

'Did you say there had been bleeding?' asked Mike.

'Substantial. He was very weak.'

'So he was covered with blood in Drummer Street bus station, and nobody mentioned that to us?'

'No; he must have cleaned up somewhere. There wasn't any blood on his clothes.'

'How very odd,' said Mike. 'Can we see the clothes?'

The clothes were produced after an interval during which everyone drank hospital tea. At a glance it was apparent they were the clothes of a taller and larger man than the Professor. And they were rather curious clothes, too, or rather, they made a rather curious assemblage. There was a pair of very old velvet trousers, rolled up at the bottoms Prufrock style. Those came with a leather belt, without which, clearly, the trousers would not have stayed up on the Professor's wiry form. Then a shirt, rather a fancy shirt, with a pattern of blurry flower shapes on a buff background. No tie. Ordinary underwear. A carmine velvet jacket, worn bald of pile at cuffs, pocket tops and lapel edges, and with the elbows repaired with leather patches of the kind used to prolong the life of very different jackets – like Harris tweed. The whole had a faintly dandyish air.

'These his?' Mike asked Imogen.

'No.'

'Odder and odder. I wonder where he got them from?' Mike turned to the nurse. 'No mistake? You are sure these are the right clothes?'

'Pretty sure. We have a labelling system when we have to take the patient's clothes off immediately. It causes endless trouble and unpleasantness if things get lost. I've never known the labelling system to let us down, though perhaps it could. Would you like me to talk to the nurses in casualty and confirm? I might have to wait until their duty rota brings them on again.'

'Thank you,' said Mike. 'If you would. They might remember, because this lot is fairly distinctive, don't you think?'

'Yes,' said Imogen. 'In fact…'

'You couldn't possibly not remember them if they belonged to your lodger?'

'I'm sure I couldn't,' she said, 'but I had a faint impression I had seen that shirt somewhere before. Not recently. I must be wrong, I think.'

'Anyway, the main thing is there isn't a spot of blood on any of these things. We'd better take them for the lab to have a look. I'll drive you back to St Agatha's, Miss Quy.'

Imogen was slightly startled by his relapse into formality, and then realised he was on duty. She asked the nurse about visiting hours; about whether there was anything she could bring. They agreed it might jog the Professor's memory if she brought something from his room to put on the bedside cabinet, and if she brought him his own pyjamas.

'Mike,' she said, as they crawled into town again in a long incursive queue of cars, '*why* would anyone attack a harmless old fellow like that?'

'Robbery?' he said. 'Did he carry money around? It's usually robbery when the elderly are attacked, and he is talking about being robbed.'

'But I think he only means about that blasted missing book.'

'Which has probably been stolen.'

'Well, I wouldn't be infinitely surprised if it turned up somewhere, having just been mislaid.'

'But it has been searched for, hasn't it?'

'Well, yes. But Mike, when he's in his right mind he's

about as absent-minded as any sane person ever is.'

'So I gather. How do you put up with it?'

As she got out of the police car at the college gate, he leaned round and picked up off the back seat a brown paper envelope.

'Some reading matter for you, m'dear,' he said. 'Philip Skellow. Remember him? That's the path. report. Thought you'd like to see it.'

And the moment she took it he drove off.

14

Imogen settled down after supper to read the long-awaited report. She felt a curious reluctance to open it, and was surprised at herself. Surely it wouldn't be more gruesome than many medical notes? Surely it couldn't be more upsetting than the notes she had seen portending certain death with concomitant suffering for people still living and in her care? And yet she did feel reluctant. Inflicted death being more terrible by far than natural death. Was that it? Religious people, of course, might think of all death as inflicted. Imogen was not steadily sure of her own position towards religious faith, except that, certainly, she was not a simple believer. Death inflicted by a human hand, with no power to give it meaning – was that the ultimate horror? Imogen shook off metaphysical unease, and opened the buff folder.

Fascinating – and not what she expected. She had expected a fractured skull, and hoped for something unusual – a very thin cranium, or suchlike, – which might exonerate, or partly exonerate, Philip's assailant, by producing unforeseeable dire consequences from an otherwise-less-than-lethal blow to the head... No such thing. Philip had not died from a fractured skull; there was none. He had not died from any of the consequences of profuse bleeding from the surface cut to his head; he had died from sub-cranial haemorrhaging at the site of the concussion. He had most probably been unconscious within some twenty minutes of the blow, and dead within an hour and a half. The blow was double – consistent with a fall, first against a hard object, and then on the floor. He had not moved after the blow. Blindness had probably occurred during the period of consciousness.

Imogen flinched. People in her profession were often thought to be case-hardened; she sometimes thought they were case-softened, more like. Certainly she had no defence against the heart-sickening thought of a young man lying helpless, slowly dying, and alone... What had happened to make him fall? If he had really been pushed by someone who then left him to die, that person was indeed a *murderer*; one against whom the natural reaction was horror and detestation. A phrase came into Imogen's head from one of her father's books: 'Such a one hath a wolf's head, whom any man may cut down!' Not now, of course, when a police force forestalled the need for outlawry or revenge.

Why had a blow to the head, not sufficient to fracture the skull, produced a lethal haemorrhage? From the moment when Imogen had lifted Philip's head, found the neck stiffening, stared puzzled at the wet blood on the floor, on her own hands, remembered from his medical notes that he was not haemophiliac, she had expected this report to find warfarin, an anticoagulant in widespread use and available as rat-poison. She had expected the pathologist to look for any heart condition which could have required it to be prescribed, although she knew his notes did not reveal any such, and it would be unusual in so young a man.

She turned the page. No warfarin. He *had* been drugged, though. With heparin. She put the folder down, and went to her medical dictionary. Heparin. Rapid in action and of short duration. Often used to bridge the gap before warfarin becomes effective. Administered intravenously. Commonly used to treat transient ischaemic attack... bruising at injection site... dangerous in combination with aspirin... She set the book aside. Normally, of course, poison is administered by mouth, tampering with someone's food and drink being infinitely the easiest form of wickedness to organise. People don't willingly allow themselves to be injected with stuff, unless they are druggies, except by doctors. She checked rapidly with the folder lying on her knees. Recent injection site in right elbow, two punctures, heavy ambient bruising, no other punctures...

Philip was not a druggy. He had been given his travel inoculations by Felicity Marshall, because he had missed his appointment with her, Imogen. But he had missed the appointment because the inoculations had gone missing, and had not been found until late in the afternoon. Felicity, poor girl, a kind person, Fran had said, who would do anything for anyone, and wouldn't have hurt a fly, had not checked the seals on the ampules; so the medication had been tampered with while the chemist's envelope containing it was missing. Felicity had realised what had happened; she had dropped a note through Imogen's door; if she had not been killed she would have come and told Imogen all about it. Somebody had killed her to cover their tracks. That somebody knew nothing about Tracy, and could not know that the story of the missing prescription, and the news that the injections had been given to Philip by a fellow student, was already known to the police. Far from covering anyone's tracks, killing Felicity merely drew attention to the significance of Philip's inoculation.

Imogen frowned at the comfortably burning fire in her grate. How had anyone realised that the inoculations were a serious matter? The path. report was only now available, and surely not being shown to all and sundry. Apart from the police she herself, the Master and Crispin Mountnessing were the only people who had seen the body, and certainly she was the only one of the three who could have realised the medical oddity of the situation. But Fran had said the police could not be trusted, that they leaked information and gave away as much as they found out when they asked questions. If that were true... Imogen got up and looked up Mike in the telephone book. There were rather too many M. Parsons in the list to conduct a ring-around at this time of night.

Then, as she picked the folder off her chair to sit down again, a slip of paper fell out of it. 'Home number,' it said, and gave the six digits. Imogen phoned Mike.

'Hope you don't mind being phoned so late,' she said.

'I was expecting you,' he said. 'When you add it all up it doesn't look too good for our missing Jack Thingummy, does it?'

'For Jack? It was Felicity I was wondering about.'

'Well, recollect young Tracy's story. Jack was usually beastly to Philip. Then he was unexpectedly helpful about the missing inoculation, and helped look for it. When it was found he talked someone – we now know that someone was Felicity Marshall – into giving Philip the jabs. Frankly, if there was anything in those jabs that ought not to have been there, like a massive dose of heparin, Mr Taverham has yet more questions to answer. Unless, of course, he was merely a pawn in someone else's game, in which case we may well find him conveniently silenced.'

'He was a bit dominant to be a pawn, Mike.'

'But not all that bright, I have the impression. And there are some high-powered brains around your place of work, you know.'

'Well, yes. Mike, it's another aspect I wanted to talk to you about. I don't see why anyone wanted to silence Felicity Marshall, unless they had got to know about the time-of-death problem, about rigor and wet blood... how could any of them have realised?'

'From us, I'm afraid. We've been asking people where they were at various times... well, no, perhaps one couldn't conclude anything from the fact that the fuzz are vague about the time of death unless one already knew something about it. I see what you mean.'

'Mike, do you think Tracy is in danger?'

'I think her best safety is nobody knowing she ever even existed.'

'Yes, I expect you're right.'

'Lock your own doors, Imogen.'

'Will do. Good night.'

Imogen went through to the kitchen to make some cocoa and heat her hot water bottle. Liz was there, bound on a similar errand.

'Hullo, Liz,' said Imogen, trying to sound cheerful. 'What's new? Settled the snow-before-Christmas controversy?'

'Oh, that,' said Liz. 'Rather lost interest, I'm afraid. But I wanted a word with you, Imogen. I thought I heard someone prowling around at the back earlier on.'

Imogen considered. The police were watching the house, surely; but she didn't want to tell Liz that. 'It's probably nothing,' she said, calmly.

Liz looked at her oddly. 'Only you were so cross about the back door,' she said.

'Yes!' said Imogen. 'And I would be *even crosser* if I found it unlocked again, make no mistake.'

'Promise, promise,' said Liz hastily. 'Has Professor Wylie turned up yet?'

'Oh, I'm sorry, Liz, I should have told you. He's in

hospital. He'll be all right, but he's had a nasty bang on the head.'

'How did that happen?'

'He can't recall.'

'Calm recollection isn't his strong suit, is it?' said Liz, callously. 'But you know, Imogen, every time I say to myself that that blasted book will turn up in one of the piles, I remember the unlocked back door. I feel terrible about it, although I'm sure it wasn't me. That left it open, I mean.'

'Don't worry about it, Liz,' said Imogen, sitting down and sipping her cocoa. 'It doesn't make sense. A thief who takes advantage of an unlocked door is a casual thief, right? And why would such a thief ignore everything in the house except one book, and that one not the most valuable? But just the fact that it is worrying you illustrates why we should try to remember to lock it.'

'Yes,' said Liz. 'I do see.'

'Liz,' said Imogen, on sudden impulse. 'Do you know anything about murder? Have you met it in your studies, I mean?'

'It's come up,' said Liz. 'Criminal law is supposed to be the easy bit; if you can't get that right you won't get anything right. What do you want to know?'

'What counts? As murder, I mean.'

'There are variations. Murder, manslaughter, self-defence…'

'Supposing you did something to someone intending to harm them slightly, and then other things happened so that the end result was their death; would that be murder?'

'I think it would depend on how slight the intended harm was,' said Liz. 'If you just gave someone a little push, just to make them step back, for example, if they were shouting in your face, and if they actually fell over, and by horrible accident had a paper-thin skull, so that falling over killed them when it wouldn't kill a normal person, then I think you could argue that you hadn't intended the death, because you couldn't possibly have foreseen it. It wasn't the obvious consequence of pushing someone. But if you intend to harm someone gravely, if you shot them, for example, intending to maim them for life, but not to kill them, and they actually died, you can't argue that you are not guilty of murder, but only of grievous bodily harm because that is all you intended. Rather obvious, really.'

'Obvious?'

'Well, if the law were otherwise there would be no convictions for murder. Every assailant, however violent, would always say they had intended to hurt but not to kill. There was actually a man who stabbed a woman in the stomach twenty times, and the doctors managed to save her at first; they sewed her all up, anyway, and she lived a few days. Then she died from a blood clot moving from one of the wounds. I think that is a risk with any very gruesome surgery, isn't it? Anyway, he pleaded not guilty to murder. He said she died from the surgery, not from the stabbing, but of course the surgery was a consequence of the stabbing. And he actually argued that he hadn't intended to kill her. The judge found that he *must* have done. You can't stab someone twenty times without intending very grievous bodily harm. The point is, I think, that you are not allowed not to intend the obvious foreseeable consequences of your actions, unless you are so loopy you really might not understand them. Does that help?'

'I think so. If you do something intended to hurt someone badly, badly enough to amount to grievous bodily harm, and what you do causes them to die, that is murder. What if you did something that actually killed a person, but you hadn't intended to hurt them at all?'

'Sounds unlikely, doesn't it? But it does happen, in the case-books. That's what makes law interesting, really, the incredible things that happen. If it was self-defence, you would probably get off entirely.'

'If it wasn't?'

'Imogen, if this conversation is seriously about somebody, then they need very expert advice, not just the impressions of a rather idle second-year law student.'

'I'm just wondering. Idly.'

'Well, for example, a tiler who sat on a roof stripping tiles and lobbing them over the ridge to fall in the street below, and who more or less sliced the head off a passer-by, got done for manslaughter. Reckless disregard of foreseeable consequences, I think.'

'But not murder?'

'For murder you need two things – a line of causation between what you did and the victim's death, and a line of intent. If the causation is there, but not the full intent, it would be manslaughter. The full intent involves *mens rea*. A guilty mind. For murder you need the specific intent to hurt very seriously, or to kill.'

'Can you imagine it?'

'*Mens rea* for murder? Certainly,' said Liz cheerfully. 'I could murder Simon at least once a week!'

'Oh go along with you!' said Imogen, laughing. But her question stayed with her till she fell asleep.

15

It was Nick Sanderson who broke the wall of silence. He came to see Imogen with an entirely imaginary sprained wrist. The moment he had the door to her office firmly shut he dropped the pretence.

'I've come to talk about Jack,' he said.

'Not to me, Nick,' she said, firmly. 'Go and tell the police.'

'Would you just listen?' he said. His face was troubled. He looked as though he had been going short on sleep, and a baffled, rather pained expression clouded his handsome, uneventful young face. 'I'm worried about him,' he said.

'We all are. Nick, if you know something...'

'I don't,' he said promptly. 'I don't know anything. That is... look, Miss Quy, he phoned me last night.'

'Phoned you? Here?'

'No; he knew I would probably be playing darts in the Pickerel, and he phoned there. He was upset.'

'Go on.'

'He was fearfully upset about Felicity. He had read it in the papers.'

'And it upset him enough for him to break cover, so to speak? Did he specially like her?'

'We all liked her. Partly that; partly it makes the corner he is in even tighter. Partly he is scared more than ever.'

'Why is he scared, Nick? Is he in hiding?'

'He had some kind of set-to with Philip that night. He didn't think it was anything much. Then when Philip was found murdered, he was afraid it would all be pinned on him...'

'Yes, we understood that much.'

'He obviously hoped that it would be cleared up, and then he could turn up again. Someone killing Felicity makes it much worse. He doesn't know what to do. It ought to put him in the clear, if it's the same person, that is, who killed both of them, because he wasn't anywhere near. But that policeman said, since they didn't know where he was they didn't know he couldn't have done Felicity; and he *wasn't* in Cambridge, but because he was hiding, he obviously can't prove it...'

'Nick, where is he?'

She got no answer. He simply stared at his clenched hands.

'He has loyal friends,' she said.

Nick looked up at her. 'He isn't a murderer, he couldn't be,' he said. 'I know him very well, I've known him since prep school. He's a great big baby really, in spite of the macho pose. I sometimes think that's what the posing and swaggering and bullying people is really about – covering the fact that he's as soft as a kitten.'

'You don't make him sound very attractive, for a friend,' she said.

'He's terrific, though,' Nick answered her. 'He's fun; he's so alive – things always seem to be happening where he is.' He stopped, biting his lip. Perhaps, she thought, he had realised that not everything that seemed to be happening near Jack was fun.

'Nick, what precisely do you want to tell me? Or is there something you want me to do?'

'I really don't know where he is; but I could hazard a guess. I wouldn't be saying anything if I was sure he was

139

going to show up in Cambridge and face the music, like I told him to. But he might be going to try to get out of the country, and that would make it much worse. You wouldn't like to come with me, and help me find him?'

'Where? And why, Nick?'

'Felixstowe. At a guess. And because I think he might talk to someone who wasn't the police. And then there would be a witness...'

'There would still have to be a long and detailed statement to the police.'

'The thing is,' Nick said, 'the police verbal people. They put any old thing they like into their notebooks. They make it up. People deny that they ever said anything like it, and nobody believes them. They can go down for years... they won't let you see a lawyer till the statements are made, so nobody ever knows what the hell you said or didn't say.'

'Nick, are you sure you haven't been watching too much television?'

He looked genuinely surprised. 'Television? I can read the papers. I can read what happened to the Guildford four and the Birmingham six. Anyway, everybody knows someone to whom it happened.'

'Well, let's not argue about it. The point is you think Jack might tell his story to someone who wasn't a policeman, and you think he might be found at Felixstowe. When were you thinking of going?'

'This afternoon? And if you can come, of course. I've got a car.'

'I can come,' she said, 'if I can get a friend to take my surgery hours here. Wait a minute, will you?'

She phoned Alison, who often stood in for one of the college nurses when she was needed. Alison was free. Turning to Nick, Imogen said, 'Meet me at the gate at two. OK?'

140

When he had gone she reflected. Anyone might think it very stupid of her to go to meet a possible murderer alone, or with only his loyal friend for company. Anyone, that is, who didn't know she would be tailed by the Cambridgeshire police. On reflecting further, she picked up the phone, and asked to speak to Sergeant Parsons.

'Mike,' she said, 'I'm going somewhere interesting this afternoon. No, I'm not telling the police where. Citizen's rights; I don't have to. But is there any chance my minder this afternoon might be you?'

Although she knew she was taking risks, they were more immediate than she had expected. Nick got them to Felixstowe, taking the A45 at ninety, in just over the hour. Imogen gave up all hope of Mike; unless the police could ignore the speed limit, he would have been left far behind, and would be bound to lose them.

Felixstowe out of season had a mournfully tacky appearance. The puddles of rainwater on the promenade reflected wind-torn scraps of cloud, and the sea heaved itself into grey bolsters and broke into off-white spray with a listless regularity, like a half-hearted performance to an audience that barely amounted to a quorum. The amusement arcade had the same down-at-heel feel to it. It was nearly deserted except for a few teenagers playing the fruit machines and a bundled up toddler looking like the Michelin man, riding a mechanical dolphin. Nick parked at the northern end of the sea-front, behind rows of beach huts, and turned off the engine.

'What now?' asked Imogen.

'Jack's parents have a beach hut here somewhere,' he said. 'They live in a huge old rectory and it's a bit far inland, so they rent this hut for the tiny tots in the family. I've been here on a picnic once, and I know Jack has a key. We've done a bit of midnight drinking here once or twice.'

'Wouldn't his parents know about it if he were here?'

'Nope. Not right out of season.'

'Can you remember which hut?'

'This end somewhere,' said Nick. 'Let's have a look.'

They tramped along the shingle together, while the wind from the Urals tore up the beach and put chilly fingers down their necks. 'This is it, I think,' said Nick, by and by. 'It's the right colour anyway, and about the right place.'

He tried the door in vain, and they peered through the window. A curtain completely masked the hut interior.

'What now?' asked Imogen.

'Walk around and look for him, I suppose,' said Nick.

They retraced their steps, and made for the arcades again. It was a nice enough little town, perched on its sandy cliffs; the tacky 'attractions' were the only blot on the landscape, as the dirty high tide mark of black weed and plastic bottles and lumps of tar were the only blot on the beach. Imogen had a curious impression that town and sea were exchanging insults at the margins, like rival gangs. For an hour they wandered around together, looking in cafés and pubs, with no result.

'I might be wrong,' said Nick despondently.

'Wrong about him being in Felixstowe? We can't tell. He could be anywhere in the town, and we could walk round for hours and not see him. It's needle-in-a-haystack stuff; but let's not give up at once.'

'Aren't you getting a bit cold?'

'We could go and find a coffee somewhere to warm up, and then give it another hour.'

Nick agreed. Over coffee in an unassuming cafe he confessed it wasn't so much that he thought he might have guessed wrong about Felixstowe; he was afraid the bird had flown.

'The thing about Felixstowe is, it's a port. He might

142

have got on a boat. Then nobody will ever believe him that he didn't kill anyone. It will wreck his life.'

'I believe the ports are being watched, Nick,' said Imogen. 'He won't necessarily find it easy to get on a boat.'

'He won't be trying to go as a passenger,' said Nick. 'He'll enlist as crew on some shacky vessel. I don't know how closely they check. Well, I do. They don't, much.'

'That seems rather strange,' she said, disbelieving.

'Well, picture it. Some seaman goes missing from a ship from a god-forsaken dump in the Third World. The captain doesn't report it, probably sympathises, but he's a hand short. Then someone presents himself, looking tough enough to be useful... what is it they used to say? No questions, no pack drill.'

'You appal me,' said Imogen. 'But you convince me. How does a respectable young man like you know all that?'

'My mother says there's a National Union of Women,' he said, grinning ruefully. 'I wouldn't know; but there's certainly a National Union of the Young.'

They tramped the streets of Felixstowe for another hour, and returned twice to the beach hut, in vain, and then gave up. Imogen, reluctant to face the hair-raising drive back up the A45, suddenly suggested that they walked to the end of the little pier and filled their lungs with sea air before returning to the Cambridge townscape.

Beyond the underpopulated funfair arcade the pier was deserted except for a cluster of fishermen, minding their rods, discussing the prospects in a little cluster of foot-stamping, frozen-looking men. Funny how it isn't called gossip when men stand around talking. Just one or two were simply leaning aimlessly over the rail. When Nick suddenly sprinted forward, calling 'Jack!' it was one of the solitary leaners who turned round. He looked beyond Nick, at Imogen, approaching along the left-hand board-walk. She thought for a moment he was going to run away, to charge off along the other board-walk, but the movement that gave that fleeting impression was abandoned. As Imogen emerged on to the space at the end of the pier, Mike Parsons, in mufti – jeans and a leather jacket – came level with her and stood quietly, arms folded, at the end of the other board-walk.

Nick said, 'It'll be much better to come and talk, Jack. Trust me.'

And Jack said, 'Thank God you came, Nick. I haven't got the fare back to Cambridge, and I haven't got the price of a cup of tea left. Dad has frozen my account. I was going to have to throw myself on the mercy of the police station here in an hour or two. Tomorrow morning, maybe.'

'This will be better,' said Nick. 'You're going to talk to Miss Quy here, and she will witness what you said before anyone got at you.'

'You can do better than that,' said Mike, quietly. 'You can make a full and formal statement, to a policeman, in a public place, with Miss Quy and your friend here as witnesses. And we promise not to get at you with anything worse than a promise of fish and chips. How's that?'

Nothing is ever simple. Nick exploded with rage against Imogen for cheating him by bringing the police. Mike robustly defended her. She hadn't said where she was going; she didn't know, he asserted, as robustly as if it had been true, that she was being tailed; it was for her protection.

'Against me?' said Jack, looking genuinely horrified.

'Against whomever,' said Mike. 'Now, for Christ's sake can we got off this bloody arctic pier, and go and sit somewhere warm, and get you something to eat before you pass out and we have to carry you?'

'Can I ring my solicitor?' said Jack.

An hour later they were all four sitting in the lounge of the Geranium Hotel. A fake log fire was dispensing synthetic cheer and palpable warmth, Jack Taverham had wolfed a huge plate of steak and chips, and communicated with the family solicitor, who had apparently given his blessing. Mike had his notebook ready. He appeared untroubled by the appearance of Nick's tape recorder.

Imogen observed Jack with some considerable interest. He was generously built – a large, but lean, young man. He had heavy features of almost classical set. He was wearing expensive, crumpled clothes. He had managed to keep his shave up to standard, even in the discomfort of the beach hut. Imogen gathered there was a primus stove and a kettle, and the kind of lounging deck chair that one could just about stretch full length on, and he had bought himself a sleeping bag. That personal magnetism which Nick had assured her explained people's attachment to him was visible even through the dejected and shabby surface that his ordeal had overlaid on him; like a tiger in a zoo cage, miserable and moping but with its native magnificence showing unmistakably.

Jack said he had not noticed Philip leaving the party. He didn't, frankly, care what Philip did. But when eventually everyone left, the rooms were full of the stale smell of spilt wine and tobacco smoke.

'Or other kinds of smoke?' enquired Mike. Jack did not answer that. He had opened the windows, and then walked out into the court to get a lungful or two of fresh air, and give the open windows time to work. It was about one in the morning, he supposed; he hadn't looked at his watch. Late, anyway. He was standing at the foot of his staircase, and he saw someone else moving.

Someone entered the college gate. Jack heard the porter call goodnight, locking up behind the newcomer. As the newcomer moved across the far side of the court, Jack recognised Philip. But instead of approaching to return to their rooms, Philip went to the opposite side of the court and stood in the shadows, with his back to Jack, facing the door of the Wyndham Library. Jack had frowned at him. He assumed Philip was taking a leak, and he disapproved of doing so in a doorway, when there were flowerbeds easily available. Then Philip disappeared, and in the dim light of the only lamp burning in the court – over the main gate – Jack just saw the library door close behind him.

'I'll catch the bastard at it! I thought,' Jack told his audience.

'Catch him at what, sir?' said Mike.

'Well, theft, of course,' said Jack.

'You jumped to the conclusion that Skellow was bent on theft,' said Mike, slowly, writing it down.

'Yes, I did. He had been standing at the door long enough to pick the lock. Nobody could have legitimate business in there at that time of night – nobody *uses* the books in there anyway – and besides...'

'Besides what?'

'Well, I had already been wondering about Philip – about where he was getting money from.'

'I think you'd better explain that, sir.'

'Well, when you share rooms you get to know things. Last term Philip was very hard up. That was part of the trouble we had rubbing along; you know, I thought we should share expenses, and he couldn't pay his whack. He had to keep counting himself out of things and leave them to me.'

'What sort of things?'

'Drink, mostly. And hospitality. I didn't mind, once I

146

cottoned on to it – you know, coming from a state school, having poor parents, of course he couldn't keep stumping up for bottles of gin. But he didn't like it much. So including him in was difficult. He couldn't share and he got touchy if I just paid for things. We got on each other's wick, really. Well, then, suddenly this term he has plenty of money. No more bothers about bottles, and some rather nice new clothes, and I couldn't work out where he got it. Not from his parents, unless they had just won it at the races or something; well, it would be the pools, I suppose. And not from a job, or not one in term. I suppose he could have worked in the Christmas vac, but then, you see, I saw his bank statement, and he had well over a thousand in it. All right, I can see you don't approve, but it was an accident. He banks at the same bank as me. They give new student account-holders those snazzy red files for statements, all the same, and I picked up Philip's thinking it was mine when I was trying to tidy the room a bit. Well, it was a whole lot healthier than mine, I can tell you. So that set me thinking a bit.'

'Surely there could have been other explanations than theft?' said Imogen.

'Well, I didn't think of theft until I saw him doing a spot of breaking and entering the library; then I put two and two together. It isn't that I blame him exactly; he hasn't had my advantages.'

'What advantages would those be, then?' said Mike coldly.

'A decent school; a character-building education. One that inculcates high standards. That's all I meant.'

'I see. What did you do next?'

'I walked as quietly as I could across the court, and followed him into the Wyndham Case. The door was unlocked of course. It was very dark in there – he hadn't

147

put any lights on, and I was afraid of making a sound, so I moved very slowly. I was feeling my way with my hands. Once I was in the room, I could see him. He was using a torch. He was running it along the shelves, looking for something. I just watched him from below.'

'From below? Then he had climbed to the gallery?'

'Yes, he was looking at the top row of books. Then he stopped. He stopped for a long time, and I couldn't see what he was doing. He was directly above me and the beam from his torch didn't show me much. Then he came down the stair with a book. He put it on one of the tables, and switched on a reading light. He was looking at the book so intently he didn't spot me. I just stood in the shadows. He was looking at the book, and at a notebook, and he seemed puzzled. So I just said, "Hullo, Philip." Well he jumped out of his skin, and then he shone the torch at me, and said, "What the hell are you doing here? Get out of it!"'

Mike said, ballpoint poised, 'Those were his exact words? Are you sure of them, sir?'

'Yes, yes I am.'

'They don't sound like a thief detected *in flagrante.*'

'No, they don't, do they?' said Jack, with a look of puzzlement on his handsome face. 'Just the same, that is what he said. So *I* said, "Put that book back at once. And the fat's in the fire now, you know; by tomorrow the whole college will know you're a thief." And he said, "Push off, thicko, and leave me alone; you'll spoil everything." So I said, "You bet I will; give me that book at once!" And he said, "Jack, just get out of here, will you; you're pissed." So I reached out to take the book, and he snatched it up from the table, and I tried to get it from him. There was a bit of a heave-ho.'

'You were fighting over the book?'

'Well, I don't know about fighting. We were tugging at

148

it. It had one of those hard shiny leather bindings, and I couldn't get a grip. So I got hold of it as hard as I could, and I shoved Philip as hard as I could, and he fell over. He fell over very hard, and he cracked his head on the corner of the next reading table as he went over. And again on the marble floor, of course. So then I said, "Are you all right, Philip, are you all right?" and he didn't answer.

'After a bit I put on some more lights, and then I could see he was bleeding. He was lying there with his eyes open and bleeding. I knelt down beside him, and I tried to stop the bleeding by putting my handkerchief against the side of his head. I kept saying, "Are you all right?" It sounds silly now – of course he wasn't all right – but then he said, "I'm dizzy. I don't think I can get up."

'So I said, "Don't try. Stay where you are and I'll go and get some help." So I ran out of the library. I thought for a moment about going for the night porter, and then I thought I wouldn't. I went to get Felicity; I thought she'd know what to do.'

'What happened to the book, sir?' asked Mike.

'It went flying when Philip fell. I never gave it another thought.'

'You went to find Miss Marshall?'

'She's a third-year medic. I thought she'd know. Anyway, it took quite a long time to get to her room and wake her. Girls have to keep their rooms locked at night, so I couldn't get in. I had to stand there knocking and whispering urgently at her. I didn't want to wake anyone else. She took ages to come to her door.'

'So it would have been quite a bit quicker to get the college porter?'

'Yes it would, as it happened.'

'But you decided against that, you said?'

'Well, if the authorities got called, Philip would be in

dead trouble. I thought we could probably sort him out ourselves.'

'By concealing the fact that a theft had occurred?'

'Well, yes, I suppose so. Well, after all, a theft hadn't actually occurred. The book was still there somewhere. Unless it wasn't the first time he had done it... couldn't have been, could it, if his bank account was already stuffed with money? I suppose I wasn't thinking very clearly. Anyway, Felicity got up and came with me. We went back to the Wyndham Library. And when we got there we couldn't get in. The door was locked. So I hammered on it a bit, softly – well, as loudly as you can bang a door softly – and I called through the keyhole to him.

'Nothing. So Flick and I conferred. He must have either got up and gone away, and locked the door the same way he had unlocked it, or he must have got up and bolted it to stop me coming back, and gone on raiding the shelves. Either way, he can't have been badly hurt, we thought. So we went back to bed. When we got to my side of the court, I said to her, "Come and have a whisky. I need one and I expect you do too." So we went up to my room, and she looked at me in the light, and said, "Never mind you hurting him, hasn't he hurt you?" There was blood all over the front of my shirt, and I hadn't noticed. I said, "No, I'm all right, it's Philip's blood," and I pulled the handkerchief out of my front pocket, all sopping wet.

'Flick looked at it, and she went a bit pale, and she said, "How long did you take to wake me?" but I didn't know exactly. She said, "He *must* be hurt," and I said, "Well, but he got up and locked or bolted that door." But she made me go back and try again. We knocked and called again, but the door really was locked, and we still couldn't get an answer, and we couldn't think what to do. So we had a quick drink, and then we went to bed.'

'Didn't you wonder why Philip didn't come in?'

'He often didn't. And I thought he probably didn't want a showdown about stealing college books in the middle of the night.'

'And then?'

'Well, nothing much. Until the college started buzzing with the news that Philip had been murdered. Then I could see I was in dead trouble. Who was going to believe me that he was pottering around locking doors after I pushed him? I was going to be the last person to have seen him, as far as anyone knew, and I had pushed him... Well, I told a few friends who were in my room talking about it that I was going to make myself scarce, and I did.'

'That was very foolish of you, sir,' said Mike, quietly.

'I thought I couldn't be in a worse mess than I was already. But now Felicity...'

'Cannot confirm or deny your story,' said Mike.

'Oh, no, I suppose not. I wasn't thinking of that. I mean, I didn't mean to kill Philip; if it was me it was an accident. But they tell me somebody seriously meant to kill poor Felicity.'

'That cannot have been an accident, no,' said Mike.

'I'd like to kill whoever did that!' said Jack. He was almost in tears.

Imogen was still quietly studying him. He was a very dislikeable young man: one might almost say a nasty piece of work. Snobbish, dominant, self-righteous, self-preserving, stupid – all those things. But not, she thought, an expert liar. He would normally naïvely put forward his view of things and expect everyone to sympathise. Anyway he was not, she felt sure, lying now.

'Don't write down that last remark,' she said to Mike.

'I haven't,' he said, showing her his written page.

'What now?' said Nick.

'I'm going to ask Mr Taverham one or two simple auxiliary questions, and put the answers in my notes,' said Mike. 'Then everybody present is going to read the notes, and sign them at the bottom as a true account of what was said. If you agree, that is, with what is written. Then we are taking both the statement and Mr Taverham back to Cambridge, where we will lock him up and telephone his father to arrange bail. On the bail being arranged, we will release him.'

'Are you going to charge me with murder?' asked Jack.

'Not up to me. But I shouldn't think so. On that story an inquest jury would find accidental death. Wait and see, sir, with as much patience as you can muster. Now those auxiliaries. The path. report allows us to say with certainty that Skellow never got up after the blow to the skull that killed him. He lived for some time after the blow, but he did not move from the spot. He cannot have got up and locked the door. Do you want to alter your statement in any particular?'

'No,' said Taverham. 'The door was locked. We tried the handle, we knocked, I pushed against it; it was solid. Locked or bolted.'

'Very well, sir. Where have you been since your disappearance?'

'Here.'

'All the time?'

'Yes.'

'You didn't return to Cambridge on the night of the first of March?'

'No.'

'You didn't murder Felicity Marshall?'

'No!'

'Very well, sir. Now what do you know about the loss

152

and recovery of a chemist's prescription belonging to Mr Skellow on the afternoon preceding his death?'

'What? Oh, yes, he lost his jabs. We found them, and took them to Felicity to give them to him. Miss Quy had gone home by the time we found them.'

'Did you take them and tamper with them?'

'Certainly not! What do you mean, tamper with them?'

'When they were found, where did you find them?'

'Someone had taken them by mistake. Chemists' bags all look the same. We just asked around till we found them.'

'Who had taken them by mistake?'

'I can't remember,' Jack said, suddenly morose.

'Try to remember. It might be important,' said Mike easily. 'Perhaps you will come up with it on the drive back to Cambridge.'

16

Back in Cambridge, Imogen asked some auxiliary questions of her own. She could see now fairly clearly what had happened to poor Philip Skellow. And it depressed her utterly. Everybody concerned could say truthfully they hadn't really intended any harm; and yet they had persecuted the poor fellow, and done him to death with their supercilious snap judgments. Not sporty, therefore 'a wimp'; not public school, therefore probably dishonest; not Jack's chosen buddy, therefore beyond the pale... The outlines of what had happened were clear, but the details were not. Jack had not come up with the name of the person who had taken the prescription by mistake; either he couldn't or he wouldn't remember.

Imogen went to see the research fellow in medicine at St Agatha's, a sensible woman called Angelica Wend. Angelica didn't think that Felicity's courses would have got round to teaching her about anti-coagulants, medicine being slow and deliberate, and pharmacology not being an early part of the course. 'You want to know who would know about anti-coagulants?' she added. 'Try the vet school. They've got some kind of an investigation going, I believe.'

Imogen rode her bike out to the Department of Veterinary Science, where David Banks, a school friend of hers, now worked. The vets did indeed have an experiment going. Rat control. As everyone knew, warfarin was becoming unreliable, because resistant rats were emerging. A range of other anti-coagulants was being tested, to see if the resistance was general, or specific to warfarin. The project was being used as a teaching platform to demonstrate important lessons in the application of veterinary drugs to the control of animal populations. A large number of fourth-year vet students were working on it. And yes, heparin was among the substances being tested. Could the students take samples of it home with them? They were not, of course, supposed to.

Imogen rode back into town, thinking as she rode, and risking her life absent-mindedly at every road hazard. She was remembering with a chilling sensation what Emily Stody had said to her about Philip – *he was a rat; and you know what happens to rats, Miss Quy, don't you?* The pieces fitted neatly together in Imogen's head. Only as she got off her bike in her front garden did Imogen remember the locked door. Clearly, if an explanation didn't explain *that*, it wouldn't work.

As she made herself a pot of tea in the kitchen, Imogen was surprised to see Roger Rumbold looking round the back garden gate. She waved to him, and he came up the path. She let him in and put a second mug on the counter, saying, 'Funny way to come.'

'Been visiting a friend in Owlstone Road,' he said. 'The back path is the shortest route. Am driven to desperate measures, because you are never in your office these days. I suspect that I have a rival in your scruffy police officer friend, though I am loath to think so because it reflects rather badly on your taste, and so diminishes the compliment you confer by liking me.'

'What's wrong with Mike Parsons?' Imogen enquired. 'Think carefully before you answer.'

'In that case I plead the Fifth Amendment,' he said,

155

amiably. 'Do I get a biscuit as well as tea?'

Imogen found him one. She was glad enough to see him, glad to sit comfortably gossiping by the breakfast-room gas fire, glad to forget any troubles worse than insufficient library funds and a leaking roof in the almshouses. The college had agreed to carry out repairs to Mrs Rumbold's flat, and she had been having a fine old time exchanging talk about old times with a plasterer, who must have been challenging Methuselah if he could really remember what he claimed to be able to remember. Lord Goldhooper had cancelled a meeting with the college council. One of the younger dons had been found in bed with his bedder, and opinions were divided about whether in the modern world this was a crime or only a misdemeanour.

'Well, what would you think should be done about it?' asked Imogen. 'After all, if he were a student these days you wouldn't do anything about it, would you?'

'Oh no. Students have civil rights, which nobody asserts ought to be shared by senior members. What I would do is install proper locks on the doors, so that no bedder can be discovered by another bedder making a bed and then lying in it.'

'Roger, you're making the whole thing up!'

'Well, you're looking more cheerful, aren't you?' he said. 'Come out to dinner?'

'I'd love to. Where?'

'What about that nice pub at Barrington? Can't afford the Garden House on the emolument of a merely real librarian. Flirt with Mountnessing if you fancy the high life.'

'Barrington would be very nice,' said Imogen, fetching her coat.

They had a pleasant evening. The barmaid in the Barrington pub was an amazing sight. She wore black lipstick and eye shadow, and her dark hair was highlighted with spray-on highlights in shining gold. One almost expected her to burst into song at any moment, doing the Queen of the Night from *The Magic Flute*. And the food was good. And Roger was good company. The thing about Roger, Imogen mused later, smiling to herself on her way to bed, was that he was always so light-hearted. Insouciance and laughter accompanied his every step. And first thing in the morning she had to talk seriously to Mike Parsons.

As it turned out, he came to see her. 'We're just putting finishing touches to this case,' he told her, settling down in the chair beside her desk.

'Heavens! I didn't think you could have...'

'Well, to the theory, I mean. First we construct a careful theory of what happened and how, then we put it to the guilty parties, then they confess. Theory stage nearly complete. Thought I would just come and synchronise watches with you in case you had anything to add. Or subtract, of course. You've been a great help, you know. Wasted on nursing.'

'Have you arrested Emily Stody?' Imogen asked.

Mike's eyebrows shot up. 'Yes, as it happens. Or, well, no; not arrested, just escorted to the incident room for questioning. Now, how did you get on to that?'

'How did you?'

'Easy. Handsome Jack, under some pressure, at last admitted that when the missing prescription was found, it was Emily who had it. Now what put you on to her?'

'Access to heparin. She's a vet; I asked a pal in the vet school. They've got a project going on anti-coagulants.'

'Wonderful!' he said grinning at her. 'You're good at lucky deduction, aren't you? Now let's tell each other the story of this nasty business, and we'll see if we've got the same idea.'

'Well,' said Imogen, 'Emily Stody had an unrequited passion for Jack Taverham. Jack set up a "joke": a plan to tap Philip on the nose and have him faint at the sight of his own blood. Emily thought to curry favour by improving on it – heparin in Philip's bloodstream would make the nosebleed spectacular, but not actually dangerous; heparin delays the onset of coagulation, but does not prolong the bleeding of surface wounds. Its dangers are internal, and more sinister. No doubt the phial of heparin was in Emily's cupboard, among the mess of stuff of which her bedder complained. She probably dreamed up the whole thing on the spur of the moment when she found Philip's jabs in the chemist's bag lying around. And then it went wrong. Instead of "improving" a joke, Emily had got her hero into an appalling scrape; she had led to his having killed someone. Jack and Felicity might not have been able to think why Philip had died from a simple fall; but Emily knew. No wonder she was hysterical the next day!'

'Was she?' asked Mike.

'Yes. I had to sweet-talk her out of the loos, and give her a tranquilliser. Of course I thought it was grief for Philip; and she wasn't in a confiding mood.'

But Felicity could only too easily guess. No doubt somebody told her, after the event, about the planned joke. And as Imogen now knew, she had seen that blood-soaked handkerchief, and at once asked Jack how long it had taken for him to wake her.

'I'll confess I'm very glad we've worked out a way that poor young woman knew what was afoot that lets out me and my colleagues,' said Mike.

'What do you mean?'

'Well, for a while it seemed as though if she realised that the jabs had been tampered with, and if she knew time of death was a problem, then she must have learned that from a leaky interrogation. In which case, you see, Imogen, whoever leaked the crucial knowledge to her would in a way be responsible for her death.'

'It might not have been leaked to her,' Imogen pointed out. 'Once it was known to any of them, Felicity was in danger. Felicity had a conscience, and was about to tell everyone all about it; in silencing her, Emily would be protecting both Jack and herself. Chiefly herself. And what was she doing, anyway, washing clothes so early in the morning? Were they muddy clothes, wet and muddy from a struggle in the lily pool?'

'You've lost me,' said Mike. 'Is this another little bit of lucky deduction going out without my knowledge and permission?'

'Just that I met her in the launderette, washing clothes early in the morning, the morning after Felicity died.'

'Did you, now? We'll ask her about it.'

'Aren't you going to ask me?'

'You were at a posh dinner all evening. Unless you have the knack of being in two places at once it wasn't you who tripped Felicity, pushed her into the pool and held her under.'

'No. I confess it wasn't me.'

'It baffles me somewhat that nobody heard anything. Two people thrashing around in a fountain ought to make some sort of noise,' said Mike.

'Over the sound of the jets?' said Imogen. 'There's a huge tower of falling water, designed to fan out all over the pool and make waterfall noises. It's on a time clock, switching off at midnight.'

'So from dusk onwards the court would be rather dark, and full of splashing sounds already?'

'Yes. But aren't you going to tell me a bit of this story?'

'Are you sitting comfortably? Philip got fed up with the party, and went off to see Tracy in the town. He came back to college late – the porter remembers letting him in at about one-thirty – and he went straight to the Wyndham Library. He didn't see Jack, who by that time had come outside for a breather, and was standing watching him. He picked the lock: a difficult lock, so it took him some time. Then he went in and looked for a particular book.'

'Why, Mike? What book?'

'The one his contact wanted. It was you who pointed out, Imogen, that fine books, like Impressionist paintings, would be hard to dispose of. One could hardly just take them round to the local Jimmy-the-fence and expect a few quid for them. Well, you're dead right; they *are* like Impressionist paintings; they get stolen to order. And there's quite a little racket going, or so the booksellers tell us. Very fine rare books going missing at the rate of dozens a year.'

'But wouldn't there be an uproar? A major search?'

'Well, missing property doesn't catch the public imagination like missing persons. It would have to be the Crown Jewels to get headlines in the papers.'

'Round here fine books *are* the Crown Jewels.'

'But most of the public thinks a book is a copy of *Woman's Weekly*.'

'I suppose you're right.'

'And there are other things. People who have had fine books stolen are usually in a position of trust. They aren't as eager as they might be to tell the whole world that they went for a coffee with the library full of strangers, or that their security systems aren't up to scratch. Shocking, isn't it? Anyway, the fact is there's a constant trickle of missing books. They don't get found. They don't turn up in book auctions; they've just gone. So most people think the thefts are commissioned by collectors who want particular volumes.'

'For libraries in South America?'

'Or Milton Keynes; just somewhere private.'

'Is this what happened to Professor Wylie's Bartholomew?'

'Could be. I'm not in charge of that case. Anyway, it seems that young Skellow was in the money because he was nicking books for someone, and that someone wanted something from the Wyndham Case.'

'I just don't want to believe that, Mike.'

'Imogen, just because young Taverham is a nauseating yobbo of the Hooray Henry kind...'

'Who leaps to the conclusion that a grammar school boy isn't honest...'

'Doesn't mean he has leapt to the wrong conclusion. Anyway, you are interrupting my story. Jack follows Philip into the library, and pushes him over, as recounted...'

'Have you got a theory as to how the door was locked against Jack when he came back with help?'

'Has it occurred to you that Jack might be lying?'

'Why?'

'Well, perhaps he didn't go to fetch help, he just went back to bed, not caring a damn. And now he sees that will look very bad, and might even hike the charge against him to something very serious. So he tells us that he went back, with help. But his only witness to that part of the story is conveniently dead.'

'Is he cold-blooded enough for that?' Imogen wondered aloud.

'Maybe not. Anyway, one thing one routinely does, faced with a problem about a door locked when it ought to be open, or open when it ought to be locked, is to ask the key-holder. Do you want to come?'

'Wouldn't that break the rules?'

'Might help. Might make it look less like a serious police enquiry, and more like a little matter of one's idle curiosity. Might throw the suspect off guard. Might interest you?'

'Yes, it might,' Imogen admitted. She put a little notice on her door saying 'Please come in and wait. Back shortly', and went with Mike.

17

Imogen hadn't been in the Wyndham Library since the morning when Philip was found. It was in many ways a magnificent, but not a cheerful room. The books dominated it, towering two storeys high up one of the walls. Blinds over handsome windows filtered the light. It was furnished with large heavy reading-tables and leather-covered chairs, and two enormous globes – terrestrial and celestial – in mahogany mounts stood in the central space.

Crispin Mountnessing was sitting at the far end of the library, writing. He looked deeply careworn. Imogen's first impression, before he looked up, was of a man much older than he had been only a week ago. He also looked slightly dishevelled, for one who was usually garnished in immaculate taste. His deep red flannel waistcoat clashed slightly with deep red velvet trousers, rather worn; his magenta and white striped shirt looked unhappy with both. Certainly he was thinking of other things when he got dressed that morning.

'Can I have a word with you, sir?' asked Mike.

'I'm very busy,' said Mountnessing, looking apprehensive.

'This won't take a moment,' said Mike. 'It's just that we have a little problem. We have a statement...' He recounted, very carefully, what Jack Taverham had told them. 'You will see at once, sir, that Mr Taverham thinks

163

that the door was relocked from the inside. But the path. report leads us to believe that the dead man could not have got up, walked to the door, returned to the spot. Now can you cast your mind back, sir, to the moments before the discovery of the body. When you arrived at the library, you found the door locked as usual, I take it? And you opened it with your key, which we are correct in saying was the only key?'

Mountnessing looked distraught. He got up and walked to the window, and stood staring into the court. 'I am extremely sorry,' he said. 'I didn't think it could do any harm; I didn't see how it could matter one way or the other. Except of course, to me. It mattered to me, and so I didn't say anything about it. I am truly sorry.'

'Please sit down, sir, and tell us what you are talking about,' said Mike.

Mountnessing returned to his chair. He appeared to collect himself, though he was clutching the edge of the table very hard. 'The night of the... calamity,' he said, 'I was up very late. I was discussing a point of Christian theology with the Dean. He had some rather good brandy. We were up very late. When I finally left him...'

'At about what time, sir?' said Mike, who had taken out his notebook and was writing.

'It must have been almost two o'clock. I had to pass the library door on my way to my rooms, and as I passed, I tried the door – a sort of nervous reflex – and I found it open. So I locked it.'

'You just stood there and locked it? You didn't go in? You didn't raise the alarm?' Mike sounded politely incredulous.

'I did not go in. I opened the door only a crack. Then I closed and locked it. I assumed that it was my fault; that it was open because I had forgotten to lock it on leaving the evening before. In fact... the fact is... it has

164

happened before, Sergeant, that I have forgotten to lock up. More than once, I am afraid, the cleaners have found the door open, through my oversight, and then they have needed to find me to lock up when their work is done. Of course such a thing should never happen. It is a breach of the terms of the bequest. It is a dereliction of duty on my part.'

'So you decided to say nothing about it?'

'Sergeant, although you might think it is a small thing to forget to lock a door once or twice, the fact is that I have enemies in the college. Enemies who would make the most of any such matter if they ever got to hear of it. I did not see how it could have any bearing… and I was very surprised that I had left it open. On the last occasion when the cleaners found it unlocked, I had made a very solemn resolution that it should never happen again, and I *thought* I had kept it; I really thought I could remember locking up the evening before. Then I thought I must have been wrong, and I locked the door as I passed. Then of course, in the morning, when I found the body' – he shuddered visibly – 'I realised that perhaps I had not forgotten, after all: the intruder had picked the lock.'

'Then it would seem, sir,' said Mike, 'that when you locked the door Skellow was lying in the library, bleeding to death. When his assailant returned with help he found the door locked, and was unable to render assistance.'

'I did not know that. I could not have known anything about it. Of course, I bitterly regret…'

'I need to get this absolutely clear, sir,' said Mike. 'If there had been lights on in the library, would you have seen them when you opened the door a crack?'

'Well, I didn't see them, so the answer must be no. There is a sort of draught box round the door, Sergeant, you can see, which would have concealed all but the brightest lighting.'

All three of them inspected the baffle round the door. A construction like the sides of a box, with a second door a yard and a half within: a miniature version of the kind of thing often put inside church doors, and for the same reason – a person entering lets the outer door close before opening the inner one, and so keeps out draughts. Certainly it seemed pretty light-proof. Imogen wandered back towards the table below which Philip had been lying, and considered.

At first Philip had been working by torchlight. Then he brought a book down and put it on this table – and switched on a reading light. Later, Jack switched on more lights. The reading lights were old-fashioned library lights with solid brass stands, heavily shaded with green glass shades which cast the light downwards to the table tops. If the two young men had switched on only the reading lights, then it seemed perfectly plausible that someone standing outside could fail to notice. The switches for the reading lights were easily found; they were little chains below each light.

'Where do the main lights switch on?' she asked.

'Over there – a bank of switches on the wall by the door,' Mountnessing said. From where she was standing Imogen couldn't see them; they were concealed by the jut of the baffle round the door. So when Jack panicked and put on more lights, he probably just put on the reading lights, whose switches he could see from where he stood. Imogen was satisfied.

She replayed the scene in her head: Jack leans over the table, grabs the book. They pull it to and fro across the table, move into the aisle, Jack shoves, Philip falls, the book goes flying... she remembered the Inspector picking it up from over there; and the floor was certainly polished enough for it to slide. She had a sudden thought.

'What happened to the notebook?' she asked.

'The book?' said Mountnessing. 'It's back in its proper place. The police having finished with it.'

Mike referred to his notes. '*Nova et Antiqua Cosmologia*: where would that place be, sir?'

'Towards the top of the left-hand bay on the balcony,' said Mountnessing, pointing. 'Do you want to see it?'

'Wouldn't mean anything to me, thank you, sir,' said Mike. But that was, of course, the point in the room where Jack said he had seen Philip searching for and finding the book.

'I didn't mean *that* book – I meant the notebook,' said Imogen. 'Didn't Jack say Philip was looking at the book, and a notebook?'

'Point,' said Mike. 'Nobody mentions a notebook. You didn't find a notebook lying around somewhere, sir?'

'I didn't find anything that ought not to be here,' said Mountnessing stiffly.

'Except a corpse, when you turned up the next morning,' said Mike brutally.

'Oh, don't remind me,' said Mountnessing, turning pale.

'One last thing,' said Mike, 'then you can get on with your work in peace. That key: where is it usually kept?'

'Upon my person,' said Mountnessing.

'You carry it always with you? Pardon my asking you, sir, but isn't it a massive great thing?'

'Inconveniently so,' said Mountnessing. 'I have a specially deep narrow pocket constructed for the purpose in my trousers.' He reached down the right-hand pocket of his trousers as he spoke, and produced eight inches of heavy iron key.

'Glory!' said Mike.

'There are disadvantages to most callings in life,' said Mountnessing lugubriously.

As they crossed the court again, Mike going towards the incident room and Imogen returning to her office, she said, 'Mike, shouldn't we just check with Jack Taverham about that notebook?'

'It was sharp of you to pick up on that,' he said. 'More trouble than it's worth, I think. We have to handle the young upper crust with kid gloves. He's made his statement; been bailed; promised to be a good boy and keep within the college; made it up with his dad; got himself an excellent lawyer. If we keep firing off auxiliaries at him we'll be accused of harassment.'

'But that must make enquiries rather difficult? In fact I've been thinking very ruefully, Mike, about how much more difficult life is as a result of the raging suspicion of the police that all these youngsters feel. They haven't any justification for it, as far as I know.'

'I wouldn't go so far as that,' said Mike. 'Depends where they come from and who their associates are. The fact is, Imogen, the odds against the police are always very long. Policemen do what they can to shorten them. They always believe that it's in the public good. It all depends which part of the odds one tries to shorten. In some police forces they like to shorten the odds against guilty people saving their skins by keeping their mouths shut. In others they may like to shorten the odds against the guilty getting away with what they clearly did because of a nasty little chink in the evidence, that could easily be fixed up. Round here we like to shorten the odds against having true confessions doubted in court; against any case we bring getting into trouble as a result of criticisms of police procedure. So we keep the rules, and try to win by diligence and superior brain-power.'

'And thus attract into the Cambridge force the kind of officer who likes to win by brains rather than brawn?'

she said, smiling at him affectionately. 'What if *I* asked Jack?'

'Couldn't stop you,' he said. 'Citizen's rights.'

And it wasn't, of course, difficult for Imogen. Jack was confined to his rooms, very bored and not ill-disposed towards her, since he felt grateful, really, for having been rescued from Felixstowe.

'I've come to see how you are getting along,' she opened.

'Not too good, really,' he said, offering her the dazzling smile that endeared him to his cronies. 'Nothing you can help with, I'm afraid. I'm not ill.'

'Worried?'

'Worried sick. Miss Quy, what is all this about that damn prescription? I was only trying to help, and…'

'Didn't anyone explain?'

'No.'

'Philip had been given a drug which impedes blood clotting. That was why a blow to the head…'

'He wasn't bleeding enough for that, surely?'

'Internally. Haemorrhaging into the brain.'

'Oh, my God,' said Jack.

'The drug is one that has to be administered by injection. And Philip did have an injection, you see. You took him to Felicity, and she gave it to him. She didn't check the seals.'

'And it had been tampered with?'

'Probably. Well, what other explanation?'

'Then it wasn't my fault! It wasn't me, it was whoever spiked Philip's jabs! It lets me out, doesn't it?'

'I'm not a lawyer, Jack. Morally speaking, I would say that organising vicious practical jokes…'

'It wasn't me, it was…' he stopped short. 'Nobody meant to kill anybody,' he said.

'Not then, perhaps. Look, Jack, I wanted your help

169

about something. Did you say that Philip was looking at a book from the shelves, and a notebook? What sort of notebook? An ordinary Jarrold's sort of thing?'

'Oh, no,' he said, frowning. 'It was big; leather-bound. It might have been one of the books from the case.'

'Then why did you say it was a notebook?'

'It was the wrong word. Just that it was handwritten. I only saw it for a split second. It was lying open on the table, beside the one Philip had carried down from the gallery. It was upside down, to me, but the reading light was on it. It was ruled in columns with entries in violet ink. Handwriting, not print.'

'*Violet* ink? One can get brown ink, red ink, green ink, I think, but usually the choice is blue or blue-black.'

'I've even known purple ink,' he said. 'But perhaps I just mean faded. I honestly can't be sure, Miss Quy; I was looking at the other book, and shouting at Philip, and he was shouting at me, and... Sorry. Hang about, I do remember one thing. The pages had gold edges – you know, like posh prayer-books. Might this help?'

'Anything might. Only the book wasn't found.'

He looked puzzled. 'Well I didn't move it,' he said. 'And it was too big to get thrown away by an oversight or something.' He lapsed into silence. Then: 'Oh, it's such a mess!' he said. 'I'm in such a mess! And it all looked so good; I was going to get a first and a blue, and go into Dad's business, and stand for Parliament... and now I might easily go to prison, and my reputation is wrecked for life. And it's not fair, Miss Quy! Really, it's not fair! It was Philip who was stealing things! And I'm the one who's wrecked. It doesn't matter what I do, now.'

Imogen said quietly, 'It always matters what people do, Jack.'

'Do you mean there's always somebody who cares? I won't have a friend left in the world.'

'What about Nick? What about Terry? Catherine? Lots of people have been standing by you, as they saw it, at some risk to themselves. But actually I meant that it always matters to yourself, what you do. You can't help standing by yourself.'

'I suppose not,' he said. 'Thanks.'

'Would you like to come across to the office with me now, and offer an auxiliary description of that notebook?'

'OK,' he said. 'Haven't anything better to do.'

But when they got there, there was nobody sitting at the desk; the door to the interview room was shut, and a murmur of voices reached them. Jack and Imogen sat down to wait. By and by Mike emerged from the interview room.

'You want to hear what's going on in there!' he said, sitting down in his chief's chair.

'I think perhaps I don't, though,' said Imogen.

'She's singing loud and clear,' said Mike.

'Who is?' asked Jack.

'Your beloved Emily. You were right, Imogen – she thought Jack would love her better if she made a fool of Philip. Then she was desperate when it turned out she might have got wonderful Jack into terrible trouble – she threatened Felicity with murder if she told anyone about the jabs, and then she saw her chance... She isn't sorry, you know. She just reckons that anyone who casts a shadow on Mr Taverham's golden path deserves to die. What a termagant!'

Jack had sunk his head in his hands. 'Did *she* kill Felicity?' he asked.

'She seems to have seen Miss Marshall coming through Fountain Court alone, in the dark. She spotted that the fountain was throwing a screen of water between Miss Marshall's course to her room and the porter's lodge, and realised that nobody was likely to be looking from the chapel and dining-hall side of the court. She seized her chance. She ran at Miss Marshall hard, knocked her off her feet and into the pool, and held her under.'

The door to the interview room was opened, and a woman police constable emerged, with Emily behind her, followed by the Inspector. Emily saw Jack, and her face lit up. She reached a hand towards him.

'You vicious little cow,' he said. 'You stupid bitch!'

At that Emily's face crumpled into an expression of such distress that Imogen was almost sorry for her.

'I only did it for you, Jack,' she said.

'What's he doing here?' said the Inspector. 'Get him out of here!'

So Jack's curious report of the size and weight of the missing notebook would have to wait.

Imogen returned to her room, very shaken. She had so disliked Emily she hadn't thought much about her. But she should have done. A little more thinking about Emily – who after all made a lousy job of concealing her feelings – and she might have been stopped before she got to Felicity. And even if you have disliked them, the thought that someone you know is a murderer is enough to give anyone pause.

18

Imogen saw the two students who were waiting for her on her return to her room, dealt as best she could with their problems, and went home. The curious news about the nature of the missing notebook could wait, she thought, till morning. She had a busy afternoon in prospect. First she was going to show Tracy round some Cambridge colleges, buy her tea in Auntie's, and take her to choral evensong at King's. Tracy needed cheering up; but Imogen was looking forward to it, too. And then she had to get to New Addenbrooke's to see Professor Wylie before the end of visiting time.

'I really hadn't a clue!' said Tracy, leaning with Imogen over the wall of Trinity Hall's riverside garden, looking at the frost-proof ducks on the wintry river flowing below them, and watching the cyclists spinning over the humpbacked arch of the Garret Hostel Bridge.

'A clue about what?' said Imogen, apprehensively.

'All this,' said Tracy. 'I thought the centre of Cambridge was the Grafton Centre, and this bit was where all the grey buildings are. I didn't know what they were for, or that they had gardens in them, or anything. You're ever so kind to show me.'

'It's a pleasure,' said Imogen. 'A pleasure to be reminded how lucky I am to live here. I just go walking or biking through, thinking about work, and I don't notice, as often as not.'

'I bet you do, though,' said Tracy.

'Which did you like best?' asked Imogen, who was keeping King's College Chapel in reserve.

'That lovely pale one like a wedding cake!' said Tracy, without hesitation, selecting St John's New Court, 'with the pretty bridge to it. That's got to be the best, hasn't it?'

'Well, I've always liked it,' said Imogen.

In Auntie's, they settled down with a pot of tea. They ordered chocolate fudge cake for Tracy, and hot gingerbread with maple syrup for Imogen, and while they were waiting, sitting comfortably at a table in the window, Fran came past, wheeling her bike. She saw Imogen and came bouncing in. 'You promised me dinner at the Chato Singapore,' she said cheerfully, pulling out the third chair and sitting down. 'But tea and a bun will do for now.'

Imogen introduced Fran and Tracy, and explained the afternoon's mission. Fran immediately attached herself to them, confessing that she had not yet heard evensong at King's. 'It's the sort of thing you keep thinking you can do any time, and then you go down without having done it, like as not,' she said. 'And right now I'd do anything that took my mind off the uproar in college.'

'About Emily?' Imogen asked.

Fran nodded. 'Where are you?' she asked Tracy.

'Romeo's,' said Tracy. 'And you?'

'I'm at St Agatha's,' said Fran.

'I didn't think you could be anywhere respectable, with hair like that,' said Tracy, coldly.

'Ouch!' said Fran, cheerfully. 'Did I say something wrong? Anyway, what's wrong with my hair? Bearing in mind that I'm not trying to look like an air hostess.'

'You don't look as if you was trying to look like anything,' said Tracy. 'You look as though it just grew like that.'

'Well, it did,' said Fran, refusing to take offence. 'What do you think I should do with it?'

'It'd look good if you took about three inches off the ends, and put it up in a bun,' said Tracy, considering. 'Perhaps with Edwardian sides.'

'What's an Edwardian side, Tracy?' Imogen asked.

'Those little curly dangling bits in front of the ears,' said Tracy. 'What do you think, Imogen?'

'Pass,' said Imogen. 'And time we were moving if we want to get seats in the choir for evensong.'

Evensong put a quietness on both her companions. She left them talking together in King's Parade afterwards, and biked off on the long haul towards Addenbrooke's.

Professor Wylie was in a poor way. He had caught bronchitis, and to her alarm was on oxygen and not in any condition to talk to her. He had to be feeling dreadful if he couldn't even rise to an elegy for his book. Imogen went to see the ward nurse. Everything possible was being done. The Professor was 'poorly' but not in danger. He would come off oxygen some time tomorrow in all probability. No doubt he would, thought Imogen. But just the same, when she got home at last she phoned the Professor's sister in Italy.

While she was watching *Newsnight* a knock on the door announced Fran, hair rolled up and sporting 'Edwardian sides', looking perfectly charming.

'What do you think, Imogen?' she asked.

'It's lovely. Mind you, it doesn't look authentically studently.'

'That's the fun; it can be let down and left hanging for everyday.'

'I approve, then. I wouldn't have thought you'd had time.'

'Tracy opened up and did it for me after hours. And I

175

took her to a disco for a bit. Know what, Imogen? There was more to Philip than met the eye, wasn't there?'

Imogen gave Fran a cup of chocolate, and saw her out. Then she went to bed feeling obscurely pleased. Unlikely friendships are like trees in flower, or sightings of kingfishers: they make one wonder whether after all the world is a hospitable place.

Next morning, as she entered St Agatha's, she was met by a brigade of policemen, marching out. A police van was parked, with hazard lights flashing, outside the gate, and the files and phones and impedimenta from the incident room were being packed away in it. As she hung up her coat in her office, Mike appeared.

'We're shutting up shop,' he said.

'So I see. Moving to the main base?'

'Moving to other things. Case closed. Well, solved anyway. The law will still have its wayward way with things.'

'Solved?' she said.

'Yup. We won't get anyone for Skellow's murder. Taverham will get off, or get only a technical conviction. Clot didn't mean it. But we'll get Stody for killing Felicity Marshall: she's the one really responsible for Skellow's death, but there's no point in going after her for that in the circumstances. I mean, she will be charged under the Offences Against the Person Act with "administering a noxious substance to injure or annoy", but the judge will pass a minor sentence to run concurrently with life for killing Felicity Marshall. She'll get life anyway.'

'But don't you have to know what Philip was doing in the library?'

'Nicking books.'

'There's no proof of that.'

'What the hell else can he have been doing?'

'But you can't convict someone on the basis that you

can't think what the hell else they were doing.'

'We aren't going to convict him. Remember? He's dead.'

'And therefore can't defend himself. Don't you have to prove it? Find the fence who was putting him up to it, check where that money came from? Find out what happened to the notebook?'

'Nope. There's nothing in that for us. No theft from the Wyndham Case, and if there was we'd know who did it, and he's dead.'

'Don't you need to know how he got in?'

'Well, either he picked the lock or our ineffable friend forgot to lock it the night before. It doesn't in the least matter. When you find a body dead in a library, the one thing you can be sure of is that the fellow did get in, one way or another.'

'But doesn't it worry you?' Imogen was deeply upset. 'Don't you want to tie up all the loose ends?'

'Crime writers have a lot to answer for,' said Mike. 'Look, Imogen, we've got two dead bodies and two true confessions. Jack says he pushed Skellow, in circumstances which are explained by the context; Emily Stody says she drowned Felicity to stop her telling the world that she had administered jabs to Skellow without checking the seals. Emily seems to have thought that Taverham would be in worse trouble if that were known. She seems to have been willing to spike someone's medicine, lie, terrorise and kill for Taverham, who rewards her devotion by calling her a stupid and vicious bitch. Seems a bit of an understatement. Her lawyer will argue that it was a *crime passionnel*. The jury will be unimpressed. These various confessions are all witnessed, signed, taped, have not been withdrawn as soon as the villains saw their lawyers. What is there left to prove?'

'It's just that...'

'You don't like the thought that the boy was a thief. Well, I don't care whether he was a thief or not. I don't like the thought that he's dead. It wasn't murder in the eyes of the law, I'll grant. But what I think about it isn't printable. Capital punishment for theft was abolished years ago.'

'I'm sorry, Mike. Perhaps I'm just bitching because the college will be dull without you here.'

'Well, I shan't be any further away than Parkside. Should be possible to have a pub lunch occasionally. And, Imogen, you've been a great help. Mostly when the public help us it takes twice as long and gets more confused than ever; you've given really useful help. I expect you'll get a letter from the Chief Inspector, but this is thanks from me. Tara, then.'

'Tara,' she said. He went; and then moments later put his head back round the door, said, 'See you soon,' and was gone.

Before the morning was out Imogen was longing for fresh air. It's a strange thing about institutions that the heating can never be got right: it's always far too hot or non-existent. A dismal bleak March it might be, and grey and chill outside – they had been lucky with the weather on the Cambridge walk yesterday – but there was no need to heat the building as though it contained a rare collection of tropical plants. Desert palms, more like; it was dry, scratchy air. So the moment her hours were up Imogen charged out into the garden, and climbed the Castle Mound. Great drifts of crocuses were in bloom on the grassy sides of the mound. The beloved view of Cambridge cheered Imogen a little. The departure of the police from the college should have been a relief, and she wondered why it was not. The whole affair had left her feeling bruised, and, on reflection, she supposed it was because of the eruption through the tranquil and beautiful surface of Cambridge of the ugly and depressing aspects of life. No, surely; surely, she, Imogen, saw enough of the downside of Cambridge life in the woes and fears of the young people who consulted her each day. Many members of St Agatha's might live in effect, on another planet, or in another century, perhaps, but surely she, Imogen, had always had her feet on the ground.

She had intended to descend the slope of the mound and walk back through the little cluster of tombstones that gave the little church on Chesterton Road below her such an air of rural charm; but on second thoughts she decided that reading tombstones was not an activity for today, and she returned the way she had come.

As she re-entered Fountain Court she saw Lady Buckmote coming towards her. 'Just the woman I was looking for,' Lady B. said. 'Can you spare a moment?'

'Gladly,' said Imogen.

Minutes later they were comfortably occupying armchairs in Lady B.'s pretty little drawing-room in the Master's Lodge. Tea and biscuits were ordered up from the buttery.

'Guess what,' said Lady B. 'Lord Goldhooper is back.'

'I thought we had scandalised him away.'

'Evidently not. Evidently the old reprobate regards bodies in the fountains as part of the antique charm, rather in the light in which one regards college silver, or an academic prize or two. Anyway, he's back. William doesn't know whether to be pleased or appalled.'

'He hasn't needed sleeping pills for some time,' said Imogen. 'I was hoping he might have broken the habit.'

'He has, he tells me. He tells me he is not going to resort to them. But it will be rough going, I think, unless Lord Goldhooper decides quickly. However, Imogen, there is something else on my mind.'

'Something that I can help with?'

'I do hope so. Imogen, the college council has met, and decided not to send anyone to young Skellow's funeral. You know, someone usually goes to represent the college when any member of the college, however junior, dies. They are sending the Dean to attend Felicity Marshall's funeral tomorrow. There's an inquest on Skellow tomorrow also; we gather the fact that he was engaged in theft is likely to emerge, and several of the fellows are inclined to think that theft of college books needs public disapproval. William thought that in view of the tragic nature of the death it was unsympathetic of them not to send somebody, but it went to a vote and he was voted down.'

'And you don't approve of the majority line?'

'I feel very uneasy about it. After all, the college has allowed Taverham to be bailed and to continue in residence – I know he's under strict supervision, but still – and what is that going to look like to Philip's family, do you think?'

'Terrible,' Imogen agreed. 'They will hate us, I should think. But I don't see what you could do about it; it isn't your responsibility.'

'The reputation of St Agatha's is my responsibility while William is Master,' said Lady B. 'I'm the academic equivalent of the vicar's wife. And you see, Imogen, while William couldn't defy the college council without stirring up mayhem, I could. I'm not bound by their resolutions. I thought I would go. It's not at all likely that the difference between me in a private capacity and a proper college representative will be immediately clear to the outside world.'

'Brilliant idea,' said Imogen.

'So I was hoping you would share the driving,' said Lady Buckmote. 'It's nowhere near as far as Skye, but I need to be back the same night if William is not to ask questions until too late, and that makes a very heavy day.'

'Do we know when it is?'

'Next Wednesday.'

'I'll arrange to be free,' Imogen promised.

19

It was dark when Imogen and Lady Buckmote left Cambridge. A lightening sky had weakened to deep violet, against which the street lights, and the lemon and amber rectangles of the few lit windows, lingered uncertainly, soon to be redundant. As they drove towards Huntingdon the sun came up, dazzling in the right side mirror like an undipped following car, and helpfully blazing in the cats' eyes down the middle of the road. By the time they reached the A1 a light mist was dispersing into the chill brightness of a fine early spring day.

The church was full of flowers. It was half-full of mourners – it was a big church, though, built for the prosperity of the past, so half-full was a respectable number of people. There were reporters with cameras at the churchyard gate. Philip seemed to have had a small family – mother, father, an aunt and uncle perhaps? Probably: one could see the family resemblance to his father. Imogen looked round discreetly, from the position Lady Buckmote had chosen, three rows back. Some local people, brought by sympathy or curiosity; a large number of young men – Philip's classmates at the grammar school? That must be it. Among the youngsters several older people – two men and a woman; Imogen guessed they were school teachers. Just before the coffin was carried up the aisle a latecomer arrived: Dr Bent from St

Agatha's. He and Lady Buckmote looked at each other with mutual surprise, and rueful approval.

The service began. How oddly life-enhancing funerals are! Only for those closest to the dead is grief strong enough to blot out entirely the renewed zest for life, for the daylight, for continuance, however deeply one regrets continuing without the dear departed. No doubt these mixed feelings account for the excellence of the parties that often follow. Imogen's train of thought was suspended as the vicar ascended the pulpit.

'Our dear son, our dear friend, our brightest and most promising pupil, a valued member of our congregation, one of whom much was hoped and expected, has been brought to burial in this church, fifty years before his expected span, as a result of a violent act. How can such a calamity be reconciled, you may ask yourselves, with the image of God as the Good Shepherd, with the promise that no sparrow falls without the Father? Such questions have troubled believers since before the time of Christ... '

Imogen's attention wandered. Not that she didn't appreciate the importance of the question being discussed. Just that, like so many others, she had ceased to expect a brave profundity in tackling it from the mouth of an Anglican vicar. And like many another good parish church, this one was full of distractions. It had a little fine old glass in the chancel and a magnificent brass rescued from the floor and mounted on the wall of the aisle, within Imogen's view. From every century since the fourteenth, monuments and the familiar patterns of armorial bearings and elaborate citations asserted the passing glories of the worldly great.

The sermon rolled on. 'God answered Job then, that his knowledge was not deep enough to justify him in questioning his God. That must be enough for us also.

However, though we may not question God, we have every right to question our fellow men. We may demand an answer from the killer to the question, "Why did you do this deed?" and here it is my painful duty to allude to a second attack upon Philip Skellow, not capable of doing him bodily harm, but most hurtful to the feelings of all who knew and loved him; I mean of course the allegation which we have all heard, against his honesty. Now it may seem to some of us here present that to justify an unlawful attack by piling false accusation upon the victim is conduct so contemptible that it is literally unforgivable. I must remind you that we may, indeed we must, preserve Christian charity towards all. It is our duty to forgive Philip's killer, both the lethal action, which only the perpetrator can know if it was deliberate, and the deliberate attack upon the honesty of the dead man. We shall forgive; but we shall also answer the attack. We may not know, any more than Job did, enough to question the judgment of our Maker; but we know enough to question the judgment of those who have labelled Philip a thief. Those of us who knew him, know it cannot be so. I urge you, with all the authority vested in me by my office, to beware against feelings of hatred or of contempt for any human creature, however deep the offence they have given. But I also urge you to preserve in your memories the Philip that we all knew; to remember that it is not in this world that the secrets of all hearts shall be made plain, and to trust that Philip is vindicated and accepted by Christ in that other world to which we are all bound, soon or late...'

'Those were strong words,' said Dr Bent, quietly, to Lady Buckmote as, later, they watched the coffin being lowered into the ground. 'Strongly felt.'

'Yes, very. Very strikingly so. I am surprised to see you here,' she added.

'I am in a purely private capacity,' he said. 'I taught Philip last term.'

'I am purely in a private capacity myself,' she said, 'but perhaps we need not say so.'

'No indeed,' he replied.

And it was just as well this mild conspiracy had been agreed, for the presence of strangers had of course been noticed; they had to give their names, to say they were from the college. They were invited to go back to the house for a light lunch and a drink.

A rather difficult social occasion, Imogen thought. But not as bad as she might have feared. Dr Bent was quickly in conversation with the teachers, including Philip's headmaster, on the subject of entrance requirements, and later could be seen talking paternally with some of Philip's friends. Lady Buckmote's social skills had been honed razor-sharp in a hard school; she sallied into the middle of the crowd and asked questions: 'Are you a relative? Have you come far?' and so on. Imogen took her glass of sherry to a window seat, overlooking the back garden, and watched. The house was one of those modest thirties semis with curved bay windows. It was light and pleasant inside, but the narrow garden was beautiful; a curved path led the eye through pergolas and serpentine herbaceous borders to a rustic seat at the far end. Hundreds of crocuses were in flower; the beds were neat, the roses well pruned and budding.

'Are you the gardener?' Imogen asked Mr Skellow, who approached offering to refill her glass.

'What is he like?' he asked her, speaking harshly.

'Who?'

'The man who killed my son. I take it you know him?'

'A blunderer,' she said, choosing the word carefully.

'A bully,' he said. 'We told Philip to stick up for himself, but he said we didn't understand. No; it's my

185

wife who does the garden,' and he moved on.

Imogen looked around for Mrs Skellow. She saw her standing in the kitchen doorway, looking distraught. Imogen made a bee-line through the packed room to her. 'Are you all right?' she said. The woman was trembling.

'I just felt dizzy for a moment.' There were tears in her eyes.

'Come and show me the garden,' said Imogen.

'I can't leave things...'

'Yes you can. I think you might be going to faint if you don't get some fresh air.'

Imogen steered her through the kitchen, where two young women from a caterer were coping with everything, and out of the back door. Mrs Skellow took several deep breaths of the fresh chill outside air.

'You're right,' she said. 'Thank you for rescuing me.'

'Let's go and sit down on that bench for a bit,' Imogen suggested.

'They'll think I'm neglecting them.'

'They'll think you are obviously looking after me,' said Imogen. They moved down the garden, and sat down.

Mrs Skellow wept quietly for a few moments. Then she said, 'I'm sorry, I'm sorry. I'll stop in a minute.'

'Cry if you want to,' said Imogen. 'Why shouldn't you cry? You have every reason.'

That produced a flood of tears. Then Mrs Skellow stopped, suddenly, and said, 'It makes Frank so cross...'

'Well, that's not very understanding of him,' said Imogen. 'I expect he's having trouble with his own feelings.'

'I suppose he is, Miss...?'

'Quy. Imogen Quy. Just Imogen.'

'He says I'm wicked.'

'*Wicked?* Whyever that?'

'I told him I was grieving about a daughter-in-law.

Somehow he thought I meant I wasn't heartbroken about Philip for himself. I didn't mean...'

'Tell me about it,' said Imogen.

'I did so want a daughter. I couldn't have any more after Philip. Frank never did understand. He said he didn't care; a son is as good as a daughter, and a daughter would have been as good as a son. The thing is, you see, he *got* a son. He doesn't realise. I loved Philip more than anything else in the world, but a son still isn't a daughter. I used to think, well, never mind, I'll have a daughter-in-law. I told my friend Molly that once. She's got two and she doesn't get on with either of them, and she told me I was maundering. But I thought, well I'm not like Molly. I won't boss her about; I won't mind *what* she's like, posh and grand or plain and common, or anywhere in between. I thought, we'll have fun together. We'll go shopping. We'll talk about clothes. I'll help if I'm asked and sit on my hands if I'm not, and she'll like me... and by and by there'll be grandchildren – a granddaughter, maybe.'

Mrs Skellow was crying again, silently. 'I've been looking forward to it for years. And now... Frank thinks its wicked to be grieving for such moonshine along with one's own flesh and blood.'

'Well, I don't,' said Imogen. 'I think it's very natural. But you must try to be gentle with your Frank. People all react differently.'

'Oh, I can't tell you how good it is to talk to a sensible woman!' Mrs Skellow said. 'Frank's all cut up about this stealing business. And that's what seems wrong to me. I don't think our Philip was a thief, I think there's some misunderstanding there somewhere. But if he was I wouldn't really care; I'd gladly have him serving twenty years for nicking the Crown Jewels if that meant he was still alive! We were so proud of him when he got into

Cambridge! Frank was walking on air for weeks, and telling everybody, even the milkman. I wish we'd made him leave school and go down a coal mine now!'

'No, you don't,' said Imogen. 'Not really.'

'No,' said Mrs Skellow. 'I suppose not. I would have thought it was a waste of all those brains. Well, now, I'd better go back to the company before they all go home. But I can't tell you how much it means to me, and to Frank, that people came from the college. That helps a lot, truly. And you don't think I'm wicked?'

'Not a bit,' said Imogen.

Later, as she drove Lady Buckmote down the A1 homewards in deepening dusk, she said, 'There was a lot of strong feeling washing around up there, wasn't there?'

'Are you surprised? While you were up the garden with Mrs, Mr was showing me a cuttings book, which went from "Local boy wins place at Cambridge" to "Scholarship boy a thief, says coroner". Gruesome for them.'

'And every one of them seems sure it must be wrong,' said Imogen. 'I've never heard a sermon like that one.'

'So what's your conclusion?' asked Lady B.

'Perhaps it's wrong,' said Imogen.

'Perhaps it is,' said Lady B.

20

Wrong or not, there didn't at first seem to Imogen to be anything she could do about it. Life went back to normal. Which was, after all, what she had been longing for it to do. Being in the middle of a murder enquiry had not been comfortable. But now that she no longer was, life seemed bland and boring. She was grateful for Roger's attention. He took her to a concert performance of *Figaro* in the Corn Exchange, and to a production of *Le Médecin Malgré Lui* in the little theatre in Bury St Edmunds, and even began to mention villas in Tuscany and ask if she had her summer holidays fixed yet. Imogen accepted most of his invitations, and stalled about the summer. She couldn't go away with Roger until she knew more clearly what she felt about him. He was funny, and affectionate, and she was very fond of him; but a nurse has to be careful. The image of a nurse evokes subliminally in too many men's minds the image of themselves as patient – tenderly ministered to, their every need preemptive, however slight. Or, worse, even, they see themselves deliciously bossed about by a uniformed and capable nanny, whose only concern is their own good. Roger was an entrenched bachelor, devoted to a demanding and bossy mother. And Imogen had learned the hard way to be self-preserving.

In any case, she was still deeply concerned about the Skellow case. Obsessed, Roger said. He didn't share her worries. Indeed, he seemed almost snappish with her when she mentioned the nub of the matter in her own mind – was Philip really engaged in theft that night? Not that he himself was immune from obsession, or seemed any less obsessed by the Wyndham Case than before. He was furiously indignant with a newspaper article which compared the Wyndham Case at St Agatha's with the Pepys Library at Magdalene College, and brought it to Imogen to show it to her.

'But what's making you so cross, Roger?' she asked him. 'Is it wrong?'

'*Wrong?*' he exploded at her. 'Wyndham was no Pepys! Pepys made a magnificent collection of books on a multitude of subjects. On literature, on the changeover from manuscript to print, on the history of handwriting, on architecture, on shipbuilding, on navigation, on natural history, on music: the whole conspectus of a cultivated seventeenth-century mind. All intricately arranged and referenced into a catalogue; all still fascinating, still useful, still consulted; whereas our own beloved Wyndham of pestiferous memory deliberately collected discredited volumes expounding disproved astronomy. Utterly useless. There really is no comparison. The man and the books are well matched, I suppose,' he added darkly.

Imogen couldn't resist egging Roger on. 'What do you mean?' she asked.

'You should hear what the Pepys Librarian has to say about our own dear Mountnessing! And, hell, Imogen, there's all that money attached to Wyndham's. The Pepys Librarian has to work for a living.'

'Yes,' said Imogen. 'Calm down, Roger. You sound like a cross child.'

And he did calm down. But Imogen was uneasy. Roger's sardonic sense of humour was one thing; but there was a vitriolic streak in the way he talked about the Wyndham Librarian which felt like hatred. And hatred is a rampant weed, she thought. She decided not to mention her unallayed bafflement over the death of Skellow to Roger any more. Well, that was all right. One has many friends to whom one doesn't talk about certain things.

But how odd to be talking to Mick O'Brien about something that seemed untalkable about with Roger! To find Mick, she got up very early in the morning and walked up to the Lammas Land, where on a garden seat she expected to find him sleeping. He was there, under a heavy mulch of cardboard and newspaper, surrounded by empty bottles and black plastic dustbin liners. The black plastic, she knew from of old, would contain mostly books, including the Greek New Testament which he had been clutching when he collapsed from cold and hunger outside her house some years ago. Trying to house Mick was like trying to cage a wild bird: he pined or escaped every time. Feeding him was easier, and she had brought a bacon butty with her. He was in a sardonic frame of mind.

'Well, and isn't it me very own ministering angel, now!' he cried, striking a raw nerve in Imogen. 'Come bearing nourishment, and bent on helping the old rascal meself, whether I want it or not!' Just the same he took, unwrapped and guzzled the bacon butty.

'I haven't come to help you, Mick,' she said, 'I've come to ask you to help me.'

He bent a beady eye on her, suddenly interested. 'Is it somebody you want taught a lesson?' he asked.

'Good heavens, no!' she said. 'Not that! Whatever do you take me for?'

'Well, I only thought you might be wanting a black eye and broken nose job,' he said, 'not a dead-in-a-ditcher.

Not you. I've got more savvy than thinking that.'

'It isn't a black eye job at all,' she said. 'It's about picking a lock.'

'Is it now?' he said. 'Well, that depends. Depends what you want to lift. There's none of my friends wanting any trouble at all with the law that they haven't got already. Now if it's something of your own that you want back, maybe...'

'I don't want anything; I just want to know if a certain lock can be picked.'

'Out of pure Protestant curiosity?'

'Yes.'

'Ah, aren't the English wonderful!' he said. 'The poor bloody Irish never had a chance in the world. I'll find you someone.'

'It's at St Agatha's: can you bring your friend there?'

'They'll not let us in,' he said, looking doubtful.

'Ask for me. There'll be a bag of groceries waiting.'

'Cheese,' he said. 'And chocolate Brazils. None of that healthy stuff.'

'Right,' she said. 'Everything in the bag will be bad for you. Promise.'

'Ah, you're a wonderful woman,' he said.

He didn't produce his friend till after dark, so that she was working late, waiting for them. That did her no harm: there was lots of note-making, filing, clerical work to be done to catch up on the lacunae produced by the upheavals of the past few weeks. Mick had been right to think the porter would look askance at him, too. Imogen had to reassure him that the two 'gentlemen' were indeed expected, and under his polite insistence she said she would walk across to the porter's lodge and meet them. They were not taking a single step on St Agatha's hallowed ground without an escort – not on the porter's responsibility.

When she was there she saw why. Improbable though it was, Mick's friend looked even less respectable than Mick himself. His upper half was clad in an amazingly dirty anorak, ripped into shreds, with the padding hanging out; his lower in a pair of filthy red trousers, rolled up at the hems. She avoided meeting the porter's eye, and led them round to the door of the Wyndham Library. There was no light on as far as she could see, but she took the precaution of knocking on the door first. There was no answer.

Mick's friend whipped out a bunch of skeleton keys – or at least she assumed that was what they were – a collection of wires, hooks, bent metal bands and keys. He inserted something in the lock and bent down, applying his right ear closely to the lock as he gently, and then fiercely, twiddled the projecting end of his gadget. He tried several; then he stood up and shook his head. 'That's a powder job,' he declared.

'You're out of luck,' said Mick. 'If Joseph can't do it, nobody can.'

'Would a different sort of key...?'

'Not a chance,' said Joseph. He had an educated, upper-class voice. 'That's a primitive lock, Miss Quy. I can do any modern lock, with one or other of these. But you'd have to get a key made to fit that one.' He smiled at her. 'We could blow the lock, but that would be a dead of night job; it would make a hefty thump.'

'A sound that could be heard by someone standing at the other side of the court?'

'Yes indeed.'

'And it would leave a smashed lock?'

'Yes.'

She shook her head. 'That's no good, then,' she said.

'You wouldn't be going to change your mind about the groceries?' said Mick, mournfully, in the tone of one who expects treachery, and is resigned to it.

'Certainly not,' said Imogen. 'Come up to my office and you can collect them. I'll make you a flask of coffee to go with them.'

'We won't sit down,' said Mick, as they went through Imogen's door. But Joseph had immediately done so, and stretched out his legs. Imogen stared at his trousers. They were stained and filthy, deep red velvet.

'Will you get out of the lady's nice clean chair!' said Mick.

'I'm wearing my new trousers,' said Joseph, staying put.

'Where did you get them from?' Imogen asked.

'We totted them from the rags skip at the dump,' said Mick. 'And you know, they belonged to a thief already! There's a lovely deep pocket for the skeletons. It's a shocking thing, isn't it, Miss Quy, how many villains there are in the poor world?'

Imogen filled the flask for them, and put the two loaded plastic shoppers on her desk.

'Explain to me about the lock, Joseph,' she said. 'Why can't you do it?'

'Old lock,' he said. 'Blacksmith's work. The key has large heavy wards, and all the tumblers are made of iron. You might get a skeleton that fitted the matrix, though most would be too small. But the skeleton won't lift the weight of the moving parts, even if it was oiled and worn smooth.'

'I see,' said Imogen. 'So it isn't just that you didn't have the right gizmo? You mean nobody could do it?'

'I don't know anyone who could. A pro would just put a little charge in and blow it.'

'Thank you,' Imogen told him. 'That's a great help.'

'Can't think how,' he said. 'But ours not to question why.'

Imogen walked the two of them across to the lodge, seeing them safely off the premises. They avenged the suspicions of the porter by loudly and affably taking leave of Imogen under his beady eyes, shaking her hand and hoping to see her again very soon.

'Oh, Joseph,' she said at the last minute, *'when* did you tot those trousers?'

'Yesterday,' he said. 'They're as new as the morning!'

Riding home Imogen thought, 'Oh, but what's the matter with me? It isn't a crime to throw away a pair of old trousers!'

When she got home a surprise was waiting. Liz and Simon had set the table with candles and flowers, and had supper ready cooked for her. Simon took her coat and hung it up; Liz put a glass of sherry in her hand.

'What's all this in aid of?' she asked, amazed.

'We thought you were looking very gloomy and sad, landlady mine,' said Simon. 'Not your usual self at all. You haven't told us off in weeks.'

'Cheeky monkey!' said Imogen, laughing. 'How kind of you both! Just what I needed. And what a heavenly smell!' A fragrance of garlic and herbs was wafting from the kitchen.

'Bourguignon,' said Liz, proudly. 'Sort of. With variations.'

'Boeuf à la mode Elizabeth,' suggested Simon.

'Who's the fourth place for?' she asked, glancing at the table.

'Fran's coming, and bringing the salad,' said Liz.

'There's a very good bottle of red in the cellar that's been waiting for a special occasion,' Imogen said. 'Let's crack it now.' She hadn't intended to drink it with her tenants, but she was touched by their concern and kindness. She vowed to remember this next time she yearned for an empty house!

Gratefully, she sat down as instructed, sipped her sherry, and listened to the chatter in the kitchen.

'Oh, do you remember that palaver we were having about snow before Christmas?' Liz asked. 'I've thought of something. Those eleven days. That'd explain it, don't you think?'

'What?' said Simon. 'Do we have a decanter, Imogen? Don't get up, just tell me where.'

'Eleven days. They chopped eleven days out of the calendar, because it had gradually got skewiff. There was uproar. People rioted in the street, demanding their days back.'

'What's that got to do with snow?' demanded Simon.

'Well, we both agreed there's often snow in January. And the day they were keeping as Christmas before the reform is the day we now call January the fifth. So they had snow at Christmas as often as we have snow by Jan fifth. Got it?'

'When?' called Imogen. 'When did they change it?'

'Oh, I don't know exactly. Some time when the populace was thick enough to think their lives had been shortened.'

Imogen jumped up, heart beating, and tore into her living-room. She looked up 'Eleven Days' in Brewer's *Dictionary of Phrase and Fable*:

'When ENGLAND adopted the GREGORIAN Calendar (by Chesterfield's Act of 1751) in place of the JULIAN calendar, eleven days were dropped, 2 September 1752 being followed by 14 September. Many people thought they were being cheated out of eleven days, and also out of eleven days' pay...'

The change had been made after Wyndham's death. So each century after his death ran not to the anniversary of his death, but to eleven days after the anniversary. She seized her notebook and turned to the note she had made herself – it seemed an age ago – about the Wyndham Bequest. She had noted Wyndham's date of death – January 8. So the true centenary of that death fell on January 19. Any rejoicing or relief that the Wyndham audit was out of time should have been postponed till January 20. That was very clear. But equally clearly it didn't help over Philip; he had died on February 15. There was no doubt; the audit was really out of time; Wyndham's crazy codicils had nothing to do with it. She was staring, baffled and disappointed, at her notes when the doorbell announced Fran.

Imogen managed to behave herself. To eat her delicious dinner, and not raise the question of calendar reform. To smile, to talk about the concert in the West Road Music Room everyone proposed to go to the following week, to compare P. D. James with Ruth Rendell mysteries, to enjoy her surprise party. But all the while in the back of her mind, subliminally, the question of coincidence sounded an insistent note.

She was almost relieved when the party broke up. She wasn't allowed even to clear the dishes into the dishwasher, so determined were Simon and Liz to treat her. Just as she was on her way to bed, Simon remembered there was a message for her. The Professor's sister had turned up, wanting Imogen, and would call again in the morning.

Imogen lay awake for some time before sleep laid thoughts to rest. When she was a child she had holidayed on Romney Marsh. It was a bleak and windswept beach, with gravel piled in unstable cliffs against the curving sea-wall, and sand lower down, covered at high tide, and so always hard and clean. There was a foghorn that boomed lugubriously. It could sound from dawn to sunset, bemoaning a worthless day, one when the nature of the world would be occluded, veiled from view, with familiar things lost, or looming abruptly over her just before she collided with them. She had hated the foghorn; but it had given fair warning that you couldn't see what was there, that you might lose your way in the most obvious excursions.

And now, as clearly as though she could hear it, she had that foghorn feeling booming in the bottom of her mind. She couldn't see something that was there. Those eleven days – they really, really *ought* to have been the answer. And yet they weren't.

21

The Professor's sister was Mrs Barclay, a brisk elderly woman, very smartly dressed in dark colours, with elegantly cut grey hair, and a martyred expression that no doubt she had earned. Showing her the Professor's flat, Imogen felt obliged to explain that she was forbidden to dust the books. Just the same, Mrs Barclay, looking round with an exasperated expression, declared that her brother could not possibly be discharged from Addenbrooke's to live in it. 'He'll have to stay with me for a while,' she said.

'I would do my best to keep an eye on him,' said Imogen, 'if he came home.'

'But you have a job to do. He's my flesh and blood. I'll have to cope,' said Mrs Barclay. She had the tone of voice of one who was used to coping and did it well. 'Now, this missing book. It would be a great help if I could find it.'

'We have all looked. Thoroughly.'

'With Edward wailing and wringing his hands while you did so, no doubt, hindered by him helping you? I am going to look again. Frankly, with Edward a simple misplacement seems far more likely than theft, don't you agree?'

'Well...' Imogen remembered that, disorderly though the toppling piles of books seemed to an outsider, the Professor had seemed to know exactly what was where.

'I'll make us some coffee and come and help,' she offered.

'Bring a duster, would you?' said Mrs Barclay. 'Now, let me see…' She reached into her handbag and produced a scrap of paper. 'This is what we're looking for.' She handed Imogen the paper. Imogen glanced at it. She knew it would say 'My Bartholomew'. It said: *'Nova et Antiqua Cosmologia,* Aldus Bartholomeus. Quarto vol. in brown calf.' Imogen stood looking at it, thunderstruck. There are limits to coincidence.

They did not find the book.

Later that morning Imogen found Professor Wylie ensconced in one of Addenbrooke's day rooms. Off oxygen, and out of bed. He had been done good to, whatever he himself thought of an institution with no serious books and no television-free zone. He was looking kempt and rosy. The doctors attributed his absent-mindedness not to scholarship, nor to old age, but to insufficient vitamins in a disorganised diet, and were administering supplements.

Imogen asked, 'Professor, how many copies of that book of yours are there in England? Can you say?'

'Only one. Mine.'

'But there's one in the Wyndham Case, isn't there?'

'No, no, no, woman! Couldn't be.'

Imogen unwrapped the grapes she had brought, and put them on the table between them. The foghorn atmosphere swirled in her mind. 'That young man who was killed in the Wyndham Library…'

'What young man?'

How had he managed not to hear of it, amid all the publicity, all the fuss?

'A young man who was found dead in the Wyndham Library…'

'It will have happened during the period of my incarceration, no doubt. What an extraordinary thing!'

'He had displaced a book, which was lying on the floor near the body. I thought it was *Nova et Antiqua Cosmologia*.'

'Must have been the other one,' said the Professor obscurely. He filled his mouth with grapes. 'There couldn't be a copy of mine in there. Wasn't published till 1708. After Wyndham's death, don't you see?'

Imogen took the point about the date. 'Even that clot Mountnessing would know *that*,' added the Professor, contemptuously.

'The other one?' Imogen asked, having left him time to eat another handful of grapes. 'The other what?'

'The other Bartholomew. There were two of them, father and son. Ricardo and Aldus. Father's book a load of old cods – *that* might be in Wyndham's. Think it is, now you come to mention it. Published 1688. Twenty years later son tried to salvage the family name. Published a revision. Quite a sensible book, really. Bloody rare. Couldn't be in Wyndham's though, could it?' he smiled at Imogen seraphically. 'Old fool forbade anyone to add to his list.'

'Two different books, with the same title...' Imogen was thinking aloud. 'Could the same title, just by coincidence, be involved...?'

'Wyndham's Bartholomew isn't rare, you know,' the Professor offered, finishing the grapes. 'The later book is the rare one. Mine.'

'But there are lots of copies of Ricardo's *Nova Cosmologia*?'

'Yes. There must be ten or twelve of those. Worldwide, of course.'

Shapes loomed in Imogen's mind, through the fog. She had that terrible sensation of panic which she remembered feeling when you *knew* there was something which you couldn't see.

'Incidentally,' the Professor said, as she got up to leave, 'should he be allowed to lock one up for days? Shouldn't somebody be after him for it? It was devilish damp and cold down there, and it was taking a liberty, wasn't it?'

He startled her, suddenly switching from the books to the rambling like that. 'Is he wandering again?' asked a ward nurse, appearing at her side. 'He gets very excited; we have to try to keep him calm.'

'Professor Wylie,' she asked, nevertheless, 'who hit you? Can you tell us who hit you?'

'Came from behind. Didn't see,' he said. She caught the nurse's eye and they shrugged at each other.

'Habeas corpus!' shouted the Professor after her as she left. 'What happened to habeas corpus?'

Spring had reached Cambridge at last. It was a beautiful clear day, crisp as a new apple, with a tender, relenting warmth in the air. The Fellows' Garden was full of windflowers, and a thrush sang ecstatically on a branch of the Magnolia Stellata that filled the island flower-bed with a constellation of fragrant white flowers. Imogen was walking, walking to breathe, to clear her mind, to think.

She ascended the castle mound, taking the turns of the zigzag path at a stride, paid the view its due of a moment's lingering on the summit, and then descended again, to walk in the churchyard of St Giles. She went right to the far end of the churchyard, where a drift of little daffodils grew wild in the grasses – the ones she knew as 'Lent lilies'.

The wall which divided the churchyard from the Chesterton Road sheltered her from the wind and made a pleasant warmth there, and she slowed down and read the inscriptions on the headstones '…and Martha, his wife…' 'beloved son…' '…erected by their one surviving son, Thomas Martin, Gent., of blessed memory…'

The lapidary affections, however flowery their expression, were touching. Sad. The children's graves the saddest. Who could fail to be sympathetically appalled by Sarah, wife of the above, of whose thirteen children none survived infancy, and all died before her? Sometimes a child had a doll's-house memorial, a miniature headstone hardly showing above the deep grass and rampant daffodils. Like this one – Imogen bent and brushed aside the herbage to read the words beneath the carved angel, wings curved round the hemispherical top of the stone, hand holding a monitory skull.

'Our heav'n-sent babe, again to heaven returned,
His parents' joys extinct, and hopes now spurned
Not e'en one year in this drear world did stay
He who now wakens to th'unending day;
His time how short, his life was scarce begun
And now for him eternity is won.'

How touching the verse was – she looked at the details above it, and then frowned deeply.

The child was Samuel Fennichurch, born February 1, 1751; died January 3, 1753.

Imogen took out her notebook and carefully copied every word on the little stone. With the foghorns of confusion blaring in her head she went to look for someone who could explain.

She had an odd impression that Roger turned white when she asked him; but perhaps it was just the cadaverous glare of the neon reading-light in the basement of the library, which he turned on to look at her note of the words on the stone. 'I expect they just got muddled,' he said.

'*Muddled*? About the age of a child? Surely not, Roger!'

'Well, you have to remember people didn't feel about children then the way we do now. They didn't get attached to them. Couldn't afford to; they lost so many – they died off like flies to a dozen diseases. Women farmed out babes to wet nurses and got on with their lives.'

'Are you telling me people didn't love their children in the early eighteenth century?'

'Well, not much. There's a book by Philippe Ariès that proves it; I'll find it and lend it to you if you like.'

'Let me get this clear: you are saying there is a book which *proves* that in early modern times people didn't love their children. They put up grieving inscriptions about them, but really they cared so little they could have been unclear about whether an infant was less than a year old or nearly two. Is that what you're saying?'

'Well, there could be other explanations.'

'Like?'

'Like a mason's book. You find the same verses on tombstones in widely dispersed places. There's a good one for a blacksmith, for example – "My forge and anvil lie declined, my bellows now have lost their wind" – which is used on a tomb at Houghton, just up the road from here, and another in Oxfordshire, and no doubt many more. There must have been books of suitable inscriptions for the masons to use. So perhaps someone just used a verse for a dead infant, without alteration, even though it didn't quite fit.'

'Wouldn't the parents have objected?' she asked.

'Might have been illiterate. Or didn't care about the details,' he said.

She left him without another word, and went to find Lady B. 'How very curious,' said Lady B., putting on her spectacles, and studying the inscription. 'What did Roger Rumbold say?'

Imogen told her. 'Oh, rubbish!' said Lady B. 'I know the Ariès book. I always think one look at Ben Jonson collapses his thesis. Do you know the epitaph on his son?' She fetched a book from her shelves.

'Farewell, thou child of my right hand, and joy;
My sin was too much hope of thee, lov'd boy...
Rest in soft peace, and, asked, say here doth lye
Ben Jonson his best piece of poetrie...'

'Yes! I would have thought that in any century, parents who had lost a child would know its life span to the nearest minute, to the exact day,' said Imogen.

'So would I.'

'To suggest otherwise is an outrage on one's common sense, I think,' said Lady B. 'But I can't unscramble your conundrum.'

Imogen went back to her office and propped the words up on her desk. She stared at them from time to time. Like staring at something in the fog.

At three o'clock Fran came by, with her right hand wrapped in paper tissues. 'Can I have some tender loving care getting a splinter out?' she asked, showing Imogen a sore and oozing finger-tip. 'It's in my right hand, and I can't manipulate a needle well enough with my left. It doesn't half hurt, too!'

'Sit down, Fran,' Imogen said, getting a bowl of water with TCP, and a needle.

'What's that?' asked Fran, looking at the propped-up note.

'A deeply puzzling epitaph,' Imogen told her.

'Deeply touching, yes,' said Fran, wincing as Imogen inserted a needle next to the sliver of wood. 'Where's the puzzle?'

'The dates. Was the child less than one, or nearly two?'

'Oh, less than one. The birthdate is written old style. Before calendar reform in 1752,' said Fran learnedly.

'Calendar reform? The missing eleven days?'

'Same reform, different bit of it. They moved New Year from March twenty-sixth to January first. We have to remember to keep track of it doing eighteenth-century history.'

'Got it,' said Imogen, expertly removing the splinter. 'Now tell me again, carefully.'

'They moved New Year. The year used to run to the end of March. So that what we call January, 1752, they called January, 1751. They changed the year end to December, so next time January came round it was 1753.'

'Got it!' said Imogen. The fog had lifted off at least part of the landscape, and she could clearly see. She rinsed the bowl, put the needle in the sharps disposal tin, and took her coat off the hook.

'Where are you going?' asked Fran.

'Yorkshire,' said Imogen.

22

When the fog rolls back it's hard to remember why one didn't see things. Things very clear and sharp. Christopher Wyndham had estates near Helmsley. Philip Skellow came from near Helmsley. Those oddly familiar armorial bearings in the parish church – Wyndham's, no doubt. And after all, by common agreement there were two keys to the Wyndham Case. Imogen spent the night in a pub in Wetherby, and reached her destination just after breakfast the following day.

Mrs Skellow was surprised to see her and, Imogen thought, glad. Mr Skellow was off for the day, fishing. The two women opened the box of Philip's papers that the college had sent home, along with his clothes and books. It was untouched in his room, likewise untouched. Imogen winced slightly at the little desk, used by a studious boy; at the pinboard with snapshots, with a school cricket team, with a picture of his mother and father. A poster above the bed showed not the usual pop-star, but Simon Rattle conducting. It felt wrong to be riffling through the box of papers. They found his bank statements, in a nice new plastic folder provided by the bank for new student accounts. It showed a deposit of £1000, made on 2 January.

'Lord help us, where did he get that from?' said Mrs Skellow. 'We haven't got that kind of money... this'll just about kill Frank! Oh, I shouldn't have let you look!'

'Hush now,' said Imogen softly. 'I think he came by it perfectly honestly. I think I know what it was for, and what he was doing in the Wyndham Library; but we need to find who paid him the money, if we can. Help me look for the paying-in book.'

It was quickly found. Philip had been methodical; he had scrawled on the stubs the names of the payers. There weren't many: mostly the Education Committee for his grant cheques, and presents from relatives. And a thousand pounds, from 'Fanfare & Bratt'.

'That's the one,' said Imogen. 'Who or what are Fanfare and Bratt?'

'Lawyers,' said Mrs Skellow. 'Very stiff old-fashioned lot. We've never had anything to do with them; well, we don't have to do with lawyers at all, really, except for making our wills, and we had those done by Shanklins.'

'Where are the offices of Fanfare and Bratt?' Imogen asked.

'In the High Street, opposite the school gate. What are we going to do?'

'Leave it to me,' said Imogen.

Fanfare and Bratt occupied a delectable late Georgian house in what was clearly the posh end of the little town. She had to insist to get to see a partner, a Mr Bratt, and he denied all knowledge of any client called Skellow. His assistant went off to check the files, and confirmed it. They did not have, and never had had, a client called Skellow.

'Then why did you pay him a thousand pounds?' Imogen asked.

'All our clients' affairs are confidential,' he said.

'I will level with you,' said Imogen. 'This is a matter of concern to St Agatha's College, Cambridge, where I work. We would rather sort it out privately; but if that is not possible we shall have to inform the police. It is likely that they would then get a warrant.'

'Look up Skellow on the computer, will you, Miss Bates?' said Mr Bratt.

'I find two entries, Mr Bratt,' the girl said, an impressively short time later. 'A Mr P. Skellow had an appointment with Mr Bratt senior on the eighteenth of December last. And we paid a Mr P. Skellow a thousand pounds on the twentieth of December last. Mr Bratt senior signed the cheque. It doesn't say what the cheque was for.'

'My father was not always methodical, Miss Quy,' said Mr Bratt there present. 'He kept confidential business in his head. I'm afraid I can't help you; we do seem to have had dealings with P. Skellow, but I haven't an earthly what they were about.'

'But we could ask your father?'

'You could ask him, certainly. But whether he would remember... My father had a stroke at the end of January, Miss Quy, and is making a slow, and I'm afraid very partial, recovery. A good deal that was filed in his once encyclopedic memory is gone for good.'

'But I may visit him, and ask?'

'Certainly. Visits do him good. He is in the Forget-me-not Home.' Mr Bratt winced slightly, speaking the name. 'Most embarrassingly titled, but the care there is of the best. I will tell the staff to expect you.'

Forget-me-not Home was a hideous Victorian mansion on the outskirts of the town, in spacious grounds which would have been agreeable enough if not disfigured by the presence of a house which looked like George Gilbert Scott powering up for St Pancras, but on an off day. Mr Bratt Senior was in a pleasant room overlooking the garden. He was sitting in a chair in the window bay, with a rug over his knees. Conversation with him was certainly difficult; rather more, Imogen thought, because he had difficulty speaking than because he had difficulty remembering. A newspaper lay on the coffee-table beside him, unopened. Imogen wondered if he was able to read. Did he know what had happened to Philip?

'I want to ask you about Philip Skellow,' she said.

He reacted at once. 'Poor boy... my flaw...' he seemed to say. Then he shook his head, miserably aware that he hadn't got it right. He took a deep breath and said, 'I can't talk, you know,' quite clearly.

'I'll talk,' said Imogen. 'I'll tell you what I think happened, and you can say no if I've got it wrong. OK?'

'Yes,' he said.

'Your firm is supposed to do the Wyndham audit. There's some kind of trust. It got forgotten; you left it very late, almost too late. When you woke up about it, you had a good idea. You had read in the papers about a boy from the school here winning a scholarship to St Agatha's – '

'Yes.' He spoke hoarsely, but his eyes were bright and clear, fixed on her face.

'You thought it would be easy for such a boy to do the audit for you, if you gave him the auditor's key.'

'Great thing...'

'You paid him. Perhaps you wanted to help him; perhaps you thought it would be no fun being hard up at Cambridge...'

Mr Bratt nodded vigorously.

'But you swore him to secrecy. The whole matter was secret. I don't know how your firm came by the Wyndham audit; it can't be that old. Did you inherit it from somebody?'

'Yes.'

'And there's some money along with the obligation, so you were anxious to carry it out and retain the retainer?'

'Useful sum.'

'And it was very clever of you to realise that the audit still had a year to run, after the apparent centenary. I suppose lawyers know that kind of thing?'

'Fellow reminded me,' he said.

'Who?' asked Imogen. An icy fear rolled over her.

But Mr Bratt smiled at her very sweetly, and shook his head.

'Mr Bratt, did you know that Philip Skellow is being branded a thief?' she asked.

'Poor dead,' he said, still smiling.

It was little less than a miracle that Imogen didn't crash on the drive down the A1 back to Cambridge. She drove like the wind, with her mind nagging and teasing at the loose ends. Perhaps avenging angels have the special care of guardian angels, for she didn't crash; she didn't even get stopped for speeding. She got back to the college at just after seven, and went in search of Wyndham's librarian. He was not in his room; he was working in the Wyndham Case, his papers spread out over one of the tables.

'Mr Mountnessing,' she said to him sternly, 'where is the second key?'

He froze for a second. Then, 'I don't have to answer questions from the college nurse,' he said, coldly.

'Of course not,' she said. She turned to go.

'Where are you going?' he asked.

She told the truth. 'To my room. I am going to sit and think seriously about whether it is my duty to persuade the police to ask you about the other key.'

He reached into his pocket and produced his key. Then he went to a cabinet at the far end of the room. He unlocked it. He removed four books. He reached round behind the row of volumes, scrabbling at something. She heard a click, as of a safety lock opening. He produced another key, brought it and laid it beside the first. Two heavy, ancient, iron keys, with elaborate wards. He sat down heavily and said, 'I'm not cut out for deception.'

'You found the key on Philip's body and removed it.'

'Not on the body. It was on the table.'

'But why did you remove it?'

'I had a lot to lose. I stood to lose my job.'

'Because an auditor would find something amiss?'

'He *had* found something amiss. The book which the Inspector found on the floor should never have been there.'

'It was the Aldus Bartholomew, not the Ricardo Bartholomew?'

'You know!' he said, dropping his head flamboyantly in his hands.

'I've guessed a lot. Tell me what happened. It might help me decide what to do.'

'That morning when I came in to work. There was a body on the floor; lights on. The incredible key was lying on the table, beside the handbook – that's the definitive booklist for the Wyndham Case. I realised the auditor had come, and come to grief somehow. It looked like foul play to me. I had a quick look at the bookcases, starting with A, up there on the right. The books are packed closely; if one is removed it leaves a gap. Well, there was a gap where the handlist would have been; I replaced the handlist. There was another gap, right beside the Bartholomew. I couldn't think what was missing. I looked around for the missing book, and I found it on the floor, under the table. I picked it up. I realised at once that it was the wrong Bartholomew. I was afraid, Miss Quy, please believe me. I might have been seen trying the door late the night before. And if there was a wrong book in the Wyndham Case, and the auditor was lying dead on the floor, then I was the obvious suspect. I didn't know what to do. And anyone might wander in, wanting to look at the library; it was already opening hours. I removed the later Bartholomew and the second key, and hid them. Then I put the legitimate copy of Bartholomew on the floor where the wrong one had been lying. Then I raised the alarm.'

'The book you hid was Professor Wylie's copy?'

'It must have been. I have no idea how it got into the Wyndham Case. I have enemies.'

'How often do you check the books?'

'I see what you mean. It could have been there for weeks, or months, I'm afraid.'

'And what did you do to Professor Wylie?' she asked.

'It's been a nightmare!' he said. 'I was beside myself. How could I have known he was going to turn up and set all Cambridge by the ears, carrying on about his book? I was afraid someone would make the connection. He wouldn't listen to reason. So I did lock him up; I admit that. I made sure he had food and blankets... it all went wrong.'

'I don't think I understand this bit,' said Imogen.

'I was going to lock him up, before he had the whole country looking for the blasted book; I was going to find a way of slipping it back to his lodging. Then I could release him; he would find the book, everyone would put the whole thing down to his absence of mind... it all went wrong.'

'Was it you who hit him?' she asked, appalled.

'It was only to shut him up. He wouldn't stop shouting and banging down there; I was afraid someone would hear him. He made a terrible fuss.'

'Well, wouldn't you make a fuss if someone locked you up?' she said indignantly.

'I suppose so. Then when I had to knock him out he took ages to come round, and then he was rambling. He was in and out of consciousness... I hadn't meant to hit him hard enough to do any damage. His clothes were covered in blood. I cleaned him up a bit and lent him some of mine, and I drove him to Wisbech, and...'

'Why ever Wisbech?'

'I thought he would get put in a hospital safely out of Cambridge somewhere, for some time. I didn't think he would just get on a bus.'

'What a performance! Couldn't you just have left the book somewhere for someone to find and return to him?'

It was his turn now to look horrified. 'A book like that?' he said. 'It's fragile, and it's valuable; it's totally irreplaceable...'

'So is Professor Wylie,' she said.

'What are you going to do?' he asked her.

'If you will kindly give me that book, I am going to return it to its owner,' she said, 'and ask him if he wants to do anything.'

Mountnessing picked up a volume loosely wrapped in newspaper that was lying in full view on his desk, and handed it to her without a word.

23

The Professor was sitting fully dressed beside his bed,
waiting for his sister to come and fetch him away to
convalesce. Imogen put the parcel gently on his lap. She
saw the expression of joy on his face as he opened it, and
the tenderness with which he inspected it, delicately
turning the pages with his clumsy arthritic hands.
'Unharmed!' he said at last. 'A miracle! It has come to no
harm. Where did you get it, woman?' and he turned a
stern gaze at her. It came to Imogen that if she were to
say, 'It was in my kitchen all the time,' he would simply
scold her, and that would be that. But why should she?

'Mr Mountnessing had it,' she said.

'The beggar stole my book?' said the Professor,
breaking into a ferocious grin. 'No wonder he locked me
up!'

'No, he didn't steal it,' she said. It was one thing to let
Mountnessing take the blame for what he had done,
quite another to let him carry the can for Roger. 'He
simply secreted it, for reasons of his own. He would have
given it back later, he says.'

'And do you believe he would?'

'Oh yes,' said Imogen, 'I do. Why didn't you say it was
Mountnessing who had locked you up?'

'Make a nasty stink,' he said. 'College scandal. Don't
want that.'

'Will you go to the police about it?'

'The police? Why should I? I've got my book back, unharmed. A fellow of the college can borrow a book of mine if he wants. Should have told me, of course, but...'

'Perhaps about being locked up and hit over the head? Weren't you on about habeas corpus?'

'I hadn't got my book back, then,' the Professor said, serenely. 'Naturally I was upset.'

'But a fellow of the college can incarcerate you and assault you if he likes?' said Imogen. 'I mean, what's a spot of GBH between friends?'

'That's the trouble with women,' he said. 'Tongues so sharp it's a wonder they don't cut their mouths. Thank you for bringing it back.' He was clutching the volume to his chest like a long-lost child.

Imogen left him, and went home to think it over.

Her thoughts were distressing to her. No doubt the police would be interested in prosecuting a man who locked up a colleague for three days and inflicted GBH. But clearly Professor Wylie would not be likely to co-operate. After due consideration Imogen decided that what she had discovered was not a matter for the police so much as a matter for the Master. Let him recall the police if he thought best.

And so she found herself once more sitting in a fireside chair in the living room of the Master's Lodge, with a glass of sherry in her hand.

'Can I stay and listen, William?' asked Lady B., assuming the answer and sitting down beside Imogen.

'It begins when you all began to rejoice that the audit was out of time,' Imogen told the Master. 'Because it wasn't. The change in the way dates are written between Wyndham's time and ours means that his date of death falls a year later in our chronology than it seems to. Someone knew that, and decided to play a trick on Mr Mountnessing. This someone stole – I expect he would say, borrowed – a book: an edition of *Nova et Antiqua Cosmologia*, by Aldus Bartholomew, which couldn't have been in Wyndham's, because it wasn't published till after Wyndham's death. The someone put the book in the Wyndham Case, alongside the legitimate one, the Ricardo Bartholomew, feeling pretty sure that Mr Mountnessing wouldn't notice it. And he didn't. Then this somebody did a little historical research, and tracked the trust Wyndham set up to carry out the audits in perpetuity. He jogged the memory of the partner in the firm, a certain Mr Bratt. Master, all this is guesswork, you understand.'

'But we guess the mysterious perpetrator to have been Roger Rumbold?'

'I think it must have been,' she admitted sadly. 'He had the know-how, and, I'm afraid, the motive. Well, Mr Bratt didn't know how to go about the audit. But he remembered having seen in the local papers that Philip Skellow had won a place here. So he paid Skellow to do the audit, and gave him the auditor's key to the Library. Philip went about the job the night he had been doped with heparin, though of course, he didn't know that. He put the handlist on the library table, and began to check. He didn't get far – just through the A's – and there in the B's were two copies of Bartholomew when the list said only one. He took the suspect book down the stairs and laid it on the table to look at it more closely. Jack Taverham burst in on him, accusing him of theft. No wonder that he didn't react like someone caught *in flagrante*, but just told Jack to push off. We all know what happened next.'

'They struggled over the book and he fell and banged his head.'

'Mountnessing came by and locked the unlocked door again, using his own key. Then in the morning, when he returned, he found the dead body...'

'And called me, and I fetched you.'

'Not quite. He found a dead body, and he found the second key on the table, and he found a book lying on the floor that shouldn't have been there. The wrong Bartholomew. So he put the right Bartholomew on the floor – he tossed it as though it had fallen when Philip fell. Then he hid the key and the interpolated book. Then he called you.'

'But didn't the police find Philip's fingerprints on the book that was on the floor?' said Lady B.

'He must have handled both volumes when he was checking them on the shelves, I think,' said Imogen.

'The terms of the bequest had been broken, and Mountnessing was protecting his job,' said the Master. 'But then why didn't our original mischief-maker blow the whistle?'

'And own up to having precipitated murder? Besides, I think he was having fun at Mountnessing's discomfiture. And you realise, the dates are out by a year; he can still pull the plug on Mountnessing at any time.'

'And the supernumerary book is the one that Professor Wylie lost?' said Lady B.

'Of course. We should have realised; Roger Rumbold knows the set-up in my house, I'm afraid, and can drop in there without anyone raising eyebrows. He knew the Professor was away indefinitely. And when the Professor turned up and began asking for his book, and trying to report the loss everywhere, it was Mountnessing who was terrified. Mountnessing who by then had the book, and had everything to lose should anyone make the connection with the book in the other incident. He tried to talk the Professor out of putting around that the book was missing; when that failed he locked him up somewhere. Somewhere damp and dark and nasty, so that when the unfortunate man described it to us we thought he was raving.'

'There is a disused undercroft in the Wyndham wing,' said the Master. 'We used to store things there, but it's too damp.'

'I expect it was there, then. Eventually Mountnessing clobbered the Professor over the head to stop him making a noise and getting rescued. Then he abandoned him in Wisbech. I was very slow; I thought I had seen somewhere before the curious clothes the Professor was wearing when they found him. They belonged to Mountnessing and I *had* seen them, but I couldn't place them. And the poor wretched Professor has been in hospital all this time because they think he is still hallucinating when he talks about being locked in a dungeon, when it's actually the literal truth!'

'Who knows about all this?' said the Master.

'I confronted Moutnessing, and he owned up at once. Otherwise, only we three. I thought it should be up to you, Master, whether to call the police.'

'What does Rumbold say? You didn't confront him?'

'No,' said Imogen. 'I didn't feel like doing that. I suppose I might be wrong.'

'I'm afraid it sounds very much as if you are right, my dear,' said Lady B., looking at Imogen with concern. 'Well, William, are you going to call the police?'

'No, I'm not,' said the Master. 'But I'm going to call an emergency meeting of the college council. I rather think we shall have to dispense with the services of both our librarians. And we shall refuse the Goldhooper endowment. If the council want to accept it against my advice, I shall reluctantly use my power of veto.'

'That's your mind made up very suddenly after all these months of agonizing!' said Lady B.

'It's not unconnected. All this terrible trouble, and both

those two young people's deaths have happened, fundamentally, because Christopher Wyndham wanted to ossify knowledge. He wanted to limit science. So he burdened his successors with all this ridiculous apparatus for preventing accessions to his books. *FINIS EST SAPIENTIA* over the door, indeed! "The End is Wisdom". When I was an undergraduate here we used to translate it "Wisdom is at an End". And that is nearer the mark! Time has moved on, and the real library is full of things Wyndham rejected. Well, you get the point. And now Goldhooper wants to do the same kind of thing. In three hundred years, shall we have the college torn by dissenting bands, administering fossilised science to keep the money intact, and acting as an impediment to the progress of reason? We should refuse; we will refuse.'

'And today, William?' said Lady B.

'We shall thank Imogen for her services to the college. And we shall dismiss our librarians. And I shall write to Skellow's parents, telling them that it has emerged that Philip was engaged on highly confidential college business, and that the imputation of dishonesty made against him is without foundation.'

'Does that leave the odd loose end for you, Imogen?' asked Lady B.

Where the devil had Lady B. got an inkling that Imogen might have a soft spot for Roger? Imogen couldn't imagine. Wincing, she said, 'I'll live.'

24

Both the St Agatha's librarians found new jobs. Mountnessing went to catalogue the library of an ancient family in Umbria, whose present head was a friend of his sister, the Contessa Amandola di Tramontana. Roger was furious. 'Trust him to fall on his feet!' he said, though it wasn't clear, really, whether Mountnessing was falling on his feet or into a lioness's den. He certainly wasn't going to be as rich as he had been. Roger himself, on the other hand, was going to be richer, setting up a new library for the outpost of a Middle Western American university in a stately home in the Midlands. Richer, but sadder. He kept pointing out to Imogen that he would be only two hours' drive away; that there were bound to be good pubs for lunching somewhere around half way, that he would have to be in Cambridge often to visit his mother... When he understood that Imogen would always be otherwise engaged, that no invitation would henceforward be accepted, he was angry.

'But what have I done?' he demanded. 'What are you holding against me? *I* haven't murdered anyone! All I have done is play a little prank on a colleague, and richly deserved! Think, Imogen; if he had known the first thing about dates; if he had checked his books – his only duty – do you know how long that book was there? Three months! Three *months*! If he could tell one edition of Nova Whatsit from another, none of this would have happened to him! You can't tell me he doesn't deserve it! Why does it cast a chill between us?'

'Not a chill. An ice age. You let that young man be branded as a thief.'

'Oh, that. What did it matter, once he was dead?'

'It most dreadfully hurt the feelings of his family and friends.'

'Naughty of me. But keep a sense of proportion, Imogen, love. Not important enough to freeze out a friend, surely?'

'Deeply dislikeable, Roger.'

'Well, even ice ages have an end,' he said. 'I'll try again from time to time.'

Curiously, the Master's brave refusal to accept the Goldhooper endowment ended happily. Lord Goldhooper, receiving a long-faced delegation from the college – the Master, the Bursar, the Dean – to thank him with dignity and refuse him, met them with hearty laughter. 'Of course you're quite right,' he said. 'I like men of principle. Have it your own way.'

'Have it?' the Bursar said, stunned.

'Have the money, and I withdraw any conditions you don't like,' said Lord Goldhooper. 'Spend it on astrology for all I shall care! I leave the administration of it to the good sense of the future members of college. There's not a lot any of us can do about the future.'

There was one last consequence to the whole affair of the Wyndham Case. Some time in June, Tracy came to see Imogen. She sat in Imogen's breakfast-room looking tense and pale. 'I want some advice,' she said. 'I need it bad.'

'What's the trouble, Tracy love?' asked Imogen.

'I'm pregnant,' Tracy said. 'They keep telling me at the clinic to get an abortion. But ...'

'But?'

'It's Philip's. Got to be.'

222

'So you'd like to have it?'

'Oh, I don't know, Imogen. I just don't know. I've been the child of a single mother, and it wasn't any fun. I know what it's like when someone is looking after you all alone, and they nearly can't cope, and all the time they wish they didn't have to. *And* I know what it's like when they really can't cope any more and you get dumped into care. And there's never any money for things. It isn't fair. I don't want to do that to the poor little bleeder. And it would be just me looking after it; I haven't got anyone except one auntie that's beaten into the ground herself by her own problems. It wouldn't have a nan, it wouldn't have cousins and aunties, it wouldn't have a dad. I just can't face it.' She was near to tears. 'They're telling me it would be wicked to have it, the social worker would take it off me anyway.'

'So you're thinking of having an abortion?'

'Only it's all there is left of Philip, isn't it? All there'll ever be. They keep saying, to wait for better circumstances; but *he* isn't going to get any more circumstances, better or worse. And I did love him; really I did!'

Imogen left her in the breakfast-room, went to the phone in the hall, and dialled a number. 'Mrs Skellow? It's Imogen. This might be a bit of a shock; are you alone? There's someone I want to tell you about.'

Praise for Jill Paton Walsh and the Imogen Quy novels:

'An admirable detective heroine.' *Times Literary Supplement*

'Imogen Quy positively sparkles on the page as an amateur sleuth. *A Piece of Justice* is one to be savoured, and enjoyed.' *Sunday Express*

'A jewel in the traditional English detective mode . . . Ms Morse has arrived.' *Observer*

'Elegantly written series still has much appeal . . . an entertaining read' *The Sunday Times*

'Jill Paton Walsh's crime fiction is like a proper maiden aunt who turns out to be good fun' *Sydney Morning Herald*

'Jill Paton Walsh demonstrates that the traditional ingredients of the woman sleuth, the academic background and a clever puzzle, are still capable of being arranged into an entertaining and stimulating crime novel.' *Manchester Evening News*

Also by Jill Paton Walsh

The Imogen Quy novels continue with
Debts of Dishonour
The Bad Quarto

With Dorothy L. Sayers
A Presumption of Death
Thrones, Dominations

About the author

Jill Paton Walsh is the author of seven highly-praised literary
novels: the fourth of these, *Knowledge of Angels*, was shortlisted for
the Booker Prize. Before writing for adults she made a career as a
writer of children's books and has won many literary prizes in that
field. She is also the author of *Thrones, Dominations*, which
continues and completes Dorothy L. Sayers' last novel featuring
Lord Peter Wimsey, and *A Presumption of Death*, which incor-
porates some of Sayers' writing and continues the Wimsey story
into the Second World War. She lives in Cambridge.

You can find out more about Jill Paton Walsh's other novels for
adults and children at www.greenbay.co.uk

Jill Paton Walsh

A Piece of Justice

HODDER

For R. H., a true original

This equal piece of justice – death . . .
Sir Thomas Browne

I

'Where's the repeat?' asked Imogen Quy. She was sitting surrounded by scraps of fabric, patterned and plain in a rainbow of colours, spread all over the floor. Pansy Whitman and Shirl Nichols were sitting in her armchairs, and the three of them were passing the pattern book to and fro. They were a quorum of the Newnham Quilters' Club, setting out to make a quilt to be raffled just before Christmas for the Red Cross funds. A little pleasant disagreement was afoot. Shirl wanted an elaborate pattern, involving piecing curves; Pansy wanted bright colours and easy shapes. Both of Imogen's friends liked quilts made with different blocks, put together on a grid with plain borders separating one from the next. Imogen liked patterns that overspilled, running across the entire surface of the work. There were many patterns like this; one block merged with the next, so that the patterns shifted as you looked, part of one block completing squares or diamonds in the next. They had lovely traditional names: 'Lost Sail', 'Compass Rose', 'Drunkard's Path', 'Delectable Mountains', 'Blazing Star', 'Homeward Bound', 'Barn-raising' . . .

Shirl was suggesting one called 'Pumpkin Patch', all curved seams. Pansy was pointing out how easy to sew was a pattern called 'Birds in the Air'.

'So boring, Pansy,' Shirl said.

'Not if we make it in lovely colours,' said Pansy.

'It's supposed to be special,' said Shirl. 'It won't raise

1

lots of money if everyone thinks they could jolly well make it themselves.'

'They won't think that, whatever else,' said Pansy. 'People can't sew these days. They're all too busy taking doctorates and working in the City. They can't so much as darn a sock. And as for cooking – putting ready-meals in the microwave is too much for some I know!'

'Nearly everyone in the Quilters' Club is ancient!' said Shirl, agreeing. 'The whole art will die out soon.'

'Craft,' said Pansy.

'What?'

'It's a craft, not an art.'

'Oh, Pansy, don't!' said Shirl. 'Such a cop-out. Why isn't it an art? Just because women do it?'

'No,' said Pansy. 'That is . . . well . . .'

'What do you think, Imogen?' said Shirl.

'Sorry,' said Imogen. 'I wasn't listening, I'm afraid. I was trying to find the repeat in this one.' She showed them a page of the pattern book. It was covered with outlines of patchwork patterns – elaborate networks of lines, making a mesh of shapes all over the page. Somewhere in the mesh was an area that repeated; that was the block. You made however many blocks were required for the size of the proposed quilt, and sewed them together. Once sewn together they made patterns larger than themselves, which flowed in and out of adjacent blocks, danced and dazzled and pleased the eye.

The pattern Imogen was studying was called 'Coast o' Maine'. It had a flowing curved wavy look to it, although it was made only of triangles and squares.

'Here,' said Shirl, running a pencil line round an area of the diagram. The moment she isolated a square of the mesh Imogen could see how the whole page was made just of this pattern, repeated. The second row was offset by half a block, making it harder to see.

'Hey, that's nice!' said Pansy, looking over her shoulder. 'What about making that one?'

'I'll go along with that,' said Shirl. The pattern looked much harder to piece than it was; it seemed to have curves running through it. Shirl couldn't bear to be seen doing anything easy.

'Right,' said Imogen. 'Colours next. You start, I'll make some coffee.'

Choosing fabrics for the blocks was an intriguing process. Every time she did it Imogen started out picking up tastefully blending scraps, in soft harmonising colours. The three friends wielded scissors, cutting sample shapes, and laying them together to see what the stitched block would look like. The carefully chosen prints and plains in gentle harmony always looked dull. Pretty, and boring. The fact was, patchwork was a folk art – it didn't like being used in good taste – ghastly good taste was the expression that came to mind. Pansy might be lazy about sewing curved seams, but she had a wonderful eye for colours – clashing, unlikely colours that talked to each other across the grid of shapes, that looked bright and accidental. That wonderful 'found' look of old quilts, that Imogen loved, that spoke of need, and thrift, and using what you had to hand, the very absolute opposite of going into Laura Ashley and buying bits specially cut up and chosen to tone with each other, needed some daring to imitate. Reaching over Imogen's pleasant, ordinary looking choice of colours, Pansy tried a square of orange cloth, printed in scarlet blotches, alongside the dark red central star, removing the lilac that had been Imogen's first guess.

'Hmm,' she said, tilting her head. 'No . . . perhaps . . .'

3

She swapped one of the soft blues for a bright turquoise, completely out of key with the other colours. It looked lovely. They sipped their coffee, and contemplated the result. Before the two friends left, they had worked out a yardage for a big double quilt, and cut out the templates from thick art-shop card. Next week they would cut out the fabric, sort it and distribute it to the members of the Quilters' Club for sewing into blocks. Imogen was always surprised at the large number of club members who liked to be given the block worked out, and cut out. All they had to do was the sewing. The fun of choosing and designing had all been greedily gobbled up by Shirl and Pansy and herself. Of course, anyone who wanted to could come to the planning session; the others must really truly prefer just to sew. And they were a good lot; kindly, unassuming, hard-working women, ready to make jam, or sew for any good cause; to arrange flowers in churches, to shop for neighbours, to baby-sit, to feed cats for absent friends. Salt of the earth sort of people. Heads down sort of people, reluctant to take credit.

Here in this modest little suburban corner, within easy walk of the centre of Cambridge the contrast, Imogen reflected, was not so much between housewives and women with doctorates – half the housewives *were* women with doctorates. It was a question of how people saw what they did. Of what counted for credit, so to speak. And one way or another, simple skills – domestic skills, the ability to make comfortable beds, and arrange rooms pleasantly, to preserve fruits in season, and make the little back gardens grow flowers and tomatoes and beans, to bring roast beef to table perfectly done at the same moment as perfectly done roast potatoes and Yorkshire pudding: all these abilities were disregarded; taken for granted by those who had them, not thought of as achievements worth crediting oneself with. Not taking credit for the altogether more arcane skills required for the quilt was part of the culture. Best not even call it an art. 'Craft' was more like it, Imogen reflected, in more ways than one.

Imogen settled in her breakfast room, with her sandwich lunch, and the newspaper propped on the water-jug to keep her company. She didn't need to go in to work that day, because the college didn't need her much during the long vacation; it was in the short hectic terms – the Michaelmas term began next week – that college nurses like Imogen were worked off their feet. The newspaper was supposed to help Imogen not worry by keeping her mind off Frances Bullion, her lodger. Not that it was up to Imogen to worry about Fran; she was not a relative, and she had a mother of her own in the Midlands somewhere, whose duty it was, one supposed, to provide all the necessary worry about Fran. Imogen wasn't old enough to worry about Fran; Fran must be twenty-two or so, and Imogen was only a dozen years older. But Imogen, whose own life had been sidetracked by a disastrous love affair some years back, and who would have had children of her own by now if life had gone according to plan, had plenty of unused affection locked away carefully, and Fran had somehow come in for a share of it. Entitled or not, Imogen just did worry about Fran. Nothing in the newspaper was nearly interesting enough to stop her.

Making coffee she confronted the worry head on. Frances so desperately wanted to be an academic. What Cambridge ineffably called a 'don'. She had got to know Imogen as an undergraduate at St Agatha's, where Imogen worked as college nurse, and although the little flat in the top of Imogen's comfortable house in Newnham was not usually let to someone from St Agatha's, Imogen had happily made an exception for Fran when she stayed on at Cambridge doing postgraduate work. In one way things fell out luckily for Fran. She was interested in the relationship between biography and autobiography, as the subject for her dissertation. And Cambridge had just established a new chair in Biography – the History Faculty had refused to have anything to do with it, and it was under the aegis of the English Faculty – and Professor Maverack, the appointed first incumbent, had agreed to supervise Frances. The problem was money. Fran didn't have any.

She had, of course, a minimal grant. It left her short of nearly everything. Imogen couldn't afford to do without the rent, even if Fran would have accepted that. She had, without Fran's knowledge, lowered it somewhat – she had wanted Fran as a tenant, wanted for once someone that she liked, whose company would be an advantage. She did her best to feed Fran, giving her dinner several times a week, while still trying *not* to feed the two undergraduates from Clare College who rented her two spare bedrooms, and whose unauthorised raids on the refrigerator made catering difficult.

A helpful professor would find teaching for his graduate students, to organise some earning power for them. But the Biography chair was new, Professor Maverack was new. He hadn't developed a network of contacts yet. Frances had struggled through the previous term without any earning power except doing a night duty on the petrol pumps at the garage on the Barton Road. This morning she had gone to see Professor Maverack to tell him that she didn't think she could continue indefinitely without some kind of teaching work. This interview would be complicated by the fact that Fran didn't like Professor Maverack. She hadn't told Imogen that, Imogen just knew. And Imogen was afraid she would draw a blank, and decide to throw it all up and get a job in an office somewhere. Imogen's own chance at getting qualified as a doctor had slipped through her fingers, and that made it much more painful for her to contemplate the same sort of thing happening to someone she cared for.

Not that Josh – the nearest thing Fran had to what used to be called a boyfriend – was anything like the sort of danger that Imogen's lover had been to her. Far from telling Fran to abandon her career, and devote herself to looking after him, Josh was given to putting his feet up on the fender, swinging back in the battered armchair, and hoping Fran would cut out a dazzling path of public achievement, and be able to support him while he minded the babies. Neither his own PhD nor Fran's seemed likely to come unstuck because of him. Imogen liked Josh.

She had abandoned the newspaper, with its thrilling headlines about glass panes falling out of the History Building, and had returned to contemplation of the patchwork block to try to stop worrying over the whole Frances saga yet again, when the front door slammed behind someone, and Frances herself called, 'Yoohoo! Imogen!' from the hall.

How seldom is worrying about someone justified! Fran came bouncing in, dropped her bag of notebooks on the floor, and collapsed in the armchair in Imogen's breakfast room, smiling happily.

'It's all right,' she said. 'He's got something for me.'

'Wonderful,' said Imogen. 'Terrific, Fran! What is it?'

'A little spot of ghosting,' said Fran. 'Quite well paid. Do you think I can do it? Whoo, hoo, haunt, haunt . . .'

'Fool,' said Imogen fondly. 'Now have a mug of coffee and tell me about it.'

'Well,' Fran began, turning on Imogen that clear-sighted, grey-eyed gaze of dauntless candour of which the owner was presumably unaware, 'there's this publisher who's after

7

him. And he's far too busy himself. But he doesn't want to turn him down in case he's useful later . . .'

'Stop!' said Imogen. 'Slow down. Start again.'

Fran began her tale again. The gist of it was that there was a publisher – a well-known one, Recktype and Diss, who had approached Professor Maverack to complete a biography for them. They were desperate for it; it was already announced in their autumn catalogue and they needed it by August next year at the latest. They would pay a large advance. Maverack himself was too busy to do it in the time – he was working on his inaugural lecture, and had research of his own in progress. On the other hand the goodwill of Recktype and Diss was not to be sniffed at; scholarly biographies did not sell like hot cakes exactly, and Maverack could see himself approaching them to publish work of his own sooner or later. He would like to oblige them if he could. All the materials for the project had been assembled by an author who was unable to complete it. So the Professor proposed that Fran should write the book – it might even be useful for her in her own dissertation actually to have written a biography herself – and he would look it over and put his name to it. Of course, every penny of the advance would be Fran's. End of money problems. Everyone happy.

'But Fran, if you are going to write it, shouldn't your name be on the title page?' asked Imogen.

'Recktype and Diss wouldn't have it. They want a famous name on it, or it wouldn't sell at all. Wouldn't get serious reviews. He's promised to put my name on it somewhere – share the credit. Frankly, Imogen, getting a share of the credit for a project with his name on it won't do me any harm at all.'

'And in return for doing all the work . . .'

'I get all the money.'

'You didn't say who this biography is of?'

'Gideon Summerfield. He's a mathematician of some kind. He's about to get the Waymark Prize.'

'I've heard of Gideon Summerfield,' said Imogen.

'Clever you. That's more than I had.'

'He used to be a tutor at St Agatha's. Retired before you came up. He's dead now, surely.'

'The prize is posthumous.'

'But the biography is urgent?'

'The publishers expect the announcement of the prize to stir some interest. They had it all organised; started in good time. They put it in their catalogue. Someone called Mark Zephyr was doing it for them.'

'I get the picture,' said Imogen. 'You do this for them. It solves problems. It pays well, it puts you in the professor's good books . . .'

'I'm taking you out to dinner to celebrate,' said Fran happily. 'Let's go to that nice pub at Sutton Gault. But I must fly now, there's a lecture I want to hear.' She jumped up, and gathered up her books and notebooks. 'If a large box arrives for me, it will be the papers from Mark Zephyr. It's coming from the publisher's office by courier.'

As she left, Imogen called after her, 'Fran, why didn't Mark Zephyr finish the job?'

'He died,' yelled Fran from the front door, letting it slam behind her.

2

Urgency in the editorial department of Recktype and Diss did not translate very easily into urgency in the post-room, and it was three days before the papers for Fran's great project arrived. Imogen was cycling home when she saw the van blocking the narrow roadway between the parked cars, outside her own front door. She put on speed, and dismounted with a screech of brakes, just as the driver had given up knocking and waiting, and was about to drive off again. Imogen unlocked her front door, and he staggered up the path with a very large box, in a very battered state. It was bound up with string, and coming apart at all four corners, and clearly from his manner of carrying it very heavy. When Imogen asked him if he could possibly take it upstairs, he mentioned his heart. Imogen sympathised, and offered some beer money, whereupon the driver took several steps towards the stairs. Imogen wondered whether to tell him now, or when he reached the upstairs landing, that the destination of the box was the top flat, but before he had heaved himself and his burden more than three steps up from the hall, the box disintegrated.

String snapped, corrugated cardboard tore open, and bundles and sheets of paper thumped and fluttered everywhere. The driver cursed, and began to seize the fallen stuff, and thrust it back through the holes in the package. Imogen stopped him – Lord knows what confusion and destruction he was wreaking – and gave him some beer money anyway.

Then she closed the door on him, made some coffee, and began to try to sort out the confusion herself.

It wasn't easy. Imogen pulled out the leaves of her dining-room table, to have room to spread things out. There was a stack of four stout box files labelled 'From Mark Zephyr'. Imogen put these unopened at one end of the table. Then there was a brown box, the kind of box dresses used to be packed in in smart shops, flattened at all four corners, but roughly intact. Imogen put that down beside the files, and turned her attention to the masses of papers that had been loose in the outer box, and were now piled inside it, and lying widely scattered on her stairs and hall floor. It was quite difficult to sort out things when you didn't know what there was, or what order it ought to be in. Imogen contemplated simply leaving it all for Fran to handle; but she had someone coming to dinner that evening, and the table might well be wanted before Fran got in. No, better sort it roughly and carry it upstairs in parts to Fran's eyrie.

But what was supposed to be here? She found a torn and exploded wrapper marked – it took a bit of finding, for the thing was torn across the label – 'Return to JS'. Then there was an ancient paper file that had worn through and dumped out its contents from the back. That was labelled, in a different hand, a small neat one, 'Recovered from premises of May Swann'. Imogen inspected the loose papers. There were dozens of letters from many different correspondents, a desk diary from 1963, wallets of holiday snapshots, a list of Christmas card recipients . . . and a number of handwritten pages, closely covered in a clear handwriting, from a lined loose-leaf block. Guessing, Imogen put the random assortment of papers into a pile with the 'Return to JS' wrapper, and the manuscript pages into the May Swann file, which she repaired with parcel tape. Then she trudged up and down the two flights of stairs and laid the stuff out on Fran's little square table in the upstairs flat. She gazed around with some satisfaction – Fran was the first tenant Imogen had ever had who kept the place clean.

Now to remove the shattered ruins of the outer box, and the snarls of snapped string from the hall, and she could get on with her cooking – it was high time, all that had taken ages. As Imogen bent the box, and trod it flat to compact it enough to put it out by the dustbins, she saw a paper caught in the split angle, where the stupid driver had tried to thrust stuff back into the box. She extracted it. It was a sheet of office memo paper, with Recktype and Diss's monogram on the top. It said, 'Send at once, to Frances Bullion, address below, Zephyr files on Summerfield. *Keep back the rest.* M. Drawl.'

From the look of it, Imogen concluded, the despatch department had made a mistake, and sent off both the stuff they were supposed to keep and the instruction to keep it. Perhaps some of it wasn't about Summerfield, and Fran wouldn't have so much to deal with. But Imogen was in a hurry now; she propped the note behind the coffee jar on the kitchen dresser, and turned her mind to her cooking.

Imogen's dinner guest was Dr Malcolm Mistral, a fellow of St Agatha's. He was a widower, who had returned to live in college after many years in a handsome house in Newton Road. He had confessed to Imogen ruefully how he missed having quiet suppers at home with his wife – the wide open spaces of high table in the College Hall and the compulsory random company of college fellows and their guests discomforted him.

'Why not cook yourself supper in your rooms, now and then?' Imogen had asked. 'You've got a little kitchen haven't you?'

Malcolm Mistral had confessed to being unable to boil an egg. His wife hadn't let him so much as pick up a wooden spoon, all his long married life.

Imogen had taken to having him for a meal at home with her now and then. He often asked her for the recipe for whatever food she had served him, and she gave it to him carefully written out with full instructions; tactfully she never asked him if he had tried the recipes, or how he had got along with them. He invariably remarked that being male, and a college fellow, was not an absolute bar to being a good cook; Meredith Bagadeuce was an excellent cook. The only complaint against him on that head was that he didn't invite Malcolm Mistral very often.

Under cover of this supposed tutorial process Imogen had gradually got to know Dr Mistral. The thought that very clever people can sometimes make very dull company was one which Imogen kept firmly suppressed. Now, over coffee at her fireside in one of the long pauses that fell naturally into her conversation with someone with whom she had so little in common, it occurred to her to ask him if he had known Gideon Summerfield.

'Somewhat,' said Mistral. 'He was a research fellow when I first came to St Agatha's. Quite a bit younger than me. Saw him around though, of course. On a college committee with him once or twice. That sort of thing.'

'What was he like?' asked Imogen.

'I don't know, really. Decent sort of chap, I suppose. Worked hard for the college. Why do you ask?'

'A friend of mine has been asked to write his biography.'

'Really? You rather surprise me. Was he interesting?'

'That's what I was asking you!' said Imogen, laughing. 'Have a chocolate with a second cup of coffee, won't you?'

'You spoil me, Miss Quy,' he said, delicately picking a mint from the box.

Imogen wondered whether to ask him to call her Imogen, and then decided that she didn't feel quite ready to call him Malcolm; so she left it.

'I wouldn't have thought old Summerfield was worth a book,' he said, thoughtfully, 'though it's quite possible to be in the same college as someone for years and years and never know the least thing about them *privately*, you know. They could be wife-beaters or womanisers, or tricksters, or fraudsters, and their fellow fellows wouldn't realise a thing. We know each other very well on a narrow ambit. Wouldn't be surprised if *you* know more about us than we do about each other, d'you see?'

'Well, the healthier a fellow is the less I would know about him, as a rule,' said Imogen. 'But that narrow ambit on which you know each other well might have given you some sidelight on Gideon Summerfield?'

'As I say, I can't think of anything interesting about him. Why does anyone want a biography? Apart from Janet, that is?'

'Janet?'

'His wife. Widow, I mean. Fiercely devoted sort of woman. My wife – my late wife – knew her somewhat. She would want a biography if it confined itself strictly to praise. Devoted her life to the great man. That sort of woman. But I can't think who would actually want to *read* it . . .'

'I think he's about to get the Waymark Prize.'

'Yes; I heard that too. Might be true, I suppose.'

'But you would be surprised?'

'Of course, he was a mathematician,' said Malcolm Mistral, thoughtfully, taking another mint.

'Well, the Waymark Prize is specially for mathematics, isn't it?' asked Imogen.

'Yes, yes. But I meant merely, talent in mathematicians can be difficult to detect. For non-mathematicians, I mean.'

'You thought he wasn't clever?' said Imogen, joyfully egging her guest on.

'My dear Miss Quy, *every* fellow of St Agatha's is clever,' said Dr Mistral, sounding pained. 'The question is, was he brilliant? So brilliant that he merits the Waymark Prize? As you know, rather oddly there isn't a Nobel Prize for Mathematics, and the Waymark is supposed to make up for that. So to get that is to rate with Nobel Prize winners.'

'And you didn't think . . . ?' Imogen felt unscrupulous to press on in this way, but she had cooked a very good dinner, and she was still hoping for a titbit for Fran, as quid pro quo.

'I believe he puzzled other mathematicians, too,' said Dr Mistral slyly. 'Of course, we don't understand each other's subjects. We can't estimate the worth of work in physics or history or law unless we are physicists or historians or lawyers. But you know in most cases you can feel yourself in the presence of a fine mind, even just talking commonplaces at high table. But Summerfield . . . well, some of his colleagues were surprised at what he had done. He was a perfectly respectable mathematician, but he didn't strike people as brilliant. Then he produced this one splendid piece of work, rather late in life, and then that was it. As I say he wasn't scintillating. I sat next to him once at a college feast and all he talked about all evening was that the Filet de Boeuf Wellington was tough.'

'His work was done late in life?'

'I only mean late for a mathematician.'

'They burn out early?'

'Not necessarily, I understand. But they usually start to be good very young – then they can keep it up for a long time. But to get much better in midstream is un-usual. So Bagadeuce told me, and I suppose he would know.' Dr Bagadeuce was St Agatha's Director of Studies in Mathematics.

'He was rather odd, I thought,' continued Dr Mistral, 'about the rumour – the rumour that Gideon Summerfield was in the running for the Waymark, I mean. Very cool about it. Very cool. Considering how hot he usually is for the glory of the college.' He visited a malicious grin on Imogen. 'Can't have liked the fellow much, *I* thought.'

Imogen offered a choice of brandy or Cointreau to complete the evening.

As Dr Mistral was sipping his brandy and talking of leaving she asked, 'What was that one splendid piece of work that propelled Summerfield to fame? Do you know?'

'You're asking the wrong man, I'm afraid. Don't know a thing about maths. It was some kind of geometry, I think. Your friend should be able to ask Bagadeuce about it; he was very excited about it when it was first published.'

'Thank you,' said Imogen. 'I'll suggest it to her.'

'Her?'

'Her,' said Imogen, firmly. He had given himself away, expecting that a biographer would be male. But then he was a harmless enough sort of man, and of an earlier generation. The world had changed a good deal since his unconscious expectations had been formed. Perhaps, she thought, as she closed the door behind him – he never stayed late – she should not pamper him, but should give him recipes and leave him to it. On the other hand, what harm did it do to cook for him now and then? And tonight he had been useful in a way.

Only in a way; it didn't seem likely to be helpful to tell Fran what an old bore she was going to have to write about. An old bore with an adoring wife. Oh dear. She hadn't heard Fran come in, so she sat up for a while, waiting for her. She lit the gas logs that made such a pretty phoney fire in the Victorian grate in her front room, got out the piece bag, and the squared paper on which 'Coast o' Maine' had been drawn out, and began playing with swathes of cloth – patterned and plain in a rainbow palette of colours, cutting bits roughly to shape and laying them out to see what they looked like. The colour choices made earlier, when Shirl and Pansy were with her, were good, but there was no harm in trying to improve them.

The piece bag was slightly dangerous to Imogen. It put her in mind of the past. Here was a piece of finely striped shirting from the uniform of a trainee nurse; Imogen had once, some time ago, owned three of those, and worked very hard in them. Here, from longer ago still, was a lovely flower print on silk from which she had made herself a ball-gown to go to a Commemoration Ball at Oxford, while she was a medical student there, before she threw it all up to go to America with Frank. How different her life would have been if he hadn't suddenly dumped her in favour of another woman! Imogen put the scissors into the the folds of silk, and cut a sample diamond from it. Once this whole line of thought would have been horribly painful to her – now, she realised, she was on the whole grateful to have had her life as it was, instead of as it might have been. Frank was a trimmer, and sooner or later would have found a wind favourable to his plans, and left Imogen. She was probably lucky he had done it sooner rather than later. She had managed; she had come home, trained as a nurse, looked after her parents, found a niche in St Agatha's College, where she was appreciated. Most of the time, anyway. It was a job with some unlooked for perks – like friendship with Lady Buckmote, the Master's wife, known to one and all as Lady B., a kind, sensible woman with a nice dry wit. She had made common cause with Imogen several times, and they were now fast friends.

The scrap of silk looked lovely in the patchwork square – was there enough to be useful? It had been bold of Imogen to buy anything so bright to wear with her very red hair. She stood up and held the silk in front of herself as she stared in the mirror above the mantelshelf. Her round, full, slightly freckled face looked back at her, framed in her carroty curls, above the dazzling orange and gold and pink of the print. A wonderful effect for a happy young woman going dancing with her lover – Imogen would never dare it now. 'Plain grey Alpaca for me, now,' she murmured, smiling at herself. It was late, and she was tired. Goodness knows how late Fran would come in – it might be any time until dawn when the young whooped it up with their friends. Imogen gathered the scraps into the bag, put out the lights, and went to bed. Talk about Summerfield would have to wait till morning.

3

'You wouldn't have some time to help me, would you?' Fran asked. It was a crisp fine Sunday morning, and Imogen had been intending a long walk. But it could wait for an hour. She trudged upstairs with Fran.

'I'll make coffee,' said Fran. 'This could be a big deal.'

Imogen took in the state of the little flat. Every flat surface – the seat of the settee, the expanse of the hearth rug, the dining table, the seat of every chair, was covered in papers. Piles of papers, files, bundles of letters, of index cards, of manuscript, typescript . . . There was nowhere to sit down.

'What can I do, exactly?' Imogen asked.

'Well, chiefly, I was hoping you might remember where some of this stuff fell apart from,' said Fran.

'Not a chance,' said Imogen cheerfully. 'It just exploded everywhere out of the box. I might be able to reconstruct my reconstruction, I suppose. What's the problem, exactly?'

'Well, Mark Zephyr's stuff is in wonderful order,' said Fran. 'It's in all those box files.

'Those stayed together.'

'Yes. And he was a careful worker. So in a way there isn't a problem . . . the other stuff *ought* to be the raw materials; Summerfield's papers from which Zephyr was working. But look at this.' Fran showed Imogen a thick, board-bound A4 notebook, nearly full of notes and script. 'Chapter One – Early childhood', it said on the first page. Then it listed sources – a nanny's recollections, interviews with family, letters home from holidays abroad . . . Imogen skipped down the long list. Three pages in the notebook began:

Gideon Summerfield was born in 1918, into a family of non-conformist artisans, living in a working-class suburb of London called Palmer's Green. His father was a cobbler, and his mother a dressmaker, and he was the youngest of three sons. The exotic name belies these simple origins, but is explained by his family's membership of a break-away missionary church serving the London poor – the Church of Christ the Carpenter – who were given to Bible readings and to using Old Testament names. Gideon's brothers were Seth, born 1916, and Isaiah, born 1910 . . .

'Well, this is a start on the job,' said Imogen. 'What's the problem?'

'It isn't in Zephyr's hand,' said Fran. 'That's all.'

'Are you sure? Perhaps he had a different style for jotting and for faircopy.'

'Compare,' said Fran, showing Imogen a note from Zephyr to Recktype and Diss. There wasn't any question really of the handwriting being that of the writer of the notebook, Imogen saw that at once. Zephyr's was small, neat and rounded; the notebook hand was bold and angular.

'Anyway,' Fran continued, 'all Zephyr's work was done on a computer – it's all printout in that spotty kind of print.'

'So the work in the notebook . . .'

'Is by someone else.'

'Well, is that so odd?' Imogen asked. 'Perhaps someone in his family had begun to jot down a recollection . . .'

'What I was hoping was that you would remember what was in this,' said Fran, holding out to Imogen the mended

22

file marked 'Recovered from premises of May Swann'.

'I'm afraid I just guessed,' said Imogen. 'I put stuff in that handwriting – like the big notebook – in this file, and all the other stuff just in a bundle. Sorry.'

'Oh it's not your fault, Imogen,' said Fran. 'It's just very confusing. There's such a lot of it; and . . . well, I'm puzzled. Mark Zephyr was supposed to be about ready to write this *magnum opus*. And he had reduced the subject to order, so it seems. Look, here's a list of sources in his spotty printout. It is stepping through Chapter One, and everything has a reference – like this.' She showed Imogen a page of Zephyr's notes. 'Childhood holidays. *Vide* MS no. 23'.

'Well, surely a lot of this mountain of stuff is original material. Somewhere there will be something numbered 23 . . .'

'Help me look,' said Fran. 'So far I can't find a single one of the originals numbered in any way.'

A short shuffle through Summerfield's diaries, childhood letters and school reports, all piled on the lefthand end of the settee confirmed it. If the documents had been numbered, it was not by having numbers written on them.

'Well, let's speculate,' said Imogen. 'Suppose this file contained an assortment of original documents, coming from May Swann, who was some friend or relative of Summerfield's. The "Return to JS" file contained some other stuff – family papers. Without help we are never going to be able to reconstruct what was in which; but that may not matter for the moment. The notebook is perhaps a family member's record intended to help Mark Zephyr . . .'

'I'm going to have to ask someone at the publishers if they know more about it, I suppose,' said Fran.

'Well . . . Perhaps don't hurry,' said Imogen. 'Unless you want to work only with the Zephyr files. I'll show you something.'

Imogen went downstairs and returned with the note from Recktype and Diss that had finished up propped on her dresser the day the parcel came.

'You weren't supposed to see most of this stuff,' Imogen pointed out.

Fran became incandescent with rage. 'That's intolerable!' she cried. 'How can they give me a job like that and not trust me with the documents? What the hell are they playing at? I could never do a good scholarly piece of work without seeing the materials! Bloody hell, Imogen . . .'

'Has it occurred to you, Fran,' asked Imogen, 'that it must be your professor they don't trust? They don't know anything about you, do they? You are flying under his colours, so to speak.'

Fran sobered up at once. 'Well, I wouldn't trust him far, myself,' she said. 'Somehow. Don't know why I'm saying that. But I did think this was a fair offer. And I do need it so badly . . .'

'It probably is a fair offer, love,' said Imogen. 'Probably some clot in the publishers didn't understand that you would need the documents; they just thought you would merrily write up Zephyr's material, and so that was all you needed. But if you do need the rest, why not work on it quietly at once, and not draw attention to it until someone notices you've got it?'

'Imogen, you are a real pal. Thank you. That's good advice, and I'll take it.'

'Well, I can't see that I've been much help really . . .'

'Just talking to you helps. Clears the head.'

'You make me sound like an embrocation, child!' protested Imogen. 'I'm off for my walk. The golden morning wastes. Feel like coming?'

'With all this to master? You're joking!' said Fran. 'Leave me in my salt mine and enjoy yourself!'

24

*   *   *

Imogen drove off in her little car to the car park at Wimpole Hall, and set out to march round the inner circuit – she hadn't time now for the longer, woodland walk. The shorter walk was pleasant enough, with the nearest thing to hill views that Cambridgeshire offered. She walked briskly, and in half an hour was ascending the gentle slope through chalky white ploughed land to the folly, set among trees on the slight summit. The folly, which had been constructed ready-ruined, to spare the expense of time, and made of brick within, for economy, and clunch and stone without, for authenticity, commanded a wide sweep of the gentle countryside, and improved the prospect from the windows of the house. Imogen walked through the gateway in the ivy-mantled tower, to the little phoney courtyard within, and saw at once a back she recognized – Lady B., sitting in contemplation on a low stretch of folly wall. Imogen crossed the grassy keep, and sat down beside her. A pair of little dogs came running up wagging and woofing in greeting, and Lady Buckmote looked round and smiled.

'Oh, Imogen! Are you the answer to a matron's prayer?'

'Depends what the matron happens to be praying for,' said Imogen, cautiously. 'If you want to share the driving on one of your hare-brained expeditions to the other end of England, definitely not.'

'No, no. Don't alarm yourself. I only want someone to make up the numbers at dinner. To be honest, I want a woman. I hate being the only female in these august gatherings. Tomorrow night; are you free?'

'I'm free, and female; but not specially august,' said Imogen. 'What's the occasion?'

'William wants to take a look at the new professor. The biography one with the funny name . . .'

'Maverack?'

25

'That's him. He has a chair, but no fellowship. The University is discreetly looking for a college to take him under its wing. William wants to dine with him before taking a view on that. He's invited various of our senior members . . .'

'I'd love to come,' said Imogen.

'You would?' Lady B. looked curiously at Imogen.

'I'd quite like a look at Dr Maverack. He's supervising Fran's PhD. I shall hear quite a lot about him these two years or more.'

'Fran?'

'Frances Bullion. My lodger.'

'Come for a quiet drink first then – sixish? We will stiffen our nerves for the evening.'

The two friends rose, and began the descent towards the model farm, and the return loop to the car park, with Lady B.'s long-haired dachshunds scampering ahead of them. At the gate to the last field Lady B. put the dogs on leads, as they walked between the strange-looking, curly-horned, long-horned, antique cattle in which the Wimpole farm specialised, under the lugubrious solemn gaze of these endangered creatures.

'That one,' said Lady B., pointing at a rough-haired, rather pale buff-coloured creature, with tight curls around its horns, 'reminds me of William.'

They looked at the amiable, baffled expression on the bullock's face and began to giggle together.

Imogen went home cheerful. She found Fran, sitting beside the Rayburn in the breakfast room, her slippered feet propped on the warm rail, her chair tipped up on its back feet, gently and thoughtfully rocking herself in the warmth of the stove.

'Sorted?' Imogen asked her.

'Not so's you'd notice. Not sorted as such,' said Fran, weightily. 'But I got clued up about one thing, at least.'

'Tell,' said Imogen, hanging her coat in the cupboard, and sitting down in the facing chair.

'I found this.' Fran held out to Imogen several pages of yellow ruled paper stapled together at the top. It was a neatly written and carefully numbered list. Against the numbers were brief descriptions – postcard, dated 23.4.68, picture Brighton Pier . . . Letter from Simon Brown, dated 3.9.68 . . . Imogen looked down the page for number 23. 'Postcard from G.S. to Aunt Emily; Postmark New Romney 5.6.79.'

'So those manuscript numbers in Mark Zephyr's list . . .'

'Were numbers assigned in this list. Yes; I've checked. They correspond.'

'So you should be able to sort out the stuff with the help of this list?' Genuinely though Imogen was interested in Fran, she wasn't a historian, or an archivist, and her mind was wandering towards the consideration of what was in the house for supper.

'Well, yes. Though I still wouldn't know which lot of things were labelled "Return to JS".'

'Does that matter?'

'Well yes, it might.'

'I do see that if JS turned up demanding the return of documents, and you didn't know which were hers . . .'

'Why do you say "hers"?'

'Well, I was jumping to conclusions, I suppose. But isn't Mrs Gideon Summerfield a J? I thought she was called Janet.'

'Aha!' said Fran. 'I hadn't tumbled to that yet. So very likely then, she is the JS to whom stuff must be returned. Or rather, some of the stuff. Makes sense.'

'But you were explaining to me why it might matter

27

ahead of the embarrassment if the documents get reclaimed.'

'Well, take number 48 on the list, for example,' said Fran. 'It's a postcard from Chartres. It isn't signed. It isn't addressed. It just says, "Enclosing this to remind you – it's as wonderful as you said it was. See you next term, Yours ever, M." So there's nothing to connect it with Summerfield at all. But it is evidence that he went to Chartres.'

'Lots of people have been to Chartres . . .'

'Oh, it isn't that it's in any way unlikely, Imogen. But to use it you would have to know the provenance of the postcard. If you saw it quoted in a biography a footnote would say, "From a card enclosed in a letter from Peter X, circa 1978," or something. If the card was given to the biographer by the great man's wife, having been found among his papers, one would be satisfied that it really had been written to him; if you don't know from Adam where the card came from, then it doesn't prove anything. It might have got accidentally picked up among other papers from a colleague's desk; it might have been sent to Mark Zephyr and just got muddled with his Summerfield stuff; it might have been planted . . .'

'Fran, why in heaven or earth would anyone plant a postcard that falsely proved that Summerfield had been to Chartres?'

'Well, they wouldn't, of course. That was just an example, a hypothetical instance to demonstrate to you that you have to know where documents came from; who has owned them between the time they date from and their coming into your hands, before you can rely on them. It's a fundamental principle of historical research. You'd be surprised how often in the history of history people have planted evidence, or suppressed it, or cunningly omitted it.'

'And is biography history? We could have macaroni cheese, if you're eating with me tonight. I can put tinned tunny fish in it.'

'Brill,' said Fran. 'I'll set the table. But Imogen, what I'm trying to tell you is, this list is in the second hand.'

'Second hand? As on a clock face, or as in a junk shop? I don't get you.'

'Neither. As in a taxonomy of handwriting. Fran Bullion's own classification. To wit: first hand Mark Zephyr's writing. Small, rounded, neat. Betrays tidy mind. Very little of it; most of his stuff is in spotty printout.'

'Like the list of MS materials you showed me earlier?'

'Exactly. That list uses numbers which are in this list – here on the yellow paper – and this list is in the second hand, bold, angular, strong-looking, uses blue-black real ink.'

'And whose is the second hand?' asked Imogen, putting a pan of water on to boil, cooking while she listened.

'Well, I rather think,' said Fran, getting up from the chair, and coming to lean against the side of the door into the little kitchen, 'that I can say with some certainty. Those Zephyr references to "MS" number 23, don't mean "manuscript number 23", you see. Later in his list we get references to manuscript material called "IG number suchwhich". MS means May Swann. And if this list was written by May Swann, then it all fits perfectly. All Zephyr's references to "MS" numbers correspond to the numbers in this list. And, Imogen, if this list is in May Swann's handwriting, then so is the work in the big notebook – the Chapter One, you remember – and various other things, including pages of notes. Which make it perfectly clear to me that May Swann, whoever she was, had a lot of the great

Gideon Summerfield's private papers in her hands, and had carefully listed them, and begun putting biographical facts in a notebook, and where is she now?'

'She must have given up on the job and handed the papers back,' said Imogen. 'Cut some brown bread for me, will you, Fran?'

4

Sir William Buckmote, the Master of St Agatha's College, greeted Imogen warmly. 'Sit down, sit down, Imogen. Sherry? How kind of you to share the ordeal of the evening with us.'

'Will it be an ordeal?' asked Imogen, smiling at him, and accepting the proffered glass. 'Satisfying one's curiosity is usually a pleasure, even if one is also appalled . . .'

'But what is it about the reputedly dreadful Professor Maverack that has so aroused the curiosity of both you and my dear wife?' the Master enquired, sitting down comfortably with his own sherry. 'I have come to associate a common front between you two with trouble for the college; it fills me with dread.'

'William! How grossly unfair of you,' said Lady B. 'Take it back at once!'

'Shan't,' said the Master, smiling gleefully at his wife. 'You two were in cahoots during the whole of that unfortunate affair over the Wyndham Case.'

'Just as well we were,' said Lady B. crisply. 'We saved the college face in more ways than one.'

'Of course my dear, of course. You are wholly benign, and so is our dear Imogen; it's just the feeling you give me of something *going on*; you know how I hate goings on. I am happiest when the nearest happening of any kind is several million light years away, and the college is safely sunk in the somnolence of centuries.'

31

'Oh, go along with you, William,' said Lady B., in sweetly feigned crossness.

'Something is going on, just the same,' the Master observed. 'Humour me; put my mind at rest. Tell me why the Master's wife and the college nurse are on parade to inspect Professor Maverack. Who is, as I say, reputedly dreadful.'

'We didn't know his reputation,' said Imogen. 'In what way is he supposed to be dreadful?'

'Well, if he were personable and charming he wouldn't be handed round from college to college looking for somewhere to give him a fellowship,' said the Master.

'Oh, but William you know perfectly well the trouble isn't about Professor Maverack *personally*; it's just that people wonder about biography as the subject for a professorship . . .'

'Well, I'm just a humble astrophysicist,' said the Master, grinning wickedly. 'You can't expect me to understand what's wrong with biography as a subject. Naturally I assumed that the subject was impeccable, and that the trouble must be caused by the man . . .'

'Arguments *ad hominem* are famously dicey,' said Imogen. 'Surely that's true in astrophysics?'

'Oh, quite, my dear Imogen, quite. But in biography, whatever else could arguments be?'

'*Ad feminam*, perhaps?' she said.

'Oh, no!' he said. '*Homo, hominem* distinguished a man from beasts and angels. *Vir, virum* distinguished a man from a woman. But you see what I mean.'

'Don't admit a thing,' said Lady B. 'And William, dear, isn't it time to go in and face the subject?'

'Lord, so it is,' said the Master, swiftly finishing his sherry, and rising. He took his gown from the back of his chair, and struggled into it, arms waving like the wings of a raven, and then led the way through his private door into the Combination Room, where the company for dinner assembled.

Dr Maverack was a round-faced man in middle age, with receding red hair, and gold-framed spectacles. He had bushy eyebrows, and a darting glance from pale blue eyes. His evening shirt was rather elaborate, with starched ruffles, and he was wearing gold cuff-links in the form of tiny curled dragons with pinhead rubies for eyes. He was surrounded by St Agatha's dons when the Master's party entered; hanging back a little Imogen remained on the edge of the group, watching. Those lavish cuff-links caught her eye while she studied him. The Master hastened forward, extending a hand in greeting, and asking if everyone had been introduced.

'Ah, here is Lanyard now,' he said, as a late-comer arrived. 'Lanyard is our Director of Studies in English Literature, Dr Maverack . . .'

The gathered company exchanged small-talk.

'How are you finding Cambridge, Dr Maverack?' asked the Master.

'A little daunting, if the truth be told,' said Dr Maverack.

'You have come to us from . . . ?'

'San Diego. And before that, Williams.'

'Williams?' enquired Lanyard.

'Western Massachusetts,' said Maverack.

'Well, no doubt you would find our entrenched tradition-alism daunting . . .' said Lanyard.

'I like the traditions,' said Maverack. 'It's the traffic that terrifies me!'

Everyone laughed. 'The thing to do,' said the Dean, 'is to find a college conveniently in the centre of things, and preferably not on the Backs, unless one is able to love one's fellow men in very large numbers and assorted nationalities, and simply not own a car. Walk everywhere; it's much better for your health.'

'Excellent advice,' said Maverack. 'I hope to follow it. But of course, I am being selected rather than selecting when it comes to a college address.'

'I hope your welcome in the department has been friendly?' asked Plomer, St Agatha's second English fellow. Did Maverack know Plomer had been stubbornly opposed to a chair in Biography? Imogen wondered. If so he showed no sign of it.

'Friendly, but cautious,' he said, smiling.

'And you have some research students?' the Master asked. 'You have, so to speak, a clientèle for the subject?'

'Oh, yes,' said Maverack. 'Young brains take to it easily; it's the older minds who think that a footnote or two in the history of literature will cover the matter well enough.'

Just as the butler announced that dinner was served, Imogen noticed that there was a third woman in the room – an elegantly dressed middle-aged woman with smoothly upswept hair, standing quietly in a far corner, apparently engrossed in contemplation of the college's portrait of Christopher Wyndham. Imogen stepped over to her as the company massed at the doors, and began the informal procession to the table.

'Who was Christopher Wyndham?' the woman asked. 'Ought I to know? Well, I don't know anybody here, so perhaps it's not surprising . . .'

'I am Imogen Quy,' said Imogen. 'I am the college nurse.'

'Holly Portland,' said the other, holding out a hand.

'Are you someone's guest?' asked Imogen.

'Not exactly. I am working in Cambridge for a few weeks, and St Agatha's offered me dining rights. I thought I'd try it . . .'

'Come with me, and I'll show you how it works,' said

Imogen, leading Holly to the rear of the rapidly diminishing press of people at the Combination Room door. 'It isn't usually as crowded as this. Everyone has turned out to see if they want Dr Maverack as a fellow.'

Holly Portland smiled. 'Never mind Leo Maverack,' she said. 'I was at grad school with him. I can't take him entirely seriously; tell me about Christopher Wyndham.' She had a soft, but clearly sounding American accent.

'A college benefactor, contemporary with Isaac Newton,' said Imogen.

'An ultra conservative, I take it,' said Holly Portland, smiling again.

'Well, yes; but how do you know?' asked Imogen, leading the way onto the dais at the head of the hall. Two long trestles stood ready laid out with rows of silver candlesticks, shining flatware and crystal glasses. The floor of the hall was bright with warm lights at all the tables, and the undergraduates were already seated; above everyone's heads the magnificent beamed roof rose into shadows, darkening towards the ridge, far above the gilt-framed portraits, and the linenfold panelling.

Holly's eyes widened. As the diners filed in and stood behind the chairs at the tables she found herself opposite Imogen, with Lanyard beside her. 'Your Christopher Wyndham is shown with a Ptolemaic astrolabe,' she said. 'That makes him conservative at least; more likely very reactionary.'

The Dean read grace, and everyone sat down.

'Has it occurred to you that the man might have been painted with his astrolabe *before* the publication of Newton's *Principia*?' asked Lanyard.

'I think the portrait was painted in 1692, give or take a year,' said Holly firmly.

'We'll ask the experts,' said Lanyard, calling diagonally

across the table to Dr Bagadeuce. 'Meredith, when was our Wyndham portrait painted?'

'1691, I think,' Dr Bagadeuce replied. 'Miss Quy, have you met Li Tao?' He indicated a young man of oriental appearance, sitting opposite. 'Li Tao is joining us for a year, doing research into mathematics.'

'I hope you'll be very happy with us,' said Imogen. 'What is your research project?'

'Ah, the ABC conjecture,' Li Tao said.

'Is that important?' asked Imogen. She could think only of the ABC murders.

'Oh, yes,' said Li Tao, 'it is very strong. It implies Fermat's last theorem.'

'But what is that?' asked Holly.

'Ah, is great mystery,' said Li Tao. 'Fermat left note, saying he had found proof. Nobody knows what proof was.'

But now the soup was served, and as serious conversation began at the top of the table, a hush spread down towards where Imogen was sitting. People were listening in, as far as the medieval acoustics allowed them to, but the truth was that the length of the table kept conversations rather local; the Master's conversation was out of earshot.

'Can't hear what the fellow is saying,' muttered Lanyard, crossly. 'We'll have to buttonhole him over port, I think.'

'Tell me what you are working on in Cambridge,' said Imogen to Holly Portland.

'Eighteenth-century Indian calicos,' Holly said. 'There's your conversation stopper. You'd better tell me about being a college nurse.'

'Alas,' said Imogen, smiling, 'all the interesting bits are highly confidential. But why should your subject stop conversation? *I'm* interested. I wouldn't have thought there'd be many eighteenth-century calicos left.'

'No, there aren't. Sometimes the only knowledge we

have of a fabric is from a tiny scrap left in a seam. My work is in establishing criteria for dating fabric; even the smallest scraps might be useful.'

As the meal progressed from soup to fish to racks of lamb, to elaborate choux pastry birds filled with fruit and cream, Imogen kept Holly talking. They were soon talking about quilts. Evidence for dating fabrics often came from dated quilts; once known it would often help to date undated quilts. From 1700, when tariffs were imposed in England to help protect English silks, linen and wool from hugely popular Indian cottons, with their bright permanent colours, there were also descriptions – records of goods seized from smugglers by the excise men, for example. One could get some idea from such records of what designs and colours were popular. The exorbitantly expensive indigo dyes, for example, were often mentioned.

Imogen, of course, was more interested in contemporary quilts, although she knew what a long tradition they were in. Holly was less interested in fabrics, or in quilts in the twentieth century; dating them got much easier, with the manufacturers' catalogues, and fashion magazines, and so forth often allowing exact knowledge of a particular print. The whirlwind of changes in fashionable taste meant that modern fabrics were marketed for quite short times – perhaps only for a single season, and then went out of production.

'It might be many years, though,' said Imogen, thoughtfully, 'before something made into a shirt, say, and then worn, and then finally tossed into the scrap bag, was pulled out and made part of a quilt. Mightn't it be forty or fifty years?'

'Well, the date the fabric was first sold gives the earliest possible date for a quilt – or a shirt for that matter. The latest possible date would be harder; but it isn't very likely someone would make a quilt entirely out of very old shirts. You could usually get the earliest possible date from one fabric and the latest possible from another. Dyes fade, and fabric wears; an expert can date things pretty well.'

The absolute eldorado for Holly, Imogen gathered, was to find in an American quilt a fabric or design which undoubtedly came from England, so settling the controversy over whether the tradition crossed the Atlantic with early settlers, or developed independently in the New World. She wasn't very likely to succeed; the earliest known patchwork was in bed-hangings at Levens Hall in Cumberland, dating from 1708.

When the meal was over and a closing grace was said, the company left the great hall, and crossed the Fountain Court to the Combination Room, where dessert and port and coffee awaited them. In this less formal setting people moved around freely, changed places, joined or left conversations as they pleased.

Rather as Imogen had expected, when she and Holly entered the room the Master was leading Dr Maverack to a central chair at the great oval table, where everyone could see and hear him. The senior members were assiduously plying their guests with choices of port or claret, fruit or nuts, and offering histories of the silver laid out before them – that splendid candlestand, Dr Bagadeuce was saying, was the only piece of college silver to pre-date the Civil War. Cromwell's men had reoccupied the castle, which formed part of the college buildings, and comprehensively sacked it. They had found all the college treasure and stolen it, melting it down for army pay. The candlestick alone had escaped, hidden in a cartload of books that the Master and scholars had been permitted to take with them to Barnwell, where they sat out the Civil War. The candlestick was duly admired. It was a ring of dancing angels, a gothicised vision of a Renaissance three graces, with wings. The angels circled, each with one hand upraised holding a candle, and the other holding an undulant banner bearing the inscription '*Lumen ad revelationem gentium*'. All the courtesies accomplished, the business of the evening was launched by the Master. 'Are you engaged in writing a biography at present, Dr Maverack?'

'Not at present, no.'

'But you have someone in your sights, I presume? May we enquire whom?'

'At present, nobody. It is some little time since I wrote a biography. I have written only three altogether.'

'Let me see,' said Lanyard. 'A life of a Duke of Northumberland; a life of Carmichael, the Victorian landscape painter, and a life of Sir Humphrey Davy. Am I right?'

'You are perfectly right,' said Dr Maverack, 'but I imagine you have been reading *Who's Who* rather than the books in question.'

Lanyard smiled. 'A useful work,' he said.

'Oh, very. But you see, Lanyard, even a man as well read and distinguished as yourself is likely to read a biography only if for some reason he is very interested in the subject of it. One may labour for years to write a scholarly biography of some nineteenth-century figure, even a fairly important one, and win very few readers.'

'You surprise me, Dr Maverack,' said Lady B. 'Every time I go into Heffers, it seems to me, I find tables groaning under the weight of new biographies. Surely the publishers' catalogues are full of them?'

'Popular biography, like popular fiction, does do quite well,' Dr Maverack told her. 'One should not deplore it, I think. Fine scholarship is bound to be a minority taste.'

'Oh, I wasn't deploring it,' said Lady B., quietly.

'You do not seem hugely enthusiastic about biography, for a man who has just been appointed to the only chair in it,' remarked Mr Sykes, St Agatha's Senior History Don.

'Ah, well, I am a theoretician myself, rather than a practitioner,' said Dr Maverack.

'There is a *theory* of biography?' said Lanyard. 'I would have thought that of all subjects it would be the most circumstantial and particular. Of what possible use can a theory be?'

'Why, my dear fellow, one can't write a word without one!' said Dr Maverack, suddenly animated. 'How can one propound the meaning of a human life without a theory of what makes human life meaningful? Everything you decide to include, or to exclude, the very choice of whose life is worth attention implies a philosophy – indeed embodies a philosophy. One might indeed suggest – I think I would suggest – that the history of the theory of biography is the history of western moral philosophy. It is, I assure you, very much more interesting than any particular human life, even the greatest.'

He had certainly got the attention of everyone present now.

'Can you give us an example of the interaction of theory and biography?' asked the Master.

'Easily,' Dr Maverack replied. 'We might start at the beginning with Plutarch. He was interested only in world leaders – and what interested him about them was their style of leadership. His comparisons between great Greeks and great Romans was intended to provide a copybook of examples in how and how not to rule. It certainly didn't occur to him that the private lives of his subjects was of any interest except in so far as it might account for some public action. And one would imagine he would have dismissed as of no possible interest the life of anyone who held no public office of any kind.'

'You mean that he had a theory of human value which esteemed only powerful men?' asked Mr Sykes.

'Precisely. But when we move into the Dark Ages we get a completely different set of values. What is important in a deeply Christian society is redemption – an account of an inner life, full of conversion stories, full of bright lights on roads to Damascus. The biographies become plentiful, and many of them are of very humble folk. They are so strange to us we have coined a special name for them – hagiography. And the lives of the saints laid down such a powerful pattern that the few lives of laymen which survive – like Asser's Life of Alfred, or the Life of Charlemagne – make peculiar attempts to force the life stories of vigorous military kings into the saint's life shape. If we are to believe Asser, Alfred was a sickly and pious boy. But most likely this is because the only model for a meaningful life story which Asser had, was hagiography. Alfred was clearly as tough as old rope.'

'Well, bring us to a more modern stage,' said Lanyard. 'How does this story go on?'

'Boswell, obviously, is the first modern biographer,' said Dr Maverack. 'By his time the idea of character has emerged; the idea of human beings as specimens, individuals. An individual is valued for colour, eccentricity; the biographer works by valiant attempts at total inclusion. An inclusion, however, untroubled by the privacy of sexual life; presumably a man's sexuality was not seen as specially important – and therefore as not specially informative about him.'

'Until Freud puts sexuality in the centre of things?' said Max Allotson, the Fellow in Psychology.

'Exactly!' cried Dr Maverack joyfully. 'Of course not everybody in our times is a Freudian, and so you do get people calling biographers muck-rakers or worse when they go pounding after the sexual history of their subjects, and relatives, heirs and assigns get very upset, and literary executors turn themselves into angry censors; but what is going on is strictly theoretical; a theory of life which puts sexuality at the heart of human personality.'

'Freudian interpretation must by now be on the wane, surely?' asked Lanyard. 'What will take its place, do you think, Dr Maverack?'

'Deconstruction,' said Dr Maverack briskly. 'A theory that human life has no meaning at all.'

'Well, but in that case why would anyone write biography?' asked Lanyard.

'I suppose there is a historical value in the discovery and ordering of archives and materials,' said Sykes.

'One of our greatest biographers, Leon Edel,' said Dr Maverack, 'called that sort of thing the kitchen work of the task. According to him the true task is to discover the lies and delusions by which all men and women defend themselves against the indignities of life, and expose them. To deconstruct, if you like, the pitiful walls of the castle of self-respect people build for themselves. I agree with him.'

'You seem to be implying,' said the Dean, 'that there are no truths by which anyone could live; no simple people finding meaning in their lives but not deceiving themselves.'

'Yes,' said Dr Maverack, smiling. 'Byron said he thought that people lied to themselves more than to other people. He was right.'

'But do you mean that all systems of meaning that attribute value to human life are false?' A note of outrage had entered the Dean's voice.

'Well, there are so many they cannot all be true, and possibly none are,' said Dr Maverack. 'In any case, the fundamental point is simply that people lie to themselves, to keep the thought of chaos, or of their own futility, at bay. No doubt some lies are more profitable than others, some disguises less crippling than others.'

'But there is no such thing as human merit or real achievement, or solidly based self-respect?' asked the Master. He sounded more amused than outraged. Had Dr Maverack missed the fact that in advancing his theory to the assembled senior members of St Agatha's College, Cambridge, loaded with academic and political honours as they were, he was putting it to people who had a lot to lose if he was right? 'Not a very uplifting thought, if I may say so,' the Master added.

'But did you expect a Professor of Biography to cheer you up?' asked Dr Maverack. 'Or to bolster your self-esteem? Surely not.'

'I told you not to take any notice of Leo Maverack,' murmured Holly to Imogen. 'He's a leading exemplar of his own theory.'

But Imogen, who had for some reason been expecting to take against Dr Maverack, was rather impressed by him. She had noticed him several times during the evening glancing appreciatively at her. He had a pleasantly eager demeanour. And there was no denying he was a lively talker.

5

Zephyr, Imogen reflected the next morning, cannot be a common name. But she had been at school with a Pamela Zephyr, many years ago. She could clearly remember an anxious little girl with blue hair slides in black hair, who struggled to rise above her alphabetical order in the weekly achievement scores read out in assembly. Imogen hadn't thought of her or seen her for years; even the appearance of the surname on the Summerfield file hadn't immediately triggered memory. Idly, now, she looked her up in the phone book. And there, among the Zacs, and Zawadas and Zinofiefs was a Zephyr. In Waterbeach – not far at all. Imogen tried to think of some sort of pretext to break the ice. But when none occurred to her she boldly dialled the number anyway.

And it was unexpectedly easy. A woman's voice answered.

'Am I speaking to Pamela Zephyr?' Imogen asked.

'Yes. And I am not buying encyclopaedias or double glazing,' said the voice.

'This is Imogen Quy, Pamela.'

'Good gracious – I remember you – you did my maths for me at school.'

'Did I? I hope I got it right.'

'Better than I could, anyway. How are you these days? Where are you?'

'I'm flourishing in Cambridge. Pamela, is Mark Zephyr a relative of yours?'

There was a pause. Then an answer in an altered tone of voice. 'Yes. He's – he was – my brother.'

Imogen was startled. She had expected, she couldn't think quite why, a father or an uncle. 'Can I come and talk to you about him? Some time fairly soon?'

'You can come and talk about anything. Come now if you like. I'm very lonely.'

'I'm due in college in half an hour. If I drove out to you after work I'd arrive around three. How would that be?'

'Lovely. I'll expect you.'

Imogen had a quiet day in college. The high point was a swift exchange of views with Lady B. 'Was he so terrible, did you think?' Lady B. had asked, putting her head round Imogen's office door.

'That rather depends on the field of comparison,' said Imogen cautiously.

'Well – as dons go?'

'I'd say I'd known worse,' said Imogen.

'At St Agatha's?'

'I don't think he'd strike an all-time low here, do you?'

'Hmm. No, not really. But I don't think they're minded to have him, just the same.'

'Well, he does seem like a strong sort of flavour,' Imogen said.

'Did you notice that he didn't mention Summerfield, when they asked what he was working on?'

'Yes, I did. Odd that, when Summerfield was . . .'

'A St Agatha's man. Yes, that's what I thought. Perhaps because your student friend is doing all the work?'

'Well, but Maverack's name is to go on the book, as I understand.'

46

'Well then, perhaps,' said Lady B., 'it's natural embarrassment about that which stopped him mentioning it. Must fly. Come for a coffee tomorrow? Just before your office hours?'

'Tenish, then,' said Imogen. 'Love to.'

Driving out to Pamela Zephyr's house, with a bunch of chrysanths in the car, Imogen reflected. She had unconsciously been assuming that Mark Zephyr, if dead, had been elderly. Wrong, it seemed, unless Pamela's family had had remarkably spread out children, or Mark had been a step-brother. She resolved to be very tactful with Pamela.

At first, when Pamela opened the door of the house – a pleasant Victorian villa, set back from the road – Imogen thought she would not have recognised her. Her dark hair was greying at the temples, and drawn back into a bun. She still wore hair slides – an elegant pair of tortoiseshell ones, smoothing her hair above the ears. She was smiling. 'Come in, do come in,' she said. 'Oh it's such a treat to see you after all these years!'

She took Imogen's coat, and led her into a pretty, cluttered sitting-room, where afternoon tea was set out on a side-table – a lavish tea with Florentines, and cucumber sandwiches, and an elaborate cake.

'Oh, you shouldn't have taken so much trouble . . .' said Imogen.

'It isn't every day one rediscovers an old friend,' said Pamela, still smiling. 'Or, indeed, sees a friend at all,' she added sadly. Suddenly Imogen recognised her – saw the expression of anxiety that she remembered so well on the little girl's face settle down on the face of the grown woman. When Pamela said, 'You haven't changed much, Imogen,' she answered, 'Neither have you,' and they both laughed merrily.

'How did we lose touch?' asked Imogen, accepting sandwiches, and a cup of tea.

'When you went to America. You did give me an address, but I lost it when we moved house.'

'That must be it. I didn't stay in America long. My engagement came unstuck. I'm still in the house in Newnham.'

'Mark and I moved here soon after you left,' said Pamela. 'You wanted to ask about Mark, but you didn't say why.'

'Someone I'm very fond of has taken over the Summerfield biography,' said Imogen.

'Well, stop them if you can. It was a horrible job. It was practically the death of Mark.'

'It was the death of Mark?' asked Imogen. She couldn't help the appalled note in her voice.

'Oh, not literally of course. Just that it clouded his last days, and I do so bitterly resent that now. *Then* of course, we didn't know it was his last days.'

Imogen said, 'You mustn't let me upset you, Pamela. I'm sorry to come raising painful queries. But I would be very grateful if you would tell me about it all.'

'People don't understand, you know,' said Pamela, getting up and wandering off to stand gazing into her garden through the french windows. 'People are surprised one should be so devastated by the death of a brother. Once one is a grown-up. I rather wonder whether I really am a grown-up. But Mark always looked after me. In lots of ways. He paid the bills, and organised things, and arranged our holidays, and brought his friends over to meet me. He looked after me ever since school, when he used to fight the boys who teased me. That's why he moved in here with me when his wife left him. She kept the house, and the children. Mark moved in here. And we were very happy, Imogen, really we were, in spite of people telling us it wouldn't work. There must be a lot of crummy families around, I think, for people to be surprised when brother and sister get on.'

'I'm not surprised,' said Imogen. 'Just jealous. I'm an only child. And I'm afraid I don't remember Mark. Was he much older than you?'

'No; he was two years younger. That's why it was so plucky of him to fight for me; he had to take on boys much older than himself.'

'Did he win these fights?'

'Usually, yes. He was quite tiny, but he got so furiously angry! They called him little spitfire, and kept clear of him!' She was smiling again at the recollection.

'Pamela, what was so awful about the Summerfield job?'

'In a word, or two words rather, Janet Summerfield,' said Pamela.

'Summerfield's widow?'

'That vitriolic, vicious, unhinged harpy!' said Pamela. 'She's deranged. She didn't want a biography, she wanted a hagiography. And Mark wasn't her man; not for that kind of job. She would come storming out here shouting about writs and copyright, and trying to take back documents, and demanding the right to check every word he wrote . . . He actually ran away from her, Imogen, would you believe that? That a man could be driven into hiding from his own house? God, it was awful.'

'Why didn't he just chuck it in? If, in effect, she was making it impossible?'

'Little spitfire, remember? He hated defeat. And unfairness, and unreasonable conduct. And another thing, I'm afraid. He needed the money rather badly. He was paying alimony, and his eldest daughter was at a private school . . .'

'Don't apologise. Why shouldn't he do a job for money?' said Imogen. 'It's a clean, clear, honourable motive. There are a lot of messier reasons for writing a biography, I think.'

'It's good to talk to you,' said Pamela. 'You have a nice clear mind, without being a cold person. Do you know what that hell-cat did in the end? You can't imagine, Imogen! She sent a solicitor with a court order and two heavies round here *the day after Mark died* to recover the Summerfield papers. The very next day! I was terrified. And of course, I hadn't a clue which of Mark's papers were his, and which had anything to do with Summerfield. They were just clearing his desk – sweeping things into cardboard crates – it was terrible. Luckily my neighbour is a lawyer – a judge, as it happens, and I ran out of the back door and fetched him. By the time he came the cardboard crates were lined up in the hall ready to go off in their car, but Max stopped them, and made them put most of it back. They were way outside their rights.'

'I should think so!' said Imogen, appalled.

'They said they were going to sort out everything back at their office and return anything not to do with Summerfield later. But Max made them sort right there, so that they couldn't take anything not to do with Summerfield. There was a lot of argument. They had actually impounded Mark's cheque book. Max talked a lot, and when his son came to see what was taking so long, he sent him to fetch the cricket team, who were all in the pavilion, and they all came over and stood around, holding their bats. That speeded things up a bit. The hell-cat's lawyer said it was threatening behaviour, and Max said how did he think he would demonstrate in court that it was threatening behaviour for a village cricket team to hold bats just before a game, right beside a cricket field?' Pamela smiled ruefully.

'Do you have any idea what was worrying her about Mark's work?' asked Imogen.

'Not really. I don't think he had uncovered any scandals – he kept complaining how boring the man was. And he was a good way through the work, too. There were just one or two loose ends to tie up, he said, and then he could complete the thing in draft, and get on with polishing up a finished version.'

'And then . . . ? What happened?'

'He went to see her. He was hoping to calm her down, and get things sorted out. There was just one thing he needed to know from her, he said. He thought she must know it . . .'

'You don't know what that was?'

'Something to do with holidays. I didn't follow it all. And it must have worked – his charm offensive, I mean, because he came back very cheerful and happy, quite like his old self, and swept me off to dinner at a posh restaurant, and we had a lovely time. Then when we got back to the car he was suddenly feeling tired, so I drove us home, and he went straight to bed. Then he couldn't sleep. He was feverish and he woke me staggering around fetching himself water. I called the doctor out first thing in the morning, and he shot Mark into hospital. But he was unconscious before he got there, and he died some time in the afternoon. I try to tell myself that there's a lot to be said for a rapid death, but it was a terrible shock to me, as you can imagine.'

'What was it? Meningitis? Food poisoning?'

'I honestly don't know. They thought it was meningitis, but their scanner was busy, and he was dead before they could get him on to it. I thought only children died of meningitis, but I must be wrong.'

'There have been some minor epidemics recently, I think. Pamela, I'm so sorry. You really have had a bad time.'

'I'm getting over it. Slowly. One of the problems is having nobody to do things with. Mark liked walking, and we went somewhere every weekend; somehow there doesn't seem enough point on one's own.'

'Well, I like walking too,' said Imogen. 'Let's go into partnership over that. Do you know the circuit of Linton Hill and the Roman road?'

'Yes; but I haven't been there for some time.'

'What about next Saturday, then? And a pub lunch?'

'Oh, that would be a treat! Are you sure you have time?'

'I've only just rediscovered you,' said Imogen. 'We have a lot of time to make up.'

Later as Imogen was leaving, Pamela said, 'Watch out for that friend of yours, won't you?'

'Yes, I will. But you said Mark had nearly done it all. So Fran hasn't a huge task ahead?'

'A few loose ends. And dealing with an unhinged widow. I don't know; perhaps it was just Mark that got on her wick, and she will be all sweet reason with another person. Perhaps. Mark often wondered how his predecessor had got on with the dreadful Janet, but of course we couldn't ask her.'

Imogen was standing in the hall, putting on her coat when Pamela said this; she froze to the spot. 'His predecessor?' she asked.

'Oh, didn't you know? Mark wasn't the first person to work on the Summerfield book. A lot of the work was already done when he took it on.'

'Who was it, before Mark?'

'One May Swann.'

'And what . . . ?'

'She disappeared. I kept hoping she'd turn up again, and take the project back; we could have managed without the money *somehow*. But she didn't.'

'Pamela, people don't just disappear . . .'

'Well, I wouldn't have thought so either. But it seems they do. The police have great long lists. She just went out one morning, I understand, and didn't come back. Hasn't been heard of since. Odd, that.'

Or worse, thought Imogen, driving herself home, concentrating intently on the road. They can't do a breath test to discover that you were out of your mind with worry, or in shock when you were driving, but either can be as dangerous as drink. She did her level best to drive safely, and got hooted at for what seemed to the driver in the car behind her excessive caution at the A45 crossover. And all the while her mind was intoning to her, 'Odd, or worse.'

6

The problem was whether to say anything to Fran. And if so what, exactly. And what moment to choose. When Imogen got in from visiting Pamela, Fran could be heard all over the house, singing in the bath. What a horrible job it would be to persuade her that her wonderful job was booby-trapped! Imogen thought perhaps she would react strongly against advice – who could blame her? Would Imogen herself have taken cautious, middle-aged advice in such a situation? And what exactly needed saying to Fran? She already knew that an earlier worker had died in harness.

Imogen sat down after supper, and took her notebook from the bookcase. She drew a line under the previous entries, which were all about the death of an undergraduate last year. A sticky label on the front of the book said 'Patient Histories'. When troubled in her mind, or when something needed carefully thinking through, Imogen often retreated to the discipline she had learned as a student nurse. You wrote down everything the patient had told you, and everything you had observed, and tried to make sense of it. Now she headed a page 'The Life of Summerfield', and began to write, not, oddly, in her current, bold, rapid calligraphy with a thick-nibbed pen – the way she wrote letters to friends – but in the careful neat, rounded and legible hand she had used as a nurse. It was always important that the next nurse on duty could read your notes – fast, if necessary.

So what did it all amount to? Summerfield was a near nonentity, except for one splendid piece of work . . . his biographers were unlucky. Mark Z. had died suddenly; his predecessor had vanished. Coincidence? Perhaps. And perhaps it was also a coincidence that his current biographer (official) had farmed out the job, taken cover, so to speak, behind a student. Imogen laid down her pencil and gazed at the flickering pastiche coal fire that burned serenely and undemandingly in the grate. There was a feel of farrago about what she had written. A feel of an imagination run riot. Imogen accused herself sternly. Was she bored? Had she acquired a ghoulish lust for excitement, so that now she was deliberately fomenting fear and suspicion? After some hesitation she gave herself a clean bill of health – she could reasonably tell herself that she was perfectly contented with the even tenor of her days – but she had nevertheless made a decision. It was too early to tell Fran anything. She must check further first.

By and by Fran appeared, rosy from her warm bath, and wrapped in a fluffy dressing-gown, offering to make hot chocolate. Imogen accepted, and the two of them listened to some Mozart together, and exchanged college gossip before bed.

When her college hours were over the next day, Imogen phoned a friend, Mike Parsons, Detective Sergeant in the Cambridgeshire police. Mike had taken a St John's Ambulance Brigade first aid course with Imogen, who had felt at the time she needed a refresher course in dealing with accidents. He had confided in her – his relationship with his wife had been shaky at the time – and they had become good friends with a habit of leaning on each other's expertise.

'I need a little help, Mike. How about a pub supper some time?'

'Is it urgent, old friend? Only I'm off to Lanzarote for a well-deserved week tomorrow. Before the season of mists gets going. Can it wait?'

'Of course,' she said, trying to disguise dismay.

'I perceive that the true answer is not really,' he said. 'Look, I absolutely must stay here and pack; but why don't you skither round here right away? I'll put the kettle on, and if you happened to pass Sainsbury's on the way you could bring some sandwiches.'

'Lunch service on its way,' said Imogen, ringing off.

Mike lived in a flat in Chesterton, not too far for Imogen's ancient bike, even with its basket full of juice and sandwiches. He greeted her at the door with, 'Can you iron, by any chance?' He had scalded a large, iron-shaped burn on the front of a polyester shirt.

'Indeed I can,' said Imogen marching in. Almost every flat surface in the living-room had clothes draped on it. A suitcase was open on the table, with a mountain of clothes piled up in it, and a pair of shoes and a pair of pyjamas topping it off.

'Where's Barbara?' asked Imogen at once. Mike had had a little trouble with his wife during the years she had known him.

'It's nothing like that,' he said. 'She's there already with her mother and the children. I could only get one week off, so I'm joining them halfway through.'

'And Barbara usually packs for both of you, I see,' said Imogen, unpacking the sandwiches, and pouring juice. Mike picked up both halves of his sandwich at once and consumed it hungrily. Luckily Imogen had bought two packs for him. When she got to the iron she saw at once what was wrong. It had run out of water and was set at high heat for steam.

'Shall I show you how to use this, or shall I just do it for you?' she asked.

'Each to his own trade,' said Mike, grinning. 'You iron; I'll dispense this urgently needed advice. What have you done? Murdered a don? Your obvious defence is provocation.'

'No. Sorry. My hands are clean of scholarly blood. I am not provoked.'

'You must have the patience of a saint to be unprovoked by that lot!' he said, throwing a sweater into the case on top of the shoes. 'Seriously, nurse, what's up?'

'It's a missing person,' said Imogen. 'Nobody I know. But I would dearly like to know more about the circumstances in which they disappeared. And about what enquiries were made and such.'

'On our patch? A Cambridge person?'

'Don't know. Have no special reason to think so. All I know is her name. Is there a register?'

'Scotland Yard keep one. You're supposed to be able to match details of DBs with descriptions of missing persons. It doesn't by any means always work.'

'DBs?'

'Dead Bodies – when you've found one with absolutely nothing on them to identify them.'

'If someone just disappears from their house . . .'

'Well, it isn't necessarily a police matter. It's not against the law to do a bunk, if you don't leave unpaid debts or whatever. The Sally Army are quite good at tracing people. You could try them. But why are you interested? What's the handle?'

'It's what she was working on. She was called May Swann, and she was writing a biography of a fellow of the college. She just disappeared.'

'Boredom?'

'That might be nearer than you think!' said Imogen laughing. 'But the papers seem to have been retrieved from her abandoned dwelling, and passed to another bi-ographer. He died, rather suddenly.'

'What of? Any hint of foul play?'

'I don't *think* so. Seems to have been meningitis.'

'But my thriller-reading friend has spotted a coincidence. I see.'

'It is a coincidence.'

'Yes. Slightly. When did she vanish?'

'I don't know exactly. About eighteen months ago would be my guess. What sort of things could I find out from this Scotland Yard register?'

'Absolutely zilch. It's all regarded as confidential and you aren't next of kin, or even best pal. I'll have to do it for you.'

'When you get back then . . .'

'No time like the present. I'll phone them. You just keep ironing!'

He went through to the hallway, and closed the door behind him. Imogen ironed two more shirts, folded them neatly and then looked despairingly at the chaotic suitcase. Mike's voice could be heard faintly through the door. 'Yes, I'm holding . . .'

Imogen tipped the contents of the case out on to the sofa, and started again.

'This is what I've got,' said Mike reappearing. He had a notepad in his hand and was reading from it. '"Aged forty-one. Lived at 13, Beachcroft Road, Edmonton. Last seen 22nd March, 1992, by landlady. Reported missing by

nephew, David Swann, 15th April, 1992. No sightings. No unidentified DBs match description. Case remains on file."
Here. Have it for what it's worth.' Mike tore the sheet from the notepad and handed it to her. Then his eyes lit on the suitcase.

'Bloody hell, Imogen – how is Barbara to believe I packed that? She'll think I've had another woman here!'

'Well, you have, haven't you? Give her my good wishes, and have a lovely time,' said Imogen, putting on her coat, and folding the sheet of paper into her bag.

Directory enquiries found seven David Swanns. It's one of the benefits of the new customer aware system that they can look for a name nationwide if you haven't a clue about an address. They were all over the place, from Peebles to Finchley. Imogen tried the Peebles one first, bearing in mind the longish interval between the disappearance and the nephew reporting it. The most likely explanation was that he lived far off, and didn't visit often. The Peebles David Swann denied all knowledge of any May Swann. He was rather curt about it. So were the next four. But Imogen allowed for the fact that she was in fact being cheeky in telephoning out of the blue like that. It was called "cold calling" she remembered, when indulged in by double-glazing sales staff. And at least they had something to offer. It was theoretically possible that one wanted their dreadful windows. She must try to be civil next time they called her. She made herself a cup of coffee before trying the Finchley number. Suddenly her luck changed.

'Oh, yes!' the voice on the phone said. A woman's voice. 'That's David's aunt. You don't have news of her, do you?'

'I'm afraid not,' said Imogen. 'I work at St Agatha's College, Cambridge. Summerfield was a fellow here, and I am trying to sort out the progress of his biography. I wondered if anyone in May Swann's family could cast any light.' She had a slight pang of conscience at giving a misleading impression. But she hadn't actually told a lie – she did work at St Agatha's, and Summerfield had been a fellow there.

'You could come and talk to David,' said the voice. 'But I don't think he can help. He did everything possible at the time. It was perfectly horrid.'

'I'm sure it was,' said Imogen.' Would he mind talking to me?'

'I don't think so,' said the voice. 'He doesn't get in till eight most evenings, though, and then he needs his supper.'

'What about Saturday? Could I try Saturday?' Fran was away for the weekend, and Imogen had two blank days in her diary.

'Fine. Come in the afternoon – my mother takes the children out, and there might be a little peace and quiet.'

'Splendid. Next Saturday, around three?'

'Who shall I say it is?'

'Imogen Quy. Q-U-Y, rhymes with "why".'

'Like Quy near Cambridge,' the voice said. 'I'm Emily Swann. I'll tell David to expect you.'

The Swanns lived in a thirties semi, in a quiet street off North Finchley High Road. Emily Swann had made tea. There were toys scattered everywhere, and a battered appearance to the furniture, but the house was bright and cheerful. David Swann was a tall gangling man of rather harassed appearance. He led Imogen into the front room, where she spotted files on his desk, labelled 'Marshall and Swann, Accountants'. He asked her to sit down.

'Now, what is all this about?' he asked.

'We are trying to find out all we can about the progress

of the proposed biography of Gideon Summerfield. And we understand that your aunt was working on it at the time of her disappearance,' said Imogen. 'We wondered if there was any connection between her work and . . .'

'If there was, I wouldn't know about it,' said David Swann. 'She didn't confide in me.'

Imogen paused, waiting.

'I didn't get on with her at all,' he said. 'I paid duty calls from time to time, since I was her last living relative. But she didn't have a lot of time for accountants. She thought they were money-grubbers – prey to greed. I thought that was pretty silly, not to say offensive. But I once remarked that her devoted scholarship was remarkably badly paid, and she never forgave me.'

'So you didn't know she was working on Summerfield?'

'Well, as a matter of fact I did. She thought because I could do accounts, and he was a mathematician, I would understand his work, and could explain it to her. I said I would try – would have given us something to talk about when I went over to see her. But the stuff was geometry – absolutely bugger all to do with accounts, believe me. So I said sorry, no can do, and she offered to pay me for my efforts.'

'Having concluded that your inability to help her was occasioned by . . .'

'My general lack of interest in anything but money. Exactly. I was seriously annoyed – to put it mildly, and so I didn't get over there for a couple of months. When I did she had gone.'

'Taking the work she was doing?'

'Oh, no, taking not a thing, as far as I could see, and leaving two weeks' rent unpaid. Nearly all her clothes were there, and her cheque book, but she had drawn two hundred and fifty pounds the day before she left, and taken a weekend case. She told the landlady she would be gone for a few days, but she didn't say where she was going.'

'If this trip of hers was connected with the biography in any way, it might have been possible by looking at her files, to work out where she had gone . . .'

'I thought so too. But the publishers had taken the files before I got there. They said when she reappeared she could get in touch, but time pressure was so great that they reserved the right to get someone else to complete the book. That's what really convinced me to report it to the police, and start a search for her. She was a crazy old bat, if you'll forgive my language, Miss Quy, but she did care about her work.'

'Had she done other biographies?'

'Several. We've got copies somewhere. Haven't read them myself. They're all about such boring people. Now if she had done a golfer, or a jazz player . . . As you see, I can't help you.'

'You are helping. Do you know how far your aunt had got with the book?'

'She'd been working on it for months. I'm not sure exactly. She always did work for ages for very little pay. You couldn't calculate her hourly rate unless you could do small fractions. It was stupid. It was just so she could call herself a writer, or a biographer or something. She could type, and file things. She could have got a nice little office job, and been quite comfortable. But no, not her!'

'And you never saw any of her work on Summerfield?'

'Well, yes, I *saw* it – it was always lying round on every table and shelf in her flat, but I didn't read it – only the monograph by the man himself that she wanted me to expound to her.'

'Mr Swann, what do you think has become of your aunt?'

'I think she's come to harm, Miss Quy. I think she's stepped under a bus in Manchester, or been murdered by a pickpocket, or slipped into a river and drowned, or lost her memory and been confined to a hospital . . . It just isn't – wasn't – like her to leave unfinished work. And come to that it wasn't like her to leave her rent unsettled. She wouldn't have gone off and done that. Of course she might have known I would settle it for her . . . but it wasn't like her. You know, Miss Quy, when people are hard up they are sometimes very particular about money . . . she was like that. The police agreed with me, when they got the picture. They put out an alert, and a description. I think they're still trying to find her. But they haven't succeeded.'

7

Why would someone just walk out on a book in progress? Boredom? It would have to be very lethal boredom to make one abandon one's whole lifestyle, and simply flee. Imogen resolved to ask Fran just *how* boring Summerfield had been. But meanwhile she cooked up another ruse, carefully designing it as she drove home. It would have to wait till Monday, of course.

And when she got in the little light on her answerphone was blipping furiously, and she found something else to worry her. The Master's secretary had been phoning at half-hour intervals all afternoon. The last message on the tape was from Lady B. It said simply, 'Please get in touch as soon as you return. Don't wait till Monday.' Imogen, out of an instinct for self-preservation, put on the kettle, and put her slice of quiche in the oven to warm before phoning the Master's Lodge.

'Trouble, I'm afraid,' said Lady B. 'One of our young men has been accused of cheating in the Tripos exam. Very mediocre student; very brilliant essay.'

'Who is it?' asked Imogen.

'Bob Framingham. Philosophy.'

'Oh, yes. I think I do know him . . .'

'He has an excuse – or an explanation, rather, Imogen. He says you gave him medication which made him exceptionally lucid and fluent.'

'I did?' Imogen was momentarily stunned.

'That's what he says. He says it accounts for his unusually good performance.'

'Well, I can't have given him anything much at all, if he came to me just before an exam. I might dole out two paracetamol to help someone calm down and sleep well the night before; otherwise I send them to the doctor.'

'Always?'

'Always.'

'I think he's going to be very obstinate and difficult, Imogen. He's getting a lawyer.'

'If I gave him even paracetamol it will be in the book.'

'Of course – you keep a book . . .'

'With everything in it. Dose, time of day, reason for giving it . . . We have to be preternaturally careful . . .'

'We?'

'College nurses. If we make mistakes our colleges are liable. As a matter of fact, someone who needs paracetamol is more likely to ask a friend for some, or skid over to Boots; it's less trouble.'

'Does paracetamol put a sudden intellectual shine on people?'

'Not that I ever heard. In fact a major reason for being so careful, and sending them off to the doctor at exam times is the very opposite – the risk of being blamed for a poor performance. I would have done better, but nurse doped me – that sort of thing.'

'The Senior Tutor is dealing with it. Could you let him have a copy of the entry in your book as soon as possible? And, Imogen – I'm sorry about this.'

'Not your fault, is it?' said Imogen reasonably. 'I'll zip over to college tomorrow and copy the relevant page of the book.'

'When you do, pop in and have a word with John

Spandrel, will you?' said Lady B. 'As Senior Tutor he's in charge of this can of worms.'

'I thought you'd better know what's going on, Imogen,' said John Spandrel. 'Have a sherry?' He waved her towards an armchair at his fireside. His room was dark and ancient, and furnished with heavy large couch and chairs. The walls were covered with prints of the college at various times of its life, and prints of Roman piazzas, and wild Tuscan landscapes. It was loud with the ticking of an immense grandfather clock, decorated by angels and signs of the zodiac, that stood under a massive ceiling beam in the darkest corner. He proffered sherry in a delicately engraved glass with a spiral stem that looked rather too good to use.

'Thank you, John,' said Imogen. 'Now what has this villain been up to?'

'It looks like a very clear case of cheating,' John Spandrel said. 'Framingham has very modest abilities, in the normal course of events. He has produced a philosophy essay in the Tripos which though not word for word throughout is remarkably like the essay of another examinee. To cap it all, both essays are remarkably like an essay submitted for the Random Memorial Prize by a third undergraduate. The other two aren't ours – one's at Pembroke, and the other at Girton.'

'Fill me in, John, – I don't know what the Random Prize is.'

'For an essay on a topic in philosophy. It's conducted rather like an exam – aspirants have to present themselves on the appointed morning, and write it on the spot. It's got considerable cachet, and it carries a bursary of seven hundred pounds. Well worth winning, in fact.'

'Is it set before the date of the Tripos exam?'

'A full month before. This year's winner was a chap called Melvin Luffincott. It's his essay that has cropped up in these other papers. It's a sheer fluke that the full extent of the wickedness was noticed; but it just happens that the assessors for the Random Prize included one of the Tripos examiners. Usually the same people don't mark both, to spread the workload round the faculty; this year someone fell ill suddenly, and Peter Prestwick did both jobs. Of course he spotted at once that there was something fishy, and raised a hue and cry. Then one of the other examiners realised one of his papers was very like . . . To cap it all, our young dolt, who says that your pills made him unduly brilliant, had folded his paper in four. He says he finished early, and just folded the paper up in boredom . . . then he flattened it out and handed it in. I ask you!'

'I don't quite follow this . . .' said Imogen.

'Well, you'd be surprised how often fishy papers turn out to have been folded or crumpled. It's nearly impossible to smuggle ready-written stuff into the exam room still pristine and flat.'

'I see. And what do the other two people involved say?'

'The Girton chap says he has no explanation; no idea how it happened. His paper was flat – and he wasn't sitting directly beside Framingham. But he does know him well. He says they belong to a discussion group which Luffincott also belongs to. And Luffincott professes himself outraged, and hotly denies having given any help, or any copy of his essay to either of them.'

'Would this Luffincott have a copy? If he had written the essay under supervision, and handed it in?'

'Well, a prize competition isn't exactly like an examination, Imogen, and a significant difference is that when the judging is over, the candidates are given their entries back.'

'And they were given them back . . .'

'Three days before the Tripos.'

'I don't envy you having to sort it all out, John.'

'I don't have to, thank God. It's a university matter, not a college one. There'll be a Court of Discipline.'

'What's that?'

'It consists of a group of lawyers, and lay senior members. They will hear the case. Framingham has the right to be represented. His tutor offers to act on his behalf, and represent him; but Framingham has declined the offer, and will have a lawyer of his own choosing. That lets Emlyn Bent off the hook, anyway. It takes a lawyer's training to be energetic in the defence of someone one thinks guilty as charged. However, the college isn't out of the woods entirely – the Court of Discipline is bound to want to take evidence from you, in view of this farrago about pills.'

'I see.'

'Imogen, we – the College Council I mean – are somewhat alarmed. We don't seem to know whether you can be compelled to attend such a hearing. It being nothing to do with the law of the land, and the days of the Star Chamber being long past.'

'That doesn't arise. I shan't refuse to attend. I would look on it as an extension of the job for which the college pays me.'

'It isn't likely to be much fun. There will be a skilled and forceful attempt to suggest that you gave inappropriate medication. We think the college should pay for you to have legal advice of your own.'

'Forgive me, John, but I don't agree. It is a very simple matter in so far as it concerns me. I kept a record in my book. I am sure I didn't give any drug capable of having the effect suggested, and I can say so if asked. Having a lawyer of my own looks over-defensive to me; as if I thought I had done something that put me in need of defending.'

'Hmm. Do think it over, Imogen. What would you say, for example, if someone suggested you might have given out something which is not in the book, and simply forgotten? The college will employ a lawyer for you. You have only to ask.'

'I really wouldn't have done that,' said Imogen. 'That would be a major dereliction of duty, which I could not possibly have perpetrated. But all right, I'll think it over and let you know.'

All that was a fairly powerful distraction from thoughts of May Swann. And Fran did not appear on Sunday evening, so that Imogen still had not spoken to her on Monday morning, when she telephoned Recktype and Diss, with a disingenuous query. She asked for an editor in charge of biography, and was put through to one Angela Kingsweir.

'I wonder if you can help me?' she asked. 'I am trying to make contact with an old friend, and I believe she was working on a biography of Gideon Summerfield . . .'

'May Swann?' said the voice.

'Yes!' said Imogen brightly. 'Do you have her address?'

'No, we don't,' said Ms Kingsweir. 'I'm afraid we can't help you.'

'But the biography . . .'

'Miss Swann abandoned it. She did not see fit to tell us, let alone to tell us why, or to give us a forwarding address. We have been put to considerable trouble and expense, and the first half of the advance is still outstanding. We would dearly like to communicate with the lady ourselves.'

'Oh,' said Imogen. 'How distressing; and how odd. Really it isn't at all like her . . . Do you think she's all right?'

'I honestly wouldn't know,' said the voice. 'But I know this project is jinxed. And she wouldn't be the first author to scarper with an advance, I can tell you.'

'What did you mean about the project being jinxed?' asked Imogen.

'It's been endless trouble. For one thing, you can't imagine how difficult it was to recover the papers from May Swann's lodgings. We had to brief a lawyer . . . The literary executor was going bananas about it.'

'Papers?' said Imogen, acting dumb.

'Relating to the life of Summerfield. They are the property of his executors. Miss Swann was lent them in good faith on the assumption that she would make legitimate use of them and return them.'

'Executors?' said Imogen.

'Of Summerfield's literary estate. Without which, of course, no other biographer can proceed. Your old friend simply left them behind her when she bunked off with the money.'

'Oh, but I'm sure she wouldn't have . . .'

'Authors,' said the voice, 'are so unreliable.'

Imogen next saw Fran on Monday evening. Fran came bouncing in, announced that she was jolly hungry, and had forgotten to shop, and could she do anything to help with supper . . . Imogen invited her, laughing, and got her to set the table while she concocted a curry.

Once they were sitting comfortably at the table in the little breakfast room, Imogen asked her how the great work was going.

'Well, I haven't started to write it yet. So in one way I don't know. I just might find myself incapable of getting words on paper, like my friend Mitchell.'

'Whyever would you find yourself incapable of getting

words on paper? Haven't you been writing essays these many years? And who's Mitchell?'

'He's a friend. Or rather, a friend of Josh's. His father is fairly filthy rich, and Mitch wants to be a novelist, so father is paying for him to stay on in Cambridge and work on a book. Mitch is very bright, and he's got lots of ideas. But somehow he can't get started. He's always doing research, or making notes. I might be like him.'

'You might not be. I would blame his father. If the fellow had to get a job it would concentrate his mind.'

'It isn't like you to be unkind, Imogen,' said Fran.

'Is "unkind" current jargon for "spot on"?' said Imogen, crisply. 'So: you haven't started to write yet . . .'

'But I've got a fairly good grip on all this paperwork now. There's just one gap – I need to find out where he spent the summer of '78. Then the tally of his days is complete, and I can get writing.'

'And Mark Zephyr's notes don't cast any light?'

'Nope. Nobody seems to have got that bit.'

'Neither Zephyr nor Swann?'

Fran looked at Imogen strangely. Then she started to say something, and stopped. Instead she said, 'Pass the mango chutney, would you?'

'It turns out that Mark Zephyr was the brother of a friend of mine,' said Imogen, passing the chutney jar. 'He died suddenly of meningitis, poor fellow. But while he was going strong he had a little difficulty with Janet Summerfield. And he wasn't the first on the job. May Swann was working on it before him, as we thought. Remember, you asked me where she was now?'

'It's a good question. I don't suppose we shall ever know.'

'You could be right. I've been ferreting around. She disappeared. Taking an advance from Recktype and Diss, and leaving all the documents from the Summerfield estate in her lodging. Everyone says it wasn't at all like her, except her publishers who reckon that authors are capable of anything.'

'Exactly why have you been ferreting, Imogen?' said Fran.

'Friendly interest.'

'In me?'

'Well, not in Summerfield, anyway. Do you mind?'

'I'm not sure. You'd better tell me about it.'

Imogen recounted the gist of her conversation with Pamela Zephyr, and with David Swann. They had finished eating, and were clearing dishes when she got to the end of the story.

'Great!' said Fran drily. 'Just great. And what happened to Ian Goliard?'

'Who?'

'The fellow who was working on this book before May Swann.'

'God, Fran – was there?'

'There certainly was. Unmistakable traces. Once one gets everything sorted there it is. Three previous folk. All stopped in midstream.'

'That's a hefty, nasty coincidence . . . It must be coincidence. Or, at least Mark Zephyr must be. You couldn't catch meningitis from a stack of papers. I am very sure of that.'

'It's a bigger coincidence than it looks, actually,' said Fran. 'All three of these projects were interrupted at the same point. Or on the same point of enquiry, rather.'

'I don't understand you . . .'

'When, for one reason or another, each of these three stopped work, they were at the point of wondering where the great Summerfield was during the summer of 1978.

73

Ian Goliard hadn't got very far. He had made a sort of calendar, tracing Summerfield's movements from birth, through school and college, and addresses and holidays. It's quite a neat idea, really. I suppose he intended to go on to attach information and documents to each place in turn. Anyway his calendar is quite full and detailed as far as spring '78, and then stops with "August – away??" '

'Fran, how do you know this was someone called Goliard and not May Swann or Mark Zephyr?'

'Different paper; different method of work; different handwriting . . .'

'Yes, I see.'

'And in any case he put his name in tiny letters on the bottom left-hand corner of each sheet of paper in his files. There might have been more, of course, not kept by his successors. But the calendar is there, has his name on it, and is very full and complete as far as it goes.'

'And it goes until . . .'

'August '78. Summerfield went on holiday. He and his wife rented a cottage in the Malverns. Or so the calendar says. They took the cottage for a month, and various of their friends came and went, joining them for days at a time. At some stage there was a quarrel and Summerfield went off for a few days – somewhere, we wot not where.'

'Alone?'

'Perhaps not; but I don't know who with. The rest is silence. From Goliard, anyway.'

'So he gave up on the project, and it was handed to May Swann?'

'That's what it looks like. She was very systematic. As you know, she assigned numbers to all the original papers she had been given. She copied Goliard's calendar headings into a notebook, putting the dates and places as headings, and listing all the material on that place and time that she had been able to find. She went past summer '78; she took the method right through to Summerfield's death. There is something on nearly every page – even if it's only business letters, or an announcement of a lecture series he was giving in a certain term. In a separate notebook she began drafting the actual text of the book.'

'But she had got well past August '78?'

'Only in a way. August '78 headed a blank page. She had *something*, however slight, on every other page from birth to death.'

'But you don't know if she was trying to fill in that particular blank when she disappeared?' Imogen was clutching at straws.

'Oh yes, I do.' Fran was almost gleeful. 'She was under time pressure. She kept a work diary. She roughed out the week's work for herself every Monday, estimating the time that the next chunks of work would take. Her last work diary entry says "Find out about August '78." It's heavily underlined. And dated 20th March, two days before she vanished.'

'Fran . . .'

'You're going to ask about Zephyr. Well, I'm only guessing. He took over May Swann's research work, and just set about checking and ordering it. I imagine he found she was reliable, and decided to accept her version of events, and simply write it up.'

'But he couldn't accept her version of this holiday in '78 . . .'

'Because there wasn't one. Exactly. And didn't you tell me that his sister said he had just one little matter to find out about and then it would be ready to write? Something like that?'

'Yes,' said Imogen. 'She did say something like that.'

'Well, what's the betting that one little thing will turn out to be August '78?'

'We can ask Pamela that,' said Imogen.

But Pamela, consulted on the phone while Fran cleared the table, could not remember.

8

'You wouldn't feel like lending me the car?' Fran asked the next morning. 'I'll need it all day.'

'Today? That's all right. I need it myself tomorrow,' said Imogen, abstractedly. She was eating toast and reading the *Independent*.

'Thanks,' said Fran. 'It's a pig of a journey otherwise.'

'Where's that?' asked Imogen. She was somewhat sleepy, the conversation about coincidence the night before having turned philosophical, and gone on rather late.

'Castle Acre. I might not be back by supper time. I'll buy the car some petrol.'

'You're welcome. Have you decided what to do about the missing summer of Summerfield?'

'Yes. Ask. What else could I do?'

'Forget it. Fudge. Simply leave it out . . .'

'You know me better than that.'

'Who could you ask?'

'Janet Summerfield. That's what I want the car for. She lives at Castle Acre, and she's not in the phone book. I'll have to go on spec.'

'From all accounts, you'll get your head bitten off,' said Imogen. 'Are you sure you've got to accost her?'

'Quite sure. Even if she didn't herself go on this blasted escape trip, she presumably knows where *he* went.'

'Fran, you must have realised that you yourself are now precisely at the point . . .'

'Which defeated all the others? Quite a challenge, isn't it?'

'Well . . .' Imogen bit back the over-anxious and certainly counter-productive 'Take care . . .' and replaced it with 'Drive carefully'. Since it was her car, she was entitled to say that.

On her way into college, later in the morning, Imogen saw that the Clare College Fellows' garden was open, and she turned into it to take a look at the autumn colours – trees on the river bank, the autumn crocus palely loitering in the grass, and the Michaelmas daisies in the borders. One of the benefits of Imogen's life-style was leisure. She worked part-time for St Agatha's College. Once she had had a portfolio of jobs, adding up to more than full-time, and had had no time to enjoy the money she earned. Then she realised that leisure was the most luxurious thing money could buy. She resigned from every college but her favourite one. Now, like most part-time workers, she put in many more hours than she was paid for, but even so she had privileges to offset against the need for thrift. She could set her own working hours, and take time for shopping, wandering and thinking.

This fine crisp autumn day, for example, she had allowed time for some filing and tidying in her office before her official surgery hour, and could on impulse decide to spend the time instead staring at the butter-yellow leaves of the sunlit flowering cherry trees, some hanging on to their branches, and others lying in a golden disc beneath them on the grass. She tried to imagine what fabrics might achieve that bright cool contrast in a quilt. It was just warm enough in the sun to sit for a few moments on a damp bench, and relish the day. The garden competed with her background anxiety about Fran. Of course it was possible that something about Mark Zephyr had irritated Janet Summerfield, and would explain, if one had known him, why she had harassed him. Not that she had harassed him to the end – hadn't Pamela said that he had come back pleased from his encounter with her the day he fell ill? And Imogen found it hard to imagine a person in their right mind not taking to Fran. You can give reasons why some people are immediately likeable – you can use words like candour, cheerfulness, warm-heartedness . . . but in the end it's a mystery. Nor, thought Imogen, do we have any way of acknowledging these forms of liking, these gentler kinds of love. 'Friendship' is supposed to cover all.

And what a narrow stereotype of friendship people have! The word wouldn't suggest an anxious landlady – and someone considerably older. Fear for Fran, sharp concern for her safety and prosperity was *ultra vires* from Imogen. She sighed. A shadow fell across her, and she looked up to see Lady Buckmote looking down at her.

'You look thoughtful, Imogen,' said Lady B. 'I hope this cheating uproar isn't worrying you.'

'No, no,' said Imogen getting up. 'Something quite other. I'm sorry; it seems a sin to gloom at these lovely trees.'

'It does rather. Are you on your way in to college? Shall we walk together?'

'Let's.'

'I've got some news,' said Lady B., as they crossed the Clare College bridge, with its prettily sagging parapet, and marble balls poised atop it. 'The college powers have offered a fellowship to Dr Maverack.'

'Really?' Imogen sounded as she felt, surprised. 'I thought the feeling was flowing rather against.'

'Well, nobody was very keen. But a worse prospect was looming. You know that colleges are supposed to take in these wandering scholars roughly fairly – shared

79

out so to speak. The fair shares system only arises when someone isn't welcome – often there's hot competition to get someone.'

'But not for Maverack?'

'Indeed not. Only news came on the grape vine that the *next* homeless eminence would be Hugo Obverse – and the thought of *him* is so horrible that the college snapped up Maverack at once. We couldn't be expected to take two googlies in a row, you see.'

'So taking Maverack is a sort of protection racket?' said Imogen, laughing. 'How does everyone know that Obverse would be even worse?'

'No contest,' said Lady B. 'Obverse is notorious throughout the English speaking world.'

'What for?' asked Imogen. So Lady B. regaled her with stories of the horrible Hugo all the way to the college gates. What hadn't this monster of academe perpetrated? Seducing his students – of both sexes – quarrelling with colleagues, getting drunk at high tables, delivering lectures in alcoholic stupors, losing examination scripts, hacking into colleagues' computers and leaving obscene jokes on the screens, getting his air fares to the States paid four times over by four different Mid Western universities, and then not turning up to give the promised lectures at any of them . . .

'But why isn't he cast out into exterior darkness?' asked Imogen. 'Why does anyone want him in Cambridge? How does he get away with it?'

'He's brilliant. A world-class intellect. And Cambridge is about intellect, not niceness. However, fear not. We will put up with Maverack, and someone else will have to suffer Obverse.'

'But Maverack is long-winded,' said Imogen, 'and Obverse . . .'

'At least sounds interesting? I fear it would pall quickly in the event.'

Hugo Obverse however, thought Imogen, as she walked across the court to her office, having taken her leave of Lady B., sounded like a whole lot more fun for a biographer than Gideon Summerfield, whose wild oats had left no traces, and been confined to a single summer well into his middle age.

Naturally Imogen was on tenterhooks for Fran's return. Anxiety was making her slightly trembly. The moment she heard the front door she trotted into the hall, where Fran was hanging her jacket on the hall stand, and said, 'How did it go?'

'Very mixed,' said Fran. 'Have you got any tonic, Imogen? I've got a smidgen of gin left, and I need a drink!'

'Tonic no. Bitter lemon, yes. Or you could have some whisky.'

'I'll go and get my gin, thanks. Tell you all about it in a mo.'

Imogen emphatically didn't feel like cooking supper. She laid out salad, and bread and cheese, and sliced ham from the deli on the corner, and a jar of home-made pickle.

'Very basic supper,' she said, when Fran reappeared, 'but you'll eat with me, will you?' She didn't herself feel very hungry.

'Swap,' said Fran. 'A tot of my gin for you, and a supper from your supplies for me.'

'Done,' said Imogen. 'Now tell me.'

'I spent the morning hanging about. She wasn't in, and her neighbours said she usually went shopping in King's Lynn on a Tuesday morning. I looked round the village – it's very pretty. Big church one end, Norman castle the other. There's a good pub. I had a coffee, and lurked around. She's got a small, very bijou Georgian cottage on the green. By and by she came home.'

'What's she like?'

'Sort of – ample. Blue rinsed. Wearing velvet and Morrissy prints. Like a ship in full sail.'

Imogen smiled. 'And were you welcome?'

'At first, yes. I helped carry the shopping bags in from the car – she has asthma, and she was a bit breathless. Then she got uptight when she realised what I was after.'

'Didn't you tell her right away? What did you say?'

'At first I just said I was at Cambridge and interested in her husband's work,' said Fran. 'So she thought I was a mathematician. Then when we'd got the shopping all stowed she made a cup of tea, and sat me in the living-room, and I explained a bit more, and she was very disconabulated.'

'Discombobulated, you mean, dear child.'

'Whatever. She obviously didn't know that Professor Maverack had farmed out the work on the biography, and I had to cover my tracks, or his tracks, rather, quickly, and say that I was his student doing a bit of preparatory work for him, and try to unmention that I was doing it all.'

'Hmm. Awkward . . .'

'Very. But then she got very friendly and helpful, and fetched out an album of family photos to show me. She said she had lent a lot of family papers, she understood they were with Professor Maverack at the moment, and they included all the loose photographs, but she had held on to the albums, as she hadn't wanted to unstick the mounted photographs. So we spent a little while looking at all these pics together. We might have been old pals. Of course I kept hoping one of the little captions would say "Summer '78". No such luck. And I kept putting my foot in it by failing to recognise her in the snaps.'

'Little blurry black and white things, about the size of a postage stamp?' said Imogen, taking her empty glass through to the kitchen, and returning to invite Fran to sit opposite her at the table.

'Partly that. And partly she kept changing. I mean, the woman sitting on more than half the sofa with me just didn't look like the slender one in a swimsuit standing on a beach in Brittany in 1955.'

'*Eheu, fugaces!*' said Imogen learnedly. 'Few of us do look like ourselves as time goes by.'

'Yes, but . . .'

'But what?' asked Imogen.

'She had done it more than once. She had kept doing it.'

'Doing what?'

'Changing. Putting on weight and losing it again. I mean, only the very young ones showed her looking slender. After that she varied between being on the plump side of normal, and being absolutely massive – like a Michelin woman. She was telling me who the people in the snapshots were, and I asked, "And who's that?" and she got a bit shirty. She said, "That's me," as though I were a half wit, but honestly she wasn't recognisable from one to another. The state she is in now is a kind of compromise between extremes.'

'And was there a photo of summer '78?'

'No. So eventually I asked her about it. And she went berserk.'

'What do you mean? Tell me more.'

'She started yelling. She said . . . Well, to tell the truth I was so startled that I'm not sure I can remember her very words, but the gist of it was that she had told people over and over again that it didn't matter, to leave it out, to just get on with the job and forget about it and it had no significance, and nobody would take any notice of her as though she had no rights, and her opinion didn't matter a damn when actually she obviously knew everything there was to know about poor Gideon, having spent every waking minute of her life completely dedicated to him, and if she said it didn't matter where he went one summer, what insolent overmighty person could dare to say it did . . . on and on. I jumped up off the sofa and backed away from her.'

'Not surprising. Golly, Fran.'

'Then she really got warmed up. About how the papers were hers, and the biography couldn't be written without her consent, and she would jolly well see to it that the matter was omitted, or the book would get vetoed, she'd get an injunction. She was bitterly disappointed in Dr Maverack, she had been promised he was a man of discretion, and she thought he had understood the biography was to chart the career of a great modern thinker, and not to go muck-raking around among the trivia of his private life . . . just on and on. Then she threw me out.'

'Not laying hands on you?'

'Oh, no. I didn't wait to see if she would. I just grabbed my jacket and notebook and ran. She followed me down the garden path, fist clenched and shouting the same things over and over.'

'She sounds completely potty. Pamela said she was deranged.'

'Well, maybe . . .' Fran sounded doubtful. 'You know, Imogen, I'm not sure. It sounds potty when I tell you about it, but at the time . . .'

'You can't have felt she was entirely normal, surely?'

'Of course not. And yet this uproar didn't feel exactly *mad*, all the same. She seemed more malevolent than out of control. I can't explain it properly. It didn't feel so much like being the butt of a crazy outburst, just random, like a gust of wind in someone's mind; it felt more deliberate.

She meant to cow me. She turned it on like a kitchen tap, somehow.'

'So what do you conclude?'

'Well, I shall have to tell Professor Maverack about it first thing tomorrow. And hope to get to him with my version before she gets there with hers. And also, it is of the first importance to discover what it is about that holiday . . . Nothing on earth will prevent me trying to crack it.'

'Fran, we might be melodramatising coincidence. But you have realised that it seems unlucky – perhaps even dangerous, to pursue that?'

'Imogen, *what is this*?' cried Fran. 'What *could* the old bore have done on holiday? And all that time ago?'

'Robbed a bank?' offered Imogen. 'Fathered a child?'

'You haven't eaten anything, hardly,' said Fran suddenly. 'Are you all right?'

'I feel a bit wobbly, to tell the truth,' said Imogen. 'I might go straight to bed.'

'Haha,' said Fran. '*I* get to look after *you*, at last. The tenant's revenge. Off you go then, and I'll bring you a hot-water bottle.'

9

Flu is horrible. Luckily one forgets from one attack to another how nasty it is, or anyone like Imogen who mixes with a lot of people and is exposed to germs would be in perpetual dread of catching it. Next morning, feeling spectacularly feverish and aching from top to toe, Imogen kept to her bed. Fran seemed more pleased at her opportunity to reciprocate kindness than sorry for Imogen's misery, but she brought breakfast in bed for the sufferer – toast and Marmite and French-style milky white coffee – and then removed the tray and produced a damp towel made piping hot in the microwave, so that Imogen could freshen up without getting up. Then, sitting in the little bright blue basket-weave armchair that occupied the corner of Imogen's bedroom, she asked, 'Will you be all right if I leave you for a bit?'

'Fine. I'll just sleep it off.'

'Only I really need to catch Dr Maverack – Professor Maverack, I mean, this morning and have a few things out with him.'

'I'll be fine. Good luck bearding the lion in his den . . .' Imogen was half asleep before the sentence was finished.

She was woken by an aggressive hammering on her front door. Someone was not only bashing the Victorian iron knocker, but whacking the door with the flat of the hand. Not a chance that anyone knocking like that would give up and go away easily. Whatever was going on? Was her chimney on fire? Of course not – Imogen got herself sitting up, and put her feet into her slippers. She got herself unsteadily across the room, took her dressing-gown off the hook, and put it on. The beating on the door continued. Moving slowly, feeling light-headed, and with her knees aching, Imogen got herself downstairs. Somehow the racket at the door felt daunting in her fragile state, and she went instead to the living-room, where the bay window let her see through the swathes of net curtain that conferred privacy to the room, who was standing on her little front garden path.

A man was knocking. A woman in a dark coat was standing behind him. Both were strangers. Imogen proceeded slowly and reluctantly to her door.

'Who is it?' she called.

'Open up, please,' said the voice, peremptorily.

Imogen put the door on the chain, and opened it a crack. The moment she did so the person outside tried to thrust it open, and step in. The chain was taut.

'Who are you and what do you want?' asked Imogen. The flu gave her voice a quavering tone, and sapped her authority.

'Is this the residence of one Frances Bullion?' enquired the woman.

'Yes. She is not at home.'

'We do not require to see her. She has in her possession certain documents which are my property,' said the woman. 'We have come to retrieve them. Please let us in and show us which parts of the premises are occupied by Miss Bullion, so that we can find what we have come for as quickly as possible.'

'Let you search Miss Bullion's flat in her absence and take things away?' said Imogen. 'Certainly not. Please go away.'

'I am entitled to recover my property,' said the woman. This must, of course, Imogen realised, be Janet Summerfield.

'This house is *my* property,' she retorted. 'And you are not entitled to enter it without my consent.'

'It's a cheap and lightweight chain,' said the man. 'I can break it easily.'

'Forcible entry is a criminal offence,' said Imogen. 'As also is the assault you would need to commit to get past me in this narrow hallway if I stood my ground. And I will stand my ground. If you have lawful business with Miss Bullion you must pursue it in lawful ways.'

Janet Summerfield suddenly offered a grimace, which might have been a placatory smile. 'Look, there's no need for this,' she said. 'It's all very simple, and there's no need at all to involve landladies. Miss Bullion has been lent some documents of mine. I require them to be returned. I can easily identify them. It would not involve ransacking the place, or breaking locks. Just picking up a few papers . . .'

'You may be able to identify them,' said Imogen coldly. 'But I can't. I don't know what is yours and what is Miss Bullion's. I cannot allow the removal from her flat of anything at all. Please leave.'

The cold draught from the partly open door was cutting round Imogen's ankles. She was beginning to shake – standing in the cold with a high temperature not being a good idea – and she was a little frightened. Janet Summerfield was brimming with hostility, and a sort of self-righteous rage. Her unidentified companion was beefy, with a thick fist, clenched round the door chain, and a stupid expression. Wherever had she got him from?

And then, suddenly, Imogen was rescued. From the street behind the visitors a voice hailed her. 'Everything all right, Miss Quy?' There was Josh, and Simon, who had been her lodger last year, with two friends. They were young, and athletic looking, and one of the friends was nearly as bulky and tall as the bouncer with Janet Summerfield. Josh vaulted the front fence, and reached the door.

'Having a spot of bother?' he enquired over his shoulder, of Imogen.

'These people are just leaving,' she said.

'Oh, good. Well, we'll wait and see them off, shall we?' His heavyweight friend opened the gate, and bowed elaborately.

'You haven't heard the last of this!' said Janet Summerfield. 'We'll be back!' But she was beating a retreat now. A wide area of black coat topped by tousled grey hair was turned on Imogen. Her companion followed her, reluctantly. Obviously he had been longing for permission to shoulder the door and break the chain.

'Christ, Imogen,' said Simon, 'who's your fat friend? Was that the bailiffs? Good thing we were passing. This is Jason, and that's Wace. They like coffee and biscuits as much as I do.'

Imogen slipped the chain and let the boys in. 'You're all very welcome,' she said, 'but you'll have to fend for yourselves. I must get back to bed . . .' She was swaying gently on her feet.

'Put the kettle on, Jason,' said Josh, and he picked up Imogen bodily, and carried her upstairs, putting her down gently on the edge of her bed. 'A hot-water bottle and some Lemsip for you, I should think,' he said. 'We'll leave the door on the chain, and let ourselves out at the back when we go. But I think we'll lurk for a few minutes in case your heavies see us leaving and think to return. What have you been up to?'

'It isn't me,' Imogen told him, pulling the blankets up to her chin, and gasping with relief at the comforting warmth. 'It's Fran.'

'Curiouser and curiouser,' he said. 'Look, I'm sharing a room with Simon, and we're only in Chedworth Street. I'll write the telephone number in your phone book, in case you need to rabbit me out of a hat any time.'

'Thank you Josh. You're a pal. And you certainly came at the right moment just now.'

'What a hero I am,' said Josh smugly. 'Get some sleep, why don't you?'

For a while Imogen lay awake and aching. Josh appeared with a mug of Lemsip, and her hot-water bottle, and she tucked it under her toes. The sun had moved round the house far enough to flood her bedroom with morning light. Outside in the street she heard passing footfalls, and the occasional car. Downstairs the voices of her visitors and the chink of their mugs and spoons comforted her obscurely. Ever since childhood she had liked that feel a house has when someone in another room is talking, moving, humming – when there is a sense of life flowing within the walls. She did not hear them leave; she must have been asleep by then.

Imogen woke to find Fran in the room. She must just have come in – she was still wearing her jacket. 'Do you want some lunch?' she asked.

'Something to drink, perhaps,' said Imogen. Her throat felt dry. 'How did you get on with the Professor?'

'Badly,' said Fran. 'I'll bring you some soup and tell you about it.' Imogen struggled up to a sitting position in the bed, and waited. Fran reappeared with a mug of consommé, a glass of water and some aspirin.

'Anything else you want?' she enquired.

'Tell me how you got on,' said Imogen.

'He was angry with me. Very.'

'What for?'

'Pestering – his word – Janet Summerfield. I have overstepped my role, it seems. I was not supposed to conduct any enquiries, merely write up the material I was given. He had given his word that no embarrassing investigation would occur. I had a lot of trouble convincing him that I had not gone and told her he was not intending to write it himself. But of course, I had twigged that she didn't know that, and I hadn't told her. Only . . .'

'You had told her enough to let her know where to come for her papers, Fran,' said Imogen.

'What do you mean, come? Was she here?'

Imogen told Fran of the morning's brouhaha, but played down somewhat the general nastiness of the episode.

'What am I going to do?' asked Fran, dejectedly. 'This is going to be terrible if Professor Maverack won't support me. And *why* won't he? His whole theory of biography is that people are shit-holes, concealing their faults, deceiving themselves, presenting a false face to the world, and the biographer is to reveal the lies by which men live.'

'Perhaps he thinks one missing holiday doesn't amount to an interesting lie.'

'What about three missing biographers, then?' said Fran. 'Why has that happened if it isn't important? You know, at first, Imogen, I felt suspicious that he was going to edge my name off the title page, and take all the credit for the book himself without acknowledging me; now I wonder if it isn't the other way round . . .'

'What do you mean, Fran? I'm not at my brightest . . .'

'I'm sorry; it isn't fair to burden you with this when you're not well. I meant that now I wonder if the plan might be to lumber me with all the responsibility for the book – and make sure his own name is nowhere to be seen. That might explain why he wants to whitewash the subject.'

'That American said Maverack was a good example of his own theories . . .' mused Imogen. 'Look, this won't do. I think you might have to give back the family papers. After all, they are hers. But it's probably worth while to make sure nothing by the earlier workers goes back to her – I don't see how Mark Zephyr's files, or May Swann's notebooks can be hers, do you? Make sure everything is in separate piles, why don't you?'

'But can they come back and try again?'

'I don't know what they can do,' said Imogen. 'I've never met this sort of thing before.' She sounded, as she felt, sleepy. She must have drowsed before Fran left the room, she was not aware of her going.

By the following morning Imogen felt better – better enough to have a bath and get dressed, and go downstairs for a while. The aches and shakes had worn off and left her feeling languid and aimless. She ate as much breakfast as she could, and she was still sitting at the table, with the crossword propped on the marmalade jar, and completely blank, when a sharp crisp knock on the door interrupted her.

She opened the door to Janet Summerfield, this time accompanied by a man in a dark suit, and a policeman. 'My client obtained an *ex parte* hearing before a judge in chambers last night,' said the suited man. 'The judge has given us a Mareva injunction, to be served on one Frances Bullion, resident at this address. Is Frances Bullion at home, please?'

Behind Imogen Fran had come down the stairs, and now said, 'Yes I am.'

'I must deliver this document into your hands,' said the suit.

'Very well,' said Fran. She joined Imogen at the door,

93

but Imogen reached out, and taking Fran's wrist prevented her from accepting the long narrow envelope.

'What is a Mareva injunction?' she asked.

'It is a writ. It prevents Frances Bullion and or her agents from destroying, defacing, concealing, or removing to any other premises the papers in dispute, until such time as an *intra partes* hearing can determine the suit between Janet Summerfield and the said Frances Bullion. It ensures the return of the papers intact and entire to Janet Summerfield, unless the said Frances Bullion can show cause before a properly constituted court why the papers should not be returned . . .'

'There is no need for this,' said Frances. 'I have not refused to return the documents. But . . . Mrs Summerfield—' Fran raised her voice slightly, addressing Janet Summerfield over the shoulder of the lawyer. 'If you remove the materials for the biography from me before I have completed the work, I cannot be responsible for the accuracy of the eventual book.'

'You will indeed not be responsible,' said Janet Summerfield. 'Another biographer will be found.'

'I am serving you with this writ, Miss Bullion,' said the lawyer. 'You must take it, please.'

Fran took the envelope from him, and at once the three in the deputation turned as if to leave. 'Well, do you want these papers, or don't you?' said Fran. 'Aren't you going to wait for them?' She put the envelope into Imogen's hand, and ran off up the stairs.

'Why did someone give you an order like that, when you were not faced with any refusal to return the papers?' said Imogen. She was shaking, not from flu, but with anger.

'On my client's sworn affidavit that a request for the return of the documents had been made, and refused, and further sworn undertaking to pay all necessary damages if the case stated turned out to be unfounded when the matter came before the jurisdiction of the court in the presence of the other party . . .'

'She is mad!' said Imogen. 'She was refused only because Miss Bullion was not at home when she called . . .'

Fran put a cardboard box of papers on the doorstep.

'Is this all?' asked the lawyer.

'No; there is a second box,' said Fran. 'I'll just get it.'

'We need a receipt for these items,' said Imogen, suddenly thinking of it.

'How do we know everything is there?' said Janet Summerfield. 'She could have kept things back.'

'These boxes,' said Fran, putting the second one beside the first, 'contain three hundred and six documents, of which most are of one page, and some forty are of two or more pages. Every original document which was given to me on behalf of Dr Maverack from the offices of Recktype and Diss is here.'

'But we will not hand them over without a written receipt,' said Imogen.

'I'm not giving you a receipt for my own property!' said Janet Summerfield.

'The request for a receipt is in good order, and should be complied with,' said the court bailiff suddenly. 'You may give a receipt for two boxes, contents unexamined, stated to contain three hundred and six items.'

'I . . .' began Janet Summerfield.

'You had better comply,' said the lawyer stonily. 'We will be in difficulty before the court if the facts are not as stated in your affidavit. If you comport yourself further in any way unreasonably you will not be a credible witness . . .' As he spoke he was writing in his notebook. He tore the page, and offered it to Janet Summerfield to sign.

And then the scene was over. The receipt was in Fran's

hands, and the boxes were picked up from the doorstep and carried to the Mercedes parked across the street.

Imogen closed the door behind them. 'It's too late, anyway,' said Fran. 'I've read it all and made copies of the useful bits. And so help me God, Imogen, I'm going to give a proper account of Gideon Summerfield, whatever anyone says – the sanctified widow, the glorified professor, or the entire personnel of Recktype and Diss!'

'Or me,' said Imogen.

'Or you,' said Fran with an emphasis of finality.

10

The aftermath of flu is very depressing. Imogen didn't feel like staying out of bed, and she didn't feel like going back there. Fran had disappeared upstairs. The post brought three junk circulars, and a summons – a request on university crested letter paper for her appearance before the Court of Discipline in ten days' time. She looked at it blankly. She had no anger to spare for it. The undergraduate had an awful cheek, trying to blame Imogen for what he had been up to, but she was suffering, as a result of Janet Summerfield's interventions, from indignation fatigue.

On a sudden impulse she put her coat on and went out. It was such a beautiful day. She walked to the end of the road, intending to take the footpath to Grantchester, not all the way, on her first day out of bed, just a little distance. But she had got only as far as the paddock, where a few lucky youngsters kept ponies, before the point where the path opened out to the view of the serpentine, willow-lined river, when she felt she had gone far enough. Turning back she saw Shirl and Pansy approaching from the other end of the road, bearing stuffed pillowcases full of scraps. She waved, and they waited for her. She had forgotten they were coming.

'You look awful, Imogen,' said Pansy brightly. 'Should you be out?'

'No, not really,' said Imogen, 'but I'm in now. Come in and we'll get started.'

'Are you well enough?' asked Shirl. 'What is it? Flu?'

'After-effects of. Don't think I'm infectious.'

'We did rather want your advice. We've got twelve blocks to arrange, and the borders to design.'

'Giving advice never killed anyone,' said Imogen, smiling. 'The table in the sitting-room is clear. Spread it out.'

But the table was not big enough. When Fran came down half an hour later the three women were crawling round the floor, with the patchwork blocks laid out on the sitting-room carpet.

'Golly,' said Fran. 'What's afoot? I like those starry squares!'

'They look like compass stars when you see them one by one,' Pansy told her. 'But look what happens when you put them together.' She moved a group of squares closer on the carpet, so that the unhemmed edges overlapped slightly, and no border of carpet was visible between them. The background fabric, which appeared broken up as small areas round the edges of the block, narrow triangles between the spokes of the patterned stars, joined up when they were laid together, making plain stars between the patterned ones. You could see the quilt as made of multicoloured compass roses on a plain background, or as scattered with plain stars in an elaborate interwoven lattice of colour. There was a visual 'click' as you saw it first one way and then the other.

'Wow!' said Fran. 'What a beautiful thing! I had no idea . . .'

'Good, isn't it?' said Shirl smugly.

'*Seriously* good,' said Fran. 'My Gran made patchwork quilts, and I thought they were all like hers. She used very tiny pieces all the same shape and just random colours and patterns all over. I never knew you could get an effect like that. No wonder Imogen is so keen.'

'This one is for a raffle for the Red Cross,' said Pansy. 'Feel like helping?'

'You bet. What needs doing?'

'We have to dream up a border,' said Pansy, 'choose the fabrics for it, work out the amounts needed, make cardboard templates, and mark and cut the shapes. Then we have to put the right amounts of each shape and colour for about a foot of border into each of these plastic bags to take to our jolly team of needle-persons to sew.'

'Is that all?' said Fran laughing. 'Give me some unskilled work. I approve of your gender awareness, by the way.'

'How about ironing swatches for us, so that they are flat enough to cut accurately?' suggested Imogen.

'Anyone who helps gets to help choose colours,' said Shirl. 'And it isn't so much that Pansy is gender-aware, I'm sorry to say, it's simply that one of the needlewomen in the Quilters' Club is factually a man. Actually Pansy is a rather unreconstructed, pre-modernist sort of woman.'

'I sew a straighter seam than you do, for all that,' said Pansy equably.

'Do all possible designs have a repeat like that one?' asked Fran, contemplating the arrangement on the floor from her viewpoint at the ironing board.

'There are lots of different effects,' said Shirl. 'But every pattern repeats. Your gran's type of work repeated with every single shape – this repeats with every block. You could have a repeat of every second or third block . . .'

By and by Fran graduated from ironing to marking and cutting shapes. The women worked steadily and pleasantly together, and chatted. Remembering that Shirl worked part-time in a firm of solicitors in Petty Curie, Imogen thought to ask her if she knew what a Mareva injunction was.

'A freeze. Stops everything exactly as it is while some dispute gets sorted out.'

'Why Mareva?'

'It's the name of a ship. There was a dispute over harbour dues or somesuch, and the ship was about to sail out of British jurisdiction. The injunction held it at its moorings while the courts heard the dispute. I don't know much about it, I'm afraid. I could look it up, or ask Bob.'

'No need,' said Imogen. 'I just wondered. The crisis is past.' Which led, of course, to Imogen and Fran telling the dramatic story of the recovery of the papers, and the job Fran was doing for Dr Maverack. Fran avoided, Imogen noticed, mentioning the earlier biographers, but she explained the missing August. And Pansy suddenly dropped a bombshell.

'If I wanted to know something about old Gideon, I'd ask Melanie,' she said.

'Who's Melanie?' asked Fran.

'Melanie Bratch. She was his mistress for years and years. She might know.'

Fran stood thunderstruck, holding a pair of scissors poised to cut and motionless, while she stared at Pansy. 'He had a mistress?' she asked.

'More than one, the horrid old goat. But Melanie was mistress in chief.'

'But . . . there isn't a sign of it, not a murmur in any of the papers we told you about.'

'A successfully kept secret?' asked Imogen.

'Hardly that. He used to have tea with her once a week, and if he couldn't make it, Janet would ring up and change the day or time for him. Used to give me the creeps to think about it, but Melanie didn't seem to mind. And she went with them in the summer more than once when they rented a villa in Tuscany. Smelly or civilised according to your point of view.'

'Pansy, however do you know all this?' asked Imogen.

'Melanie is my best friend. Well, one of them.'

Fran turned to Imogen, her brow furrowed, her eyes wide. 'Janet Summerfield must have kept back stuff. She must have removed evidence of a mistress . . .'

'So why all the heat about getting papers back, if she censored what she lent?'

'A mistake. She made a mistake. There was *something* in those papers that she realised too late would give the game away about the mistresses . . .' Fran stopped, puzzled. 'But I can't think what it was. There wasn't anything . . . I hadn't a clue.'

'Pansy, are you absolutely sure?' asked Shirl.

'Absolutely. Melanie was crazy about him.'

'She couldn't have been fantasising?'

'Over ten years? Why would she? It would have been a very prolonged and elaborated fib. Anyway the point I'm making is, why not ask her?'

'Wild horses wouldn't stop me,' said Fran. 'Where is she?'

'Just up the Histon Road. She lived in Buckden for years, but she's moved into sheltered housing – old people's flats. I've got the address.' Pansy reached into her handbag for her address book, and in her eagerness to take the precious information down Fran put down the iron on a swatch of cloth, and scorched it while she wrote.

Shirl scolded, serenely, and cut the scorched area out of the piece. 'Remind me not to ask for your help making shirts or curtains,' she said.

'I don't know what kind of light it casts on human

nature,' Fran said to Imogen later, as they cleared up the threads and clippings from almost every surface in the sitting-room, after Shirl and Pansy had departed, 'but it's the only interesting thing yet to emerge about the great Gideon.'

11

It was, on account of the flu, some few days since Imogen had been in college, and a large bundle of files for new undergraduates awaited her. She worked hard all morning on filing, and scanning, reading rapidly over the forms new students filled in, looking for anything medical of which she had better be aware. At twelve she felt jaded. 'Serves you right, Imogen,' she told herself. How often had she scolded a flu victim for getting back to work too quickly? But served right or not, she felt like a sherry before lunch, and on impulse decided to exercise her privilege, conferred on her by a grateful college, and go and have a drink in the senior common room.

It was a handsome room, in the Victorian wing of the college, looking out on to the stretch of the garden that contained the Castle Mound. The tall windows were in full sun, and motes of dust hovered like minute insects in the slanting beams of warm light. The room had the anonymous comfort of a good club. On a side-table were arrayed pretty well all the national papers, as well as yesterday's *Cambridge Evening News*. Lord knows against whose names the original requests for the *Sun* and the *Star* had been entered, but the universally approved result was that everyone could read, or at least glance at, the pop papers, and nobody had to buy them. The college fellows could display very well-informed disdain for the gutter press.

Imogen helped herself to sherry from the range of

decanters on a handsome sideboard, selected *New Scientist* which was offering an article on pollen dating by a college fellow, and settled in one of the vast pneumatically soft armchairs. At once someone who had been sitting comfortably at the far end of the room rose, and moved towards her. Professor Maverack. She lowered her eyes to the printed page, and feigned to be lost in reading, but undeterred he sat down opposite, and said, 'May I join you?'

Imogen nodded. One cannot, after all, say 'no'.

'I am told,' he said, after a decent interval, 'that Frances Bullion is your lodger.'

'Yes,' said Imogen.

'Rather more, I gather – she is a close friend?'

'I am pleased to think so,' said Imogen coldly, levelling her steadiest gaze at him.

'Forgive me. I don't mean to be impertinent. I have been asking around to find, if I can, someone who might have some influence with her, and Dr Bent suggested you.'

'You are her supervisor, aren't you?' said Imogen. 'Don't you have any influence over her?'

'Not enough,' he said. 'I'm sorry, I'm not going about this very well; but I do need to talk to someone about Miss Bullion. I realise that it's a delicate matter, but . . .'

Overcome with curiosity, Imogen tried to thaw her voice a bit. 'I can always be talked to,' she said. 'It's a large part of my job.'

'Thank you,' he said. 'You see, I'm afraid I may inadvertently have got Miss Bullion into trouble. And yet . . . I may be fanciful. I hope I am, but . . .' He halted, looking miserable.

'Dr Maverack,' said Imogen sternly, 'I hope you are not going to tell me that you gave Frances the Summerfield biography, knowing that it was likely to lead her into personal danger. Because if you did that, how can you expect any friend of hers to listen to anything you say?'

Oddly, he seemed relieved. 'I have less explaining to do than I thought,' he said. He looked round, making sure that no armchair in easy earshot was occupied. 'Please believe me, I had no intention whatever of leading her into danger. I simply thought the money would be of use to her. Of course I knew the project had been in difficulties; I had no idea *what* difficulties. Indeed, I can still hardly believe . . . I am probably just imagining things . . .' He seemed to collect himself. 'Frances has surprised me in two ways. Firstly, in discovering the existence of more than one former biographer; I knew of one, but only yesterday when she visited me did I know there had been three – *three*! Secondly, I had supposed that a research student would be, shall we say, biddable. That if I told her to ignore the remaining unanswered questions – if I told her that there always were loose ends and lost knowledge in any biography, she would simply accept it, and leave sleeping dogs alone. Whereas in fact, she announced her intention to defy me, and to pursue the truth, as she calls it, come hell or high water.'

'I take it you want me to try to dissuade Fran from further investigation? But I might say that I thought such a devotion to the truth was a sign of a good scholar, and that you ought to be delighted rather than discouraging.'

'I don't suppose you are a statistician,' he said. 'But what would you say the chances were of three people coming to a sticky end, or vanishing off the face of the earth or something, in succession, and all of them working on the same thing, and the accidents being just pure chance, pure coincidence, nothing to do with the work in hand?'

'It is a bit strange, isn't it?' she conceded. 'The only one I have any knowledge of is Mark Zephyr, and he died of meningitis, and I honestly don't see how that could possibly be connected with working on a biography.'

'Well, I don't know anything about any of this string of mishaps,' he said. 'But the thing is, if they are coincident accidents, then the odds are long – longer with each successive person. And if they aren't coincidences, then they aren't accidents. Or so it seems to me.'

'And if they aren't accidents?'

'Then it would seem to be very dangerous to work on the Summerfield book. And Miss Bullion . . . and you see, I feel very badly about it. It is my fault she is – might be in a position of danger.'

'Dr Maverack,' said Imogen, 'can you tell me exactly why you off-loaded this commission on a student instead of doing it yourself?'

'It looks a bit bad, you mean? Yes, I see that it does. And it's ironic, really. I thought it would be boring. What interests me professionally is the discovery of deceit. The demolition of the pathetic false idealisations of self by which people live . . . I thought old Summerfield was not capable of being interestingly demolished. Too unimaginative to have erected for himself a grand false façade. I checked up with some mathematicians, and found that the maths is thought to be genuine – a real discovery, though an appendage to Penrose, it seems. Penrose discovered these funny patterns which don't repeat to infinity in any direction, but if you rotate them have some kind of ghostly five-sided quality. He set the mathematical world by the ears with them. They are huge fun, I am told. Summerfield came up with a variant kind, ghostly heptagons. Also fun.'

'Not easily demolished?'

'Not by a non-mathematician, for sure.'

A thoughtful silence fell between them. Then, 'Dr Maverack . . .'

'Do call me Leo. I hardly recognise myself otherwise.'

'A doctorate by way of false façade?' said Imogen, amused in spite of herself. He had the grace to blush slightly. 'Leo – should we tell the police?'

'I've tried that. They let me make a long and involved statement to a very young policeman, who wrote it down in full. They said they would report my statement to officers in charge of the relevant investigations. But they clearly regarded me as mad. They were very concerned to know what I took the motive to be for suppressing biographers. And of course, I didn't know.'

'Naturally I have wondered about that too. Janet Summerfield certainly seems fierce enough . . .'

'But it is she who wants the biography; cares passionately that it should be out in time for the Waymark Prize . . .' he said.

'But if there is a dark secret, she would want it kept dark?'

'What dark secret?'

'His mistress, perhaps?' offered Imogen.

'Oh, that. But everybody who knew him knows about that. You couldn't possibly expect to keep it secret.'

'Fran said there was absolutely nothing about it in the papers she was given. She found out by sheer accident.'

'Really? How very odd. Melanie isn't a disgrace of any kind, anyway, not nowadays. Rather a feather in the old bore's cap, I would have thought. She was a very beautiful woman.'

'You knew her?'

'I knew them all, long ago. When we were all young. Before I went to America. But, look, Imogen. Whatever is behind all this the obviously best thing is for Frances to get an anodyne book written as fast as possible, and for her to stop, absolutely stop ferreting around for more material, and then she'll be out of harm's way, and we can all relax. However, she reacted very forcibly and volubly to this suggestion coming from me. Really, I am hoping you can make her see sense.'

'I could try. But not with much hope of succeeding. She is very much her own woman.'

'Don't I know it!' he said, ruefully. 'I'm all for equality; truly I am. But it does make the fair sex combative!'

Imogen stood up. The tactfully muted bell had signalled lunch, and she intended to eat in hall today. Very much in spite of herself she was rather liking Leo Maverack. 'There's something else I can and will do,' she told him. 'I have a friend in the police here. I'll try to find out if they have really put your statement in the bin, or if there is anything happening.'

'That's a good idea,' he said, hauling himself out of the deep cushions of his chair. 'That would be good to know. But the main thing, you know, is to safeguard Frances, in case . . .'

'There is mischief rather than accident at work?'

'Precisely.'

'I'll try,' she told him.

Later, as Imogen was leaving college, she saw, as she strolled through the gateway arch, pinned on a board that was covered three deep with handbills, posters and announcements, an announcement for a special lecture in the Mill Lane lecture room – Dr Holly Portland on the dating of eighteenth- and nineteenth-century printed silk and cotton textiles. Imogen stopped and noted the date and time in her diary. She would go to that, and take Shirl and Pansy with her if they were free.

Imogen had expected Fran to be difficult to advise; somehow she had not expected a flaming row. Within a few minutes of the conversation beginning Fran had extracted the confession that Imogen had been talking to Professor Maverack. She froze, and regarded Imogen coldly across the room.

'And are we to expect in due course monographs on the contributions of landladies to twentieth-century biographical scholarship?' she enquired.

'Fran . . .'

'No, Imogen. This is not a minor medical emergency. Unless there is a swathe of your early life which you have never mentioned to me, the truth is you have no relevant expertise, and no standing. You are in no position to tell me whether I should or should not investigate something to do with my professional work.'

'Fran, calm down a minute . . .'

'You have the damn cheek to discuss me behind my back with my supervisor . . .'

'Fran . . .'

'I'd be bloody angry with you if you were my mother, Imogen, and you're not even a second cousin twice removed. Just mind your own bloody business, will you?'

And with that Fran flounced out, banging the door.

'Whew!' said Imogen, sitting down abruptly. When the shock wore off in a moment or two, misery would engulf her, she knew. But before it did the phone rang.

'I'm back.' It was Mike's voice. 'How about a spot of lunch, and a walk?'

'Oh, oh Mike. That sounds nice. Next Sunday?'

'Sooner. Today if you like.'

'Aren't you at work?'

'I've taken a few extra days leave to recover from the holiday. Are you all right, Imogen? Have I put my foot in it somehow? You don't sound your usual delighted-to-hear-from-you self.'

'Mike, of course I'm delighted. I'm just upset about something – nothing to do with you. And today would be wonderful . . .'

'You do rather sound as if you could do with some cheering from big brother Mike Parsons. If it's nothing to do with me, is it anything to do with disappeared persons?'

'Remotely. I'll tell you about it on this proposed walk.'

'Certainly, I could find out if anyone is working on Professor Maverack's report,' said Mike. 'But I'm pretty sure his impression will be right – they will have taken his statement to humour him, and put it on file, and got back to work.'

They were standing on the top of Linton Hill, just beyond the water tower, where the trees thinned out, and a splendid view spread out below them. Not that Linton Hill is *high*, exactly, – it must be a rise of less than a hundred feet, but in so flat a county it nevertheless gives a dizzying prospect. The mere fact that the land is softly folded, and you can see a long way on the blue level landscape below, and look down on the little town – or is it a big village? – is refreshingly heady. Last year there had been a blazing fluorescent yellow field of rape down there at the foot of the slope; this year there was a field of flax, grey-blue, and looking like a lake of standing water under a cloudy sky.

'But Mike, why? *Why* aren't the police interested?'

'Their job is solving crime, not solving conundrums.'

'But this might *be* crime; several crimes.'

'Well . . . What have we got here? A funny coincidence. And a worry on your part that something might happen to a friend of yours. A friend who is so far in bouncing good health.'

'But . . .'

'Bear with me. I'm answering your question. Now, if there had been a string of three crimes – something, we know not what, that befell Ian Goliard; a disappearance which indicates a crime against May Swann, and a death from apparently natural causes, which you are implying was not natural at all . . .'

'I never said that. Meningitis is . . .'

'You are implying that. You must be. If these crimes have taken place, the motivation of the criminal is unusual – bizarre. It isn't anything like the motives the police are used to. It isn't lust, jealousy, filthy lucre, revenge or rage. It isn't self-defence. It is some arcane matter to do with biography. The biography of a dead don who seems to have lived a boring and law-abiding life. Honestly, Imogen, what a farrago. And the police are busy.'

'I see. And if something were to happen to Frances, what then?'

'That would take a bit of laughing off, I agree.'

'So three dead bodies could be coincidence, but a fourth . . .'

'But we haven't *got* three dead bodies, woman! Your May Swann may turn up any minute – dead or alive. And who knows what happened to Ian Goliard? Perhaps he won the pools, and swanned off to Florida.'

'Could one find out?'

'Might be able to. Tell you what, I'll try. All right? Now, aren't you ever going to ask me about my holiday?'

12

'I'm sorry,' said Fran.

'No, I'm sorry,' said Imogen.

'But I didn't mean . . .' said both at once. They laughed.

'Of course I've no right to be worried about you,' said Imogen.

'Since when didn't a best friend have a right to be worried?' said Fran. 'I'm just on edge, I think. I'm so bloody determined not to be bullied and deflected and pushed into doing a job badly, that I'm firing off with all guns in every direction at friend and foe alike.'

'Good description,' said Imogen, ruefully. 'But the rebuke was in order.'

'Whether or no, let's make it up. I've got a lot to tell you,' said Fran.

It was a fine morning, and the two women went through the back door into the tiny garden. An old, solid wooden bench, weathered silver-grey, stood on a small area of York paving slabs, under the kitchen window, facing south. A china rose scrambled up the fence beside it sporting a few brave, late blossoms. Beyond the tiny lawn an ancient gnarled apple tree filled the garden from fence to fence, covered with hard little green apples and dappled golden light. They sat, closing their eyes and tilting their heads to the bright October morning.

'I saw Melanie,' said Fran.

'And?' said Imogen, opening her eyes, and sitting up.

'I learned a lot,' said Fran. 'She talked and talked. I had trouble getting away.'

'Tell, tell.'

'Well, I have to précis. She knew Summerfield all their lives, pretty much. Before they were students together. They met at a tennis club in Palmer's Green. She was mildly sweet on him, but she had a lot of other boyfriends. Then when he went up to Cambridge, Janet made a dead set at him, and Melanie played it cool, and lost him. She kept right on seeing him – them – though. There was a tight little group of friends, who kept up with each other. Odd thing – Professor Maverack seems to have been one of them, until he took a job in the States. Did you realise *that*?'

'He told me,' said Imogen.

'You didn't say . . .'

'You bit my head off before I had a chance. Go on.'

'And – get this! – another of the group was one Ian Goliard.'

'Ho, ho. The plot thickens . . .'

'You bet. Now Melanie knows a good deal about Ian Goliard.'

'As, like, where he is?'

'No, she doesn't know that. But she knows he took on the biography in the first place as a tribute to an old friend. He's very rich, I gather: it wasn't for the money, it was to be an elegant memoir of the great man. But he quickly went off the idea. According to Melanie he was being hounded by Janet, who was loading him down with family papers and old diaries and such, enough to fill an entire encylopaedia, whereas what he had in mind was a slender volume, devoted mainly to a great scholar's contribution to the world of learning . . . and whereas on the one hand she was demanding that he devoted months to reading Giddy's laundry lists . . .'

'Whose?'

Fran laughed. 'Isn't it odd? I've got so used to thinking of him as a monster patriarch, and she calls him "old Giddy"! You know, Imogen, she has such an affectionate, amused tone when she talks about him, she made him come real to me. Somebody really *liked* him – you know that? Where was I?'

'Goliard. On the one hand forced to read laundry lists . . .'

'And on the other hand she became venomously hostile when he proposed to retrace old Giddy's steps, and visit some places in the life. Melanie says Goliard was a poet; published in small presses, and he rather wanted to spread himself on background landscapes – places where the great man had trod – that sort of book. When it became clear Janet would obstruct him, he took himself abroad. Just dumped the project back to the publishers. Melanie knows he did; he left her to post the papers back, under plain cover.'

'And where did he go?'

'Thailand, probably. Or perhaps China. He's rich; and he has boyfriends all over the place. He can lie low in comfort for as long as he likes. His friends have never had addresses for him. One writes care of a bank in London.'

'Well, that seems to complete the strange prehistory of the biography. All the hands in the papers accounted for.'

'Yes. And it seems clearer than ever to me that there is something Janet Summerfield doesn't want known . . .'

'And that that something has to do with a place, somewhere . . .'

'Where he spent the missing summer of '78. Looks like it, doesn't it?'

'Well, did you ask Melanie about it? What did she say?'

'She was hugely helpful, but it doesn't help.'

'Explain.'

'Well, it seems that usually they all went on holiday together.'

'All?'

'Janet and "Giddy" and Melanie – they called her Melon, and Ian and several other friends from Cambridge days. Someone called Meredith, even, once, Maverack. They would rent a chalet in the Alps, or a cottage on Exmoor or the Lakes, and all descend on it with cases of wine, and hampers from Fortnums, and the Scrabble board – she says he was a demon at Scrabble – and they would tumble about, getting into each other's beds, and sleeping late, and walking every afternoon. Old Giddy used to call this their summer Saturnalias.'

Something in Fran's tone made Imogen ask, 'How does that strike you, Fran? As a way to carry on, I mean.'

'Yucky. Pathetic.'

'I expect it seemed immensely liberated to them, at the time.'

'Oh, yes, so I gathered. It gave Melanie her chance. But I wouldn't have taken it, in her place. It must have been hellish painful, especially when the holiday was over and they all came home, Janet and Gideon to married bliss in Bottisham and Melanie to a lonely flat.'

'Wherein she was visited weekly . . .'

'He was sent.'

'What?'

'Janet sent him. She reckoned that if the old goat had deflowered the virgin Melanie, it was up to him to keep her serviced until she found an alternative source of satisfaction. She didn't, so it went on for years. Till he died, in fact.'

'My father used to say "nowt so queer as folk",' Imogen remarked.

'Spot on,' said Fran. 'And queerer than you yet know,

Imogen. Because pretty soon Melanie and Old Giddy didn't normally fancy sex together. Just because it had happened once or twice under the influence of wine and Tuscan sun, during one of the Saturnalias, didn't mean that they really wanted a steamy affair continuing indefinitely.'

'Well, but what made them . . .'

'He didn't fancy confessing to Janet that he wasn't required; Melanie didn't fancy confessing to her arch rival that she didn't have any pull; they were fond of each other. So sometimes it was a cover for another assignation, and sometimes they just had a cup of tea and a quiet chat. They intended originally, I gather, to tell Janet some time; then they got used to their weekly tête-à-tête . . . anyway they never did tell her.'

'And can you put all or any of that into the biography, for all, including Janet, to read?'

'If I like. Melanie doesn't seem to mind. While Summerfield was alive she wouldn't have liked to precipitate a row with Janet, but now she seems very laid back about it all.'

'How *very* odd, though,' said Imogen thoughtfully, 'that one might need to keep it secret that one was *not* sleeping with someone . . .'

'Well, they're all more or less bats,' said Fran cheerfully. 'But I sort of understand. Don't you think – if he visited Melanie constantly for all those years, and it wasn't sex, then it would have to be love – true affection. And it might be much easier for a lawfully wedded wife to think of her dear one as oversexed and needing auxiliary supplies, than to think of sharing his true affection . . . *I* think . . .'

'I expect you're right,' said Imogen. 'It sounds very romantic, but it still might be true. How clever of you to work it out . . . But do I gather Melanie doesn't know about the missing August? She sounds as though she would know just about everything.'

'Yes; but not that. She remembers August '78 very clearly. They rented a cottage at Colwall, in the Malverns. They were going to climb the hills and look down at fair fields full of folk. But what actually happened was a terrible row. The cottage was too small; someone had brought a friend, and it was crowded. Someone accused Gideon of cheating at Scrabble. Hard words were spoken, and Gideon left.'

'With or without Janet?'

'Without Janet, but with Meredith's friend. Melanie hasn't a clue where they went. They came back four days later, not speaking to each other. It cast a dampener on the summer's entertainment for everyone.'

'I should think it did!'

'But Melanie honestly truly doesn't know where Gideon went. She was very cross with him about it at the time, and so she never mentioned the episode to him afterwards. The next year Meredith turned up without friend . . .'

'No wonder . . . but Frances, where do you go from here?'

'Don't know, quite. I'll mull it over.'

'You won't be satisfied with all that new material, and simply record the story as you've just told me, and be damned to those four days?'

'Nope,' said Fran, stretching, and getting up. She wandered across and put her nose into a big blowsy rose, which responded by shedding its petals lavishly at her feet.

'I think I've got further than any of others. It would be real cowardy custard to give up now. Incidentally, what's so cowardly about custard? Do you know?'

'Haven't a clue. I've known some custard in my time that would require a tad of courage . . .'

'Haven't we all?' said Fran, darkly.

13

Holly's lecture on the dating of fabric was at five in the Mill Lane Lecture Rooms. It was a cold and blustery evening, with bursts of rain on the gusts of wind, and a wintry feel to the world. When Shirley and Pansy arrived to pick up Imogen the three friends decided to drive, and park in the Lion Yard, if there wasn't any room in Silver Street. A sullenly dramatic light overhung the city; wet streets, gleaming, a cloudscape above full of lowering blackness and silver cloud rims; people scuttling under rain-glossed umbrellas; the buildings looming in the daylight dimness – the few shops on their route showing golden rectangles of warm lighting, and casting angled rectangles of light across the pavements.

The lecture room was very thinly packed; not more than thirty people at most, but the weather gave a painless alibi for that. Imogen sat between Shirley and Pansy, and all three of them had brought notebooks and pencils, in the expectation of enlightenment. Holly was sitting at the table at the front, putting slides into a carousel, while a technician set up the projector. She looked up and waved at someone, and looking round Imogen saw Professor Maverack, making his way to the front. The lecture room had filled up considerably in the last few minutes. Professor Maverack stood out somewhat, since the audience was predominantly of women, and Imogen was briefly surprised to see him, until she remembered that Holly had talked of him as a friend. Presumably it was the lecturer rather than the subject that had brought him. At the very last minute a group of dignitaries filed in; governors of the Fitzwilliam, committee members of the friends of the Fitzwilliam, and Holly stood up to the microphone, and began.

Imogen learned an enormous amount in the next hour. How wildly desirable to Europeans Indian printed calicos had been, right through the eighteenth century – soft, wearable, washable with their lovely printed patterns in fast dyes. How the Indians had mastered the skills of mordant dying long before western manufacturers. How frantic attempts to proscribe the wearing of calicos, and impose huge tariffs on them in protection of the wool and silk weavers at home had failed miserably. All that had been achieved was making people hoard every scrap and cutting of the precious calico, to reuse in quilts. Holly's slides traced the progress of printed designs – the East India Company's men in London sending requests for patterns in the English taste: 'Those which hereafter you shall send we desire may be with more white ground, and the flowers and branches to be in colours in the middle of the quilt as the painter pleases, whereas now the most part of your quilts come with sad red grounds which are not equally sorted to please all buyers . . .'

The English needlewomen were soon imitating Indian patterns in their needlework, and the Indian print makers imitating English needlework in their printed cottons, until it was impossible to disentangle the taste of the makers from the taste of the wearers of the fabrics. The history of fashion could be dimly traced in the inventory of cotton goods seized by the excise men from smugglers . . . Imogen watched entranced while Holly showed slides of old fabrics. Her last set of slides however was most interesting of all. She was discoursing on a new industry in America, of faking old quilts. Old quilts had become highly collectable, and so naturally people were trying to turn a dishonest buck by making new ones look old. Holly showed a faded and worn quilt of great charm. Then she showed close-ups of the wear and fading on one of its pieces, alongside a faded piece of a truly old bedcover. You could see the difference at once. On the fake the wear and tear was random – or rather – look closely, Holly exhorted them – it was concentrated in places where it could be seen. On the really old pieces the wear was concentrated at the edge of the patches, where they pulled on each other, and over ridges where the seams overlapped, and the cloth was at its thickest, and over lumps in the carded but unspun wool with which the quilt was filled. In the fake piece the fading turned into the seams; in the old piece the material in the seams when you unpicked them was still bright. But in any case, Holly said, and Imogen could see what she meant, anyone with any kind of eye for it could see at once from some indefinable atmosphere in the patterns on the scraps whether they were old or not. She finished with a long sequence of slides of quilts, each one dated, and ranged in order from the bedhangings of Levens Hall, the oldest surviving patchwork, datable to 1708, right through to quilts made in the fifties. Like those timed sequences which show you flowers opening on the stalk, the sequence showed the changing shapes and colours of fashion. Once Holly's historical prospectus reached Imogen's own lifetime she found it amazingly recognisable – the quilts might have been made from her own clothes and those of her friends. She still winced at the sulphur yellows and bright turquoise patterns of the fifties! And though the fabrics changed, the blocks and their repeating structure remained, done in a thousand hues, a kaleidoscopic mosaic of prints, but themselves strongly traditional, handed down the generations of women, their folksy names and persistent appearance and reappearance telling of mother and daughter, and church sewing circle, reaching way back.

After the lecture Holly was surrounded by admirers, Leo Maverack among them, and Imogen slipped away, and had a drink in the Anchor with her two friends before going home. She went to bed with a book, and instead of reading, let her mind wander over the many quilts Holly had shown. Some of them, of course, had been made by prosperous housewives, with time and money to spare, because they preferred their own handiwork to what could be bought. But many – most – were made by poor and ordinary women from practical need. And who were all these people, with a nimble needle, and an eye for colour and pattern? The least of them achieved a charm and prettiness found in very few designed and manufactured things; the best of them had made visually stunning pieces, that would steal the show if hung on the walls of art galleries instead of spread on beds, and washed and worn to bits. Imogen had recently read a whole book on the question why all the great painters were men. It offered a number of reasons, of varying degrees of plausibility, but had not suggested that the reason was that the women worked in textiles instead of oil or watercolour.

Imogen felt an enormous and heart-warming solidarity with all these women of the past – mute inglorious Elizabeths and Janes, whose work didn't count as art. She began to dream up her own masterpiece, based on one of the blocks she had just seen.

There was a light tap on the door, and Fran's voice, very quiet.

'Imogen? Are you awake?'

'Come!' called Imogen. Fran came in, and sat in the little nursing chair, over which Imogen cast her clothes at night, unceremoniously dumping the clothes on the floor.

'I thought you must be awake,' she said, 'since the light was on.'

'I'm just thinking,' said Imogen.

'Funny coincidence; I've been thinking too.'

'What about?'

'About biographers, actually. Being one, that is. Suppose, for a fr'instance, one had a subject who had one glorious year . . .'

'Like Keats?'

'. . . and one spent ten years researching him and writing about him. It's quite a thought, isn't it – the proportion of one's own life engrossed in someone else's? You could in theory spend all the years of your own life elucidating someone else's, and that couldn't be sensible unless the subject was immensely more important and interesting than oneself. Well, no doubt the subjects of biography ought to be that – worth their own years and a stretch of someone else's to the world – but when you look actually you find that lots of published biographies are about folk of quite modest importance – people dimly heard of but nearly forgotten, or some famous person's wife, or . . .'

'In my experience people's wives are often more interesting than they are,' said Imogen drily.

'Well, the remark wasn't intended to be gender-specific; a famous person's husband would be an equally clear example.'

'I rather think my remark wasn't gender-specific either; I meant that given a couple, the less famous one is often . . .'

'I hadn't noticed that; but I expect you're right.'

'The real question is, why do people spend long years celebrating minor stars in the constellation?'

'To earn a living?'

'To enable themselves to be professional writers?'

'To make some worthwhile contribution to the state of knowledge?'

'To defeat oblivion?'

'Both for the subject and for themselves . . .'

'Well, your biography appears to be a short cut *to* oblivion for the biographer . . .'

'I'm being careful – honest.'

'The sooner you get round to researching autobiography the better I'll like it.'

'I never know quite what I do to earn your affection, Imogen,' said Fran, 'but what I really came to ask is, do you want a few days in Wales?'

'With you? Sounds good. When?'

'Leave tomorrow, or the day after?'

Imogen reached for her diary, and saw the snag at once. 'I've got to be in Cambridge the day after tomorrow, Fran,' she said. 'Could it wait till next week?'

'Blast!' said Fran. 'Oh, well, I'll have to go by myself. Unless you could change your appointment?'

But it was the Court of Discipline. 'I would if I could, love,' said Imogen regretfully. 'But Wales won't run away . . .'

'Another time, then,' said Fran. 'Good night.'

The Court of Discipline was held in the Old Schools. Oddly, though Imogen had passed down Trinity Lane times without number, going through King's College on her way to and fro, or taking the spectacularly beautiful way through Clare College, she had never stepped through the somewhat forbidding arch into the looming Victorian Gothic building. But inside the courtyard one came face to face with a pretty, church-like medieval building, modestly completing a courtyard the Victorian improvers had tried hard to make grand. Imogen entered by a door in the south range, and found herself in an interior which the incumbent University Registry had tried hard to make office-like. She was directed upstairs.

The accused young man had, as was usual, requested that the hearing be held in camera, and that the two junior members of the University, who could have made up a panel with the two senior members, not be appointed. It was very rare for anyone to want two of his fellow students to adjudicate; even rarer for anyone to want the hearing to be held in public. When Imogen arrived, therefore, there were three men sitting behind the table – the chairman and two senior members – and the defendant was sitting stiff and white-faced beside his Senior Tutor. The lawyer he had threatened to use was not there after all.

The proctor entered a formal complaint on behalf of the University, and the University Advocate acting as prosecutor began to state the case to be answered.

The defendant had written a brilliant, even flawless answer paper. The question had involved some working out in logic – and the defendant's calculations were on a sheet of paper that had been folded, and then flattened out again. The sheet in question was the third of nine sheets he had used. It was the only one that had been folded. It carried the crucial material on which the high marks awarded to him had been based. In addition to having been folded, it had a little groove visible on all four quarters of the paper. The Advocate took up a clean sheet of paper, folded it, clipped his pen to the folded paper, removed the pen, flattened the paper and invited the panel to compare the sheet to the defendant's exam paper.

The two sheets of paper were passed round, and carefully examined; tipped this way and that in the light by each person in turn. Imogen sat quietly at the back, watching. In particular she watched Framingham. He was sitting very erect, and very tight-lipped. In front of him on the table was a notepad in which he occasionally scrawled something. The set of his head on his shoulders was odd, she thought – as though he had a stiff neck. His face was tilted a little upwards, and his glance was bent downwards to compensate. Defiance? Obstinacy? Misery, certainly – he positively radiated it. Well, it couldn't be fun, after all, to be accused of cheating.

The Court was carefully stepping through the situation. Luffincott's winning paper for the Random Prize; the startling resemblance between Framingham's final paper and Luffincott's prize essay; the folded exam paper . . . things were certainly looking rather bad for young Framingham.

The University Advocate began to put questions to him directly. 'Why was the sheet of paper folded?'

'I finished early. I was shuffling the papers, and messing about. I must have folded that one without thinking.'

'Precisely into four?'

'It's a nervous habit. Some people chew their pencils, I fold paper.' He extended his notebook to them. The page he had been writing on was folded in two.

Odd, Imogen thought. She had not seen him do it. The Advocate thought it was odd too.

'Your nerves impelled you to fold only one of nine sheets of paper, and that one the most important to the argument in your essay.'

'I did it without thinking. It's just chance it happened to be that one. I suppose it was on top.'

'And your nervous habit extends to clipping your pen to the edge of the folded sheet?'

'I told you. I was messing about.'

'Most people spend the time anxiously checking what they have written. You were not anxious?'

'No,' the boy said. 'Why should I be? I knew I had done well.'

'You knew that you had written precisely what had won the Random Prize for another man.'

'In a way. But not the way you are suggesting. I had discussed the matter with Luffincott, and with others in our group. We had worked out the best approach to the problem in conversation together. What's wrong with that? You don't accuse Luffincott of pinching his ideas from me!'

'It seems that Luffincott has been a high-flyer during the whole of his career at Cambridge, and if he has worked out an original approach to a crux in logic nobody is surprised; whereas your supervisor is very surprised to discover that you have done so.'

'I don't get on with him,' said Framingham. 'He doesn't like me.'

'Are you saying he has made a false report of your ability out of personal dislike?'

'Not exactly. But I didn't like him so I didn't work hard for him. I messed him about. He doesn't know what I can do.'

'So you are saying that in spite of your supervisor's view of your abilities, you did write this paper entirely yourself?'

'Yes.'

Both Framingham's college tutor, and his head of college, sitting either side of him, tried to draw his attention.

'. . . that is, yes, but under the influence of some medication. I remember feeling exceptionally alert and fast-reacting.'

'And you wish to call a witness, I believe?'

'Yes. Miss Quy.'

Imogen found herself called forward.

'You remember giving me pills?' Framingham asked her.

'I have a record of giving you something to help you sleep. You came to me late in the afternoon of 4th of June, and told me you were worried about the exams, and could not sleep. I gave you two paracetamol.'

'It can't have been paracetamol. It was a mind-bender. It put me on a high.'

'I have a record in my medication book,' Imogen said. She could not help feeling agitated. She was being accused of lying. 'Two paracetamol.'

'It can't have been just paracetamol. You can get that at Boots. Why would anyone ask the college nurse for it? Everyone knows you can give them things which help with exams.'

'Everyone knows wrong then,' said Imogen. 'A college nurse cannot give anything which requires a prescription. If it were not available from Boots, in fact, it would not be available from me. At any time when exams are in prospect we are doubly careful, in case someone should feel slowed down by some medication, and not do their best. I have never heard of anyone claiming to have been stimulated by medication so as to out-perform their best.'

The Senior Tutor cleared his throat, and said, 'Miss Quy, may we take it that there is no possibility of mistake? That you are morally certain that you could not have given any other drug on this occasion?'

Imogen paused. She thought very carefully. 'I cannot actually remember giving Mr Framingham any pills. It is not surprising I can't remember – I am consulted many times a week all term, and many dozens of times in the run-up to exams. That is why I keep a register of every single pill given out. Now that the question has arisen, I am resting my answers on two things – first the entry in the book –' She brought the book out of her bag, and put it on the table, 'and second the very fact that I don't remember the occasion. For me to have given any very potent medication to Mr Framingham or anyone else would be unprecedented – I could not possibly have done such a thing and then forgotten about it. Indeed I could not possibly have done such a thing at all.'

Framingham's tutor asked, 'Is there any possibility that you intended to dispense paracetamol, but actually inadvertently gave something else? You are not a qualified dispensing pharmacist.'

'No,' said Imogen, 'indeed not. That is one powerful reason why it would be wrong for me to dispense prescription medicines to undergraduates. But the sort of mistake you ask me about could not occur – or rather could not occur without being discovered. We run a kind of double-entry book-keeping. Amounts of medicines purchased are entered here –' she showed them a page of the register – 'amounts given out are entered here – and we have a regular audit of the medicine cupboard to make sure that amounts tally with the amounts in the book. Any discrepancy would cause an investigation at once.'

'Miss Quy,' the tutor said, 'can we be quite sure that paracetamol is incapable of causing an exceptionally fine performance? The lay public is often told that individual reactions to drugs are varied and somewhat unpredictable.'

'I am not a pharmacologist,' said Imogen. 'I can only say that in all my training and all my scope of experience I have never heard of any such effect being reported. As far as I know paracetamol is an analgesic, pure and simple.'

'Thank you Miss Quy,' said the tutor, and she stood down.

Framingham's tutor was summing up. He asked the Court to have due regard to the terrible consequences for his pupil of being found guilty. Not only would he be deprived of his degree, and sent down from Cambridge at once; he would have very great difficulty getting any kind of job with a reputation for cheating hung round his neck . . . Surely the Court should be exceptionally certain of the case against him before making such a finding. And there was some room for doubt . . .

Not much though. By and by the Court retired into private session, and Imogen left. She retreated to her office in college, taking her dispensing book with her, and carefully replacing it in her filing cabinet. She locked the filing drawer, having realised how crucial the book was.

When, later, she was leaving college for the day she walked into an aftermath. A trunk and a pile of gear with a bicycle propped up against it was stacked in the porch. Framingham was leaning against the gateway arch, head down. As Imogen stepped past him he suddenly began to shout at her.

'Bitch!' he cried. 'Bloody unfeeling bitch! You could have got me out of this; just one word from you would have given me the benefit of the doubt! What did it matter to you? You could have helped me, you bloody self-protecting hellcat, you cow!'

Imogen stopped in her tracks, stunned. The head porter arrived, shooting out of his glass-fronted booth like an avenging angel in a bowler hat, but before he got there a couple of passing students had lifted Framingham bodily out of the college on to the pavement, where his taxi to the station was just pulling up to the kerb. Several pairs of hands helped his luggage away with him.

14

'You are shaking Miss Quy. Let me help you. Let me take you to the Combination Room and sit you down with a drink.' The speaker was Dr Bagadeuce, St Agatha's Fellow in Mathematics. Imogen realised that she was indeed trembling, though whether it was with anger or not she hardly knew. She never recalled being the object of such hatred before in her entire life. She let Dr Bagadeuce accompany her to the Combination Room, and pour her a whisky – it would be silly to try to ride her bicycle home when feeling so agitated.

'What a contemptible lout he is,' said Bagadeuce. 'You must try to ignore him. He richly deserves his fate.'

'I suppose he does; if we are all quite sure . . .'

'He's done it before, you know.'

'Done it before?'

'Cheating. It's addictive. Or rather, it is when you get away with it. He was in trouble over his A level papers. The exam syndics gave him the benefit of the doubt.'

'What was wrong with his A levels?' Imogen asked.

'A couple of folded pages. Crucial pages.'

'Did the Court of Discipline know that?'

'Oh, no. We try to proceed fairly. In a court of law, as you know, a previous record is inadmissible; and this one was a doubt, not a certainty. He would have cried persecution all the way to the Court of Human Rights in

Strasbourg . . . In the Middle Ages we could have tarred and feathered him, and quite right too!'

Imogen was rapidly getting over her own trauma, and focusing her attention on her companion. Surely that last remark was a little over the top? He must have seen her looking at him curiously, for he said, 'Some of us love the college, Miss Quy, and serve it all our lives. To see its good name dragged in the mud . . .'

Imogen looked up sharply. His face was set. She thought he might not be joking. 'Surely nobody will blame the college?' she said, gently. 'Such an action is a personal one, nothing to do with anything any other member of college has done or not done. Neither his supervisor nor his tutor could have known what he was thinking of doing . . .'

'I suppose you are right,' he said. 'In these dishonourable days such crimes are quickly forgotten. And at least, this time, it was only a junior member of college . . .'

'This time?' said Imogen in astonishment, whereupon Dr Bagadeuce coloured slightly, and bit his lip. Then he said, 'I hope you are sufficiently recovered? It is getting rather late.'

'I'm fine now,' she told him. 'Thank you for your kindness.'

Whereupon he got up and left.

'This time?' Imogen thought. *'When was the last time?'* But she was weary of thinking about cheating. She finished her drink and went home, pushing her bike rather than riding it through the dusk.

The house when she reached it was empty and dark. No lights on in the upstairs flat, no friendly elephantine footfalls, or tuneless singing drifting down the stairwell. The tenants Imogen had to keep loneliness at bay, even the well-loved Fran, were an uncertain quantity. Of course,

Fran was away; Imogen could have gone too if it had not been for the wretched Court of Discipline. Imogen lit the fire, and then put the kettle on. She picked the freesheet off the doormat, and sat down with it at the breakfast-room table with her cup of tea. There was a knock at the door. Imogen got up reluctantly, and opened it to Josh.

'Oh, come in Josh. I've just made a cup of tea. How do you like it?'

'With no tea, sugar or milk, and lots of gin and tonic,' he said grinning.

'Cadge,' she said. 'Rotter. Why do I put up with you?'

'We have a lot in common,' he said.

'Oh? What's that, then? Ice?'

'Yes please. We are both devoted to Fran. Me in a predatory, and you in a maternal mode.' He sat himself in the battered armchair. 'And talking of Fran, I dropped in to ask you if she happened to mention to you when she would be back from the goose chase.'

'No,' said Imogen, frowning as she tried to remember. 'No, she didn't. She asked me to go with her, and she mentioned a few days, but I didn't think to ask how many were a few. Didn't she tell you?'

'She said she didn't know how long it would take.'

'How long what would take? Did you say wild goose chase?'

'Yes I did. She was looking for a village in Wales.'

'Which village in Wales?'

'She didn't know. The one in which the cursed Summerfield spent a few days in 1978.'

'What made her think he went somewhere in Wales?'

'That Melanie had a dim recollection that it might have been . . .'

'Josh, how in heaven's name did she mean to find which village? Did she have some clues?'

'She was going to drive around in her father's car, borrowed for the occasion, and scrabble around in hotel registers . . .'

'I shouldn't think hotels keep their registers that long . . . But surely we can just ask Bullion père how long he lent the car for?'

'He's abroad for three months. That's why the car was available.'

'Well, she left the day before yesterday. She had to pick up the car . . . It's early to be worrying yet, Josh.'

'Oh, I'm not worrying yet. I'm just wondering when I should start to worry. Well, the truth is, I thought she might have phoned.'

'I would have thought she might have phoned you,' said Imogen. 'I wouldn't have expected her to phone me.'

'Well, the truth is . . .' said Josh. He was looking very unhappy. 'We had a little spat just before she left. So she might not phone me while she's still feeling cross. And the longer it takes her to find her village in Wales the crosser she might get . . . I wish she would phone. Or come back. I hate being cross. I want to make it up with her.'

Imogen looked at him sympathetically. Of course he didn't like being separated from Fran in the middle of a quarrel; she could remember only too well what such tribulations felt like when one was young . . .

'What was the spat about, Josh?' she asked. 'Was it serious?'

'Not at all. Perfectly stupid. I just suggested that the trip was ridiculous. Over the top. Unlikely in the extreme to be worth it. Impossible. You get the idea. I said I would go with her to the ends of the earth if the end in question had a grid reference. Was precisely specified. I would go with her to any particular village in Wales. But not to an unspecified one . . . She told me to please myself, and left.'

'Hmmph. More gin?'

'No thank you; too much is depressive rather than bracing. Look, could I ask you – would you let me know if she writes, phones, returns to base?'

'Certainly. Would you do the same for me?'

'I haven't got you worrying now? You always seem so sensible . . .'

'Like you, I'm not worried yet. And the sensible demeanour is a cunning disguise. Designed to conceal a tender heart, a paranoid tendency and insane ambition to be beloved of all who know me . . .'

Josh laughed, and gave her a peck on the cheek as he left.

Those who worry, of course, do so most in the small hours. Imogen lay awake, thinking. Fran was such a sensible girl, really, in spite of her wild enthusiasms, and passionate statements of principle. She was just what a sensible but not insensitive person *would* be when young. Could she really be scouring Wales without any clues at all to where to look? Imogen concluded that something somebody had said to Fran must have offered a clue. Wales, after all, was an extensive principality. Bitterly she resented the Court of Discipline which had prevented her from going with Fran; Fran would have confided in her, and they would have been pleasantly occupied in the quest together. That wretched boy! Cheating is a miserable sort of crime, Imogen reflected, and an odd one; not like straightforward theft or GBH. The most likely victim of such a crime is the perpetrator himself. Or herself, of course.

Unavoidably now, as she lay sleepless, she was turning over the cheating incident in her mind. Had she been right to assert so categorically that paracetamol could not possibly give someone a high? What if it had that effect in combination with other things – the boy might have been taking other things? Sighing, resigning herself to her own inability to forget it and get some sleep, Imogen got up, put on her faded tartan dressing-gown and her sheepskin slippers, and plodded downstairs.

The Family Medical dictionary confirmed her in what she had said to the Court. It did not mention interactions, malign or otherwise. Imogen went through to the kitchen, and helped herself to a stack of three chocolate digestives, and a glass of milk. The house felt forlorn. She *hated* living in an empty house. And how silly she was being! If Fran had been there, the house would still have been dark and silent at this hour, and Imogen would not have considered waking her up to chat! But then if Fran had been there, Imogen would probably have been fast asleep herself.

Still cross with herself, Imogen went into the spare room, and hauled out from the bottom drawer of a chest of drawers a battered cardboard folder containing her notes on toxicology, made during her nursing training. Below the familiar folder was another – labelled 'Old notes on Tox'. It came from Imogen's years of training as a doctor, before she abandoned her career for love . . . She took both files downstairs, and lit the gas fire to sit beside. The American clock that her father had so loved ticked encouragingly in the quiet room, counting while the fire steadily hissed. An owl hooted a little way off; it must be hunting in the trees along the river bank.

'Poor mouse,' thought Imogen.

There was very little about paracetamol in Imogen's nursing notes – or at least very little except recommendations of it as a pain killer, all the way from arthritis to z-plasty. She turned to the other folder, and pulled out a stack of sheets of paper, written over in a handwriting that no longer looked like her own. Aconite, antiseptics, barbiturates, DNOC . . . Imogen was about to turn the page. DNOC. Weedkiller and insecticide. At one time used to treat obesity. Absorption through the skin, as well as by injection or inhalation . . . initial feelings of well-being, followed by fatigue, thirst, hyperpyrexia, convulsions, coma and death . . .

Imogen read this entry several times, and then went, thoughtful, back to bed, where paradoxically she fell asleep at once.

In Imogen's life housework was an activity of last resort.
She did quite a lot of it, because she hated living in an
untidy house. The last resort was resorted to quite often,
in fact. Hoovering the stairs was the very worst job – quite
hard work, involving heaving the heavy vacuum cleaner
up and down three flights, and clumsy – the damn thing
wouldn't stand on a stair while you used it, being just
too large and heavy . . . and in a mistaken fit of design
consciousness, Imogen had chosen a plain stair-carpet in
soft moss green, which showed every speck of either light
or dark coloured dirt. Fran's few days in Wales had now
extended to five, without a phone call to Josh, and Imogen
was wrestling with the vacuum cleaner, and wondering why
all dirt was always either lighter or darker than the surface
it fell upon . . . She started at the top of the stairs, and while
she was up there Hoovered Fran's rugs, and then worked
her way down, slightly out of breath, and miserable, and
cross.

Dust accumulated on the white-painted woodwork, the
moulding of the angled skirting boards that ran down
beside the stairs, between the turned banister rails, on
every pleasant detail of the Victorian house. Imogen ran
the snout of the vacuum cleaner over the paintwork, which
was quicker than using a duster, and nearly as efficient.
Towards the bottom of the stairs, when she had worked
her way backwards almost into the hall, there was a little

fragment of paper sitting on the skirting among the dust. Imogen zapped it with the crevice-cleaner tool on the end of the cleaner hose. It stayed put. She tried again, and then realised it was not a tiny piece of paper irresistibly stuck to the base of the wall, but the corner of a larger piece that had fallen behind the skirting, and was protruding by a bare quarter inch. She tried to ease it out, gripping it by her finger nail, but she couldn't do it. She put the vacuum cleaner down, and went to her work-box for a pair of tweezers.

It was a postcard, or something. The skirting board had parted from the wallplaster by a quarter inch or so – such are the ways of old houses – and whatever it was had slipped into the gap. Not a postcard – a photograph. A scuffed, creased photograph with battered corners, a greyish black-and-white print. It showed a group of people leaning against a farm gate. They were very small – there was a lot of background. A man with string round his trousers below the knees, holding a hayfork; a young woman in a print dress and wellington boots, and a man in an open-necked shirt and flannels, hands in pockets, standing between the two. Imogen sat on the bottom stair, smoothing the picture and staring at it. At first she couldn't imagine who it was – friends of her parents? But although she didn't Hoover often, the picture surely couldn't have been there that long! In fact how could it have got there? Imogen recollected the papers bursting out of the box in the arms of the delivery man, and falling everywhere in the hall – fluttering through the banisters, skithering down the wall . . . this photo, presumably, lodging unnoticed in the crack between plaster and woodwork . . . Perhaps the corner had been lifted into view by the noisy suck of the crevice nozzle just a moment ago.

The picture might have – must have – come from the

Summerfield papers. The smiling young man was the great Gideon. But Imogen's first thought had been that the photo belonged in the dress box upstairs, on top of her wardrobe – the box full of ancient snapshots taken on dozens of annual holidays on her father's box brownie and its successor simple cameras; and she had thought this because of the familiar, well-loved outline of the mountain in the distance, behind the field-gate with its three figures. Imogen could say within half a mile where the picture had been taken; she had spent her childhood holidays roaming around the Tanat valley while her father fished, and her mother snoozed in a deck chair in the farmhouse garden, her knitting neglected on her lap.

Stamping on the spiralling mist of recollection, Imogen spelled it out to herself. She was possibly looking at evidence of where Summerfield spent the missing month in the long-ago summer. Very probably, really, when you took into account that Fran had never mentioned Wales in connection with him, and yet the picture proved he had been there at least once. Could it be coincidence that Fran had suddenly decided to depart for Wales, and – awful thought – was it coincidence that she had been gone longer than expected? Imogen felt suddenly sick. What could she do? Who could she talk to? Whose help would be any good? Josh? Mike?

Josh first – he might know something.

As it happened, he didn't. He should have asked Fran if she had any clue to help her in searching the principality, and he hadn't.

'You see, she couldn't have seen this –' said Imogen, waving the photograph. 'So if she did have a lead it was something else.'

Josh shook his head. 'I just don't know,' he said. 'But

141

it feels all wrong. She's not vindictive – usually we make things up in a few hours. I really thought she would have rung me by now . . .'

Imogen put in her hours at the College, and then went to see Mike. They showed her into his office, where the filing cabinets towered above and around him, and a glass screen offered precarious privacy from the next-door office. Mike shared the tiny space with an officer called Robinson who looked up, nodded briefly, and went back to his form-filling.

'People don't get to be missing persons until they're most definitely missing,' said Mike, when Imogen had told him her story. 'But I don't like the feel of this much; not in the light of what you tell me, and what you say about other biographers of this chap. Even so, most likely she's just happily perusing her researches, or she's even on her way home right now.'

'There's only one hotel in the valley,' Imogen told him. 'And the pub. But there are dozens and dozens of people doing bed and breakfast. The local policeman . . .'

'What powers you credit me with!' said Mike. 'I don't know any of the many thousands of policemen in Wales. But all right, I'll see what informal channels might reveal. Satisfied?'

'Too worried,' said Imogen, smiling at him wanly. 'But grateful.'

Imogen knew, really, that she would have to go herself. She would have to drive herself there, put up in the pub, ask questions, discover if Fran had been, or was still, in the valley. If nothing was wrong she would find Fran easily, and Fran would be furious with her; the last row would be nothing compared to the fury that would be visited on a landlady who followed her tenants around, leaning

on them worse than the bossiest and most impossible parent
. . . but until she did something about it she wasn't going
to sleep at nights. Why hadn't she panicked at once, and
gone in pursuit earlier? The mere fact that earlier there
hadn't yet been enough rational cause for alarm didn't
in the least convince her now.

She set about preparing to go. She told the bursar of
St Agatha's that she was taking a few days' leave, and
arranged with her semi-retired friend Mary to work her
college hours for her – after all it was full term. She told
Lady B. what she was doing. She told Shirl and Pansy that
she would miss the next sewing session; she cancelled the
milk. She packed a suitcase, locked the back door, and
opened the front door to carry her case to her car, which
lived parked outside the front garden, under a street light.
Mike was standing at her gate.

'I rather thought you might,' he said. 'I wish you
wouldn't.'

'How can there be no good cause for alarm about Fran,
and any cause to worry about me?' Imogen asked him
crisply.

'I didn't come to argue,' he said. 'I'm on my way home
for my grub. I came to tell you she isn't in the hotel or the
pub, and that PC Emlyn Jones is on the lookout for her
or anyone answering her description. OK?'

Imogen could almost feel pallor spreading over her
cheeks. So long as every responsible adult around her
was refusing to take the thing seriously she could calmly
with the upper part of her mind regard it as an internal
truth only; something that was in a way a game of her
own. If Mike was suddenly listening to her then with a
leap the sense of danger sprang nearer.

'There isn't a law against going to Wales,' Imogen said,
trying for her usual robustly independent tone.

'Story of my life, that,' said Mike. 'When anyone wants a bit of unofficial help it's oh, Mike, dear Mike, couldn't you just, Mike? And the next minute it's the letter of the law and my advice isn't wanted, thank you very much. Just make sure you phone me every day, my girl, or I'll have PC Emlyn Jones after you like a flash, law or no law. Got it?'

'Mike, I'm very sorry, I didn't mean . . .' she said, but he was stomping away down the pavement back to his car, saying 'hmmph!' over his shoulder. He grinned at her over the open driver's door as he got in, and waved.

Suddenly sure that if she didn't go at once she might think better of it, Imogen swung her case on to the back seat, ran back to check that she had locked the front door, and drove herself away.

She didn't like motorways. England spooled past her windscreen, looking for many miles almost as she remembered it from long ago. It had always been a long journey from Cambridge. She had set out with her mother and father, Thermos flask propped in a wicker basket, rugs tucked round their knees, luggage roped to a roofrack that whistled in the wind as they drove, the road atlas – a pre-war job bound in crumbling leather, open on her mother's lap. She was always car-sick. The remembered nausea was the one thing she didn't regret in the memories – car-sickness had disappeared for good when she learned to drive.

West of Cambridge the landscape is self-effacing and gentle. The church spires rise from the trees which cluster in the villages, having been banished from the sweeping gentle undulations of the vast open fields. The chalky pallor of the ploughed and combed soils shows off the almost fluorescent green of the winter wheat. The skies were full of little woolly clouds, as though the heavens regretted the lack of earthly sheep . . . Of course, something was wrong; less birdsong,

fewer wild flowers in the verges than she remembered;
Milton Keynes had once been nothing but fields, a mere
name on a signpost; and the A5, while no doubt becoming
safer, was losing the quality of the great Telford road that
swept through England and Wales to Holyhead; the little
toll-houses standing mud-spattered and forlorn on one
side or the other of the dualled and thundering roadways.
Further along the road the landscape changed, the western
configurations of hill and farms, less crop, more livestock,
less anxious churches content with modest towers among
the surrounding hills. Imogen was soothed. This quiet land
of village and green and pub, this landscape cultivated in
several senses, was a gentle law-abiding place in which,
surely, hardly anything ever really happened, and serial
murder was diminishingly rare.

She stopped in Shrewsbury, and found a pub supper,
and was quite startled to find the conversation in the bar
all about cattle rustling. Peaceful appearances could be
deceptive anywhere, it seemed. What was that Housman
poem her father used to quote?

> *High the vanes of Shrewsbury gleam*
> *Islanded in Severn Stream*
> *The bridges from the steepled crest*
> *Cross the water east and west.*
>
> *The flag of Morn, in conqueror's state,*
> *Enters at the English gate.*
> *The vanquished eve as night prevails,*
> *Bleeds upon the road to Wales.*

And indeed she drove on into a spectacular conflagration
that made driving difficult as the setting sun blinded west-
bound drivers. At Oswestry she stopped for the night.

The bed-and-breakfast place she remembered from so long ago was still in business with quite different owners, just as shabby and comfortable as before. Imogen fended off night-thoughts by sitting in the family living-room, watching television with the grandparents until she could hardly keep her eyes open.

16

The valley was entirely familiar, deeply etched on Imogen's younger mind. She had both remembered, and forgotten it. What she had remembered was the appearance of the valley, and the mountainside, the stout, four-square houses, the Methodist chapels painted black and white, the tumbling river winding noisily along the valley floor, the very shapes of the shadows cast across the road by the looming heights that made up the southern wall of the valley. This escarpment stood permanently in the light, its steep north-facing sides dark all day long, all year round. What she had forgotten was how she felt about the place; the tension between pleasure at the beauty, and claustrophobia; how could people bear to live on the shadowy side of the valley?

She was sharply aware of why she had never, since her parents' death, returned here. And yet she had been happy here as a child. At the head of the valley the road wound over the pass to Vyrnwy, and the village came into view. Wildly unexpected, the little terrace rows of Victorian houses stood on the hillside in stripes, as though a thoughtless child had left his toys scattered. No rural beauty; above the rows of houses the slate quarry left the gouged and broken holes and mounds of spoil heaps, grey in sunlight, navy-blue in rain. And here was the pub where, Imogen remembered, flinching, from her adolescence, the language at the bar changed from English to Welsh as a stranger entered, and changed back again as they rose to leave.

She had a little trouble finding the farm she had stayed in as a child. The road had been straightened at the foot of the mountain, and the well-remembered hair-raising bends had become milder. By and by she found her way. The farmyard was as muddy and richly odorous as ever, and a pleasant young woman was working, feeding the pigs, who crowded along the trough outside the sties. An old horse looked over his stable-door, and harrumphed.

'I'm very sorry,' she said, smiling at Imogen. 'But there's no bed and breakfast here now. You would find somewhere in the village, easy.'

'I'm an old guest here,' said Imogen. 'My name is Quy, Imogen Quy. My parents used to spend every summer here . . .'

'Why, goodness!' said the woman. 'Imo, is it? Don't you remember me? I'm Gwenny!'

'Gwenny! – Heavens, Gwenny!' said Imogen, astonished. Gwenny had been a little, bird-boned creature, scampering everywhere – and now she was a tall, hefty, muscular figure, with bronzed arms, and stout, reddened working hands.

'You will have tea, now,' said Gwenny firmly, leading Imogen indoors.

The farmhouse was changed considerably less than Gwenny. Dark and cool, with low beams, a deep window-seat in the mullioned window bay, covered in tatty cushions, and bearing a sleeping dog at one end, and a sleeping cat at the other. The floor was made of great slabs of local slate. An iron range filled the huge chimney nook, with five doors shut on the ovens, and one open to flood the room with warmth from the fire. In front of the fire Gwenny's dad sat rocking in his elaborate old chair, reading a newspaper. His slippered feet were propped on another sleeping dog.

'Look who's here, Dad,' said Gwenny. 'Do you remember Imo?'

The old man looked at Imogen steadily with watery eyes. Then he heaved himself up from his chair, and reached for a photograph from the mantelpiece. He handed it to Imogen, who found herself looking at a picture of herself in a cotton sunhat, no more than three feet tall, throwing hay in the air with a tiny garden fork. Behind her rows of men worked with real hayforks, her father one of them. Memory flooded back to her, bringing the scent of hay, and the smart of sunburn on her back. The crossed straps of her summer dress had been stamped on her painful skin in white, she remembered . . .

Gwenny took the simmering iron kettle from a hot ring, and was already wetting the tea.

'We thought you would be coming back,' the old farmer said, replacing the photograph between a studio portrait of his dead wife, and a snapshot of a prize-winning pig, with a ribbon from the Oswestry show pinned to the frame. 'Long enough, you've been about it.' He regarded her critically. 'You have a good colour for a city lass,' he said. 'None of that pasty look, I'm glad to see.'

Gwenny put up an ancient little gate-legged table, and spread a white cloth over it. A stout brown teapot accompanied bone china cups, delicate and pretty. Flapjacks and scones and jam were set out, before Gwenny announced 'elevenses' but the old man grumbled bitterly at the absence of gingerbread. 'Not a patch on your mother at the housekeeping, Gwenny,' he said.

Imogen sat in the chair brought up for her, and tried not to eat too much of the elevenses. She and Gwenny had serious talking to do. Little by little she led the talk round to Fran.

'No,' said Gwenny. 'No, I haven't heard of anyone just

recently. Dad? There hasn't been anyone in the valley, isn't it?'

'There might've been someone at the Doctor's, Gwenny,' he said.

'True enough. There's a doctor has the old cowman's cottage, down the English road a bit – you remember, Imo, where old Williams used to live – he has people staying with him, and nobody knows about it unless they come up to the shop, or a meal in the Fisherman's Rest. But there – the doctor is from Cambridge, Dad; Imo will know all about him and his friends. There's nowhere else could have a stranger staying without we knew all about it, Imo, except perhaps in August when it's people by the three dozen coming here. It will be some other valley she's in.'

'She would be looking for somewhere where someone might remember a holiday maker from long ago. Someone called Dr Summerfield. The name doesn't ring a bell with you, Gwenny?'

'Dr Summerfield? No. Sorry, Imo. Unless – a lady doctor, is it? There's someone comes bothering the Evanses now and then.'

'I wonder if she's anyone I know?'

'She wouldn't be a friend of yours, Imo, she's a menace, so she is. An antique dealer lady. She won't take no for an answer, but pesters, and pesters, and keeps coming back. Harassing people . . .'

'Well, the one I'm thinking of isn't an antique dealer. Has this person been harassing you, Gwenny?'

'Not me. Evans. Up at Quarry Farm. Over and over.'

'Funny you should mention Quarry Farm,' said Imogen, producing the battered photograph from her bag. 'Where would you think this was taken, Gwenny? Up that way somewhere, I should think. It might be a clue to what my friend Fran is looking for.'

'That's the gate to Evans' three acre top field,' said Gwenny without hesitating. 'And there won't be any English up there, Imo. They won't have them set foot on their land. Funny, that,' she added, sipping her tea, 'when you think that old Granny Evans was English. Wasn't she, Dad?'

'Old David Evans took his sheep down to Shrewsbury Fair just after the war, and came back with a wife,' said the old man. 'Talk of the valley, it was. She couldn't speak a word of the language, and the Evans hadn't a word of English.'

'How did she manage?' asked Imogen.

'She learned,' he said. 'That was a fine woman. Gone now,' he sighed. 'She could *swear* in Welsh, something frightful!' he said, grinning. 'What a trimegant! The Evanses were all chapel, and she was Church. She'd have the pony trap every Sunday, and gallivant off to church, and all the rest of the family would have to walk to chapel. Talk of the valley, in her day . . .'

He meandered off into recollection of his youth.

Imogen realised that when he had described a wife brought into the valley 'just after the war' he had meant the First World War. He would have gone on all day, wool-gathering, lost in recollection, but she gently extricated herself after an hour.

Gwenny walked with her to the gate.

'I would make up a bed for you, and you could stay here, where you belong,' she offered, but Imogen could see that one pair of hands would be overworked already, without guests.

'Thank you, Gwenny, but I'm booked in at the Inn,' she said.

'I hope they air the sheets down there,' said Gwenny suspiciously. 'You'll catch a chill . . .'

'I'll be fine!' said Imogen. 'Gwenny, you don't happen to know the name of the Doctor who has Williams' cottage now?'

'Funny, but I don't,' said Gwenny. 'He gets called "Happy Chappy", or "The English" mostly. I haven't ever seen him myself. He isn't here much.

'You know what rich English are like, buying the place up to use it like a holiday camp . . . Happy Chappy, that's what he's called. I hope you find your friend, Imo.

'And don't go home without coming for another cuppa, will you? Makes a change for Dad. He likes to talk to people.'

17

It came on to rain in the afternoon. Imogen looked in the boot of her car for warm waterproof clothing. She found a good Aran sweater, one she had knitted herself long ago, and her bicycle cape – capacious and hooded. She was going to look like a walking tent wearing these, but what was the point of vanity so far from home? She left the car pulled off on the verge of the main road, and began to tramp up the muddy track to Quarry Farm. What was it, she wondered as she walked, the ladies of Cranford had said? What was the point of vanity at home, where everybody knows us? And what was the point of vanity in town where nobody knows us? Something like that.

The Evanses had certainly barricaded their farm. A sequence of gates across the track as it rose up the valley side were padlocked, and crested with spirals of barbed wire. Warning notices decorated the stiles. NO ENTRY. TRESPASSERS WILL BE PROSECUTED. KEEP OUT. VISITORS BY EXPRESS APPOINTMENT ONLY. DANGER – SHOOTING. WARNING – FIERCE DOGS AT LARGE. These signs would have been more alarming had each one not been accompanied by another, saying, in Welsh, 'Come on up'.

It was Imogen's smattering of Welsh that led to her not taking the signs seriously enough. She could see the farm, snuggled into the mountainside some way above her, a dozen trees planted round it for shelter, its barns and yard between her and the house. She doggedly climbed the stiles, and ignored the notices. When she had still a quarter of a mile or so to go she heard a shout, far off. She stopped and looked around. A man was standing at the entrance to the farmyard, looking down the track towards her and shouting. She waved and continued towards the last gate.

When he fired his gun she stopped. He had not aimed at her; just discharged the thing into the air. He was shouting again. She cupped her hands around her mouth, and yelled back, 'I need to talk to you!'

'Get out!' he was yelling. 'You'll be sorry! Get out!'

Imogen tried shouting *'Boro da!'* but it's hard to sound inoffensive and friendly when calling across another mountainside at a distance of a quarter of a mile. She took a few uncertain steps forward, and then she saw the dogs. Not the familiar black-and-white sheep dogs, with their narrow sharp-eyed faces, and harmless barking at strangers; these were huge black dogs, of uncertain breed. The man had let them out of the barn – the door was standing wide now – and they were hurtling downhill towards her. Imogen's courage failed her, and she turned and ran.

It was only a few paces back to the last stile; Imogen would have made it, even encumbered by her flapping cycle cape, if she hadn't tripped and fallen. She caught her foot in a hummock of grass and went flying. The wrench shot daggers of pain through her ankle – she heard the bone snap – and then the dogs were upon her. One of them sunk its teeth in her forearm, snarling and dragging at her – the other had got a grip on her cape and was tearing at it and snarling. Terrified, and in agony, trying to wrap her face in her free arm, Imogen heard human cries, and a sequence of high-pitched whistles. The dogs released her arm and clothing and raced away. She tried to sit up, and fainted.

When she came to she was being carried. Someone had hold of her by her armpits, and someone else by the knees, walking between her legs. Every step jolted her painfully. Her left hand was warm and sticky. The two who were carrying her were talking together – urgent, agitated voices, rather short of breath, presumably from the effort of carrying her uphill.

'Mother will kill you for this, Daffyd!' said the voice at her head.

'I didn't know, see! I thought it was *her*!' said the other. Then one of them stumbled, and the flash of pain in her leg was followed by oblivion.

It felt like a long time later when she came round again. She was propped on a sofa, in a dark, warm kitchen with a huge old range, and battered table and chairs very like Gwenny's. Her leg was up on the sofa, held between cushions. Her arm was dangling, her hand immersed in a bowl of warm blood. She frowned down at this ghoulish sight, and finally worked out that it was a bowl of warm water, into which her arm was steadily bleeding.

The same voice as before was saying, 'I thought it was *her*, see!'

'But it's a little, thin woman she is!' said a woman's voice, crossly.

'She was wearing a cape sort of thing, Mother. Made her look large enough . . .'

'We are in trouble now, right enough, whatever she looked like! What are we to do with her now?' said 'Mother'.

'Phone Gwenny Floyd, and ask her to come and fetch me,' said Imogen. Immediately she had spoken she felt a heaving sensation, and leaning over her bloody bowl she was very sick.

'You are a friend of Gwenny's is it?' said the woman. She was almost crying with vexation. 'Whatever will people think about us? There's crazy, those boys are!'

Imogen was beginning to shiver violently. Her teeth rattled together in her head. She looked at her ankle, which was aching in a somehow sinister way, and saw that it was thick and swollen. She was going to need a doctor. A high-pitched humming sound was ringing in her ears – someone had left a untuned radio set on, and she wondered why they didn't turn it off.

The cross woman brought her a clean bowl of warm water, and then a cup of tea, and a warm wet towel. Imogen shook her head.

'Sip it and you'll feel a little better, my dear,' she said.

'I need a doctor,' said Imogen.

'Help is coming, don't you worry,' the woman said.

'Have you got a bandage?' asked Imogen faintly. 'My arm is bleeding.'

'I'll bind it up for you in a minute,' the woman said. 'But better let bites bleed for a little first . . .'

She could be right, Imogen thought. A flow of blood being the best way to clean a deep puncture like a dog bite . . . The hot sweet tea was right for shock too, though not if she was going to need an anaesthetic. She was woozing gently, in and out of consciousness perhaps. It occurred to her that the high-pitched hum was in her own head.

It was later again. There were voices around her.

'. . . and to cap it all, she's a friend of Gwenny's' – that was 'Mother' who sounded so cross with her menfolk, and so kind to Imogen. 'Whatever am I going to say to Gwenny?'

Then a new voice, saying, 'Just thank your lucky stars, Mrs Owen, that it isn't worse. I'll be able to make her comfortable. The problem is the bites. She will need a tetanus injection right away—'

'My tetanus protection is up to date,' said Imogen.

'Ho, ho, a sensible woman, and wide awake, I see,' the

doctor said. 'Good, good. In that case we don't need to move you. Now, I'm going to put a splint on your tibia, and I have to get it quite straight first. So just a little painkiller . . .' He produced a surprisingly large syringe with a little clear liquid in it. Imogen flinched at the sight of it, and then braced herself – how often had she silently accused a patient of cowardice? Very gently and efficiently he emptied the syringe into her uninjured arm, and she slid into peaceful and total oblivion.

She awoke in a very large bed, under a sloping ceiling. A hefty oak chest of drawers stood against the wall on her left, with a mirror hanging behind it. The bedside table was adorned with a lace mat, and had a tea tray on it, with a cup of tea standing in its saucer. Imogen could see it was cold without moving to touch it – it had a brown scummy surface. The sun was pouring through the window in the dormer and it was already late – the light had the brightness of mid-morning. Very gingerly Imogen tried to move – first her arm, which she at once felt was bandaged. It was sore, and the bottom of the bandage was anchored round her thumb, but all her fingers moved freely, and it didn't hurt too much. Even more carefully she tried moving her leg. There was a splint on it below the knee, and it hurt enough to make her stop. She looked at the ceiling for a while, and then moving very slowly, shifted herself up on to the pillows a bit, so that she could see round the room. At once her attention was drawn to the patchwork quilt under which she was lying.

It entirely covered the huge bed. It was in soft and faded colours – pinks, white, lilacs, blues, pale greens and browns. It had only two shapes – fat diamonds and skinny diamonds. Imogen stared at it appreciatively. 'Where's the repeat?' she wondered. As sleepiness ebbed away she looked

more carefully. And she couldn't find it. She kept thinking
there was an area where the pattern repeated, and then
noticing that one or two pieces were different . . .

The quilt was a masterwork. It had no repeat; it could
not have been made conveniently block by block; it had
been sewn in a single mind-blowing piece, each little patch
stitched to the whole. What Imogen kept seeing in the
swirling kaleidoscope of colours and patterns – she could
see no two pieces the same – was ghostly shapes, a sort of
irregular seven-sided shape which appeared in the pattern,
and disappeared the moment you looked closely. A ghostly
heptagon – a non-repeating pattern . . . *What was it Fran
had said?* Imogen sat up abruptly, ignoring the pain in her
leg, her scalp prickling and her spine shivering. Suddenly
she knew exactly where Gideon Summerfield had spent his
missing weeks of that long ago August; she knew why that
was a secret worth killing for. And when you know why
you know who. Or so Mike once said.

There was a knock on her door, and Mrs Evans came in,
carrying a tray. 'You don't look so bad, now,' Mrs Evans
said. 'I brought you breakfast in bed. And to explain . . .'

Imogen felt astonishingly eager for the breakfast. Thick
creamy porridge with sugar and milk; a rack of toast with
butter and marmalade . . . a pot of tea.

'Let me guess,' she said cheerfully. 'You've had a lot of
trouble with someone trying to buy this quilt. Someone
called Janet Summerfield, right?'

Janet Summerfield had given them no peace. She had tried
asking; she had tried offering lots of money. She had
tried threats, of the 'You'll be sorry . . .' kind. She had tried
cheating. Well, they were almost certain it was her doing –
a woman had turned up saying she was from a museum of
textile arts in Nottingham, and trying to get them to lend

the quilt for an exhibition. But they were not foolish; they had telephoned the tourist office in Nottingham asking for a number for the Textile Arts Museum, and found that there wasn't one. Then there were three break-ins to the farmhouse – all on market days, when everyone was out of their houses, but Mrs Evans had hidden the quilt by then; putting it away in the dower chest together with her mother's jewellery whenever she went anywhere.

'The dower chest is too heavy to steal, see, Miss Quy, and it has a hefty old lock on it too. The burglars had a try the third time they came, but they only scarred the wood a bit.'

'Do call me Imo,' said Imogen. 'It's Gwenny's name for me.'

'In the end we told her we would set the dogs on her next time she set foot up here,' said Mrs Evans. 'And she must have believed us; she hasn't tried again for nearly four years now. I'm sorry our Hugh thought you were her, truly I am. He isn't too bright, Miss . . . Imo. And she gave him such a bad time, see, he's jumpy about her.'

'What did she do to him?'

'She locked him in her garage. Then she put a kidnapper's note through the door here, saying he'd be safe if the quilt was put in a binbag beside the road, after dark. Silly, it was. Everyone knew where he would be if she had got him; there's only the one garage in the valley with a door that locks. And there's only her that's batty about the quilt, see? PC Jones went and got our Hugh back, easy. She hadn't been cruel, mind; he had blankets, and plenty of food in there. But he was frightened.'

'Naturally he was,' said Imogen.

'So when he saw you coming he thought you were after him . . .'

'Don't worry about it,' said Imogen. 'It was a mistake.

It's forgotten about. Just tell me about the quilt. Who made it?'

'Granny Vi made it. The house is full of quilts, Imo, but she always prided herself on this one. It's on the spare bed to keep it from too much wear, see.'

'It is magnificent,' said Imogen. 'And quite old, I imagine. Do you know when it was made?' But Imogen didn't need Holly's lecture to tell her that the quilt was older than Gideon Summerfield's precious piece of geometry.

'It must have been before the war. I can't remember the spare room without it,' said Mrs Evans. 'And I don't want to let it go, you see, not for ever so much money. She offered us five thousand pounds – *five thousand*! And Mr Evans would have taken it, just to get rid of her, but I wouldn't have it. It's my word goes inside the house, and his in the farmyard, so she didn't get it. And do you know, Imo, all the while, if I thought she liked it, I might have let her have it – goodness knows we could do with the money – but I didn't think she wanted it, somehow. She didn't look at it, like you were doing; how can you want a quilt you don't want to run your eyes over? There, I'm running on and on about it; you'll think we're all batty as owls in the valley.'

'No, I won't,' said Imogen. 'You sound perfectly sane to me. And you are quite right about Janet Summerfield. She doesn't want the quilt. She wants to destroy it. You must never let her have it.'

'Do you know her, then?' said Mrs Evans, eyeing Imogen curiously.

'I've met her. I'm just guessing what she would do with the quilt.'

'But your guess is the same as mine. I can see why Gwenny likes you. She'll be over to see you as soon as she can, by the way.'

'Did the doctor say I could get up?' asked Imogen.

'That wasn't the doctor. There isn't a doctor till Bala one way, and fifteen miles the other. That was the vet. I'll ring him and ask him.'

But just for now Imogen was glad to have the breakfast tray removed from her knees, and to wriggle down again into a comfortable position, and lie back against the pillows. She contemplated the quilt, timeworn into a state of exquisite delicacy, and wondered how it had been planned and sewn. In its Venetian frailty and beauty it seemed to her to be as much an object of desire and joy as an impressionist painting, or a Greek amphora.

18

The vet thought that if a cow could walk on a bone he had set, then a woman could. Although it was illegal for a doctor to treat a cow, it was perfectly legal for a vet to treat a woman; and as far as Imogen could tell the vet had been both kind and competent. Imogen got up, and made her way downstairs leaning on a borrowed walking stick. The question uppermost in her mind was Fran. She had been giving it careful thought. Fran had not seen the photograph that had, on her chance recognition of it, brought Imogen directly to the valley. She was at large somewhere in Wales, inspecting, or trying to inspect, ancient hotel registers. She would very obviously be in danger – perhaps great danger – if she turned up in this place, asking questions about Summerfield in 1978. Or rather, she would, if she did that, *and Janet Summerfield got to know*. So the first question was where was Janet Summerfield?

Imogen carefully sat herself down at the kitchen table, in the comfortable warmth of the range, and, she hoped, out of the way of Mrs Evans and her daughter, Megan, who were cooking. She leaned on her arm, and immediately stopped, wincing. She asked if either of the two women knew of any visitor to the valley – she was sure there would be a bush telegraph to tell them immediately if Janet Summerfield showed her face there.

They confidently denied all knowledge. Megan Evans had been serving at the hotel bar only last night, and helping in the dining-room. The place was very quiet, she said. Only a few fishermen, and without their wives. 'Wrong time of year for the crowds,' she told Imogen, putting a cup of tea in front of her.

Imogen embarked on a description of Fran. Had either of her hostesses seen or heard tell of anyone like that?

They shook their heads. Any English in the valley, they told her, would be at the Inn, or at Mrs Jones's, who did bed and breakfast, or at the Happy Chappy's cottage. Sometimes he lent it to people, or had friends staying. In summer, mostly. Someone in the village would have heard, they were sure, if anyone had arrived at the cottage. It always got around as soon as dusk fell – you could see the lights down the valley side from various windows in the village. People went to draw their curtains, and they saw at once if there was anyone in down there.

'You keep a watch on the Happy Chappy?' said Imogen, amused.

'Nothing much to do here, except gossip, see?' said Megan, ruefully. 'There's nothing against him.'

'Except he has funny friends,' said her mother.

'This friend of yours; would she have been driving a Rover? An old one? 3.5 litre coupé?' asked Megan.

'Golly, I don't know,' said Imogen, startled. 'I can recognise a Nova, because I drive one, but beyond that . . . and anyway, Fran borrowed her father's car; I never clapped eyes on it. What's a Rover whatdyecallit like?'

'It's women like you,' said Megan, 'that give the sex a bad name. That's a gorgeous car – and someone was driving one here the day before yesterday. I saw it parked in the Inn yard, with half the kids in the school gawking at it over the playground fence.'

'I just don't know what car she was driving,' said Imogen helplessly.

'If it was her,' said Megan, 'then she didn't stop long. Couple of hours, then it had gone.'

'I rather think that's a relief,' said Imogen. 'If harm comes to someone their car stays put . . .'

'There wouldn't be any harm would come to her, here!' said Mrs Evans, sounding shocked. 'There's hearts of gold they are here. Maybe we talk a bit about rich English, but there's no one would hurt a stranger . . .' She stopped in full flood, and flushed as she looked at Imogen, arm bandaged, leg stuck out stiffly splinted beside her chair.

Her embarrassment was cut short by a knock on the door. The new arrival entered without waiting. A policeman, taking off his helmet as he came in, and revealing a shock of carrot-red hair.

He greeted Mrs Evans and Megan with a flood of Welsh, and then turned to Imogen. 'Miss Quy, is it?'

Imogen admitted it.

'You've had a nasty experience, I hear,' he said. 'Sorry to hear that. Will you be thinking of making an official complaint?'

'No,' said Imogen. 'I will not. I have had an apology, and a good deal of care and kindness, and that will be that.'

He put away his notebook and pencil, and sat down at the kitchen table, tenderly putting his helmet down beside him, two-handed. 'How are you feeling, now?' he asked Imogen. 'Over the shock, are you?'

'More or less,' Imogen said.

A plate of scones, a dish of jam and a pot of tea had appeared beside the policeman as if by magic, and Megan and her mother retreated to the far end of the kitchen and busied themselves.

'I might have bad news for you, see,' the policeman said, demolishing a scone with two large bites. 'We have found a body. A woman's body.'

165

'Please – no!' said Imogen softly. A horrible feeling of dragging flow was spreading over her – face, guts, limbs, as though the shock had liquefied her and she was draining away.

'When did – the person – die?' she managed to ask at last.

'We don't know, see. Forensic are on their way. But we have some clothing and bits found with the body, and if you could manage to come down to the station with me and identify . . .'

'Yes,' said Imogen. The possibility of action, even such a ghastly action as that, galvanised her. She struggled to her feet, reaching for her stick.

The station was down the valley some way. PC Jones was gentle with Imogen, in a beefy sort of way. He sat her down at a battered wooden table in the back of the station, and offered to wait till a woman PC was available. Imogen said there was no need. He brought a large cardboard crate to the table, and took out of it a sequence of plastic bags, containing a biro, scraps of cloth, sodden fragments of a leather bound diary, a gold watch . . .

'Take your time,' he said. 'Look very carefully, if you please, at each item in turn . . .'

Imogen recognised none of it. With the watch she was quite certain; she had never seen Fran wearing that. Fran's watch was a jolly waterproof plastic thing with Minnie Mouse on the dial. Her relief was almost as debilitating as the shock of dread had been. She found herself trembling, laughing.

'None of this is hers,' she said.

'That's good then,' the policeman said. 'Good news for you, and for Miss Bullion's friends; bad news for someone else.'

He was visibly relaxing, and Imogen realised that he had been bracing himself to deal with her distress had any of the pitiful relics been Fran's. She warmed to him. 'Yes,' she said. 'Is it a case of foul play?'

'Yes indeed,' he told her. 'Very nasty blow to the back of the head.'

'And you can't say when?'

'The body was in a shallow grave in the peat, Miss Quy. Waterlogged ground. Up on the mountain. People always think the mountains will be dry, but they're soaking wet. Bogs all over them. And the peat preserves bodies nicely – been known to keep skin on the bones from the Iron Age till the present. It will take expert forensic to tell us when.'

'How did you find it?'

'Farmer was digging a channel through to dry it off a bit for his sheep.'

'I see.'

'Nobody is going to ask me,' he added, ruefully, 'and you don't like to claim to know, really, based on what happens to dead sheep – people think you're being flippant, see. But I reckon she's been dead maybe eighteen months, two years, that sort of time. And nobody is going to be able to remember a thing about it – not who was in the valley, or who came through, or anything. Police work is very difficult, Miss Quy. Nobody local has gone missing, that I do know; so we will be looking for a missing person in the whole of the bloody kingdom – all fifty million of them.'

'If you're right about the timescale,' Imogen told him, 'try matching your body against the missing persons register for May Swann.'

It took Imogen a little while to organise her return home. She couldn't drive her car; but Lady Buckmote, on being appealed to, joyfully rose to the occasion. She would drive to Shrewsbury, bringing her son ('He might as well make himself useful now he's passed his test,'), and Megan Evans would drive Imogen in her car as far as Shrewsbury, where she would be glad to go shopping. From Shrewsbury Megan would take the bus back up the valley, John Buckmote would drive Imogen's car back to Cambridge, and Imogen and Lady B. would motor home together in comfort. Lady Buckmote could not wait, she said, to hear how a respectable woman like Imogen contrived to be set upon by savage dogs in a remote part of Wales – and in term time, too!

Before leaving Quarry Farm, Imogen took her little camera from the glove box of her car, and got a couple of snapshots of the quilt. Then she and Megan set off for Shrewsbury. The journey started early, with diversion to make a farewell visit to Gwenny, just long enough for Imogen to be weighted down with a bag of scones, a jar of honey, a pot of home-made lemon curd, and fierce admonitions to come back sooner next time.

'Do you know just where they found that body?' Imogen asked Megan, as they drove out of the village.

'Up there – where the tarpaulin is pinned over the ground – do you see it?' Megan waved vaguely to her right, but didn't take her eyes off the road. 'It's right above the cottage.'

'Happy Chappy's?'

'That's it.'

'Megan, exactly what is Happy Chappy called?'

'His real name? I don't know, really. He's always called that. He's a miserable man – really stuck-up – never talks to anyone here, pulls a face if you give him good morning. And one of his friends called to him across the road, some name like 'happy' – 'cheery' or 'jolly' or something, and it sort of stuck. It's sarcastic, you would call it.'

'Did someone tell me he came from Cambridge?'

'I don't know,' said Megan cheerfully. 'From England somewhere, sure enough.'

19

As soon as they were back, Lady B. took Imogen immediately to Addenbrooke's to have her leg X-rayed, and safely plastered up. The casualty officer in Addenbrooke's expressed admiration for the skill with which his colleague in Wales had dealt with the fracture – and all without the benefit of X-ray, as Imogen told him.

'I believe he *is* good,' Imogen agreed. 'Good enough to treat a cow.'

'Oh, he mustn't do that,' said the casualty officer, looking alarmed. 'It isn't legal.'

'Well, of course,' said Imogen, wincing as he removed the splint, 'vets do train much longer than doctors.'

'Relatively simple organisms, people,' he said cheerfully.

'From the neck down, anyway,' she said.

'What? Oh, quite. Hold quite still now . . .'

Imogen's return home, garnished with fresh plaster, still warm, and assisted by Lady B., took on the shape of a great event – she opened the door to a rush from the breakfast room of Josh and Fran, colliding with each other in the hallway, and both talking at once.

'She's been back several days, Imogen, but I didn't know how to let you know . . .'

'Where have you been? *What have you done to yourself?* I've been so worried about you!'

'Since when,' said Imogen, smiling severely at Fran,

'has it been any business of a tenant to worry about a landlady?'

'I'll leave you then, m'dear. I see you're in safe hands,' said Lady B. 'William will be fretting.'

'Thank you,' said Imogen, squeezing Lady B.'s arm before releasing it, and transferring her weight to Fran's extended hand.

And Imogen's injury at least served to divert attention for the moment – it caused Fran and Josh to rush around making her comfortable and fixing a sandwich supper and a mug of chocolate, and gave her time to think carefully what she was going to tell Fran. But for the moment Josh and Fran were too eager to tell her what had been happening to them to pay much attention to exactly how and where and why Imogen had broken a leg.

Fran had relented, it seemed, and phoned Josh almost as soon as Imogen had left in search of her. She had borrowed her father's car.

'I was a bit afraid of it at first, it's a socking great thing with lovely paint work—'

'Is it a Rover 3.5 coupé?' asked Imogen.

'Something like that. I don't know really what it is.'

'Giving the sex a bad name,' said Imogen, obscurely.

Fran ran on: 'Anyway, I trollied round tourist bits of Wales for a while, but it wasn't any good. Nobody could remember him, and the hotels don't keep their registers long enough. Actually I found two that had kept their '78 registers, and it took ages to go through them . . .'

'Fran, what made you think of Wales?'

'Melanie thought that's where it was.'

'Oh, of course.'

'You must be awfully tired, Imogen, what with that long journey, and then going to the bonesetter. We must let you sleep . . .'

But they were still standing there, looking at her expectantly.

'This thing is,' said Josh, 'that Fran didn't realise how upset I would be if she didn't phone. And I didn't realise how upset *she* would be . . . and when we realised we could see, really, that it must be because we were, well, a bit over-sensitive about each other, so we decided . . .'

'. . . to get engaged,' Fran finished for him.

'My dears, I'm so glad!' said Imogen. 'And truly amazed.'

'What's amazing about it?' asked Josh. 'Don't you think we suit each other?'

'You'll do beautifully,' said Imogen. 'I just didn't think people got engaged these days.'

'Well, they don't really. But the thing is,' Fran said, 'we can't get married very soon; we don't see how we can live together till we can afford a place, so we have come to an understanding. And that's an engagement in the language of your generation, isn't it?'

'In my generation,' said Imogen crisply, 'an engagement got announced in *The Times* and led to the purchase of a ring.'

Fran held out her left hand. It was adorned with a Christmas cracker ring, set with a big glass ruby. They all laughed.

'Do something for me, Josh,' said Imogen.

'Anything I can,' said Josh.

'Could you take my camera from the car, and get the film in it developed and printed urgently. I need big prints – seven by fives should do it. The film isn't finished, but you can make the camera rewind, and I don't mind junking the rest of the film.'

'I thought your car was in Wales,' said Josh.

'*WALES?*' said Fran. 'Oh, Imogen!'

'John Buckmote should have brought it back and parked

it outside by now,' said Imogen, avoiding Fran's eye. 'I'm spaced out. I really must go to bed.'

'We'll talk in the morning,' said Fran. 'I can see it wouldn't be humane now.'

Josh, it turned out, presumably anxious not to upset his testy dear one just as things came clear between them, had not told Fran that he had confided in Imogen, or that Imogen had been concerned enough to go in search of her. Fran of course had not seen the photograph. Over breakfast Imogen explained how she had found it, how she had recognised the shape of the hill in the background, how she had driven off . . .

Fran studied the photograph carefully. The great Gideon; Melanie, slender, smiling, leaning against Gideon, and wearing a flowery frock; a farmer; the pale shape of a hill rising behind them.

'So off you went,' said Fran cheerfully. 'What did you find?'

'I'm afraid I might have found May Swann.'

'*May Swann?* What did she have to say for herself?'

'Nothing, I'm afraid. If it was May Swann . . . she was very dead.'

'Dead. And in Wales . . .'

'It becomes clearer by the minute, Fran dear, that we are stumbling around in something very dangerous. Of course the body may not be May Swann's . . . but—'

At that moment there was a cheerful rap on the back door, and Josh bounced in. He tossed on the kitchen table between them a packet of photos, with the logo of a one-hour print service on the envelope.

Imogen opened it while Josh bestowed a good-morning kiss on Fran, and spread the prints out on the table. Only a faint impression of the delicate and subtle beauty of the quilt had survived transformation to glossy photographs. But when Fran disengaged herself and sat down again Imogen had the gratification of seeing her face as she looked at the prints. She picked up the nearest one, and frowned at it.

'This is Gideon's maths,' she said. 'His famous pattern. Made into a quilt. It's beautiful; but how bizarre . . .'

'What perhaps you can't see from a small photo,' Imogen told her, 'is that it's an old quilt.'

'It can't be older than 1979,' said Fran.

'It's much older,' said Imogen. 'Made in the 1920s, I should think.'

'But . . . Imogen what are you saying? And where is this astonishing quilt?'

'It's on the spare bed in Quarry Farm, in the Tanat valley,' said Imogen. 'And I think it tells us very clearly where your Summerfield man spent the summer of '78, and why that is a secret worth killing for. And why a biographer just back from a trip to Wales may be in great danger.'

'We've got to call the police,' said Josh.

'You mean he stole his maths?' said Fran, bemused. She was holding a print in each hand, and staring at them. 'This is it, all right – an as-it-were Penrose tiling, but with ghostly heptagons, instead of pentagons . . . He didn't invent it at all; he lifted it! The rat! And golly, that does explain a sudden rush of brilliance to the head of a nondescript man, which stood to be explained, and which most people who knew him were baffled by! Imogen, this is dynamite! Wait till I tell Prof Maverack!'

A flash of affection accompanied Imogen's dismay. Trust Fran to consider only the impact on her project of a new discovery. A true seeker after truth! But how reckless!

'Fran, you can't tell *anybody*! Certainly not Maverack,

who was once in the Summerfield circle! Haven't you heard
what I'm saying? Listen again . . .'

'Call the police,' said Josh.

'Janet Summerfield has been persecuting the people in
that farmhouse, trying by every means fair or foul to acquire
the quilt,' said Imogen. 'And it's only because it happens to
be in a tight little enclave of Wales, where the English stick
out a mile, and up an unmade track over private land, and
in a farm with guard dogs that she hasn't managed it.'

'She can't get the quilt herself, so she's taken to killing
anyone who comes close to finding out about it?'

'It certainly looks like it, doesn't it?'

'I'll call the police, if you won't,' said Josh. 'I'm not
taking risks with Fran's safety.'

'We need to think. Will police enquiries make Fran any
safer? I'm not sure.'

'She'll be safer if the mad woman is locked up.'

'What I feel like doing straight away,' said Imogen, 'is
talking to my friend Mike Parsons, of the Cambridge police.
Getting his advice. Will you hold your horses till I've done
that, Josh?'

'I suppose.'

'And, Josh, I suddenly don't feel very safe in a house
containing two women. You wouldn't like to move in with
us for the moment, would you, and offer a little manly
protection?'

She watched them exchange glances. Fran said, 'Imogen,
I thought my rental agreement with you ruled out having
anyone living in the flat, besides me?'

'I'm a free woman,' said Imogen happily. 'I can vary my
terms.'

Shirl drove Imogen into work the next day. Work was
possible, but biking to work was not. Although Imogen

had sentimentally invited Josh under her roof she didn't want to live permanently under his eye. She could easily analyse the sentimentality; just because her own life hadn't dealt her winning cards in the love suit didn't mean she wasn't willing to speed love on its way for others. In fact she was probably more willing. Heaven keep her, she reflected, from the sourness of frustrated middle age!

Imogen had thought of something she could do. She could find a way to tell Janet Summerfield that Fran had found out where Gideon was in August '78. If the woman thought that Fran was convinced that he was at Tenby, say – she would perhaps relax, and then Fran would be safe for the moment. As long as she could refrain from telling anyone the fascinating truth for a little longer.

However the simplest way to convey misleading information to Janet Summerfield was to ring her up and tell it to her, and for that purpose Imogen proposed to use her office phone, so not getting overheard.

'Summerfield, J' was of course not in the Cambridge book – she lived at Castle Acre – but directory enquiries provided it. Imogen waited till the end of her office hours, when the last minor ailment had been dealt with. In fact, she reflected ruefully, being injured herself was wonderful magic medicine – it made everyone cheer up at once, and make jokes. In fact, a fake plaster would be a handy thing to have around . . . When peace returned, and she had put up the 'closed – next clinic at—' sign on her door, she rang the enemy.

'Mrs Summerfield? I met you once, when you came to collect papers from my tenant, Miss Bullion – no, don't hang up, please, I have some news for you.'

Silence – but not a cleared line.

'Miss Bullion, as you perhaps know, was anxious to discover where your husband spent some weeks of 1978.

She has found the answer, and will now be able to complete the biography in time for the publisher's deadline. I thought you might like to know that.'

'She has found . . . what has she found?' There was no mistaking the note of anxiety – even terror – in the voice.

'That he spent the time in a hotel in Tenby, that has miraculously kept its registers for the past fifty years.'

'*Tenby?* Is she quite sure?'

'Very. She seems exuberant.'

'As well she might be, succeeding where others have failed. Tell me, did she say he was alone – or was he with someone in this Tenby hotel?'

Imogen was taken by surprise by this question. She shouldn't have been.

'No; he seems to have been with someone.' She spoke on the spur of the moment.

'That will have been Melanie,' said Janet Summerfield. Suddenly her voice sounded desolate, bleak. 'Well – I'm glad the book will be finished with no more trouble. It was kind of you to put my mind at rest. Surprisingly kind – in the circumstances.'

'Don't mention it,' said Imogen, putting the phone down, and aware as she did so how ridiculous it is to say 'don't mention it' to someone who just has.

She stomped across to her kettle, and made herself a cup of coffee. She was feeling guilty at telling such whoppers, and told herself that it was perfectly ridiculous at one and the same time to suspect a woman of being a serial murderer, and have scruples about telling her lies.

20

'I think I'll talk to you off-duty,' said Mike. 'Can you come to supper tonight?'

'Certainly I could; but won't Barbara find this all boring?'

'She owes me,' said Mike, 'considering the amount of talk I put up with about college architecture.'

'College architecture?'

'She's doing a training course to be a local guide. You must have seen them, leading little bands of multiglot foreigners around, waving headscarves on walking sticks as rallying points.'

'I've seen them.'

'One can train to do it. Barbara has fluent Spanish, so she thought she might escort disorientated Dagos . . .'

'Sometimes I wonder why I like you, Michael Parsons. But I'd love to come to supper. Isn't it short notice for Barbara?'

'Good chance for her to practise. She's doing a cookery course too.'

'What energy – I'll look forward to talking to her about it.'

'It isn't surplus energy,' he said, 'it's revenge for the long hours I work.'

Barbara didn't mention Mike's working hours, however, but seemed very pleased to see Imogen. Barbara had made the little house very bright and cheerful; now it was all done she needed an occupation. The Cambridge Guide course was fascinating – she gave Imogen a thumbnail history of St Agatha's full of graphic detail. Did Imogen know that the college had nearly pulled down Old St Giles, and built a Victorian church in its stead? Did she know that the bumps in the linenfold panelling in the hall had been inflicted by Civil War soldiers, billeted in the college, who had used the hall to stable their horses? They had fixed rings for tethers to the panels . . . Imogen was more than willing to be told, and the food was delicious, though perhaps rather rich.

After supper, over coffee, she gave Mike an account of the journey into Wales.

'It was you, was it?' said Mike. 'I might have known!'

'What was me?'

'Setting PC Jones on to May Swann. He's found her.'

'So it was her?'

'He found a DB that matches her. A murder enquiry is in progress. Someone in records let me know because mine was the last enquiry after her. And, Imogen, I need hardly tell you that amateur detectives are unwelcome in murder enquiries. If they are on the wrong tack they are a fearful waste of police time; if they are on the right tack they are putting themselves in personal danger.'

'I am chiefly concerned in getting Fran out of personal danger.'

'But she has come home safe and sound. You have no real reason to think she is in danger, honestly, have you?'

'The danger seems to centre round that quilt.' Imogen was putting off telling Mike that she had rung Janet Summerfield with a cock-and-bull story about Tenby.

'Well, look at it our way,' said Mike. 'Found – one DB, on a remote patch of mountainside, head bashed in.

Deceased known to have been carrying best part of two hundred and fifty pounds, empty purse found with body. No special need to explain presence of visitor in famous beauty spot overrun with tourists half the year. Theft is the obvious motive.'

'But . . .'

'*You* tell us that some five miles away from the interment of the victim, on the further side of the local town or village, is a farmhouse containing a quilt that you think might explain the crime via a tangled and extensive chain of guesswork . . . but May Swann probably didn't find the quilt at all. Your friends at Evans's farm didn't mention anyone except Janet Summerfield, now did they?'

'She didn't have to find the quilt to be in danger. She merely had to convince someone that she might be about to find it.'

'And then they would kill to stop her? They would kill to protect the reputation of a famous man against a recherché and far-fetched resemblance between an academic paper and a patchwork quilt?'

'Mike, there's too much coincidence here. Isn't it very strange that Summerfield's biographer should be found dead within a few miles of that quilt?'

'That sort of coincidence is like ley lines – look for it and you find it everywhere. People don't murder for these strange and curious motives, Imogen. Murder is very risky. People do it for down-to-earth, gutsy reasons, like money, lust, rage, jealousy.'

'Cambridge people might murder for what you call fancy reasons, Mike. Things of the mind matter a lot here. You can get thrown out of the University for stealing other people's work.'

'But murdered?'

'So you don't think that the mysterious fate of biographers is going to play much part in the enquiry into May Swann's death?'

'I think they will be looking for tramps and drop-outs who might have been in the valley at the material time . . .'

'Mike, what would it take to get you to take this seriously?' asked Imogen, desperately.

'A confession. We like confessions. As you know, we regularly beat them out of people . . .'

'I don't think you should say that even as a joke.'

'I suppose you're right,' he said, suddenly thoughtful. 'But the truth is most crimes are solved because someone confesses. Most confessions are made willingly enough; and most are not later revoked. Most motives are humdrum. A policeman's life is not a thrilling one . . .'

'What do you think I should do next?'

'My dear girl, I think you should do nothing. Nothing first, second or last. I can't believe your Fran's life is in danger from a serial murderer obsessed by biography. Stop worrying.'

'And what will you do?'

'Confidential. I *might* just make sure that someone digs out Professor Maverack's statement and draws it to the attention of the murder enquiry officers. Just as I might dig out the death certificate of your Mark Zephyr, and confirm that the cause of death is given as meningitis. But I can't say that I will.'

Imogen considered. She understood confidentiality. She needed to, in her job. There was no point in pressing him any further.

She steered the talk back to Barbara, and it rambled around the colleges, and arrived at the wrought iron gates at the entrance to Newnham College, which had once, Barbara said, been damaged in a riot.

'A *riot*? In Newnham?' Imogen was amazed. 'What was it about?'

'The undergraduates objected to women being given the titles for their degrees.'

'Oh – I think I remember something about that. You could sit for a degree, but you weren't allowed to call yourself a Cambridge BA?'

'That's it. I think. It's complicated. In 1920 Cambridge voted against admitting women. In 1921 they were admitted to "titular" degrees. They couldn't be full members of the University till 1948.'

'Heavens!' said Imogen.

'Among the other reasons given for the foot-dragging,' said Barbara gleefully, 'was a desire to be different from Oxford, which had let women in in 1919.'

'And there was a riot?'

'When the vote was taken in 1921. The undergraduates massed outside the Senate House while the votes were counted, chanting "We won't have women!" and then they surged off to Newnham and smashed up the gates with a stolen handcart. The Union offered to pay for the damage later. We are supposed to be able to point out to the tourists the signs of the repair to the iron work, but I admit I can't see it. Have a look yourself, next time you're passing, Imogen.'

'I will,' said Imogen. 'Golly. The past is a foreign country all right. I wonder what the undergraduates of 1921 would have said if they had foreseen mixed colleges and slot machines dispensing condoms?'

'They'd have said Hurrah if they had any sense,' said Mike.

'The women perhaps wouldn't have,' observed Barbara.

'My mother always hated the idea of mixed colleges,' said Imogen. 'But I just thought she was an old stick-in-the-mud. I wish I could talk to her about it now. She was at Girton; and it seems there was no love lost between Girton and Newnham . . .'

The conversation meandered along about the relative merits of co-ed colleges and schools until it was time for Imogen to go home.

Cambridge colleges are immortal. In the distant past some foundations were lost to the chances of time; recently, though a few have been born and nearly all have been metamorphosised in harmony with modern ideas like the equality of the sexes, none have died. None have died, and therefore none have paid death duties. The custodianship of their buildings, and their traditions, like the music in King's College and Trinity chapels, is a burden lovingly discharged. Colleges with canny bursars have prospered. St Agatha's was not among the very wealthy, has never had anyone like J. M. Keynes as bursar, and though it is not on the Backs, and has only a modest antiquity to its buildings, it feels, nowadays, the chill of the *Zeitgeist*. Once every five years, therefore, in the winter vacation, a judicious space after Christmas, it throws a splendid party for a group of its alumni; a concert is performed in the Wyndham Library, a feast is given in the hall, the Master makes a speech in which the underlying appeal for money is gracefully disguised in elegant rhetoric. The handsome Jacobean courts are available for returners to occupy – in their own old rooms as far as possible, while any money-making conferences the bursar may have rented rooms to are shunted off into the Waterhouse building on Chesterton Lane. Retired senior members are expected to turn out and recognise, or, at a pinch pretend to recognise, their sometime pupils, and a good time is had by all.

Quite often, in the course of the jollifications, or a little later, the college receives windfall gifts. A purchase of books for the library is sponsored; a bit of restoration and repair, which the Master has ruefully mentioned in his speech, and promised to undertake 'as soon as funds are available' is suddenly possible, with a donor's name discreetly inscribed nearby. A new scholarship is endowed – the possibilities are many. And the effect is not necessarily felt at once; many of the guests go home and alter their wills rather than handing out largesse immediately.

These gatherings require Imogen to man her office all day, and be on call at night, or sleep in the college for the duration. So many tottery old fellows on sticks, negotiating the undulant worn treads of the stairs to hall and chapel – drinking better port than they are used to, and therefore often more – losing their pills as they unpack in unfamiliar rooms – even falling in the river, or off bicycles imprudently borrowed, under the impression that riding a bike and propelling a punt are skills once learned never forgotten . . . There is nearly always a need for first aid, or worse, an ambulance. Imogen, who usually rarely recognises anyone who was up while she held her post, manages to enjoy it for all that. A plangent atmosphere of nostalgic joy prevails. On finding that their college still remembers them, the old boys, and latterly girls, are touched in both senses.

A short while after her return from Wales, Imogen, no longer in plaster, but still walking with a stick and aware of the irony, settled in to a student's room near her office for just such a weekend. There were rather fewer incidents than usual, and she decided she could afford to attend some of the events herself. The interesting one was a speech by Professor Maverack.

Maverack came up trumps, and delivered exactly the right sort of thing. He hoped that his eminent audience all kept

183

diaries, even if they had not written memoirs. Of course he realised how difficult it had become to get such things published, even if they recounted eye-witness experiences of important historical events, but one never knew who might be the subject of biographical research, or indeed of biographies, in the future; in the age of the telephone the raw material for biography, and for history, come to that, was becoming very thin. He hoped none of them was so modest as to think they had no need to keep copies of their letters . . .

When he had finished, St Agatha's new librarian, a sharp and efficient Oxford graduate, stood up to say that the college library would be glad to receive gifts of manuscript memoirs and diaries, and, although careful archiving and cataloguing cost money, could promise to make them available for any future need. The lives and opinions of all members of college were of the greatest possible value to the college . . .

Thoroughly and subtly flattered the company dispersed towards lunch and a free afternoon.

Professor Maverack caught Imogen's eye as he left, with a little bevy of eager questioners around him. She was standing quietly at the doors, waiting for the last person to struggle up the stepped aisles in the tiered seating of the lecture hall, and get safely on level ground.

'That should do it?' he said quietly as he passed her.

'Oh, I should think so!' she said, laughing.

The slabs of roast meat, roast potatoes and vegetables glistening with butter that would be served up for lunch were too much for Imogen in the middle of the day. She slipped across the road for some filled rolls and a pastry, wrapped herself in her thick winter coat, and took them into the Fellows' Garden to chomp peacefully on a bench.

The glory of the gardens crested in May; but Imogen liked the sight of the thickly populated herbaceous borders all tidy and labelled, and the snowdrops nearly ready to flower drifting between. The great weeping copper beech still held on to most of its rust brown leaves; and trees in lace are as pleasing as trees in leaf. She sat on a bench in a kind of outdoor alcove made of curving shrubbery, and tipped her face upwards into the pallid sun.

She had finished eating, and was thinking of going to her office to make herself a cup of tea, when a sound from beyond the bushes caught her attention. Audible between the bursts of birdsong was a human voice, quietly crying. Imogen got up and walked round the shrubbery, to find herself staring at Janet Summerfield, who was sitting weeping on a bench opposite hers.

'Can I help?' said Imogen. It was almost a conditioned reflex.

'No. Go away,' was the answer, and then, 'Who are you? Do I know you?'

'I am Imogen Quy. The college nurse here. If you are in any way unwell I can help you.'

'But you have helped me,' said Janet Summerfield. She stopped crying. 'You were kind to me. You told me that Miss Bullion would be able to finish her work; and that *was* kind when I had been – shall we say *abrupt*? – with you. You must be a very nice person.'

'I try,' said Imogen, blushing slightly. 'Do you want me to make you a cup of tea, find you an aspirin, get a taxi to take you home?'

Mrs Summerfield shook her head.

'Do you want to tell me what is wrong?'

'Dr Maverack's talk upset me,' Janet Summerfield said. 'I don't think it is fair – do you, Miss Quy?'

'I don't quite see . . .'

'Holding out a hope that their stupid diaries will be snapped up eagerly, when I know too well that even Gideon can't get a biography – without – without lots of trouble. I shouldn't have come, but I thought some people might remember me, and it would be nice to pass the time of day with some of Giddy's – some of my late husband's friends.'

'Well, isn't it? Nice to meet old friends, I mean.'

'I haven't spotted anyone yet. Except Dr Bagadeuce. He seems very busy. I suppose they invite people from lots of different years . . .'

'Yes they do. I'm sorry there's nobody here you know. Would you prefer to go home?'

'That's it, I wouldn't. It's like the grave there. Quiet as death. Nobody to talk to from one week's end to the next. Never be a widow, Miss Quy – it's the loneliest thing on earth. You could go out of your mind wanting somebody to talk to.'

'Haven't you any friends?' Imogen asked her quietly. Imogen's professional demeanour was firmly in position.

'I've quarrelled with all the old ones. Not that there were many. I need to make new ones. Will you be my friend, Miss Quy?'

So, suddenly Imogen faced a moral choice. Easy to say yes – and make oneself into a betrayer by and by.

'No,' she said. 'I can't be your friend. Because, you see, I know why you did it.'

'You know?'

'So do others, now. I've told other people.' But though this sentence was supposed to deter Janet Summerfield from launching an instant attack, Imogen knew she wouldn't. She didn't feel in any danger at all.

'And you think it's dreadful? You think there isn't anything to be said for me at all?'

'Murder is dreadful,' said Imogen quietly. 'I do think so. Yes.'

'I tried to talk him out of it first,' said Janet. She was staring at Imogen wide-eyed, like a child trying to get out of trouble with a parent. 'He wouldn't listen. He didn't care about me at all. Can you imagine what that was like, Miss Quy?'

Imogen bit back the question burning on her tongue – *whom did you try to talk out of it?* – and said instead, 'I'm not sure that I can; tell me.'

21

'I had a life of my own, once,' Janet Summerfield said. 'I had a good singing voice. I used to do concerts. Recitals – *lieder* – that sort of thing. I didn't know when I married him that Gideon would not be able to work with a single note of music audible from anywhere in the house – even someone humming while they worked in the kitchen, or singing scales at the bottom of the garden. I always thought mathematicians were musical – didn't you think they were?' She turned to Imogen a tear-stained face with an expression of mute appeal.

'I think many of them are,' said Imogen. 'What bad luck for you.'

'I couldn't practise enough, you see. I just had to give it up. I had to give everything up. Well, if you weigh in the balance a second-rate voice, against first-class mathematics . . .'

'But it doesn't really work like that, does it?' Imogen mused softly.

'It did for me. I really admired Gideon. He was much the cleverest person I had ever met; that's why I married him really. I admired him. He couldn't have wanted his work to succeed any more than I did. It was what I lived for. You do see?'

'The Dorothea Brooke syndrome?'

'Oh, but my Gideon's work was *real*. Not rubbish like Casaubon's. It was worth sacrificing oneself for.'

189

'You were the conventional old-fashioned wife, you mean, putting her husband first in every way . . .'

'Not conventional – that wouldn't have done for Gideon at all. He was a free spirit, Miss Quy. He *despised* convention. We all did.'

'All of you? You had a lot of friends?'

'We did once. Not latterly. Gideon didn't like visitors. They interrupted his work.' She fell silent.

'These friends,' Imogen prompted her. 'Melanie Bratch, for example?'

'Melanie wasn't my friend,' said Janet. 'She was Gideon's. He went off with her one summer, just to pay me out. I said the wrong thing, and he took umbrage and off he went with her. She was too young, you know, Miss Quy, to know what she was doing. I never blamed her. And I didn't mind him having a mistress. He was oversexed, you see. I couldn't keep up with him. I didn't mind; people sometimes wouldn't believe me, but I didn't. You expect creative people to be oversexed, don't you? Think how Picasso carried on with women! And my Gideon always came home. Always slept the night in his own bed. I didn't mind – not if it helped him work.'

'And you didn't mind if this got into the biography?'

'What? – Oh, no, I didn't mind that. Ian Goliard wouldn't have put it in, he said it was distasteful, the precious old twat! So I took the stuff about Melanie out of the files. But of course I thought any other biographer would find out and put it in. What has all this got to do with it? I was telling you about Gideon.'

Of course his biography has got to do with it! thought Imogen, but she kept quiet. A nasty feeling was engulfing her – like the shiver of fascination and revulsion that came over her in medical school when she was about to be asked to look at a lurid slide of injury or disease.

'I wanted children at first. Well, you do, when you get married – or you did in those days. But Gideon was afraid of the noise and the mess. He needed a regular life, with his meals nicely cooked and on time, and quiet and order in the house. So that was that really.'

'So for him you gave up music, and children, and latterly even friends?'

'Yes. I was always a support to him, Miss Quy, and happy to be, until . . .'

'He was a monster!' exclaimed Imogen. 'And yet you still want a flattering biography of him?'

'I want his work acknowledged. I want him to be famous as a great mathematician. Then at least it will have been worth it, all those years. Someone will say he owed a lot to a devoted wife!'

'They say he is about to be given the Waymark Prize. You would be happy at that – even though it is too late for him to enjoy it?'

'He didn't deserve to enjoy it!' She sounded suddenly ferocious. 'He would have wrecked it! He didn't give a damn about me! He just laughed when I told him how I felt about it—'

'I don't follow you, I'm afraid,' said Imogen. She was speaking softly.

'Let me put it plainly. The one sure thing about Gideon was his pride in his work. All those years he put it before everything else. Before me, certainly. Well, I understood that. To be honest, I wouldn't have amounted to much as a singer – it was easier to put my mind to helping Gideon than to pursue work of my own. I was disappointed at first; people treated him as just another don – not anything special by Cambridge standards. Then he published the new non-periodic pattern, and people woke up to his genius. I was really quite happy for a while; quite a few years. He liked it too. He got invited abroad to give lectures, and I went with him. And time went by, and people began to mention the Waymark Prize. And then he suddenly went dotty, and started to say he didn't deserve it and he was going to confess! Miss Quy, I *had* to stop him – you couldn't blame me, could you?'

'He was going to confess that he had cheated – that his great work was really someone else's?' asked Imogen. Once you actually looked at the awful sight directly, the feeling was different – neither revulsion, nor fascination, but a kind of cold, detached distress.

'I did everything I could think of! I implored him! Can you imagine the shame – the humiliation? I couldn't bear the disgrace. After everything I had done for him he was going to drag us in the mud, and he laughed. He said it was nothing to do with me. And it wasn't as if he had pinched work from a colleague – was it? It wasn't *mathematics* he took – just a pattern that some stupid old cow of a Welsh farmer's wife botched up! I kept telling him it took his genius to see what was special about the pattern anyway. But he wouldn't listen. So I had to kill him. Do you see?'

But Imogen was not sure what she saw. Just possibly total mania. 'How did you do it?' she asked.

'We – I – put stuff in his food. And I didn't care. I'd rather go to prison for murder than live through the disgrace!'

'It was so easy you weren't afraid to go on to kill others . . .'

'What do you mean?' cried Janet, springing up. 'What others? What are you talking about? There weren't any others!'

'I think there were at least two others,' said Imogen, standing her ground.

Janet Summerfield sat down again, and fixed an icy stare on Imogen.

'I'm sorry I talked to you,' she said. 'You aren't kind at all, you're a vicious sort of bitch. Now you listen to me. You can't prove anything I've just told you. Not a thing. There isn't any evidence. The hospital pathologist filled in the form, and we got permission for cremation . . . There isn't any proof of foul play. And I shall deny every word of this conversation. And if you repeat a word of it I'll have a libel lawyer on you in three seconds flat, and I'll strip you of every penny you possess. Understand?'

'I understand you all too well,' said Imogen, sadly.

Janet Summerfield got up and strode away across the immaculate lawns, her tent-shaped ample coat billowing in the chill breeze. Imogen sat watching her go, and wondering about that very curious change of pronoun.

'I got a confession for you, Mike. But it's for the wrong crime.' Imogen was standing in front of Mike's paper-laden desk in the police station. 'Oh and it was unwitnessed, and retracted at once. But perfectly genuine, I do believe.'

'Sit down,' said Mike. 'Tell me all about it.'

Imogen launched into a précis, as accurate as she could make it, of what Janet Summerfield had said.

'I take it this woman is bonkers?' said Mike when she had finished.

'Stark raving. Aren't murderers often?'

'Philosophical question that. Difficult one. Was the Yorkshire Ripper bonkers? Sane people don't go out at night looking for women to murder – ergo, the Ripper was mad. But mad people aren't responsible for their actions – ergo, the Ripper wasn't a murderer. What's the proof he was mad rather than evil? Well, he must have been because sane people don't go out at night looking for women to murder . . .'

'I see the problem,' said Imogen. 'Do you like philosophy,

193

Mike? I'm surprised; I had you figured as a practical man.'

'It's rather acute and relevant to what you tell me this morning,' he said. 'When a mad person confesses to a murder, it is possible that they are really mad, and therefore not really a murderer – or that they are really a murderer and not really mad, or that they are so completely round the twist that they will for motives obscure to we normal folk confess to murders that they never committed, literally.'

'You mean, aside from the question whether such people are responsible for their actions is the prior question, did they actually perform the actions confessed to?'

'You got it. Well, what do you think?'

'If she did kill him I must admit I understand her reasons. The trouble with vicarious careers, vicarious glory, is that one's self-respect is at the mercy of the lead actor; and when the great Gideon got an attack of conscience he thought it was no business of his wife . . . whereas she had sacrificed every other desire in life to foster just the reputation he proposed to self-destruct.'

'She had a motive then. Marriage is one continuous stream of opportunity. What about a method? I think you've told me twice now that meningitis is an A1 rock-solid non-suspicious cause of death.'

'I did tell you that; but since we last spoke I've discovered something. There's a drug called DNOC; it kills rapidly in a high enough dose, with symptoms – euphoria followed by high fever and collapse – that are rather like those of meningitis.'

'And is this stuff for sale at Boots?'

'No, of course not. It's a garden chemical; but some years back it used to be prescribed as an aid to slimming . . .'

'Golly . . .'

'And Janet Summerfield is unrecognisable, Fran told me,

in her photo album because her weight went up and down so dramatically.'

'So she might have been prescribed these things . . .'

'And she might have hoarded them.'

'That's an awful lot of mights, Imogen.'

'Well, I agree that it's bizarre, but patients often do hoard pills instead of taking them. Or throw away prescription forms instead of collecting the medication, even when it's free.'

'And we are talking about one very crazy lady, in whom hoarding lethal drugs would be merely a bagatelle beside the other mad things she has done . . .'

'I'll bet the maddest thing she ever did was marrying that man in the first place.'

'You're almost certainly right about that,' said Mike. He was rocking himself back in his chair, chewing a pencil, with an expression of deep thought on his face.

'And then, she said "we" and then corrected herself. And that's really *extremely* odd, Mike.'

'A mistake of one word in a great outpouring? Surely not. She's so used to regarding herself as just a suburb of her husband's life she's probably lost the use of the first personal pronoun.'

Imogen frowned. 'The distinction between singular and plural is deeply embedded, isn't it? Could one utter a sentence in the wrong number?'

'But she corrected herself at once, you say.'

'All the same . . .'

'Well, what "we" could there be? Do you mean she had an accomplice? Who else might have liked to murder Summerfield? Hang about – didn't you say he had a mistress?'

'Yes, he did; but I don't see . . .'

'Well, neither do I, I must admit. And I'm really not

supposed to go on fishing expeditions. Of course, in view of what you tell me I could go and interview Janet Summerfield—'

'Nothing stops *me* from going on fishing expeditions,' said Imogen. 'The mistress's name is Melanie Bratch . . .'

'You know, murder enquiries are intrinsically dangerous, Imogen. And you live alone in the vacation, or with only your precious Fran in the house.'

'We have just acquired Josh as a bodyguard,' Imogen told him. 'And I will be careful.'

'Well then, since this is not yet an official enquiry, why don't you talk to the mistress before I talk to the wife? See if you can find out anything. And let me know immediately you have done it. OK?'

It was, of course, more than flesh and blood could bear not to tell any or all of this latest development to Fran. Fran's reaction startled Imogen, who had been thinking of it as a dismally sad story. But Fran was ecstatic.

'Corrumbers, Imogen! If we could prove *that*! And if any of that is true – think of the story line! Our hero in a moment of weakness steals his theme – enjoys the glory for many years, and then when he is about to gain the ultimate crown repents – suddenly conscience driven, he is ruthlessly silenced. Wow! What a book I will be writing! The first biography of a scholar to combine detection and moral drama! I'll be famous!'

'That'll be all right, then,' said Imogen drily. She had instinctively been seeing matters through Janet Summerfield's eyes – the wife's tale – but Fran of course, as was quite proper in a biographer, had seen Gideon as the central protagonist. Interesting, thought Imogen – do I always tend to see the world through women's eyes? More, even, than the fiercely egalitarian Fran? Well, after all, you wouldn't expect a young person nowadays to have much sympathy for the Dorothea syndrome.

'Fran, what do you think about that I/we business? Do you think someone who was acting alone might have said "We . . ."?'

'Hmm,' said Fran. 'I don't think I would. So you mean somebody else was involved?'

'If so, who? Who else had a motive? Melanie?'

'I don't see what her motive was. *She* wasn't going to bathe in reflected glory, surely? And, Imogen, she's nice. She just wouldn't have. If you talked to her you'd see.'

'I shall be talking to her. Do you want to come?'

Fran considered. She leant back in the battered armchair by Imogen's fire, and thought about it for some time.

'In one way, I'd love to,' she said. 'But if you want confidences, two are better than three, aren't they? You have a talent for being confided in, Imogen, and I think I'm rather too bright and bouncy for it. You'd better go alone. But I want a playback of every syllable she says – right?'

22

Melanie readily agreed to see Imogen. But on opening the door to her, said, 'I'm not sure I can help, Miss Quy. I told that nice young woman Frances Bullion everything I could about Gideon. But I don't mind talking to you, of course. It's nice to have a visitor. I'm very lonely since Gideon died.'

Melanie took Imogen's coat, and gestured her to sit down. A little tray sat ready on a coffee table, with biscuits and two glasses of sherry. Melanie was moving around slowly, on two sticks, her need for sheltered housing very apparent, but she seemed mentally quite alert and capable. Imogen studied Melanie – in whom the beauty she had once had was still, if not quite visible, deducible. The flat was neat, and rather crowded – Melanie had brought more things than the planners had considered necessary for sheltered old ladies.

'It isn't Gideon I want to ask about,' Imogen began. 'It's Janet. I need your advice, and this conversation might upset you.'

'Why might it? I don't know very much – or care very much – about Janet. She made the man I loved miserable for many years.'

'I have a problem, you see. She has been behaving in a rather crazy sort of way . . .'

'That's nothing new.'

'But it leaves me in a dilemma how to react to something she told me.'

'What did she tell you?'

'That she – and some other person not named – had killed her husband by putting something in his food.'

Imogen was watching Melanie closely as she said this, but she saw no expression of terror on the other woman's face.

'She's really gone off her trolley, then,' said Melanie. 'She made a lifetime's occupation of being the great man's wife; why would she put herself out of a job?'

'Because he was about to own up to having pinched his theorem from somewhere, and she couldn't stand the disgrace.'

Melanie suddenly looked rather grey. 'Janet certainly would have hated that,' she said. 'Enough to kill for? Possibly. Oh, poor, poor old Giddy! I can't bear to think about it!' She covered her face with both hands, and began to weep quietly.

And so it was evident to Imogen that Melanie believed this story at once.

In a little while she recovered her composure. 'I suppose she told you she had sacrificed everything to his need to do great work?'

'Yes, she did. He certainly sounded very selfish, in her account. As though his work had cost her dear. Isn't that right?'

'It's the wrong way round. From the moment he married her she drove and hounded him. She shooed away his friends, and shut him into silent rooms, and organised every moment of the day for him to work in it. She wouldn't even let him out for lunch, sometimes. He had to have sandwiches and a Thermos of coffee at his desk so that he didn't have to stop. Even on holiday he had to sit there with paper and pencil part of every day, in case he got inspired. It absolutely quenched him. His sort of work came freely or not at all – he couldn't force it. And she let him know in no uncertain terms that she wasn't doing all that just for an average sort of Cambridge man – she wanted glory. Poor Giddy couldn't live up to her. He used to come to me for a bit of peace.'

'But she had made large sacrifices for him?'

'Twaddle. The first time she got a bad review for a recital she gave it all up and blamed him. He would have liked children; she said the noise would stop him working . . . Heavens! I've suddenly realised what he would have been going to confess – he was going to say he got his pattern from some quilt – right?'

'Yes. Did you know about that?'

'Not really. But I remember when we ran off together that summer long ago, there was a quilt in the farm where we stayed that he was awfully struck by. It rained a lot, and he copied the pattern in his notebook – every piece, right to the borders.'

'Did he ever tell you he had based his discovery on it? Or that he was going to confess?'

'No. But then the one thing in heaven and earth we never mentioned to each other was his sanctified work.'

'And I can take it that the other person who might have been involved in killing the poor man was not you?'

'No it was not. I would have died myself sooner than harm Giddy, whatever he had been up to.'

'Do you have any idea who it might have been?'

'No. I know who his friends were – apart from college friends of course. Ian; but he was abroad a lot. Leo – he went to America. He's back now, of course, and I see him now and then, but he didn't get back till after Gideon's death. Meredith – the trouble is I can't think

what motive any of them would have. We were just a group
of friends; rather jolly friends in our youth. And then life
separated us and scattered us, the way it does. When we
were young we were all hungry to achieve something, to
get famous – and most of us managed some contribution.
Most of us got realistic, and more modest year by year.
It was only Janet who was implacable. I didn't give a
damn about Gideon's maths – I would have hated it if
he had become any more famous, I saw less of him when
he was glorying around on lecture trips. I just liked him,
for himself. He could have given up maths and taken up
knitting for all I would have cared.'

'And you don't know anything about these successive
biographers?' Imogen asked.

'I know Ian got very fed up with it. He came to see me
before he went back to Italy. Mind you, a biography written
by Ian would have been – well – mannered. Oblique. Mostly
about Ian.'

'He's in Italy? Are you sure he's all right?'

'I got a postcard only last week. It's on the mantelpiece.
You can look if you like.'

The card showed the view of Florence from the Piazzale
Michelangelo. The message read: 'Traffic awful. Crowds
awful. Glad you're not here. Ian.' It was postmarked five
days ago.

'I'm not much help, am I?' said Melanie, smiling ruefully
up at Imogen. There was a glint of tears in her eyes. 'What
will happen to Janet? Will they get her for it?'

'They'll try,' said Imogen. 'I rather hope they succeed.'

'You know, the only clever thing *I* ever did,' said
Melanie, showing Imogen to the door, 'was busting in
on Janet's circle of satellite young men and carrying
off Gideon for three days . . .'

*　　*　　*

Medical diagnosis is an arcane mixture of hunch and logic. When Imogen was training as a doctor – a training she had thrown over to go to America with her fiancé – diagnosis had been what most fascinated her about her studies. A crime, like a disease, throws up symptoms all over the place, and the needful art is to see the pattern. Patterns in these matters are like Pascal's wheelbarrow – *c'est infiniment simple, mais il fallait y penser* – it's infinitely simple, but someone had to think of it – clear only with hindsight.

Sitting comfortably in her quiet, sunny sitting-room, Imogen set herself to the game of hunt-the-pattern. And part of the pattern is obvious enough. Having harried Mark Zephyr as she had been harrying Fran, Janet suddenly invites him to dinner and is kind and helpful. Whereupon Mark contracts meningitis, and dies. Just as Gideon himself had crossed swords with his wife, caught meningitis, and died. Could these deaths have been unrelated? Surely not. But there is a problem. For Janet has emphatically denied knowing anything about Mark Zephyr's death; and the only evidence against her on her husband's death is her confession made to Imogen. So why would she own up to one and hotly deny the other? I am missing something, thought Imogen.

Well, one possible reason, however unlikely, is that she did commit one murder, and she didn't commit the others. Think it through . . . Mark had dinner with Janet . . .

Imogen got up and went to the telephone. She dialled Pamela Zephyr's number. 'Pamela . . . Yes, I'd love another walk soon. Next fine weekend . . . Look, can you tell me something? That last evening, when Mark had supper with Janet Summerfield, was there anyone else there?'

'Yes, there was, now you come to ask. Some woman doctor with a funny name.'

'You can't remember the name? It might be important.'

'No . . . I don't think I can . . . It was very odd sounding; one of those names like Vivian, or Evelyn, or Hilary . . . Sorry, my mind's gone completely blank.'

'Well, would you let me know if it floats out of your subconscious any time? See you soon.'

Imogen put the phone down, and moved back to her sitting-room. She wasted a whole valuable hour, sitting thinking in her armchair, turning things over and over in her mind. It was nearly seven when she got up and went through to her kitchen to fix herself some supper. She saw the answerphone blinking as she went through the hall, and stopped to play her messages. The window-cleaner announced himself for tomorrow; Shirl wanted to know if Imogen would drive her to a quilt display at Hemingford Grey, in Lucy Boston's house.

'Lucy Boston made some of the loveliest quilts ever!' Shirl said. 'And you can see round the house and garden and be shown the quilts if you just look up P. S. Boston in the phone book, and call ahead to say you're coming! Shall we go soon?' Then call box blips, and Fran's voice. Fran said she wouldn't be in for supper. She sounded pleased.

'Dr Bagadeuce has asked me to have dinner with him in his rooms. He says he has something really good to tell me about Summerfield. Byee!'

Imogen put the phone down and went into the kitchen. She looked abstractedly into her fridge, having forgotten what she was doing, her mind on other things. There is a certain level of formality in college life that has become unusual in the world outside. Imogen thought of the Maths Fellow as Dr Bagadeuce, and addressed him, when she had any occasion to, as Dr Bagadeuce. But he was not a medical doctor, and she did know his first name. Dr Bagadeuce had one of those funny names like

Hilary or Vivian – a name that could be that of a man or of a woman. Dr Bagadeuce was called Meredith . . . Imogen could almost hear the clicks as everything fell into place.

She ran back to the phone and dialled Mike's number.

23

For once Mike wasn't dismissive. He was galvanised at once. 'Get there. We're on our way,' he said. And the police were there before Imogen, though she ran out of the house at once and drove herself hell for leather into college. There were police cars parked at the college gate, blue lights flashing. Mike was in the porter's lodge, wearing jeans and a sweater.

'There's no way out of his rooms except down the staircase into the Fountain Court, it seems,' said Mike. 'We've got the college gates staked out. But we have to get there without being seen, and his windows overlook the court . . .'

Hughes, the senior porter, was visibly distressed. 'It would be much better if you let me telephone through to Dr Bagadeuce and tell him you are coming . . .' he was saying, his face a picture of misery.

'No!' said Mike sharply. 'French!' – he gestured to one of his uniformed colleagues – 'Stand here and make sure that *nobody* uses a phone!' To Imogen he said, 'It would only take a split second to flush food down the toilet, if we alarm him.'

'It won't worry him to see me walking across there,' said Imogen. 'My office is just beyond his staircase. And I could have anybody with me if they're in plain clothes.'

'Off we go then,' said Mike.

In fact Imogen's usefulness as a cover for Mike was limited, because he set off straight across the college lawns, instead of using the paths round the edges of the court, which she never did. But Dr Bagadeuce did not happen to glance out of his window. His rooms were on the ground floor. His 'oak' – the solid outer door closed when the inmates wanted privacy – was shut. Mike hammered imperiously upon it. And then, meeting no response, hammered again.

'Be patient, can't you – I'm just coming . . .' said a voice from within, accompanying the sound of keys being turned. 'What is it?' said Dr Bagadeuce, opening both outer and inner door. 'I'm otherwise engaged . . .'

Mike roughly shouldered him aside, saying 'Police', and disappeared within.

Dr Bagadeuce took a step towards Imogen, as though he was perhaps thinking of leaving, rather than returning to his room. The sight of two uniformed policemen standing behind her changed his mind. 'The invaluable Miss Quy,' he said, drily, seeing her. 'Well, you had better come in. I might perhaps need a witness.'

Imogen followed him in. Fran sat facing her across a table laid for dinner. The table was set behind the ample settee which faced the fire. It was covered with white damask, and laid with college porcelain and silver. Mike was standing beside it.

'Don't move, or touch anything, Miss Bullion,' he said to Fran. 'Just tell me who is eating what here.'

And Imogen saw that there were as many as six separate serving dishes on the table – three at each end.

'I don't understand . . .' said Fran. 'What is this?'

'Just answer the question,' Mike told her, sharply.

'He is a vegetarian, so he has made a separate meal for me . . .'

Dr Bagadeuce stepped forward, moving from behind Imogen with swift steps. 'It will be getting cold,' he said, taking one of the dishes up from the table. 'I'll put it to keep warm . . .'

'No you don't,' said Mike, grabbing the dish. 'I'm sending it to be analysed.'

'Ah,' said Dr Bagadeuce, and he sat down on his settee. He had turned very white.

'No doubt you can tell us what we shall find,' said Mike, coldly. 'Miss Bullion, have you eaten any of this – what is it? – stew?'

'No,' she said. 'We were just about to start . . .'

'Thank God,' said Imogen.

'I think,' said Fran to Dr Bagadeuce, 'that the implication of all this is that my friends believe you were about to poison me. Were you about to poison me?'

'Yes, Miss Bullion,' he said quietly. 'I was. I was determined to avert a disaster to my college.'

'And you think it is not a disaster to the college if a senior member murders a graduate student?' she said, incredulously.

'I did not expect to be found out,' he said. 'But you are right; I have brought about a worse calamity. I suppose I have no chance of persuading you, when you see what sacrifices I am prepared to make for St Agatha's, that you should not publish your discoveries about my late colleague?'

'But I appear to *be* the sacrifice,' said Fran.

'You might like to tell us what, on analysis, will be found in Miss Bullion's portion of that stew?' said Mike.

'I would not like. Why should I help you?' he said.

'It will be contaminated with DNOC,' said Imogen.

'You pestiferous meddling person,' he said, snarling at her. 'One might expect a college servant to put the college first!'

'Come, Dr Bagadeuce,' said Mike. 'Time to go.'

'Do you have to march me across the court in full view, like a common criminal?' Dr Bagadeuce said.

'You are a common criminal,' said Mike. 'But no; if you prefer we can leave via the gate on Chesterton Lane. We have police cars at every gate.'

'I want her with me,' said Dr Bagadeuce, gesturing at Imogen. 'I want a witness to ensure my safety.'

'I will see you off college premises, Dr Bagadeuce,' she said. 'And the moment you are driven away I will telephone your lawyer. I'll see you at home, Fran.'

A little group of them, therefore, walked across the second and third of the college courts, avoiding the main gate, going towards the back gate. Their route led them under the colonnade by which the chapel was approached, and past the large marble slab in the wall on which the names of college members who lost their lives in two world wars were inscribed.

Beneath this memorial Dr Bagadeuce halted. 'Look at this,' he said. 'Look how many lives were given from this one small college for the defence of England. No doubt for all these young men their college was an important part of the England they died to defend. If I was ready to kill, Miss Quy, I too would have killed for my college. But who will understand, let alone memorialise me?'

'Not I, I am afraid,' she said.

'Don't give me that!' said Mike, furiously. 'You are not just *ready* to kill, you have killed two people already. The victim we have just rescued would have been at least your third, perhaps your fourth.'

Dr Bagadeuce turned on him, snarling. 'You can't prove that! And you'd better be careful of saying what you can't prove! I shall deny everything you can't prove!'

'I shall prove enough,' said Mike. 'More than enough, trust me for it.'

24

You might think that narrowly escaping being poisoned
would put you off your food, for a day or two. But Fran had
had no supper, and declared herself ravenous. So Imogen
took her out to supper at the Red Lion in Grantchester.
They were just easing the car out of its parking space
outside Imogen's house – parking was very tight these
days – when they realised that the car lurking behind
them ready to nip into the vacated slot, was Mike Parsons
in a patrol car. Mike was very ready to be invited to join
them, so they all piled into 'Rosy', Imogen's ancient little
Nova, and tootled off to Grantchester. They settled down
at a corner table to eat and talk.

'My saviour!' said Fran to Imogen tucking into game pie
and chips. 'What would it have done to me?'

'What would what have done to you?'

'Dinner with Dr Bagadeuce.'

'It would have made you feel on cloud nine at first. Then
over-excited, and feverish. Then brought on a very high
fever, and with it convulsions, coma and death. It would
have looked very like meningitis.'

'So he might have got away with it?'

'Perhaps not, this time. He was pushing his luck, going
on doing it.'

'What I want from you,' said Fran, looking hopefully at
Mike, 'is a blow-by-blow account of how you worked all
this out.'

'Not me,' said Mike cheerfully. 'All down to Imogen.'

'Imogen then. Tell me all.'

'Well, to start with we both suspected Janet Summerfield of murdering biographers. She seemed so steamed up about everything. The mystery was her motive. After all, she it was who wanted the biography.'

'But she didn't want anything about that crucial summer . . .' said Fran eagerly.

'. . . because investigating that might lead someone to the quilt; she was terrified that the great Gideon would be unmasked as a cheat.'

'Why didn't she just get rid of the quilt?' asked Mike. 'She was ruthless enough.'

'As I know to my cost the approach to the quilt was guarded by fierce dogs. The owners were hostile. She tried all she could think of, but in vain.'

'So she hoped just to contrive to get a biographer who would let it rest, and use just what she wanted used. I see,' said Fran.

'Well, so, the moment I clapped eyes on the quilt – no, I tell a lie, I was a bit foggy at first – but little by little as I looked at the quilt I perceived that it was older than Summerfield's discovery, and that it provided the missing motive. So then I thought about method. Fran – do you remember telling me that you had embarrassingly failed to recognise Janet Summerfield in her family photographs because she kept losing weight and putting it on again?'

'Yes, – she certainly did,' said Fran.

'Well, I happened to be browsing in my medical dictionary the other day when my eye fell on DNOC. It used to be prescribed, long ago, as a slimming drug. So there I seemed to have it – motive, opportunity and method for Janet Summerfield to have killed Mark Zephyr. And then I found myself talking to her at the college party. So I said, "I know why you did it," and she suddenly poured out her heart to me and confessed – to having murdered her husband.'

'Right murderer – wrong crime!' said Fran.

'Exactly. So I prompted her about the others, and she hotly denied any knowledge. So hotly that I began to wonder if in fact there could have been someone else. Now, what does the name Meredith conjure up, Fran?'

'Some elderly female of posh extraction?'

'But it's also a man's name. It's Dr Bagadeuce's first name.'

'So the "Merry" they were all talking about in those jolly holidays they took . . . ?'

'Could have been – was – him. And the Cambridge doctor near whose cottage in Wales poor May Swann was disinterred, the English man they called "Happy Chappy" because of his silly name, was likewise him.'

'But the motive and method applied only to Janet,' said Fran.

'His motive was related to hers. And do you know, he actually told me what it was, only I wasn't listening.'

'He told you?' said Mike.

'It was some time back, and about something else. He carried on rather madly about the honour of the college.'

'I don't get this bit at all,' said Mike.

'Well, it is fairly mad, I admit,' said Imogen. 'But it certainly doesn't do the college's reputation any good if one of its senior members is exposed as a plagiarist. And there are people – Dr Bagadeuce is one – who spend their entire lives devotedly serving the college, achieving nothing in the eyes of the outside world, but only their precious place here, in Cambridge . . .' She looked at her companions' expressions. They were both staring at her, looking unconvinced. 'Well, all right, he's plain crazy. But, Mike, I don't see how you can be a policeman in Cambridge, while not understanding a Cambridge sort of motive for crime.'

'Let me disillusion you, lady,' said Mike cheerfully. 'A diminishingly small proportion of crimes in Cambridge are committed by senior member of colleges.'

'Correction,' said Fran, winking at Imogen. 'A diminishingly small proportion of *discovered* crime in Cambridge is attributable to college fellows.'

'Mock away,' said Mike. 'But if you're not careful, I shall remember my official responsibilities, and not tell you what either of them said when questioned.'

'Oh, Mike!' Fran and Imogen both protested in unison.

'Well, since I have two lovely ladies hanging on my every word . . .'

'Is he always like this?' Fran demanded.

'Only when about to get a lot of credit for clearing up a murder or two,' said Imogen crisply.

'I deserve a lot of credit for listening to your paranoid suspicions,' said Mike. 'Even if it is later apparent that they were justified. Now do you want to hear about this or not?'

'Of course we do,' said Fran. 'Be quiet, Imogen.'

'Well, Janet won't repeat her admission to you, Imogen, that she dosed Summerfield's dinner. She says that Dr Bagadeuce had the run of her house, was an old and trusted friend, and could easily have stolen the slimming pills from her bathroom cupboard. She says she hoarded multiple packets of the stuff, and that at some time, she doesn't know when, it disappeared. She says she thought one of the cleaning agency's charwomen must have taken them. She says there is a black market for them since doctors stopped prescribing them. Someone who nicked them could have sold them. She absolutely denies that her husband was going to confess to cheating.'

'Can she get away with this?' asked Fran.

'Probably not, in view of what Dr Bagadeuce says. He denied everything at first, until we told him that samples of the assailant's blood had been recovered from May Swann's clothing, and could be DNA profiled, and compared with his. Then he confessed.'

'I hope that was true, Mike,' said Imogen.

'The confession? You can bet it was.'

'The statement that the blood sample could be matched.'

'As true as I'm sitting here,' said Mike. 'What do you take us for? I used to think you read too many detective stories; now I think you read too many newspapers.'

'Sorry, sorry . . .'

'According to our dear Merry Bagadeuce, Janet Summerfield appealed to him for help in talking Gideon out of a public breast-beating. He appealed to Gideon's self-respect, and his loyalty to the college, and Gideon wouldn't listen. Gideon said his self-respect demanded that he owned up and gave credit where it was due. "Imagine giving credit for abstruse mathematics to some silly old biddy doing needlework!" Bagadeuce said. Having failed to talk the man out of it, he and Janet together decided to kill him. She handed over the DNOC tablets, and he cooked up a delectable meal with them . . .'

'*That's* why she said "we" killed him . . .' said Imogen.

'Yes. Must be. Well, then he gets incandescent with rage over her stupidity. Fancy commissioning a biography in those circumstances! Stupid cow, he calls her, thinking she could suppress awkward questions, and the biographer wouldn't ever find out about the quilt. But of course, there was now a lot to lose. Who would want to murder an old friend to keep something dark, and then have it come out and get published abroad anyway? Seeing off Ian Goliard was no trouble, he tells us. The man had various things in his own life that were best kept dark; he just succumbed to pressure and went abroad. But Mark Zephyr couldn't be shaken off. And there was plenty of DNOC left.'

'But was that both of them, or just him?' asked Imogen.

'Depends whom you believe. *He* says she invited Zephyr to dinner, in the full knowledge of what he, Bagadeuce, was cooking up in the kitchen; *she* says she doesn't know what we are talking about.'

'What about May Swann?'

'Well, he says they became frantically anxious that the quilt might give Gideon away; Janet went and stayed in his cottage and tried repeatedly to get it, and failed. Then May Swann, all innocent, telephoned Janet and told her that she had found some indication that Gideon had spent time in the Tanat valley, and was off to look for confirmation; and so Bagadeuce went at once to his cottage, and waited for her to turn up. He met her "accidentally" in the pub, bought her a drink, and lured her on to his land, by telling her that he thought his was the cottage Gideon had stayed in, and then he clunked her on the head with a flat-iron he kept for decoration on the stove, and buried her on the hillside above his garden.'

'And then I came along and began to ask questions about the same thing,' said Fran, looking queasy.

'Dr Bagadeuce kept trying to persuade Janet to quash the biography; but she had got crazy for the glory of that whatsit prize, and she was sure the biography would say what a noble wife the fellow had, so she wouldn't. And, young Fran, it's just as well you have a caring landlady, or you might be six feet deep by now.'

'What will happen to them now?' asked Fran.

'Remand in custody. At the trial, I don't know. A couple of good defence lawyers will make hay over the sheer ramshackle nature of the reasoning. She might get off, even. He won't if that DNA test sticks, as I think it will.'

'Aren't confessions enough?' asked Fran.

'Well, she hasn't confessed, except to Imogen. You'll have to testify, Imogen.'

'Oh, Lord,' said Imogen gloomily.

25

Over the next few days, with St Agatha's buzzing with gossip, Imogen found herself explaining her trains of reasoning, and the accompanying trains of event, over and over again to various listeners. It is a sad commentary on human nature that people who profess themselves horrified and appalled by some calamity, speak with shining eyes, and eager expressions, so that if you could not hear their words, but only watch them, you would suppose they must be delighted.

So the members of St Agatha's, all trying to be appropriately dismayed, displayed the usual *schadenfreude*. There were many senior members who had smarted in the past under some pompous rebuke from Dr Bagadeuce on the subject of their loyalty to the college. People who had been sniped at for baby-sitting their children, or being absent when a college meeting was in progress. Junior members who in general could not help rejoicing when a senior member trod on a banana skin – and what a banana skin being arrested for murder was!

The feverish atmosphere was deplorable, no doubt, but understandable. Imogen told her story to her colleagues. She forgot to tell them that she was visiting Dr Bagadeuce in prison, and bringing him his letters, and such treats as remand prisoners are allowed. She was not quite the only person to maintain horror in parallel with kindness; Lady Buckmote had also been visiting.

Fran, meanwhile, had become famous in the courts of
St Agatha's; courted and questioned, and celebrated and
invited to dinner. She complained to Imogen that the fuss
threatened to slow down her delivery of the Summerfield
biography. Leo Maverack was over the moon, and he
invited Fran and Imogen for a 'tête-à-tête feast' in his rooms
the following week. To Imogen's surprise and pleasure,
Holly Portland was there, making up the fourth in the
party. Holly could, and emphatically did, confirm that any
quilt made in the twentieth century would be very closely
datable.

'What a story it is!' Fran said happily, and not for the first
time. 'Poor mediocre chap driven to overperform; tempted
to steal his discovery; struck with late-onset remorse –
losing his life as a consequence . . .'

'It is truly a brilliant story, said Leo Maverack benignly,
giving Fran a smile of fatherly smugness. 'I wish I hadn't
given it to you. I wouldn't have if I had had any idea that
dull old Gideon would prove so fascinating. Oh, don't
worry!' he added, seeing Fran's expression. 'I wouldn't
dream of getting it back from you now. Indeed, just the
opposite. I understand that Recktype and Diss will be
glad to publish under your name, and with only a brief
introduction from me. Your career as a biographer has
started very well.'

'But . . .' said Fran, flushing with pleasure, 'How very
kind of you, but I thought they needed your name to
make publication of it possible.'

'So they did, when they thought the great Gideon had
lived a blameless, and therefore boring, life. Now it turns
into a morality play and climaxes with a murder or
two, they think they could sell it with a dog's name
on it, and yours will do very well. I did suggest you
might write an afterword about the death and hard

times of the biographers . . . or will you be too proud and scholarly to do that?'

'Not at all,' said Fran, 'it's part of the story. But, Dr Maverack, don't you get anything out of the project at all?'

'Oh, don't worry about me, m'dear!' he said, gleefully. 'I told you originally that I was too busy to write it myself? Well, so I was; I am writing a book of my own on the theory of biography. Its main thesis is the need to deconstruct the self-flattering falsehoods behind which people shelter, and which biographers often collude with. Your biography of Summerfield is going to give me just the most perfect example possible in support of my thesis. I am going to puff your book extensively in the course of mine, and we are both going to benefit.'

'Would somebody mind very much,' said Holly, 'telling me whatever it is you are all talking about?'

Eagerly they set about telling their stories all over again.

At the end of the evening Imogen asked Fran to ride her bike home, while she got a taxi. Her leg, healed but still unreliable, was aching. Holly at once offered Imogen a lift. Leo Maverack escorted everyone to the college gates, seeming reluctant to let them go.

'It's a fascinating thing about that quilt,' said Holly as they waited at the traffic lights at the end of Sidgewick Avenue. 'A really *new* quilt pattern – not just a variation in the placing of light and dark fabrics – is most unusual. So many millions of quilts have been made, by so many people, over so many years, that just about every possibility has been done before. Your Welsh farmer's wife must have been a genius in her way.'

At Imogen's front door they said good night.

'Oh, Holly,' said Imogen, 'I'd love to have you to dinner

to meet some of my quilt-making friends. How long will you be around? When are you going back to the States?'

'I'm not going back, after all,' said Holly. 'I've been offered a research fellowship in textile history, right here in Cambridge. Dinner with you any time. Oh, and Imogen – watch out for that old fraud Leo Maverack – I'm sure he fancies you!' And she drove off before Imogen had time to congratulate her.

Imogen let herself into the house, and put some hot milk on the stove for chocolate – enough for Fran too. She took two paracetamol to quiet the aching in her healing leg. Funny that – Holly apparently used the word 'fraud' as a term of affection. For everyone else in Cambridge it was a term of abuse – serious abuse.

The paracetamol did not help her sleep. She lay awake, thinking. About the possibility that paracetamol makes you think. About the dreadful disgrace of cheating – gets you thrown out of Cambridge. About the miserable steal of taking your maths from someone's quilt . . . about Janet Summerfield and Dr Bagadeuce's shared contempt for 'some old biddy doing needlework . . .' It really wasn't as though their precious Gideon had stolen from a colleague. Not in their eyes. And yet Holly thought the quilt-maker must have been a genius.

And it was a few days later before the final penny dropped. Imogen was walking on the Roman road by the Gog Magog hills, on a lovely sunny and crisp late spring day. Her companions were Lady Buckmote, and Pamela Zephyr. They were there for the exercise, and each other's quiet companionship, and the conversation was intermittent and largely about the scurrying behaviour of the dogs, and the identification of various songbirds serenading them as they passed.

Imogen told Lady Buckmote that what with Professor Maverack's book, and Fran's book, the college could expect a little glory to make up for the disgrace of Dr Bagadeuce's homicidal devotion had cast upon it. Though of course, one had to weigh in the balance also the loss of the Waymark Prize.

'Oh, no,' said Lady B. 'We got that. Haven't you heard? It went to Li Tao, for his work on number theory.'

'For the ABC conjecture?' exclaimed Imogen.

'Mathematics is a deeply mysterious subject,' said Lady B. 'What's the time? I must be back at my car at five o'clock, because I'm dining in Girton this evening. I never miss this one. It's the night of the year when the college MAs all dine without their gowns, in commemoration of all those women graduates who were denied the titles of their degrees in the past.'

'When were women let in?' asked Pamela.

'Not fully till 1948. And I often wonder what became of them all – learned ladies, dispersed in the world trying to get teaching jobs in competition with certificated graduates from London and Oxford . . . Perhaps most of them just got married and disappeared into remote places. Anyway, I like going gownless in their memory.'

Imogen drove home, and went straight to the phone.

'How's your leg?' asked Mrs Evans. 'And those bites?'

'I'm fine,' said Imogen. 'Back to normal. I've been thinking about Granny Vi. Did she have university education, do you know?'

'Grandad always said she was too clever by half. But I don't know about educated. Why don't you ask her?'

'*Ask* her? But I thought . . . surely someone told me she had gone . . .'

'Gone to England, not to meet her maker. She's in a

nursing home in Shrewsbury. Very pretty gardens, and the matron so kind . . .'

'But however old is she?'

'Ninety-four in August. She can't get about without a zimmer frame, only with a wheelchair. But she's as sharp as needles to talk to . . .'

Imogen got the telephone number of the home, and arranged to visit Granny Vi. And since her leg still ached if she drove a long distance, she extracted Fran from the task of writing the great life, and took her along for a weekend break.

The home to which Granny Vi had retreated was a large Edwardian mock-Tudor mansion, on the outskirts of the town. Imogen and Fran found a bed-and-breakfast place, booked in for the night, had a pub lunch, and went on their visit. Mrs Evans senior was sitting sunning herself in a conservatory overlooking the garden, her eyes shut, her head tilted into the light. A patchwork square lay neglected in her lap. She was wearing a rather squashed straw hat over her spiky grey hair, but the brim did not shade her face when she looked upwards at that angle. The matron pointed her out to her visitors, and they approached. Fran's shadow fell across the wrinkled and freckled face of the old lady, and she opened her eyes at once.

'Mrs Evans?' said Imogen. 'We've come to see you.'

'Am I Mrs Evans?' she said, surprisingly, squinting up at them against the light, with bright brown eyes. 'I suppose I am. Miss Violet Margery Passmore is who I am *really*, you know.'

'Didn't you get used to being Mrs Evans, in all that time in Wales?' said Imogen, smiling.

'Not really. Of course, young women now don't change their names when they marry, so I understand. Cheeky monkeys! But if a married woman can keep her old name,

I think I might be allowed to have my old one back, don't you?'

'Of course; whyever not?' said Fran. 'I'm certainly aiming to hold on to mine.'

'And what is that, dear?'

'Frances Bullion.'

'Yes. A nice solid, twenty-two carat sort of name. But do I know you? You have probably come to see one of the other old ladies. There's quite a choice of old ladies here! But I'm sure I don't know anyone called Bullion.'

'No, you don't know me. But it is you we have come to see. I'm with Imogen here – Imogen Quy.'

'Oh, yes; my daughter-in-law told me you might come. You are very welcome, you know. One doesn't make many *new* acquaintances at my age. You'll be quite a thrill! Are you going to take me out to tea?'

'Certainly we are, if you would like that,' said Imogen. 'Can you manage the car, and steps and such?'

'Given time I can,' said Granny Vi. 'They do a very nice cream tea at the Stanhope Hotel.'

'The Stanhope Hotel it is, then!' said Fran.

Granny Vi hauled herself to her feet with the aid of her walking frame, and set off down the terrace at a steady pace. Fran picked up her needlework, and they followed.

It was quite all right for her to go out with friends, the matron said. Imogen didn't even have to declare herself as a nurse.

'Kidnapped!' cried Granny Vi, as Fran drove her out of the gates. 'Oh what fun! Spiffing!'

'But it wouldn't be if we had really kidnapped you,' said Fran.

'As long as I get my tea,' the old girl said. 'The buns in the home are always stale.'

It was a bit of a struggle for Granny Vi to get herself out

of the car, and up the steps, and into the hotel. She was frail, and slow. But she gave Imogen the curious impression that she was *good* at being frail; quite practised and skilled at it. There was no mishap. The Stanhope produced an excellent tea, in a comfortable sunny lounge. Cucumber sandwiches, and scones, and Madeira cake, and a choice of Darjeeling or Earl Grey in a proper teapot, and porcelain plates and cups.

'None of those horrid little dangling paper bits attached to teabags, either,' Granny Vi pointed out. 'Just real, mashed tea. Lovely.'

'You're right, it is good,' said Imogen.

'Now my dear, I didn't get to ninety without realising that I don't get tea for nothing,' said Granny Vi. 'What do you two want of me?'

'Well, I am writing the life of a dead don, you see,' Fran told her. 'I am a biographer. What he's mostly famous for is inventing a pattern – this pattern.' Fran took a sheet of paper out of her bag and held it out to Granny Vi.

'I can't see too well these days,' Granny Vi said. 'But it looks familiar, I must say.'

'We think he didn't invent it; we think he saw a quilt that you had made,' said Imogen.

'Typical,' said Granny Vi. 'Bloody typical, if you'll pardon my French.'

'Typical of what, exactly?' Fran asked.

'Men. Dons. Just *hate* the achievements of women. Well, I must remember that times change. They did, thenadays. In my days.'

'We want you to tell us about the quilt,' Imogen said. 'When did you make it?'

'Can't remember exactly. The thing about a farm, you know, is that one year is much like another. It might have been in 1935. Some time before the war.'

'It's brilliant,' said Fran. 'And it is a non-periodic pattern, isn't it? Where did you learn the maths?'

'Cambridge,' said Granny Vi. 'Disgusting place. In my time, that is.'

'What do you mean?' asked Fran. 'It's rather good, now.'

But when Granny Vi had been Violet Margery Passmore, reading mathematics at Newnham College, women had still been outsiders. She had come up to Cambridge without having realised that the battle was still raging there; women had long been able to take degrees at London, Oxford, Durham. She had thought of the struggle for access to education as a battle already won; just a little tidying up still needed . . . She had assumed that by the time she took her degree – three years away, and three years seemed for ever to a young woman – it would all be sorted out. She turned out to be good; had been expected by her tutors to emulate the famous Philippa Fawcett, she who had come above the senior wrangler in the lists.

And then she found Cambridge once again voting to deny her her degree. Worse; she had been terrified. When the result of the vote was announced, a mob of male students charged from the Senate House and battered at the gates of her Newnham, trying to break in, and shouting obscenities at the young women within. Violet Passmore had been in the town visiting a friend. When she returned to the college and saw the uproar, she had boldly, and unwisely, tried to push her way through the howling crowd of men, to get round to the back gate, and get in. She had been pushed, and pulled, and man-handled, and finally had her nose broken by a punch to the face.

A policeman had rescued her, and bundled her unceremoniously through a downstairs window, flung open by one of the tutors. She had landed, blood streaming down her face, on the floor inside. And it was too much for her. Too much, she declared, all these long years later, for any self-respecting woman. To go through that sort of ordeal to take an exam that would not even confer a proper degree? She had left Cambridge in disgust without taking finals, and married a young farmer with land in Wales.

Being a farmer's wife offered a good life, but short on mathematics. The farm accounts didn't challenge Mrs Evans much. But at least Mr Evans respected her intelligence, and he never punched her in the face. He even purported to like the slight kink left by the healed break in her nose.

'He was a lovely man,' Granny Vi said, fondly.

And it was amusing to work out patterns for quilts. She had loved patchwork ever since Gwenny's mother at the farm nearby first showed her how to make them. Only now it was so hard – her eyesight was failing.

Fran offered indignation and admiration in lavish amounts. Granny Vi ate doggedly, stuffing herself with tea till all the plates were empty. Then they took her for a little drive around – 'I don't get out much, these days,' she had told them. And then they took her home.

'Don't you ever regret that degree, and that lost life as a mathematics scholar?' Imogen asked, as they were just about to take their leave.

'No point in regrets. Regrets kill you at my age,' said Granny Vi briskly. 'And anger is wasted on such duff-heads. I soon saw that.'

'Can we do anything for you, before we go?' asked Fran.

'Yes please; will you thread a dozen needles for me? That will keep me going till tomorrow.'

Imogen and Fran set about threading every needle in Granny Vi's needlecase with white thread. It had to be white, these days, otherwise she couldn't see her own stitches.

'So you see, Fran,' said Imogen that evening, as they settled down to play travel Scrabble in their twin-bedded, over-cosily furnished room, 'it *was* from a colleague that your Gideon stole his work.'

'Does it matter whether it was from a colleague or not?' said Fran. 'I wonder. I've drawn X – you go first.'

'You'll never guess who I've just been talking to,' said Fran to Imogen a few days after their return home.

'You'll have to tell me then, if you want me to know,' said Imogen absently. She was browsing in a quilters' guild catalogue, looking for fabric samples.

'Ian Goliard.'

'Really? How? Where? What's he like?'

'Leo introduced me. In college this morning. He's, well – ineffable.'

'Tell me more.'

'Very long and weedy. Very posh and dreamy. Congratulating himself mightily on escaping all the unpleasantness.' Fran put on an affected voice. '"But my dehah! How perfectly frightful for you! I don't know *what* I would have done in your place . . ." That sort of thing.'

'Well, I suppose it should be a great relief that he's still alive. We shouldn't expect him to be nice as well,' said Imogen.

'Oh, he's perfectly nice. And hugely useful. He has kept loads of letters – though admittedly most of them are to rather than from the great Gideon.'

'*To* the great Gideon? But how has he got them if he sent them?'

'He's a bit of a card. And not very modest; he obviously kept copies to assist future biographers. His

own biographers, that is. I'm afraid I let slip that
I hadn't read him – Goliard that is. He's a poet,
did you know? Anyway quick as a flash he produced
this –' Fran waved a thin pamphlet on crunchy paper
– 'Poems; privately printed – and autographed it for
me before I could ask him to!'

'Are they any good?' asked Imogen.

'Look and see. You tell me,' said Fran, tossing the
pamphlet on the table. Imogen began to read:

> 'The river parts and joins again
> Around the islets of Coe Fen,
> Where come and go our learned men.
> Down from the fields of Grantchester,
> Where pub-bound scholars still confer,
> It brims and roars across the weir . . .
> So green is never another stream,
> Flowing these ancient lawns between
> Its surface bright, its depths unseen
> The willows lean with casual grace,
> Their fronds caress the water's face
> Their greenness glorifies the place . . .'

So great was the contrast between the quality of the
words and the beauty of the hand-laid paper it was hard
to avoid the sense that a fine empty book had been disfigured by printing this stuff in it.

'Ugh!' said Imogen, putting it down again.

'It's a bit, well – derivative, don't you think?' said Fran,
grinning. 'Sounds as though every line was lifted from
another poem that one has certainly seen somewhere, but
can't quite remember. *Borrowing* must have been a habit in
that lot of people!'

*   *   *

Naturally Imogen had told Lady Buckmote all about Granny Vi. And Sir William Buckmote, St Agatha's respected and influential head of house, got to hear about her too. And that is how it happened that on a glorious sunny day in early summer a very frail old lady was wheeled into the Senate House, among flocks of gowned and capped and fancy-dressed academic eminences, to receive an honorary degree. A reception for her in Newnham was to follow, at which, she had confided to Imogen, she intended to make a gift to her old college of the mathematical quilt; and at her earnest request she was pushed there in her wheelchair, so that she could once again cross the river at Garret Hostel Bridge, and admire what must be one of the loveliest vistas in Europe.

Quite a little bevy of people paused at the apex of the bridge, to admire the often recollected view. A light breeze swung the pendulant willow fronds, and billowed in the sleeves of the gowns, and fluttered the downy white hair of the old lady, who stared so eagerly at the arcadian vista of bridges and gardens. The bright new academic gown she was wearing seemed far too big for her, and emphasised her tiny bent frame.

'You know,' she said, addressing nobody in particular. 'I loved this place so much. And I always felt excluded, I never felt I belonged. But I do now – very much so!'

The green-brown river below them, swirling and sparkling, made endlessly recurring, but never precisely repeating, patterns of reflected light.

Jill Paton Walsh

Debts of Dishonour

Hoping to attract a generous endowment, St Agatha's College, Cambridge invites fabulously wealthy Sir Julius Farran to dine. The evening is a disaster for everyone but Imogen Quy, the college nurse: Farran invites her to come and work for him.

She declines, but when Farran dies, suddenly and shockingly, she has to look into it. His death left a large hole in his company accounts that could mean financial ruin for St Agatha's.

To save her college, Imogen starts to cast her cool eye over the financier's heirs, employees and enemies. What is right about the death of Sir Julius? What is wrong about it? And why did it happen? After all, her name rhymes with 'why'.

HODDER